FALLEN EAGLE: MISS GHOST

BY IRENE COLETTI

FALLEN EAGLE

Irene Coletti

Tate Publishing *& Enterprises*

 TATE PUBLISHING
       & Enterprises

Fallen Eagle: Miss Ghost

This novel is a work of fiction. Names, descriptions, entities and incidents included in the story are products of the author's imagination. Any resemblance to actual persons, events and entities is entirely coincidental.

Book design copyright © 2006 by Tate Publishing, LLC. All rights reserved.
Cover design by Lindsay B. Behrens
Interiror design by Janae Glass

Published in the United States of America

ISBN: 1-5988621-9-7
06.08.02

Dedications

I dedicate this book to Eddie, Gabe, Eric, Judy, Joey, Rosey, Matty, Rocky, Jacky, Vicky and FiFi. My beloved friends, a special thank you for your help, from this world and beyond.

Acknowledgments

I would like to thank my husband, Eddie, as well as Gabe, George and Carol. Thank you for putting so much time into making this story come to life.

CHAPTER 1

Sitting on my porch waiting for Glenn to join me, I see an eagle fly by. I look up smiling, knowing how much we have in common. A friend of ours catches my eye as she stops her car across street. The car door opens, letting her son out. He runs up to the house, joining the rest of the children playing in the yard. Then she waves.

I smile as she yells, apparently to no one. "Good-bye, see you later."

As she starts to drive off, she notices me sitting on the porch. "See you later, Vicky."

I smile and nod as if to say, "Okay." I see Don come out of the house, bringing snacks for the children playing in the yard. As he re-enters the house, he carries on a conversation as if someone were there listening. It would seem strange, if you didn't know what you were seeing.

Glenn, my husband, walks out of our house to join me. I recall how lucky we are to have neighbors like that. See, that's Don Bergen's house. He's my brother. He lives there with his wife, Jacky, and that's who my story is all about.

Even their house has a story. If I try to explain, you may not believe. But I know in each of us there's a love story. I mean a real love story that would take more than a lifetime to achieve. If I ask you if you love your mate and you answer, "If I didn't, would I be with him this long?" you could say that's love, I guess. Though the answer I am looking for is, "I love him so much that when he's not around, I worry about him. I can't sleep or eat when he's out of town; I'm so afraid that one day there'll be someone out there trying to take my place." But there's no greater love story than the one

I'm about to share. It's so incredible that even after hearing it, you still won't believe me. But it's a story that must be told.

This is a story I feel compelled to tell the world. A story about my family and friends, but most of all about Jacky and Don, and the love that broke all boundaries. . Now, you may shake your head and feel you've entered the twilight zone. However, if you're a romantic at heart, you could say, "Why not? Anything is possible." You might secretly find yourself connecting with our inner circle.

Glenn gets up to leave and I jump up and throw my arm around him.

"Do you have to go?" I ask, trying to hold back the tears. Glenn knows how upset I get when he is out on the road.

"Don't do this to yourself, babe. It's only two days."

"But I don't want you to go."

He laughs. "It's going to look funny trying to get on a plane with you on my back. I'll tell Randy you said 'Hi.'" Randy is Don and Glenn's agent.

Glenn gets in the car and backs up to Don's house, and waits. We watch Don kiss Jacky goodbye. Anyone else might think Don was acting strange.

You must wonder what I'm talking about, so I'll share my story. You can listen, and even pass judgment. But when I get through, you'll wish that you were part of, as we call it, our inner circle.

CHAPTER 2

I grew up in a small town outside of Dallas. I wasn't the kind of kid who couldn't wait until I graduated to get out of town. You see, my family and closest friends share a secret that could never be explained. If broken, we could never live with ourselves, nor would we want to. So, as I sit here on my porch watching the people of the town go about their business, I know that the secret we share is safe.

Did you ever hear that old expression, "If you want something bad enough, somehow you will get it?" That's what happened to Jacky, a shy little girl, who could not accomplish in life what she accomplished in death.

We actually met Jacqueline Boilean, or Jacky, as she's known to our friends, Little Eagle, as Don would call her, because our parents were best friends in college. Jacky was a little girl with blond hair. Though shy, she had an energetic personality when it came to people she loved. What most people didn't know was that she was just as complicated as she was fun.

When Jacky's parents left on one of their many trips, she came to live with my family at the age of two. Jacky's parents were wealthy jet setters, so I thought. Besides their home here in Linden, Texas, they also had a home in France where Jacky's father was from. Whether it was because of their lifestyle or her father's job, they traveled abroad often; this left them less time with Jacky. I would not know why until Jacky and I were getting ready to go to college, why they were gone so much. The fact they traveled regularly was tough on them, but at least they had Jacky's best interest in mind when they allowed her to live with us.

Any child would find it difficult to be separated from their parents by such a great distance. However, Jacky wasn't your typical child; she had a unique way about her, as if she knew from the first time she saw my brother what her destiny would be.

She thought of my family as hers and in many ways we were. My father would call Jacky and me, "1 and 1-A." We were more like sisters than friends. My brother Don called her his little eagle. Because Jacky often lacked self-confidence, Don thought he had to look after her more than me. When you saw the look on her face after Don spoke to her, you knew what she thought of him.

After a time, everyone assumed we were sisters. I was five months older than she was. We dressed and even talked alike. We even let our hair grow long, although we had totally different personalities. . I was the vocal one. I spoke my mind regardless of the consequences. I was athletic and played on the basketball and softball teams at school. I also loved to ride. Horses were our passion. That was one thing Jacky and I had in common.

When Jacky was at the barn she became a completely different person. You'd be amazed to see the transformation she underwent. She had all the confidence in the world; none of the other riders could hold a candle to her. Watching her was poetry, as she and the horse became one.

I have two brothers: Ray the oldest, and Don, the middle child. Ray was in his last years of high school. He was the quiet type, always keeping to himself. I guess you could say that Ray was the only one who really knew our mother. Don was just five-years-old when Mother died giving birth to me. I think deep inside Ray thought it was my fault, not that he ever said that, or made me feel that he loved me any less. Ray had to grow up fast. With Dad being at work, Ray was responsible for Don, Jacky, and me until Dad came home. It wasn't until years later that I understood how much Ray was a part of my life and how much responsibility he actually had.

Don had more in common with Jacky then me. Even though he was a lot younger than Ray, he shared the responsibility of watching us when he got older. Not that we needed him to. Sometimes I wonder who was watching over whom. I felt a responsibility to look after everyone. Father used to call me his Little Miss. Don was a tough guy and had the attitude to go with it. All he cared about was his music. He spent all his time writing songs. If anyone got in his way, God bless the poor soul. Don was a perfectionist and could fly off the handle quickly. Later in life, it showed in his music. If the lyrics were not right, no matter what anyone said, he would not change his mind. But when it came to Jacky, it was eerie. He put aside whatever he was doing just to sit and talk to her.

My brothers treated Jacky just like all brothers treat their sister, but other than that, they were cool. As for me, I was glad there was another girl around the house. Sure, Jacky and I had our fights, like sisters do, but we got over them.

I never thought Jacky's parents were ready for children—I think even Dad knew that. My dad felt sorry for Jacky. I wouldn't understand why until later in life. So he cared for her just like she was his own. He always knew the right thing to say when she'd question why her parents didn't take her to France.

Their trips lasted longer and longer, until months turned into years. Sure, they called her, but I think in the beginning it bothered her. Even my brothers felt badly when holidays came and she just got a phone call or an expensive present to make up for their absence. As time passed, Jacky didn't want to call them anymore, but Dad made sure she did.

Dad, on the other hand, was the best. He always knew what was going on. He seemed to be more a friend to us and made it easy for us to go to him if we had a problem. Never once did I ever hear him say he didn't have time. Dad loved a house full of kids, that's why he welcomed Jacky into our family. He also welcomed Glenn when his father died. Dad was my idol. A person I hoped I would end up like.

I remember when he started dating the first woman after Mother died. Her name was Judy McNeil. She was a few years younger than Dad, but we knew she made him happy.

We all were glad for him. She was a caring person who had lost her husband a few years earlier. She knew how much Dad loved Mother, just as Dad understood how much she loved her husband. Even though we thought she was old, she seemed so cool. She always knew what to say to us when it came to boys.

Jacky and I got a kick out of Dad and her when they were together. They'd act like two kids on their first date. I remember how Jacky would laugh at dinner. Dad and Judy would look at each other and make funny faces. It was like they were kids again. Jacky would kick me under the table to get me to laugh with her. Whenever Dad asked what we were laughing at, I would just say, "Nothing." Jacky always got me in trouble with Dad that way. But it didn't have to be just Dad; it could have been Ray, Don or anyone. With Jacky being the shy one, they automatically assumed it was me. Usually it was.

I remember the time at the stable when Donna and I came up with a prank to blow everyone's minds. Donna Jones was Jacky's and my best friend. We had known each other since first grade. Wherever Jacky and I went, Donna was right there with us.

Donna's mother insisted she take riding lessons. Only because she wanted Donna to hang out with the children of the parents she was trying so hard to impress. Donna agreed, knowing Jacky and I spent all our time at the stables.

Donna had more in common with me than with Jacky. Donna loved to have fun and would pull pranks just as much as I did. She was outspoken, but never without me to back her up. I guess you could say she was an instigator. Donna's mother figured if she was going to ride, she should learn the proper way. So they hired the best teacher and bought her the best horse they could find. That put her into the social standing that was so important to her mother.

Donna's family did not come from money. Her father was a young struggling screenwriter who hit it big. A producer bought his script and made it a huge hit. They moved to Texas and he wrote three more blockbusters. They didn't want to live in California and raise a child. So, every Saturday she would have to take lessons like all the daughters of her mother's circle did.

That morning Jacky, Donna and I got to the barn early. Don was picking us up because Dad had to work. Donna's instructor arrived at the barn promptly at ten. She expected everyone to be there, saddled up and in the ring, when she arrived. Donna dreaded it. She didn't have anything in common with any of the girls her mother wanted her to associate with. Jacky and I felt the same way.

Now you have to remember, whenever we pulled a prank, Jacky could never know about it. If she did, she would try to talk us out of it. While her class was doing their normal posting, trotting and going over their small jumps, Jacky and I were at the other end of the arena having fun. I could see Donna was bored to death and looking for my signal to do what we planned. When I motioned, she came over and told Jacky that the trainer would appreciate it if she could show the class the proper way of taking a six-foot jump. Everyone knew that Jacky and her horse Jazzman were the only ones that could make that jump without a fault. Jacky was the best. The instructor always wanted Jacky to join her classes. She even went as far as telling Dad that she would train Jacky for free. She knew that if Jacky took it seriously, she could be one of the best. Jacky didn't want any part of it. All she wanted was to be with Jazzman and have fun.

"Are you going to do it?" I asked.

"If you do it too." Sure, The Duke had jumped that high before, but he was not the jumper Jazzman was. I trained Duke more to do tricks than to jump. I guess you could say The Duke was a prankster, too. I agreed, knowing that I had other plans.

As we trotted across the ring, Jacky looked up. I didn't know that

Don and Glenn came early to pick us up. They sat in a corner where I couldn't see them. If I had known, I wouldn't have done what I did.

Jacky sat up in her saddle and trotted off. After making one turn around the ring, Jacky lined Jazzman up. Every eye was on her, including Don and Glenn's. She closed in on the jump and urged him on, together they flew over without a hitch. It was beautiful. She made it look so easy. Everyone gave her a round of applause.

Then Donna yelled. "You're next, Vicky."

I looked over at her. After watching Jacky, I didn't feel like doing what we planned, but Donna egged me on.

Then I heard one of the girls make a crack, "She's not going to make it."

That was like giving me a loaded gun. "Okay, Duke, let's get this right."

I kicked him and we galloped once around the ring to set up. I knew the jump was six-foot high and that I had enough room to do what I had planned. Plus, The Duke had done it many times before. I also knew that if I didn't line him up right, and I made a wrong move, I would not walk away. But I had all the confidence in the world in him.

As I approached the jump, I pulled back to slow him down, then pulled on one rein, pushing my foot into his right foreleg. Down and under the jump we went. As we laid on the ground quietly, The Duke waited for me to give him a command to get up. I lay there with my eyes closed. I could hear everyone running over in a panic. I tried so hard not to laugh.

"Call 911," I heard the trainer yell. Then, "Call the vet."

"Jacky, call Dad," I heard Don yell.

Oh no, I thought. *I didn't plan on Don being here.* I was ready to play along, saying that The Duke slipped. I knew that if Dad found out, he'd flip out. I had pulled tricks before and the result was being grounded for a month.

I gave Duke a nudge and we jumped to our feet. And before I could say I slipped, Donna came running over and could not stop laughing.

"That was great," she laughed.

That was all it took. Don grabbed my jacket. "Let's go home."

As we walked out of the ring, the trainer approached Jacky. "And you know better," she said. "Who gave you permission to take that jump while I was teaching a class?"

When I heard that, Donna and I turned and left the ring.

Back at the barn Donna came over. Before I could tell her to get lost, she said, "You should have seen their faces," she laughed. "You scared the daylights out of them." She didn't see Don standing there.

"Go home, Donna, before I call your parents," Don yelled at her. Donna ran back to her stall.

Don helped Jacky clean up Jazzman, and put him up. The Duke was all lathered up, so I had to give him a bath. I dropped the reins to the ground so I could pull the saddle off. Glenn walked over and picked them up.

"Are you mad too?" I asked.

"That was kind of stupid, don't you think?"

"It was just a trick I taught him."

"A dangerous one at that," he said.

I put The Duke in his stall and gave him some hay. "Okay, boy." I patted him on the neck. "That was great."

As I backed out of the stall, Glenn closed the door behind me. "That sure was." He smiled.

I grinned and ran to the car were Jacky and Don were waiting. Of course, Dad flipped out and again I was grounded from going to the barn for a month.

CHAPTER 3

As Don got older, he knew that music was going to be his life. He did have a good voice, and he and his best friend, Glenn, formed a band. Actually, it was Jacky who came up with the name.

As years passed, Jacky seemed to attach herself to Don. She was like a puppy that followed him everywhere. Whenever Don worked in the garage, Jacky would be right there doing something. She'd rather be playing with his headphones or some kind of equipment he had in the garage than her toys. She was fine just sitting there watching whatever he was doing. Don didn't mind; it was as if he got a kick out of her being around. He'd put his earphones on her, and she'd mimic him when he rehearsed.

One afternoon when Jacky was hanging out in the garage, Don's friends came over. Don told them they had to come up with a name for the band. After they had rejected every name, Jacky yelled, "Little Eagle!" That was one of her favorite toys. Don won it for her the day the carnival came to town. Dad had asked Don to baby-sit, and Jacky tagged along to the carnival with Don and his friends. To me it was the ugliest little thing, but she thought it was the best toy anyone had ever given her. So after that Don called her his "Little Eagle."

Tim, one of the band members yelled, "No way, that sounds stupid!" Remember that they were not that much older than we were, so considering something a girl came up with was ridiculous.

Tim, being a Beach Boy fan, suggested something to do with summer or the beach. Joe agreed. Glenn didn't have much to say at all, he just stood there, hoping they would make a decision.

After a brief silence, Jacky yelled, "Summer Boys."

Again Tim said, "That's just as stupid as Little Eagle."

The smile on Jacky's face disappeared. Don looked over at her. He knew that coming up with a name for the band made her feel like she was part of the group. That's all Jacky ever wanted, to be part of whatever Don did. He lifted her up on his workbench and whispered, "How about 'The Boys of Summer'?"

She didn't answer, but the smile on her face was enough.

"Okay, how about The Boys of Summer?" he asked the band. "It's about the beach, surf boards, and girls."

Tim smiled when he heard the word girls. "That's it," he yelled. "That's it! We're The Boys of Summer."

But there were times when she was not happy. As we grew older, the band would practice, and we'd just sit there in a tizzy. Every time Don sang, he'd look at us as though he was singing to us. He'd wink at Jacky, causing her to giggle. But when their girlfriends came in the door, they'd kick us out. That would devastate her.

Jacky seemed to take it harder each time. It wasn't until later that I found out she had a crush on him. Sometimes I'd tease her about it, just to see her go crazy. However, as we got older she'd ignore the teasing and never acknowledge my words.

I remember the first time I realized how bad she had it for Don. It was a rainy, cold Saturday afternoon. Don and his girlfriend rented a few movies. Jacky and I were watching TV at the time and, just like an older brother, he took over the set. Me, being a tomboy, got up and changed the channel and Don hit the roof.

"We got a few movies. If you're going to sit here, I don't want to hear a peep out of you," he commanded.

I was mad, but Jacky jumped up and yelled, "Great." I knew all she wanted was to be there because Don's girl was there, so we sat and watched the movie.

As the movie played, I could see Jacky off to the side, watching every move they made. Don put his arm around his girlfriend and the expression on Jacky's face went from happy to sad. I'd seen her sad before, but this time was different. It was as if her heart stopped.

In spite of the dark room, I could see the glassy look in her eyes. She tried rubbing them, but it didn't help.

Don turned when he heard her sniffling. "The movie get to you again, Jacky?"

She laughed and played along, but I knew better.

The doorbell rang, Don yelled, "Don't move," when he saw me ready to get out of my seat. "I got it!"

It was a delivery. "Jacky, it's for you."

Jacky got up and ran over. Along with the package, there was a card from her mother and father. Don opened it.

"Read it!" Jacky yelled in anticipation.

"Dear Jacky," Don started out, then stopped. He knew what the next line was.

"Read it!"

He looked at her and read on. "I'm sorry we cannot be there with you, but hope you like the doll."

Jacky started to cry. Don knelt and said, "Everything will be okay. Don't forget, we're your family, too."

Jacky smiled.

His girlfriend said in a joking way, "Jacky's got a boyfriend."

Even though they were only five years older Jacky was still a child. You could see the hurt in her eyes as she ran up the stairs. Don yelled, "How could you be so insensitive? She just got a letter from her parents saying they couldn't be here again."

Hurt, his girlfriend grabbed her coat. "I was just joking." She walked out the door. Don didn't run after her, he ran up after Jacky. I followed slowly.

Watching from outside her room, I dared not go in. As usual, I knew Don would make things right.

As she cried into her pillow, I knew it was more than what was in the letter. It was about Don and the first time she saw him show affection to someone other than her in our house.

He brushed the hair from her face. "Eagles don't cry." She lifted her face from the pillow.

"Yes, I am an eagle," she replied, trying to hold back her tears.

"Well then, why don't we go down and order a big pizza and watch the rest of that movie." He smiled at her and that's all it took.

She jumped up, as though she had forgotten everything that had happened, and followed him down the stairs.

As she passed me, she had the biggest grin on her face. "Are you coming?" she asked.

I nodded and watched her hurry to catch up to him. I knew then that it was more than a childish crush and wondered about Don. Did he have any idea how she felt about him? But it was kind of harsh, how he snapped at his girlfriend. When it came to Jacky, it seemed that Don was much older than he appeared.

As time passed, Don and Glenn devoted all their time to the band. Don had known Glenn since the first grade. It was like having three brothers, the way he spent so much time at our house.

Glenn's mother, Barbara, had Glenn late in life. Dad worked with Glenn's father, who passed away when Glenn was sixteen-years-old. So Dad helped in any way he could. Barbara worked nights, which left Glenn sleeping at our house. Dad watched Glenn at night when Barbara went to work, and Barbara would be there when we got up in the morning. It took a lot of pressure off Ray. Because Dad left so early, Barbara was there to give us breakfast and make sure we got to school before she went home.

Don and Glenn spent every waking moment writing songs. They were going to be the best band ever. Glenn was very charismatic. He was considered a real ladies' man around school, which left every girl in town trying to get a date with him.

I remember when I came home from school; he would run over to me when I walked in the door. Jokingly, he'd throw his arm around me and say, "If you were just a little older, I'd marry you." He'd make me laugh. What he didn't know was how much I wished I *were* older.

Glenn liked to joke. I think he did it to hide his feelings. Like when his father died, Glenn didn't cry and he would never talk about it. Barbara tried everything she could to get Glenn to open up, but it didn't help. Finally, she asked Dad to talk to him. She hoped that he would open up if there was a father figure in his life. .

Even thought I was eleven-years-old, I remember that night as if it were yesterday. It was late and I thought everyone was in bed. As I came down the stairs, I saw Dad walking towards the kitchen. He didn't hear me behind him. As I passed the kitchen, I heard crying coming from down the hall. I stopped outside Glenn's room. Dad was sitting on the edge of the bed rubbing his back, trying to comfort him. When Glenn woke, he was terrified. When he opened his eyes, he jumped up and threw his arms around him.

"I miss him so much, I wish he was here," Glenn cried out. It must have awakened Don; I heard his door open. I put my finger to my lips to tell him to be quiet. As we watched, we realized that all the joking Glenn did was to hide what he was feeling.

"I miss my father," he said. "It is so hard to be strong for Mom. ."

"Why would you think you have to worry about your mother?" Dad asked.

"I know when she thinks about him because she'll lecture me that I must be the man around the house."

Dad smiled, "Why don't you let me worry about your mother."

I looked at Don. It was the first time we had seen Glenn open up. He cried in Dad's arms until he fell asleep.

Don headed back to his room. Like me, he understood just what Glenn was going through. I tip-toed back to the kitchen and up the stairs to my room. I couldn't understand how we could live in the same house not knowing what Glenn was going through. I learned something that day about myself. I knew that Glenn was part of our family and that we needed to be part of him.

CHAPTER 4

By this time it was getting obvious that Jacky had feelings for Don. It was the weekend and Jacky and I spent the evening in our room. Dad was on a date and Ray went to a baseball game, which left Don in charge. Don and Glenn spent the evening in Don's room writing songs. Jacky and I were just hanging out. . I wanted so much to ask Jacky what she really felt about Don, and if she really knew what love was all about. I never asked her up front, I just assumed by the way she was behaving around him.

As I sat there watching the TV, I looked over at her every once in a while, just to see the expression on her face. She looked so innocent as she pasted picture after picture in her scrapbook of Don. Her smile seemed to get bigger and bigger. How could I ask her? I knew she was in love with him; I didn't need to hear the words come out of her mouth. I smiled.

"What are you smiling about?" she asked, taking me off guard. I had to come up with something fast.

"I was just going to ask if you want a Coke."

"I'll go with you." She jumped out of her chair. I knew she hoped Don would be in the kitchen. As we ran downstairs, we sounded like a heard of horses running through the house. We stumbled into the kitchen, banging into the wall.

Don popped his head out of his room, "Keep it down!" He slammed the door.

Before Jacky could say a word, I ran over to Don's room and knocked on the door.

"What do you want?" he yelled, as he opened the door.

"I just wanted to know if the door's still on its hinge." I ran back to the kitchen.

The look on Jacky's face made me laugh. She would never think of aggravating him the way I did. "You're going to make him mad," she said.

Don and Glenn came out of his room. Jacky sat there, as if she didn't know me.

"You're asking for it." Don stalked toward me.

I backed away and moved closer to Glenn.

"He's not going to save you, if you keep it up."

Glenn winked at me. As he shook his head up and down, Don caught him, and we all laughed.

Later that night, as I was coming out of the bathroom, Jacky stopped me to show me the picture of Don she had put in a frame. She said she was going to leave it on her nightstand and every night, the last thing she would see before she closed her eyes would be Don. I just smiled. She had answered my question.

CHAPTER 5

On Don's 21st birthday, Dad threw him a party, with the band as the entertainment. Don was excited, for he was going to play for everyone we knew, and that was basically the whole town. Dad rented a big hall. He knew Don was serious about singing and figured that's what he wanted to do. However, Dad hoped that singing would not interfere with him going to college, so I think Dad did it, not only for Don, but a little for himself. He had never really heard Don play, so that was a big night for him, too.

Jacky and I just turned seventeen. Up until then we had not experienced what real love was. However, that night we were prepared. I would be ready for a few guys I had my eyes on at school. As for Jacky, it was Don. We spent the entire day shopping for clothes and birthday presents. Jacky was worried she wouldn't get the right one. I laughed, for every one was too childish, or something that a sister would buy her brother. She wanted that perfect gift. I was really worried about her. I felt she was in for a big letdown.

Jacky hadn't heard from her mother and father in three months. In fact, she hadn't even seen them for a year. My dad had been picking up on Jacky's feelings for Don for a long time, not to mention the ongoing conflict with her parents. He was worried about her and he didn't want her to be around Don when all the girls in town would be hanging all over him.

When we got home from shopping, Glenn was just leaving the house. As he passed us, he said, "See you girls tonight, especially you." He pointed at me, and kept walking. "And don't forget our dance," he yelled as he opened his car door.

I knew I had no chance with him, but I was going to be dressed to kill, just in case. I watched him with a dead stare as he jumped into his car and drove away. At that moment I knew I was kidding myself. *Me and Glenn*, what was I thinking?

Don was watching TV in the living room. He told me to be ready early, that we were going to meet Dad at the party. "You and Jacky will be driving with me, but I need to pick someone up first."

Jacky and I spent the rest of the day dressing and undressing, never really thinking we looked good in anything we put on. We put on our makeup, only to take it off again. During this whole process, Jacky would ask, "Do you think Don, will like this?" or, "Do you think this makes me look too young?" I'd laugh and make faces at her, and she'd run in to the bathroom and start all over again. We were so excited about the party, I didn't stop to think about Jacky and how she was in for a big letdown.

When it was time, Don yelled from the bottom of the stairs, "Let's go, it's getting late! You have ten minutes."

We were ready, and we were dressed to kill. We had spent two hours on our hair and another on our makeup. Even though we bought the best dresses from the local store, we didn't think it was possible to look as fantastic as we did. Jacky was dressed all in black, with her long blonde hair down her back, while I chose to wear red. Jacky said red made my long brown hair stand out.

Before going downstairs, we stood together, facing the mirror. As we looked at ourselves, I believe we both knew a new chapter was about to be written in our lives.

Before we left the room, I stopped her. "Before we go, I wanted to tell you something."

"Is this going to be about Don?"

"Yes, it is. I don't want you to think that because we're all dressed up, it means Don is going to notice you differently. I just don't want you to get hurt."

"I'm not going to get hurt. All I know is, if it doesn't happen tonight, there will always be another time. I know we'll be together one day."

I remember hearing that all the time growing up. It was as if there was no doubt in her mind that one day Don and she would be together.

Don called us again. As we walked down the stairs, I notice Don standing at the bottom of the steps. When he saw Jacky, you could see the surprise in his eyes. I don't think he expected to see us looking as good as we did, so grown up.

He simply said, "Looking good."

With that little comment, a huge smile crossed Jacky's face. I don't think it would've mattered what Don said, Jacky smiled and giggled at anything that came from his mouth. I, on the other hand, didn't believe he meant any of the nice comments he ever said; he only saw us as his little sisters. Although Jacky was a beautiful girl, his comment was merely words and no more.

"Don't go driving the boys crazy tonight," he said to her when she got to the bottom of the stairs

"There's no one there that I want to see."

The way he looked at her when she said that made me think, *Maybe he does know how she feels.*

When we got in the car, we jumped in the front seat. Don immediately ordered us into the back. "We're picking up Sherry."

I didn't say a word, but you could see the devastation on Jacky's face. We didn't even know a Sherry existed.

We stopped at Glenn's house first. As he was getting in the car, he asked Don if he had called Sherry. Jacky looked at me with a look I had only seen once before. I glanced up at Don; he was looking back at her in the mirror. Our eyes met and I knew he had to understand what was going on in her mind. I was relieved.

I knew it was just a blind date when Glenn said, "Thanks for doing this for me; I owe you one, buddy." Jacky, too, looked relieved.

When we got to Sherry's house, Glenn jumped in the back seat with us. He sat beside me, placing his arm around me and giving me a big squeeze. "Man," he said, as usual, "if only you were just a little bit older." Everyone laughed.

Although I had heard these words often before, in my head I was thinking, *Oh yes! If only you were just a few year younger!* I was in heaven.

He kept his arm around me the whole time until we reached the party. Then he said, "By the way, you owe me a dance, babe."

I giggled. It's funny, when you think you're all grown up and a guy like Glenn says that to you, you giggle, you experience rapid heartbeat, and you're left standing there with a silly grin on your face. Then reality set in, remembering he called all girls babe. Jacky sat there, not saying a word, staring out the widow.

Not knowing anyone, Sherry tried to make conversation. You could tell she was nervous by the way her voice crackled when she spoke. She asked me what my name was and I answered. Then she asked Jacky. Jacky hesitated until I nudged her. Don, looking back through the mirror, seemed agitated by her behavior. He didn't need this right now. Tonight was all about him and the band. I thought, *if he's ever going to say a harsh word to her, it will be now.*

When we got to the party, Glenn and I got out of the car. Don walked around to open the door for Sherry and the three of them walked inside. Jacky just sat there. I got back in the car and grabbed her by the arm.

"You've got to get yourself together. This is Don's night. Now get out of the car."

She didn't say a word, she just opened the door and stepped out.

"Are you coming?" Don yelled, stopping to look back at Jacky. "Remember, Jacky, you owe me a dance." He proceeded to walk inside. Jacky smiled. Again, Don made it right.

Inside, Glenn and Don checked over the equipment. Jacky and I joined Dad, Judy and Glenn's mother and sat down.

Dad looked at us and it seemed he was seeing us for the first time. "You girls look . . ." He didn't know what to say. "My girls are all grown up."

I was sitting with my back against the stage when Dad looked up. Looking up, I watched as she glided in the door and made her way across the room. She was a knockout. She had to be a college girl, since I had never seen her around school before. After witnessing her entrance, I knew I wasn't even a thought in Glenn's mind. Besides Glenn spotting her, so did everyone else in the room. I heard "WOO" then looked up at Dad. He had a smile on his face until Judy kicked him under the table. Knowing everyone in the room saw her, Glenn strutted across the room like a rooster in a hen house. *Boy*, I thought, *he is so out of my league.* .

When the band was ready to play, Don began to sing. It was like he had a spell on the crowd. I never really had any idea how good he sounded until then. Dad was just as surprised as I was. We knew he could sing, but we never thought he was this good. All the girls in the hall were jumping up and down and running up to the stage.

Sherry was right there, putting the moves on him. You could tell that the band was feeding off the crowd. Jacky stared at Sherry, as she stood, staring at Don while he sang to her. She made all the right moves and said all the right words.

When the band stopped for a break, Don walked to our table and sat down. It was obvious that Jacky was upset.

"What's wrong, Jack?" Don asked.

"Nothing," she answered. .

Dad met Don's eyes and Don knew.

He looked at Jacky and said, "I think there is." As usual, he knew she was upset about Sherry. Still, no matter what her problems were, he could always cheer her up. It was interesting to see sometimes. At first it appeared that music was all there was for Don, but there was also a caring side to him, evident in the way he treated Jacky. I don't believe he knew all the reasons for the way she felt and I wondered how he'd cheer her up this time.

He returned to the stage and, not only did he dedicate the next song that Glenn sang to Jacky, Don walked down to the table where she was sitting and asked her to dance. It was amazing to see her transformation. You could see that she completely forgot about Sherry and the ride over to the party. She put a smile on her face and that did it.

Everyone was in shock, most of all Jacky. As I watched her and Don on the floor I knew he cared for her, but in a sisterly kind of way, and what she was feeling was just a childish crush on him that would pass in time. I couldn't have been more wrong. What she felt for him was not natural—for someone so young to be so in love. He smiled at her and she smiled back. He had made her day and, surprisingly, in front of all our friends.

That night I realized Don and Glenn were going to make it big one day. So did Dad. He still hoped they'd stay in college, but he knew that if they didn't, they'd be fine doing what they loved.

I guess Jacky and Don had something in common. They both knew what they wanted and they were going to get it. That bothered me. I wasn't worried about Don. But would Jacky ever have a chance with him?

The whole night was not a loss for me; there was a boy from school who had been trying to impress me for some time and that night I got to be with him. We danced the rest of night, until Glenn tapped me on the shoulder and asked if he could cut in. After our dance he walked me back to Jeff, the boy from school, and said, "Behave, this is my girl." My heart stopped for a few seconds and I stood there in a daze staring at him. Then I realized that it was only a dance with an older boy.

CHAPTER 6

As time went on, Jacky did start to date. Well, I guess I shouldn't say that. They were kind of one-timers, more for me than for her. You know, double dating and all, but her true love would always be Don. At times I thought she was getting over him, but I was wrong. She kept what she was feeling to herself.

Don and Glenn were going to college in California. To pay for it, they sang on weekends. They were getting better and better, and there were agents calling them all the time. Glenn and Don's talent for writing gave the band the extra push they needed. They wrote one chart-topper after another. It wasn't long before they were one of the biggest groups of all time, and soon their visits home were few and far between. But that never changed Jacky's mind about Don.

Jacky and I practically had the house to ourselves. Dad started to get serious about Judy, and to watch them together was like watching two teenagers in love. He loved showing her off on holidays. Dad was happy and he deserved someone in his life. He had been alone for so long.

Judy was a few years younger than Dad and kept herself in shape by working out three times a week. She even got Dad to go to the gym with her. Her philosophy on life was, *take it as it comes.* . She was a caring person, and when it came to Jacky and me, she was all ears. As we got older we felt that we could talk to her about anything.

Like everyone in town, Dad knew Judy's husband, Charlie, for years before his death. Dad understood about losing someone you love. He understood her first love would always be Charlie, and she understood that mother would always be Dad's. Judy was more a child than us sometimes.

I remember Dad would come home and tell us something about the band that he heard on the radio and Judy would get so excited that Dad would have to tell her to settle down. Jacky and would laugh so hard that we got her to laugh with us.

In 1972 we got a call from Don telling us that he wouldn't be home for Christmas. The band was performing somewhere in California and the show was going to be a big jump in their careers. By then they had an agent and were performing more than ever. Don told Dad that he, Glenn and the rest of the band were going to take some time off from college. Dad said it was fine, he knew that's what they wanted. They were on their way to living their dreams.

One day Dad, Jacky, and I were driving back from the mall and on the radio the man said, "And the number one hit is . . ." It was The Boys of Summer! We started screaming and yelling out the window, "That's my brother!" It was unbelievable. They had made it big. We were so proud of them. Dad couldn't wait to get home to call everyone he knew.

Although their visits were few and far between, nothing changed for Jacky. She was seeing other guys and so was I. My crush on Glenn was just that, a crush, he was making the headlines about being a ladies' man. I could never fit in his category. He was a big star, and there were so many glamorous women around him. But unlike Jacky, I didn't have to be hit in the head to know it would never be. Not that I didn't wish.

Jacky started to see a guy in our school. She had dated Bob for about three months, the longest she ever dated anyone. I thought she was finally getting over Don, until one day when we were on a double date. Matt, the guy I was seeing, turned on the radio, and there was the band. I turned it up and looked back at Jacky. She jumped up and said, "That's Don and Glenn!"

Bob said, "They suck. That's not my kind of music."

I thought Jacky was going to go through the roof. For someone who didn't say that much when she was around people, she sure let off on him.

"Are you out of your mind?" she yelled. "How can you not like them? They're the hottest group around. Tell me, what kind of music do you like anyway?"

Bob seemed lost for words. As long as she had been going out with him, I had never seen her act the way she did that night. She totally lost it. Everyone has their opinion, and I don't think he meant to say it that way. He was one of those guys who had to say the opposite of what you say, especially when your girlfriend goes crazy over one of the guys in the group. He got out of the car and started to walk.

Matt yelled, "Get in the car, Bob, I'll drive you home."

"I'm not getting in the car with her," he yelled back.

"Drive us home," I told Matt, "then you can catch up with Bob."

He agreed.

When he dropped us off at the end of the drive, I turned to Jacky. "What were you trying to do back there? It was uncalled for. What were you thinking?"

"I don't care. I don't have to care for him or anyone. When I get married it will be to Don and no one else!" she yelled.

"Listen to me, Jacky." Do you hear yourself? You sound like you've lost it. Do you want Don to think you're crazy?"

She sat down on the steps and started to cry. I sat beside her and asked, "What's going on? What made you go off on Bob that way? I thought you liked him."

She looked up and smiled.

"Oh, Jacky, you do like Bob," I said. "What's so bad about that?"

"I feel like I'm losing Don," she said. "We don't hear from him that much anymore. He's so busy. If he were here I would never have gone out with Bob in the first place."

"That's a good thing," I said. "If it's meant to be, then it will, but you need to live now and enjoy yourself." She just stared at me. As I continued to look at her, I pulled back. I'll never forget the look in her eyes that night. They went black. It was as if I was looking into an empty shell. I couldn't turn away. I felt as if I was looking into her soul.

"Vicky," she said. I listened to her words, but it was not her voice. "I know Don and I are meant to be together. Ever since I was old enough to understand, I knew my destiny was with him." She paused to give me time to comprehend what she was saying. "I don't have long."

I opened my mouth to say something, but the words would not come out. She scared me, but I felt she was preparing me for what was to come. I turned away from her and rubbed my face. I had to get a grip. I sat quietly for a few seconds, trying to figure out what just happened. Then I looked at her and the expression on her face changed. It was Jacky's face again.

She smiled. "Anyway, I guess I don't have to worry about Bob anymore. He'll never come near me, not after tonight." She got up and went inside.

I couldn't move. I sat for a bit, trying to figure out if maybe I blacked out, or this was all a dream. I wanted to run inside and grab her and ask her what had just happened, but I didn't believe it myself. Or did she even realize what happened?

After that night, there was more to come. There was something about Jacky that I couldn't explain, but I did feel that she was trying to tell me all her life that what she felt was truth.

CHAPTER 7

A year passed and I never experienced anything like I did that night. It seemed Jacky didn't realize what happened, but I learned to take what she was telling me about Don more seriously.

Just before Jacky's and my eighteenth birthdays, we decided we were going to the University of California. It wasn't that far from home, I guess. The real reason was it was closer to Don. Dad had Judy in his life now, I didn't feel as if I were leaving him alone.

We were excited and couldn't wait to start college. I know Dad called Don to let him know what we decided, but I never told Jacky. We had the rest of the summer to just be teenagers and we did make the best of it. Jacky never saw Bob again, but she dated other guys, although she never got too close. She was enjoying herself and so was I.

It was Donna's birthday, and we were going to take her out. We knew that Donna was feeling bad that in a few months we would be leaving. Donna wanted to go with us, but her mother had other plans for her, just like she did her whole life.

After taking Donna to the movies, we headed over to Joe's Pizza Shop, where all our friends hung out. Everyone knew we were going to California and asked us if we'd see the band. I let Jacky answer whenever they asked about Don and Glenn. Her face always lit up when one of the girls asked if Don was seeing anyone, or how it felt living in the same house with them.

She just answered with a big smile and replied, "No, he's not," and "No big deal."

It was the only time she spoke up, when it came to them. I wished she were like that all the time.

When we got home, we were amazed to see a limo in the drive. We couldn't imagine who we knew that could own a car like that. As we walked around the car, trying to look in the tinted window, we asked ourselves who it could be. All of a sudden we looked at each other.

"Don! Glenn!" Jacky yelled.

Why not? They were on top and what other way to come home than in a limo?

We were so excited we ran into the house, almost falling in the door. Looking around, we heard voices in the kitchen. Jacky pushed to get ahead of me, so when she stopped, I crashed into her.

Jacky's parents were sitting at the table with Dad. *Oh, No*, I thought. Jacky's face went blank. She, like me, wanted to die.

"Come sit down," Dad said, smiling. "Look who's here to see you, Jacky."

Slowly she walked over to them like they were strangers. And they were. She hadn't seen them in years. Calling her every few months didn't take the place of them being there.

She looked at Dad for reassurance, but there was nothing he could say. I sat down, with Jacky in between her parents.

Her mother, Michelle, couldn't believe how much Jacky had grown. I could tell Michelle felt awkward, trying to find the right words to say. She knew that so much time had passed, and that she really didn't know anything about Jacky.

"Look at you," she said with a French accent. "You are so beautiful."

Jacky didn't acknowledge her; she just sat there. Dad tried to keep things going by telling them about Jacky's riding ability, and how she won all the shows she entered. But it was hard for her to respond.

"Mike's been telling us that you're thinking about college," Jack said. "We would really like you to come to France and go to college there. We've been looking at a few of them, and we came up with one we think you may like."

The expression on Jacky's face said it all. She went blank, staring straight ahead with tears in her eyes. She began to shake.

"No!" She stood up, knocking her chair to the floor. "Vicky and I are going to the University of California. We planned it for a long time. This is not going to happen!" She ran out of the room.

All I could do was sit there. It hit me as hard as it hit her. We never thought this day would come. I looked over at Dad. He, too, was lost for words. *What were they thinking? They could have gone about it differently. If only Don were here, he'd know what to say.*

I tried to get Dad's attention without Jack and Michelle noticing me. I kicked him under the table, but I could see it was just as hard for him as it was for me. We never thought that one day her parents would come to take her home.

No one spoke. Dad finally turned to Jack and in a firm voice said, "What were you thinking? You can't come walking in here after all these years, telling her what you want. Sending a gift and making an occasional visit doesn't make it right. You don't even know who she is."

"Mike," Jack shot back, "are you telling me what I can and can't do for my daughter?"

"Yes, my friend." Dad lowered his voice. "I'm talking about a little girl you left here a long time ago, and that little girl is all grown up."

Jack looked down, thinking about what Dad had said. "You're right, Mike, as always. What was I thinking? I should have let you know what we planned, instead of rushing in here trying to make up for what we had lost. Can you forgive me?"

Slapping Jack on the back, Dad chuckled. "You'll find the apple doesn't fall too far from the tree, my friend."

Michelle knew just what he was talking about. She smiled. "What can we do, Mike?"

There was something about Dad and Jack that I didn't understand. Something only they shared. Jack seemed to listen without questioning what Dad had to say.

Dad asked me to go check on Jacky. I didn't want to leave, hoping I could find out what was going on. Dad looked at me as if to say, "Go," so I went.

When I got to our room, Jacky was lying on her bed, crying and clutching Don's picture in her hand. I sat down beside her.

"I wish Don were here. Maybe he could think of something to do."

"I'll never see him again," she sobbed. "They're going to take me away and I'll never . . ."

"No," I stopped her. "No matter what happens tonight, you'll always be with us. You'll be eighteen soon, and they can't do anything about it. No matter what happens, you can always come home and you'll see Don. But first, give them a chance. I think Dad can work things out."

I don't know if that made her feel any better, but she stopped crying and sat up. "You know, Vicky, you're my family and Dad is my father."

I wondered if going to France might be the right thing for her. I knew Don was dating, as a matter of fact. The band was having a great time out on the road. Their reputations for wild parties, and the woman that followed them around made headlines. When Don spoke with Dad, he explained the press had a reputation for blowing everything out of proportion. As hard as Don and Glenn tried to cover things up, Dad knew the truth. I couldn't find it in me to tell Jacky. I couldn't imagine what she might do.

Dad yelled, "Jacky, Vicky, can you come down?"

Jacky hesitated. As I left the room, I asked her to give her parents a chance. She nodded, and I left.

Dad was standing at the bottom of the steps, looking in the other room where Jack was sitting. When I got to him, I looked to see what he thought was so interesting, but all I could see was Jack staring at Mother's picture on the wall.

"Dad?" He didn't answer. "Dad!"

He seemed startled. "Sorry, baby, I didn't see you standing there." Then he walked in. I remember thinking, *What was that all about?*

When Jacky came downstairs, Jack gestured for her to come and sit beside him. When she did, he looked over at me standing in the door next to Dad.

"Come, Vicky, I think you need to hear this, too.

"Jacky," he began, "I'm sorry about the way we got off on the wrong foot. We should have asked you first before telling you what we want, but this is your decision. I'd like to take you, and Vicky, if Mike says its okay, to France to attend college. I know you've been looking forward to the University of California, but they have great schools in France, and maybe you can let us make it up to you." He grabbed Michelle's hand. "Maybe we could get to know each other again. I know we haven been there for a long time, and we'd like a chance to make it up to you."

I looked at Dad. He knew it was a great opportunity for me, for both of us. I was excited; I already had visions of being there.

"Could we tell you in the morning?" Jacky asked.

"Sure, baby." Then he asked Dad to walk him out.

Jacky sat as if she were in a coma, trying not to make eye contact with Michelle. Michelle smiled at me when I looked over at her. Then she asked, "How are Don and Ray doing?"

Jacky's eyes lit up. That was my cue to get up and leave them alone.

As I walked towards the door, I heard Dad and Jack talking on the porch. "A long time has passed," Dad said. "There is lots of catching up."

There was a pause.

"Can you forgive me Mike?" Jack asked. I stood silently still so as not to be heard, hoping to find out the secret that Dad and Jack shared all these years.

"How can I ever thank you for all you have done?" Jack asked. "You know, Vicky reminds me so much of Victoria. You know I couldn't watch her grow up in my condition. It took a long time to put Victoria to rest. Being a father, not to mention a husband, I always thought Jacky was in better hands, and I know if I stayed, I would have lost Michelle forever."

"You don't have to apologize, I know what you wanted from me and I knew what I had to do, if not for you, for Michelle. You're my best friend and nothing could change that. Besides, I couldn't imagine our lives without her; she's brought so much love to us."

Looking through the screen, I could see Jack resting his head in his hands.

"Look," Dad patted Jack on the back. "I knew what you had to do, and if Victoria was here she wouldn't have it any other way. She knew how much Michelle loved you, and always hoped you'd take her home to France and make things right. But she knew that you weren't ready. All she ever wanted was for you to be happy and, if it was living next door, then that's what had to be. You know, she never stopped loving you, either."

No one spoke; they sat there thinking of the love they shared. Then Jack said, "How can I ever repay you? Again you have taken a back seat to my escapades."

Dad laughed. "What do you mean?"

Jack looked up at Dad. "She knew you loved her, and the funny thing is, so did I." Dad looked surprised. Jack smiled. "Didn't you think it was funny? Besides sharing the same apartment, spring break, Christmas, and Thanksgiving together. We were inseparable. You had to know, just like you knew that I couldn't live in France, especially after Victoria got pregnant. Just like you, I was worried."

Dad laughed. "Watching you the last few months, you would have thought you were the one who was carrying a baby. Taking my daughter to a country her mother loved is enough."

I thought, *What Dad and Jack share is something you never see. They have their secret, their own love story. I wish I'd known her; she seems like someone I'd admire.*

As I walked out the door, Jack yelled, "Hope to see you all in France."

Dad put his arm around me and we stood silently, watching Jacky saying her good-byes.

It was great seeing Jacky and her mother together. The awkwardness between them was cute as they tried so hard to be what the other wanted. I knew it would only be a matter of time before they got comfortable with each other. If they had the time together, they'd once again find that bond that only a mother and daughter share.

"Jack's a great guy," Dad said. I knew that he was happy to have Jack back in his life again.

As the car drove off, Jacky stood there confused. Even for her mother, could she leave the only place she knew? Most of all, could she leave Don?

Jacky walked toward the house and I could see she wanted to be alone.

"I'm going to bed." She kissed Dad goodnight.

After Jacky went inside, I turned to Dad. "Why? Why did you care for Jacky all these years and never say a word?"

"I never told you this before because I didn't think you'd understand. See, baby, Jack, your mother, and I were the best of friends in college. We were inseparable." He chuckled. "We were always there for one another. What you don't know is that Jack and your mother were in love. He would do anything for her. I think he fell in love with her the first time he saw her.

"I remember it well. . It was our first day. I was standing against the wall waiting to register when I saw her walk in. She was so beautiful, so innocent looking. She was so nervous that she dropped her books. I walked over to help, but Jack got there before me. His joke made her smile. I guess you could say he swept her off her feet.

"Two days later I was sitting in a bar when they walked in. It was her laugh that made me look up. It was that childish way she had. There wasn't a seat in the room except the two chairs at my table. When they walked over, she said, 'Like some company?' The words couldn't come out fast enough. I said, 'Sure.'

"As the night when on, I could see why your mother fell in love with Jack, he had it all. He was rich, funny and had that 007 thing going for him."

"He sure does," I blurted out.

Dad laughed. "See? That's just what your mother saw. On school break, your mother insisted that we spend two weeks at each other's homes so we could get to know each other better. Your mother loved to be around family, no matter whose it was. So we spent two weeks in France, two weeks with your grandparents, and the last two weeks here in Texas.

"France was great; she loved all the excitement. We met Jack's family and they got along fine, but deep inside she didn't have that 'home' feeling that she was looking for. Jack felt it too and so did I. You could tell by the expression on her face.

"Then it was off to Jersey. Your grandmother was so excited about us coming that she threw a party that included every family member who lived within a hundred miles. It lasted until the day we left for Texas. Since we were going to school here, we made it our last stop.

"It was quiet and peaceful on the farm. Your mother loved to sit right in this very spot. I would come downstairs in the middle of the night and she would be sitting there in the dark. When I asked if there was anything wrong, she smiled and said, 'Listen.' I guess I was so used to farm life I didn't know what she was talking about.

"'Listen,' she said again. As I listened, I realized I had forgot all the little sounds that come out in the quiet of the night. As she pointed them out, it seemed as if I was hearing them for the first time.

"She laughed. 'You know I could get used to this.'

"That night I knew things were changing. I knew Jack's father had his life planned out for him and it didn't include your mother. Jack knew it to, but he would have given up everything to be with her, if she had let him.

"It wasn't until that last year that everything fell apart. I guess you could say we were growing up and we knew what we wanted out of life. Jack's father came to the States for graduation and they would return to France together—not that it was Jack's doing. When he left, he wanted your mother to go with him, but his father disapproved. Your mother told him to go and that she would follow later, but we all knew it was impossible.

"He called your mother day and night, promising her he was coming back for her, but your mother knew that if Jack didn't do what his father asked, he'd lose everything, and she could not allow that. Jokingly, she would say, he was too debonair and charismatic to ever be poor.

"When she decided to tell him, I told her that I would do it for her, but she insisted on flying to France and telling him face to face.

"The day she got back, she cried all night. I stayed with her that night. She knew, just as Jack and I did, that Jack's father would never agree to a marriage between them. She told me she knew the first time we went to France on spring break that she would never be accepted. Then, out of the blue, she asked me if it was possible to love two people at the same time.

"She took me off guard. I wanted so much to tell her I loved her since the first day I saw her, but when a picture of Jack came into view, I went blank.

"'I loved the both of you since that first time we met,' she said. Then she threw her arms around me and kissed me on the cheek. I just sat there holding her in my arms. He laughed. I didn't want that moment to pass.

"Months had passed and we had not heard a word from Jack. When we planned to get married, I asked Jack to be my best man. To our surprise, he was married too. After the wedding he decided to buy the house next door. Jack's father had died by then and he inherited the business. I guess by buying the house next door, he was keeping his promise to your mother that he would return one day. We got on with our lives as if nothing had ever happened; never once talked about the love we both shared."

I looked at him. "Yes, baby," he said. "Till this day he still loves her. You've got to remember that Michelle was carrying Jacky at the same time, so when your mother died giving birth to you, it took its toll on her. They had become best friends.

"They stayed here for three years; then Michelle gave Jack an ultimatum. I guess when she died, part of him died too. He was never the same, especially when he looked at you and saw your mother. That's when he decided it was time to take Michelle back home. I agreed to keep Jacky here. I felt it was the right thing at the time."

Dad stood there looking out. I guess with Jack being here, Mother was on his mind.

"Good night, Dad," I said, but he didn't respond. I reached over and kissed him good night and went inside.

When I got upstairs, Jacky was just getting into bed.

"Are you okay?" I asked. She smiled and said yes. I didn't say too much. I knew she had to figure this out for herself. I was ready to turn off the light when Dad came in the room. He
walked over to Jacky's bed. Usually, when Dad came to tuck us in, Jacky would jump up and throw her arms around him—it was a game they played over and over since she was a little girl—but this time she just lay there.

"Like to talk?" He sat on the side of her bed. She started to cry.

"Do you want me to go?" He hesitated and brought his hand to his face, trying to wipe the tears before they rolled down his cheek—a sight I have seen many times.

"I can be selfish and say no," he said, "but I would be thinking of myself. You and Vicky have a great opportunity to see the world, something I could never give you and your father can."

"But I'm going to miss you, Dad."

He smiled. "I could never give you or her, the opportunity your dad can. Your dad is a great man; you'll find that out in time. You're like him in so many ways. All I ask is that you give him a chance. You'll find what you've been missing all these years."

Dad looked at me. "What do you want, Vicky? You know that no matter what you two decide, I'll understand."

"I know," I said. "I'll let you know in the morning."

"Well," he said, "it's getting late and Jack will be here early. His plane leaves at eight a.m."

I kissed him good night. "I love you."

"Well, what's this all about?" he asked.

"Can't a girl tell the best person in the world she loves him?"

He smiled. "Go to sleep." He walked out the door.

About two in the morning I heard Dad walking down the stairs. I wanted to talk to him about what Jacky and I decided. I needed a few minutes with him alone.

I waited a bit and started down the steps. Dad was sitting in his favorite chair, looking at a picture of my mother he kept hanging on the wall. As I watched, I thought I'd never really noticed that picture before. I can't remember the last time I'd looked up at it. I noticed the placement of the chair to the picture. How many times had I seen my father sitting alone there at night? At that moment I realized he was never alone. He was always sitting with her.

Although I wanted to walk in, I decided not to. He raised his glass of wine to her as a show of gratitude. I knew it was something that could be shared only between them. There would be other nights to talk with him, but this was a night of souls coming together, something I could never be a part of. I turned and went upstairs so he wouldn't see me.

When I got to the room, Jacky was staring at Don's picture. She was confused, and when Jacky got that way, the only thing to do was listen to her talk about Don. Even when Don wasn't around, talking about him seemed to calm her.

I walked over and jumped into her bed, throwing the blankets up to our necks.

"What am I going to do, Vicky?" she asked.

"What do you want to do?" She didn't answer. We sat there just looking down at the picture of Don.

"Do you ever think I'll be with Don?" She turned and looked into my eyes. I pulled back. Her eyes were as black as night. It was that same look I saw that night on the step when I felt I was looking in to an empty soul.

She scared me; I had to say something. "Don't be silly," I said, but that look was still there. She didn't move a muscle.

"Jacky," I yelled, "you're scaring me."

She smiled as if nothing had happened. "What's wrong?"

"You just scared the heck out of me."

She didn't know what I was talking about. "If I go to France, I'll never see Don again."

I never heard her doubt herself, when it came to Don. Trying to joke, I said, "Just think, if we go, we'll come back so sophisticated. What do you think Don will say when he sees you for the first time? He'll never think of you as his little sister, will he? You know what they say about the French!"

That got her thinking, and she got up and looked in the mirror. She walked back and forth keeping her eyes on the mirror. "I'll be like one of those women that are so prim and proper." When she turned, she saw Dad standing in the door. We all started to laugh, and Dad shook his head and walked away smiling.

She ran over and jumped into bed. "Do you want to go?"

Sure I do, I thought. But this was her decision, not mine. "Only you can make that decision, though it would be a new chapter in our lives."

As we lay there I could see the thoughts going through her mind. Slowly her eyes closed and she fell asleep.

I got up and went to my bed. I couldn't stop thinking about the look in her eyes; that was the second time it happened. It came and went and she had no recollection of it. I had to do something, but what? How could I go to Dad, or for that matter, anyone? They'd think I was nuts. I had to keep this to myself. I stared at her. There was more to Jacky than I knew. There was something supernatural about her, something that she had no idea of.

The next day when Jack and Michelle came for breakfast, she told them we decided to go to France and that we wanted to spend the rest of the summer here with Dad. They agreed, and after breakfast they left for the airport. Jacky drove and I stayed home with Dad. I think in some small way she was happy her parents were in her life again.

CHAPTER 8

The rest of the summer, not much changed. Jacky was still worshipping the ground Don walked on, and I still had a major crush on Glenn. The guys were doing great. We couldn't go anywhere without hearing their music, no matter where we were or who we were with. People constantly asked about them. The only downside was that Jacky and I were still nonexistent to them. However, there was an upside; Jacky and I got to act like celebrities. It was funny watching Jacky acting so cool when one of our friends would ask about the guys. We couldn't go anywhere without being asked if we could set one of them up with the band. Jacky always tried playing off how much she cared about Don or the band, but her feelings became evident anytime she heard something negative spoken about them; she'd give a look as if she was ready to do battle.

I couldn't imagine going off to France without seeing Don or Glenn, but as summer neared its end, it didn't seem likely I would. They were still on the road, moving from one state to another. They had long days and hard nights. Sure, they were excited about their road to fame but it takes a toll. They never expected it would happen in such a short time. I remember sitting at the dining room table, Dad told us he spoke with Don that morning and he was in Atlantic City, New Jersey. After dinner that night, we were watching an entertainment show on television and the band was doing an interview before their performance in New York that same day.

I wrote Don a letter, telling him about everything that was going on; about Dad getting engaged to Judy, and Ray moving out, even if it just was down the block. When Jacky came in the room, I asked her if she wanted to say anything to Don, which she could add to my letter. But she told me no, she'd write to him herself.

I was curious, and that night as we walked to the mailbox I asked her what she had written, but she simply replied, "Nothing." I could tell by her tone she wanted to change the subject, so I said nothing more about it.

A few days later we received a phone call from Don, who was still on tour with the band. He apologized that they wouldn't be home before we left for France. I was surprised when he asked if Jacky was okay. Usually he'd just say, "Tell Jacky I said hello. I'll be there for Christmas and I'll see her soon."

This call was different. He told me he'd call back in a few days to talk to Dad, but to please give everybody his love. Before he hung up he said, "By the way, Glenn says hello, and we'll see you at Christmas."

I couldn't believe it. Don had never spoken about Glenn and me in the same sentence. Not to mention, this was the first time Glenn had acknowledged me outside of a joke. Then with a chuckle, Don said, "Goodbye, and take care." I never wanted to end a call with him; it had been so long since the last call, and you never really knew when he was going to call next.

At dinner I told everyone that Don had called, and what we had spoken about. At the mention of his name Jacky quivered with excitement. "Did he say anything about me?"

"He'll be home for Christmas and will see you then," I replied. You could see a smile appear from ear to ear. It was good to see her happy. Suddenly the doorbell rang, so Jacky went to answer it.

"There's something really strange going on with Jacky and Don," I told Dad. "Jacky wrote him a letter a couple of weeks ago, but when I asked her what she wrote, she said it was nothing and changed the subject."

Before he could respond, Judy and Jacky came in. "I forgot my key," Judy said as she kissed Dad. She sat down and joined us for dinner. I was going to miss watching them together. More importantly, watching Judy made me aware of the mother I desperately needed in my life.

There was a brief silence at the table while everyone enjoyed their meals. Looking over at Jacky, I could see she thought the same thing about Judy. Sure, Jacky's mother was alive, but she was as absent in her life as mine was.

"How was work, girls?" Judy asked. "Are you ready for the big trip? I'll be in town tomorrow. If you need anything I could pick it up for you."

Jacky shook her head. "If we pack one more thing, they won't let us on the plane."

Judy laughed. "I'm not going, but I'm so excited for the both of you."

As she talked you could see why Dad loved her so. I knew she cared for us just as much as she cared for Dad.

"Judy," Dad said, "settle down. You'd think you were going with them." We all laughed.

After dinner Dad and Judy spent the rest of the night watching TV, while Jacky and I spent the remainder of the night in our room. Neither of us spoke a word about Don and Glenn,

but it was killing me. I don't know why I was so stressed out. Maybe it was the strange thing that was going on with Jacky and I wasn't able to tell anyone, not even her. Or maybe it was that she was keeping a secret from me.

When I turned out the light there was silence in the room. Then Jacky said softly, "Vicky, are you awake?"

I don't really know why, but I didn't answer her right back. I thought she would just go to sleep, but again she called my name. "No!" I said, trying to ignore her.

She began talking anyway. "I wasn't going to tell you, but I told Don to tell Glenn you were asking about him."

What set me off I couldn't explain, but I jumped up and turned the light back on.

"What the heck is going on, and what exactly did you say to him?" I yelled. "When are you going to grow up and move on with your life?" I got no response. Finally I shouted, "You know Don has a girlfriend!"

Her expression went blank. She started to cry. "All I said was tell Glenn you said hello, and that you hope to see him at Christmas."

I didn't know what to say. The look on her face was as if she lost her best friend.

"What did I do wrong?" she sobbed. Her head dropped.

I didn't respond. I reached over and turned off the light, I could hear her crying as I lay there.

About two a.m. the door to our room opened and woke me up. I opened my eyes to see Jacky heading down the stairs. She always did that when she was upset. I had to talk with her and apologize for what I had said. After waiting for a few minutes, I got up and followed her. As I reached the bottom I noticed a reflection from the fireplace. Jacky was sitting in Dad's chair. When I reached the door, I could see she was holding a picture of Don, the one she kept close to her all the time. I heard her whisper, "I'll be with you one day."

What had I done? "Jacky, you will be with him one day." I stepped into the room.

"Vicky, I'm sorry if I hurt you, but I know how you feel about

Glenn. You and I are so different, you hold your feelings inside and are afraid to share who you really are, while I need to share my feelings so I can cope with everything around me. Sometimes I wish I could hold back like you, but I can't, no matter how hard I try. Can you forgive me?"

I didn't really know what to say, but I had to say something, if not for her, for myself. "Listen to me, Jacky; I don't know why I said what I did, it feels like things are getting weird around here. Can you forgive me?"

She smiled. "I can never be mad at you."

"I know it seems like so much is going on and you're getting no results, but all this has to mean something. Maybe one day you will be with Don." I laughed. "You know he can never keep a girlfriend. Maybe you're the answer. I know it's been upsetting to you, that I'm trying to pull you two apart, but I didn't want you to get hurt." I waited to hear a response, but she just held my hand real tight. "I hope you can forgive me."

I sat there holding her in my arms when we heard a familiar voice from behind us. "It's nice to see my girls all grown up."

We turned and saw Dad standing at the door. "Oh boy, you heard everything?" Jacky blurted.

I was glad I didn't say to much. Sure, Dad knew all about Jacky's feelings for Don, but I didn't think he knew how I felt about Glenn. He saw how I lit up when Glenn came into the room, not to mention the numerous times he goofed on me.

Dad walked in and sat down. "I want to share something with you, Jacky. Remember the many times you came downstairs when you were upset and couldn't sleep, and you came crying to me? I'd hold you in my arms right in this chair. You'd close your eyes and fall asleep, and you'd say Don's name. In the beginning I just thought it was because he was always there for you while you were growing up. I figured you needed someone to rely on. But when I found the picture of him under your pillow, I began wondering. I thought it was just a phase you were going though. But I continued to see the same feeling for him as you got older. I understand how you feel, but remember how young you and Don still are. I'm not going to tell you how to feel or what to do, but I will say, when you don't expect things to work out, they usually do. Sometimes you just have to move on with the present. . You never really know the possibilities around you unless you take the time. Love is one of the strangest things to ever want. If you expect it, you may never find it, but there's that rare occasion when you least expect it and it's staring you right in the face. In the meantime, you need to realize the possibility of missing so much while you wait, the kinds of things you're unable to get back later in life. I don't know what else to say. I just don't want to see you missing out on life. If things are meant to be, they'll happen."

He took her hand. "Do me a favor; enjoy the rest of your summer. And then, when you go to France, remember my words, enjoy yourself until you get that surprise knock on the door."

Jacky threw her arms around Dad and said through her tears, "I'm going to miss you. I'm sorry for any trouble I caused you."

He pushed her away and with his hands on her shoulders and replied, "You have been and will always be a daughter to me. Sometimes I don't know who the parent is around here—you girls mother me so much. Even when you were very young, you always acted as though you needed to take care of your brothers and me. I don't think I could've been much of a parent without the help of my children."

Jacky tried to smile, though tears streamed from her eyes. "She's the mother around here; she's the mother I never had."

"But you and Vicky know how to hold a family together." Dad put his arm out as I walked over to him. "She's right, you know." He hugged me. "You're the one who deserves to sit in this chair. Your mother would be very proud. I want you both to know, no matter how old you get, the two of you will always be my little girls."

I looked at Mother's picture and felt she was looking down on us. As we sat there, Dad held Jacky as he had done so many times before, when he carried her to bed.

I remembered times when Jacky couldn't sleep. I'd be awakened by Dad coming into the room. He'd sit with her, talking about what was bothering her, then tuck her in. I remembered how he'd never leave the room without stopping by my bed, even if I didn't need him. It reassured me, knowing he was there. My father had a simple way of wiping away our problems with a kiss. That was the sign of a great father, not only to his kids, but to Jacky and Glenn as well.

There were also those times when, as we got older, he still had to tell us when to go to bed. And as Jacky and I went upstairs, I'd asked him, "Will you be up to tuck us in?"

He'd smile and say, "I sure will."

He'd come up a short time after we were already in bed. He'd stop first at Jacky's bed, pulling the covers up over her head. Jacky always found this funny; she'd always throw her arms around him and say, "I love you, Dad." You could see him melt in her arms. I found it cute, the amount of time it took him to collect himself before making it over to me. Watching him walk over to my bed, I'd hear him clear his throat and wipe his eyes. When he got to my bed, he'd begin by telling me a story.

This night was no different. When we left to go up stairs, even though we were eighteen, I felt the need to ask him to tuck us in. When he came up, as usual he walked over to Jacky, tucked her in, and sat down at her side. "Look, I'm just a phone call away, so if you ever need to talk . . ."

She stopped him, jumped up, and threw her arms around him. "I'm going to miss you, Dad," she said.

"Now, Jacky," he said, as if she were that little girl he held late at night on his lap, "I'm going to miss you, too, but I'll be coming to see you at Christmas. Now lie down and I'll tuck you in." He looked over at the picture of Don and smiled. "I always wondered where that picture got to." Then he kissed her on the forehead and said, "Goodnight."

She replied, "I love you, Dad."

As he walked over to me bed, he wiped a tear from his face and cleared his throat. This time I didn't know if I could hold back my tears. Then I collected myself and he sat down next to me. "Remember when I told you about Jack, your mother, and me?" he asked. I nodded.

"Don is a lot like Jack, you know. When he was growing up," Dad said, "he wanted the whole world, but never saw the important things standing right in front of him. Yes, he has a heart of gold and would never let you be without; on the other had hand, Glenn is a lot like me. Like I've always been there for Jack, Glenn is always there for Don. What makes Glenn and Don different is the fact that Glenn knows what he wants after he reaches the top. But there's a sad part of Glenn; he holds everything inside. I often tell him he's going to get an ulcer someday." He smiled when he said that, and so did I.

"And you," he continued, "you're so much like your mother. Everything you do reminds me of her. Maybe that's why I let you care for us like I do. You know, sometimes when I look at you, I see her for a second, and then reality sets in." He pulled the blanket up to my chin. "I'll never forget that night when you were born. I was there, holding your mother's hand. She knew the second you were ready to come into the world. She looked at me like she was telling me everything would be fine. She squeezed my hand, and I knew she was taking her last breath, and simultaneously you inhaled. It was like she timed it perfectly. She knew, I don't know how or why, but she knew what she had to do. It was like everything she did was to make sure you were all right before she closed her eyes for the last time. She was a remarkable woman."

His voice cracked. He still missed her, after all these years. He didn't say much after that, just sat there.

"Dad," I said, "all these years I felt that Mom was here to tell me what to do. Things would come to me out of the blue. Or when I wasn't thinking about it, things just happened. I always felt there was someone there guiding me. I want to believe it was Mom. I never knew her, but I feel like I do."

He was at a loss for words after I said that. Then he kissed me and said goodnight. Watching him leave the room, I realized there was more to Dad than just being a father. And maybe when he sat in his chair downstairs in front of Mom's picture, telling her about his day, maybe Mom heard him.

I often recalled these moments, with Jacky wiping the tears from her face as Dad held us close, listening to him talk to us. I thank God daily that I had, or we had, a father who was so understanding and so willing to sacrifice himself for his children. I only hoped that when love found its way to my door, a man like my father would be standing there knocking.

I thought about Glenn. He was like Dad, and if Dad was right about him, I hoped that when I answered that knock on the door it would be him. I called out to Jacky, but she was asleep. I know if anyone understood Don more than Dad or me, it was her. I knew she was asleep, but I said goodnight anyway, sank my head into my pillow and closed my eyes.

Chapter 9

Two days before we left for France, Don called home. We all ran for the phone, but Dad got to it first. "Hey, Don! Where are you? Wow! You're leaving for Japan?"

Jacky and I started to jump up and down. Jacky motioned and mouthed, "Maybe he'll come to France." As Dad kept talking, Jacky and I tried so hard to maneuver the phone away from him, but he just told us to settle down. Dad and Don remained on the phone for about ten more minutes before Dad said, "Goodbye," and hung up.

When we complained about not getting to talk to Don, he simply replied, "We had a bad connection. He was at the airport getting ready to go to Japan. But he did mention that he'd be visiting both England and France within the year. He also said not to worry; he'll still see all of us at Christmas and let us know his schedule."

Jacky and I ran upstairs to our room, we were so excited. "Boy," I said, "I can't wait to see him over the holiday, so he can let us know when he's coming to France."

"You know, we could actually see them in England, too. It's not that far from France," Jacky said. Funny, with all the packing and running around, we were getting more and more excited about going to France. We were looking forward to starting college.

We had been packing off and on for weeks, and I thought we had everything we needed. We spent every dime we made on clothes and things for school. As the day drew near, we felt we were ready for anything that came our way. Like Jacky said, we were ready for a new chapter in our lives.

Then Dad yelled, "Judy's here!"

Jacky and I hurried downstairs and found Judy standing at the bottom. "Okay, girls, what's all the excitement?"

"Don called! He's going to be on tour in England, then in France," I replied.

"Yes! We're going to see him there, and we'll probably get backstage passes," Jacky said.

"That's wonderful. We'll probably see you there." Judy looked at Dad.

Surprisingly, he agreed. "Why not? We could use a holiday."

You could tell Judy was as excited as we were. She kissed Dad as we all threw our arms around him. "Okay . . . okay," he said, "let's go to dinner. This will be the last time we'll all be together for a long time."

I grabbed Jacky's hand as we ran for the car. Dad agreed to take us to our favorite restaurant. "Okay, Don's favorite place." We were so excited, it seemed as though we were in the car forever.

In the restaurant, the jukebox was playing one of the hits from the band, and their pictures plastered the wall; it was the group's home away from home. Don and the owner had a special relationship. When Don was still in school he worked for Joe, the owner. You could see that he cared for Don as if he were his own son. Joe lost his son at the age of fifteen. He was hit by a drunk driver walking home from school. So when Joe would tell Dad and the rest of the town how he inspired Don to pursue his music career, Dad didn't mind. Besides, it was kind of cute. Don remained as close as he could with Joe. Don sent photos, records, and other memorabilia to hang the in restaurant.

Later that night, before Dad paid the check, he said, "I have something important to tell you."

Jacky and I looked over at him, not really knowing what to expect. We could see he was getting sentimental.

"Dad . . ." I began.

"No, princess, this isn't one of those times where you have to help your father with his words. I want to tell both my girls how proud I am of them, and let you know how much I love you. I feel as though I'm going to lose you to the world. I know it's time for you to go, but I want you both to know Judy and I love you so very much, and we'll miss you with all our hearts."

I didn't know exactly what to say. Dad had said these things before, but they never had so much meaning as they did now. I felt tears rolling down my face. I looked at Jacky, and of course she was crying too. We held each other's hand tightly under the table. Secretly, we didn't want to leave him, either. We realized Dad would no longer be a daily presence in our lives. Together we got up and walked over to him and hugged him. I couldn't believe we were crying in front of our whole town.

Joe came over. "What's wrong? Was there something wrong with the meals?"

"Nothing's wrong, Joe," Dad said. "Everything was great. It's just that my girls are leaving for college in France. I'm going to miss them."

Joe smiled. "That's wonderful. In fact, that's cause for all of us to celebrate." One thing about our little town, everyone knows everyone. The whole restaurant yelled, "Congratulations!"

Jacky and I had no idea that everyone already knew of our plans. We never thought we made that much of a difference. However, as we stood there in front of everyone, they were all smiling and cheering. They were our extended family. We were going to miss them, too.

Suddenly, "Sad Eyes" began playing over the jukebox, and Joe brought out a huge chocolate cake. It was Don's favorite. Then Joe walked over to the door, and yelled, "Dessert is on the house."

Donna came in and joined us at our table, saying how she was going to miss us, and how she wished she were going, too. Joe asked about Don, and where he'd be touring next. Dad told him Don was going to Japan, and maybe to England. Joe was so excited he made Dad promise to tell Don that he said hello.

The next morning, Ray and his girlfriend, Ruth, were there to see us off. I sat down on the steps, looking across the street at the house that sat empty. Weeds covered the fence that wrapped around the grounds. The paint was fading from lack of care. It had been empty ever since the young couple died. Although it had been shown many times, there was always a reason why it had never sold.

Funny, the house seemed to be waiting for the right couple. It brought back so many memories of Jacky and me, how we used to sit and stare at the young couple that owned it. I wish I knew then what I do now about love. Now I could relate to the way they held each other's hands when they walked down the street, as if they were the only people on earth; or the way they sat on their porch at night when everyone was doing the same, every eye was on them; watching them as they sat on their front porch, holding each other ever so close. People laughed, and others were upset that they carried on like they did. But that didn't seem to bother them.

Jacky would run out of the house when she saw them sitting out on a cool night. She said, "That's going to be me and Don one day."

Now I was getting homesick and I hadn't even left. I was going to miss this place. Then I heard a voice from the end of the porch saying, "Are you ready?" I looked to my right, and there was Ray, sitting alone.

Ray was unique in that he seemed to walk through life, not damaged by all that happened around him. Things affected him, but he'd always work though them. I thought Dad and I were close, but the reality was that Ray knew what Dad had gone through during and after our mother's death. It was funny how he, too, never mentioned it. I guess because we were children, they didn't want to burden us which such sadness. Ray resembled Dad in many ways in that he, too, was a quiet person, never saying much. He would listen to the events of others, not speaking unless it was absolutely necessary. I never really considered myself close to him, because of the age difference. However, he had impacted my life.

I walked over and sat down beside him. "I guess I'm as ready as I'll ever be. Will you come and visit?"

"I sure will, Little Miss," he said, smiling.

I recalled all the times I'd heard those same words growing up. I knew those words. Looking up at him, I smiled.

"There's that look I remember so well," he said. "I don't know why I never recalled it before. You don't remember me taking you to the park every day. When it was time to go, you'd cry and pout all the way home."

At that moment, I remembered. He'd make me smile, forgetting that we'd ever left the park, and then he'd say, "Who's my Little Miss?" When he said that, I didn't know how to respond. I thought it had been Dad all along. Whenever I needed consoling, or hurt myself, or just needed caring for after school until Dad came home, Ray had been there. I thought it had been my father, but it was Ray.

Then Ray told me, after our mother died, it was the hardest on Dad. He became a single parent raising three young children alone, while having a full time job. I didn't realize, nor could I ever imagine the tremendous pressure he was under. That went for Ray, too. And there was the added pressure when Jacky came to stay with us. And we can't forget Glenn.

Remembering, I couldn't believe it. It was Ray on the playground and it was Ray that had to pick up Jacky when she had to leave school early because she was sick.

"Now that was a real nightmare," he said laughing. He put his arm around me, pulling me close.

"What was Mom like?" I asked.

His hand fell to the arm of the chair.

"I know no one likes taking about her," I said. Maybe because it was a subject no one ever talked about.

I saw the hesitation in his face as he searched for the right words. "At first when you were born, I couldn't help resenting you." I looked at him and he returned a smile. "You were a constant reminder of her. From the beginning Dad tried to step up, but he couldn't manage to get over her death and move forward. Part of him died that day. Even today he isn't the same person he was when she was alive, but he did learn to move on. Mom's death didn't really affect Donny as much; he was still so young. When I look at him today, I wonder if he remembers anything about her. I remember sitting at her feet as she held Donny in her arms. I could feel the love as she rocked him. Mom had an energy that was hard to explain, but you could definitely feel it. And now, looking at you all grown up, it's like looking at her. She was a great woman." He stared at the garden. "She loved her plants."

I knew he wanted to be alone, so I headed for the door. I just couldn't believe all this time it had been Ray. Ray was the one I ran to when Dad wasn't around. It was all getting clearer. I looked at him differently. I wished I'd spent the time getting to know him again. Without a word, I walked back over to him, put my arm around him, and kissed him on the cheek.

"What was that for, Little Miss?"

"No reason. I just like hearing you call me that."

He handed me a small French-to-English translation book. "You're going to need this when you get there."

As we loaded the car, I caught Dad alone. "If you want me to stay, I will."

"Don't be silly. This is your chance to really experience life. Your time is now. I want you to enjoy every minute of it. Do me a favor, just be yourself and you'll make me proud. You always have."

I had heard him say those words in the past, but as my eyes caught his, I could feel the love he had for me. Taking his hand, I said, "Make me a promise, Dad."

He nodded. "Anything, dear."

"Promise me we'll talk at least once a week."

"You know we will. Why do you ask such a thing?"

I simply looked at him. It was as though I was spending the night away from home for the first time. "As long as I can hear your voice I'll never fear being so far away from home."

He put his arms around me and held me close. "All you'd ever have to do is tell me you wanted to come home and I'd be there, no questions asked. Don't ever be afraid of experiencing new things. You'll feel better once you get there. Always remember, I'm only a phone call away."

Jacky walked over to Dad. "Vicky always took care of me," she said, "but now I'm going to take care of her. All those years Vicky watched over us, this time I'll be the one who will be watching over her."

"Let's go or you'll miss your plane!" Ray urged.

I turned to Ray. "Don't you have any wise words for your little sister?"

"No, Little Miss, there isn't anything I could tell you that you don't already know. You're a great kid. I don't have to tell you how I feel."

"No, you don't, I know exactly how you feel."

Suddenly, he grabbed me and held me tight. "I haven't said it lately, but I love you."

I felt tears running down my face. I held him tight. "I love you, too Ray." I should have thought of something more to say as a way of thanking him for all the lonely nights when he was there for me, but Ray was right, we understood each other.

"You'll always be my Little Miss," he whispered.

We all piled in the car. Jacky, Ruth, and I sat in the back seat, Dad, Judy, and Ray in the front. You could feel the tension in the air. Everyone was just a little sad.

I don't remember anyone speaking. After we arrived at the airport, Ray checked our bags, so I decided to get a few magazines for Jacky and me to read during our trip. Judy was there as I walked in the store.

"Here, I got you something to read on the plane," she said. "I'm going to miss you." She cried. I hugged her and cried with her.

As I walked over to the counter, I noticed Dad talking to Jacky. Watching him with her made me more proud of him. I don't ever remember her not being included as part of our family. He hugged her, and kissed her on the forehead and motioned for me to come over.

"Are you ready?" he asked.

"Yes, Dad."

"It's time to board, but I want you both to know, I love you so much."

As we said goodbye, part of me wanted to stay. I wanted so much for Dad to tell me not to go, but I knew he wouldn't.

In minutes we were aboard the plane, leaving behind everyone and everything we knew. I knew we were beginning a new chapter in our lives.

Jacky ran to her seat, making sure she got to sit by the window. Like a child, she was so excited. As I waited to get to my seat I felt uneasy. Maybe because I was leaving for an unknown place I wasn't sure of. As I leaned over to sit down, I looked down at her. The feeling I felt that night on the steps came over me—as if it was telling me we were making a big mistake.

CHAPTER 10

We didn't say much on the flight over, thinking of what we were giving up and what was ahead. I kept myself occupied by studying the translation book that Ray gave me before we left the house, so I could at least understand something when I got there. You'd never know that I'd had three years of French in high school.

When I opened the book it read, "You will always be my Little Miss." I wanted to cry. As a matter of fact, I felt a tear roll down my face. He knew that when he called me Little Miss, I believed everything was going to be fine.

Jacky stared out the window. I think we all know who she was thinking of.

To say we were at a loss for words when we arrived would be an understatement. When we got off the plane, I could feel the excitement and I was looking forward to a great adventure. We had no idea who was going to meet us, just assumed it would be Jack and Michelle. As we waited I kept thinking, *Of course they'll be here, they wouldn't dare not show for their daughter's arrival.* Jacky and I both knew that they were attempting to make amends for their absence in her life. That was the whole idea of us coming to France in the first place.

Walking through the airport to get our baggage, I could see the nervousness on Jacky's face. "I don't see them," she said.

I noticed she never used the terms "mother" or "father" when talking about Jack and Michelle. She simply used the word "them." You couldn't blame her, I guess.

As we exited the airport, we searched for them. I'm not really sure how much time passed, but it seemed like an eternity. I don't think either of us believed it. We had left all we knew to begin a new chapter in our lives, and we felt as if we were alone.

After thirty minutes, we noticed a fancy black limousine parked at the curb. At that point I was so disgusted, I had no idea it might be there for us. A man stepped from the front of the car. Although he was staring right at us, he looked uncertain.

Jacky and I looked at each other. "What do you think?" I asked. She shrugged. "Walk over and ask who he's waiting for," I said.

You could tell she was nervous; she shook her head no.

"Come on," I said. "I'll go with you."

As we walked over to the man, I felt Jacky's grip on my shoulder getting tighter and tighter. I couldn't help but giggle, thinking about how she'd said she was going to take care of me. Stumbling though my book, trying to put a sentence together. I said, "*Faire tom parler.*" But by the look on his face I didn't say it right.

He smiled, but didn't answer. I turned the page again and found the right phrase. "*Parlez-vous Anglais?*"

"*Oui, Mademoiselle,*" he said.

I understood that, I knew that much from school.

"*Oui, Mademoiselle,* I speak English." That's why he was smiling. He'd let me go on because he was getting a kick out of it.

"Are you waiting for anyone?" I asked.

"*Oui,* I am. I'm waiting for two children."

"Would their names be Jacky and Vicky?"

"*Oui, Mademoiselle.*"

"Well, we're Jacky and Vicky," I said, "but we are not children."

"I'm sorry, *Mademoiselle,* but *Monsieur* Boilean said only that I was to pick up two children. I assumed you would be much younger."

Being the tough person I was, I wanted to tell him I was not a child. But of course, I didn't say that. As the man opened the door and took our bags, Jacky and I glanced at each other. We really didn't care who arrived to pick us up at that point, but it would have being nice if her parents had been there to meet her.

The drive home was exciting; there was so much to see. We weren't in Texas anymore, that was for sure. I was amazed when we drove down each street; they were so small. I wondered at times if the limo would be able to make it. Everything seemed medieval. All the houses and even the streets were made from cobblestone or brick. It seemed that the driver went out of his way to show us some of the landmarks on the way. At one time, he pointed out the window.

"Oh, wow!" Jacky yelled. It was the Eiffel Tower. She jumped to the window. It was a sight to see. I glanced at the driver as he watched her. He seemed to get a kick out of the way she got so excited. Her eyes were wide open, as though she was trying to absorb everything she could. I noticed the driver smiling at her. He too, saw the innocence in her.

We drove for a bit and then he stopped and rolled down my window. In front of me was the most beautiful building I'd ever seen—Notre Dame. Jacky leaped over to my side of the car and stared, not saying a word. I couldn't help looking in her eyes—I mean, she was practically in my lap. I could see she was thinking of Don, but there was something else. I didn't put it together until later.

From the first minute we landed in France, she knew what her destiny would be.

Before the driver pulled away I asked her, "How would you like to get married there?" She smiled and went back to her side of the car. It was the first time she didn't have an answer concerning Don.

As the driver pulled away, he noticed Jacky just sitting there with no expression on her face. I guess it did seem odd; one minute she was so excited and the next she looked as though she had the world on her shoulders. I looked up at him and smiled.

We sat back in our seats and talked with the driver some. He really wasn't a bad guy. He spoke with a French accent, we couldn't understand a word he was saying most of the time. Then, without warning, Jacky gave me a look. You know the look. I knew she was up to something, but I had no idea what.

"Excuse me," she said to the driver.

"*Oui, Mademoiselle?*"

"*Savez-vous Monsieur Jacques?*"

"*Oui Mademoiselle, Monsieur* Jacques. He's my employer," he replied.

"Well, I am his daughter," she said with a smile on her face.

"Are you, *Mademoiselle*? I didn't know Mr. Jack had a daughter until today."

That hit home. She hadn't expected that. She just nodded and sat back.

"I guess I'll be driving you around as well, *Mademoiselle*."

Jacky looked at me with surprise. "Can you believe this? I have my own limousine." I simply smiled and looked out the window.

"And now you have a castle," I said. The driver looked back and chuckled.

"Unbelievable! How cool is this" she yelled as she looked out. The driver had turned onto a property that seemed to be as big as a national park. He continued down the drive until we came upon the biggest house we'd ever seen.

"Is this where we live?" Jacky stuttered.

"Oui, *Mademoiselle*, this is your home." He stepped from the car and opened our door. He took our hand as each of us stepped out. We just stood there in disbelief.

In a few seconds Michelle came out of the house. "Hi, girls," she said in her French accent. "How was your trip?"

"Fine," I said.

"I'm sorry we could not be there when you arrived, but your father had an unexpected meeting. You must be exhausted. Let's get you both inside and I'll show you to your rooms."

Inside, the house was magnificent, the kind of thing you only see on TV. We started upstairs and I noticed the staircase wrapped around each floor, allowing you to see every room. I always knew Jacky was rich, but I just never thought she was this well off. The house was enormous.

"Here's your room, Vicky," Michelle said. "Jacky, your room is down the hall." As they walked down the hall, Jacky looked back. I threw my arm up as if to say, "everything's okay."

I walked into my room, breathless. I unpacked and checked out the rest of the room. I could get used to living like this, I thought. I didn't think Dad even knew they had this much money. I walked over to the bed and sat down, remembering that back home Jacky and I shared a room no bigger than the bathroom. Now I had this room all to myself. I felt an emptiness inside. For the first time, I felt alone. I thought about Jacky. If she felt the same way, I had to be there with her. I started down the hall to see where she was, but I couldn't find her anywhere.

"Jacky," I yelled, "Where are you?" I didn't hear a thing. I made a left at the end of the hall, and there were four more rooms. I walked on and called out and finally heard her answer, "In here."

I walked into this large room, and if you think my room was big, you should have seen hers. She was sitting on the bed looking like she had lost her best friend.

"What's up?" I asked.

"Look around," she said.

I didn't know what she was talking about. "What am I looking for?"

"Did you ever think they had this much money? Didn't they want me here with them? What did I do that made them leave me behind?"

I didn't know what to say. I knew they'd left when my mother died, and that her death had taken a toll on Jack, but I was not the one to tell her. "I don't know what to say about all this, but I do know that, if we just give it time, you'll find out." Before she could say anything, I added, "We're here now. When the time is right you'll ask why, but until then, let's just have a good time."

She sat down and I thought, *if only Don was here, everything would be okay*. I looked over to her nightstand and there was one of the pictures of Don, big as day. I laughed. "I see you brought Don with you."

She jumped off the bed. "Look in here." She walked over to two doors that opened into the wall. There was another bedroom.

"Woo!" I said. "Whose room is that?"

"No one," she said. "That's if I need more room. What would I need more room for?"

I laughed.

"What's so funny?" she said.

"That's if you need to park your 747," I said, hoping to get a laugh out of her. But I didn't.

Jacky heard her mother walking down the hall. She ran out of the room quickly, before I could stop her. "Why is Vicky staying so far down the hall?" she demanded. "Why can't she stay in the room connected with mine?"

Michelle hesitated. "I thought you and Vicky would want to have your own rooms, don't you agree?"

"No." Jacky stepped back. "And if we needed our privacy we could close the door. So if you don't mind, Vicky will move into that room."

I walked out into the hall. "Jacky, my room is fine." I looked at Michelle. "I'm sorry, but that room will be fine."

"No, it's not!" Jacky yelled back.

Michelle said, "Vicky, I'll be happy to have your things put in that room."

All I could think of to say was, "Thank you."

Michelle walked down the hall and turned back. "Dinner will be ready soon."

You could tell that she was hurt. All she was trying to do was make us comfortable.

Jacky went back into her room. I ran in behind her. "What's wrong?" she asked when she saw my face. She knew I was mad.

"Don't you ever do that again," I yelled.

"What did I do?"

"You put me in a spot with your mother. You've got to apologize."

"What?"

"You heard me; you've got to tell her you're sorry. If you don't, I will. And I want you to do something for me."

"What would that be?"

"Until you understand why they didn't come for you, let it be, please?"

She hesitated. "Okay, we'll do it your way." She started down the stairs.

I felt like we got off on the wrong foot with Michelle, and if we were going to be here for the next four years, I thought we needed to get to know her.

We walked into the gigantic dinning room. There was a huge table in the middle of the floor and a big, big chandelier hung right above it. It was amazing. All I could think about was the party we could have.

Her father and mother were sitting at the far end. "Up here, girls," Jack yelled. Jacky walked over and sat beside him and I sat beside Michelle.

The more they talked, the more comfortable they got with each other. I still felt a little weird around Michelle. It was as if she was jealous of the relationship Jacky and I had. Maybe I was wrong and I was just upset about the whole room situation, but I hoped we could overcome it in time.

As for Jack, I felt I knew him for years. Maybe it was the way he made you feel when he spoke to you or his distinguished black hair with just a little bit of gray on the sides. He reminded me of James Bond. I could see why Mother fell in love with him. In fact I could see were anyone would fall head over heels when first seeing him.

During dinner Michelle asked, "How's your father doing?" She seemed to care for Dad. She told me all about him and the things he'd done for her. He must have been there for her when Jack was going through Mother's death.

After dinner I told Jack I needed to call Dad to let him know we'd arrived okay and he led me to the phone.

While I was talking, Jacky yelled, "Tell Dad I'd like to talk to him." When she said that, I noticed the look Michelle gave Jack.

I gave Jacky the phone.

"She'll be fine," Jack said. "Just give her time." I really didn't know what he meant, but I smiled.

Jack stayed near the phone while I joined Michelle. I had to make things right before another night went by. I sat down across from her. "I don't know what to call you."

"Why don't you call me, Michelle?"

After I said what I did, I felt silly. Of course I should call her Michelle. What else would I call her? But she never said anything else. I had to say something to break the ice. Before I went to bed, I had to let her know that I was not a threat.

"Michelle, when she calls my father Dad, it doesn't mean she doesn't love you or Jack. It's that we're the only family she knows. She's never been without us, and we've never been without her. Don't let it bother you when she calls my father Dad. She'll always be a part of us; that will never change. But you're her mother, and I know she loves you, because she's that kind of girl. She's a wonderful person. She knows what she wants and she will try hard to get it. She doesn't give up. That's what I respect about her. Her feelings get hurt easily, but she forgives more easily than anyone I know. To know her is to get up in the morning and figure what she'll do today to make you feel glad that you do know her."

Michelle took my hand. "You really love her, don't you? Your dad said you're always there for her and I'm grateful for that." She paused. "I'm sorry I wasn't there for her. One day I'll tell her and I hope she'll understand. I'd like to make it all up to her."

"Just get to know her first," I said.

"I'm glad you decided to come, I'd like to become your friend." She put her arms around me and hugged me.

I think she needed me to let her know that I was not a threat when it came to Jacky. I so wanted them to get to know each other, so they could have the relationship I never had with my mother. I felt she needed my approval. "Just talk to her, you'll see."

Jack and Jacky walked into the room. "What's going on here?" Jack asked jokingly.

Michelle replied, "Oh, just getting to know each other."

"Well, Jacky," I asked, "what did Dad have to say?" When I said "Dad," I looked at Michelle and was relieved to see her smile.

"Do you mean, did he say anything about Don?" Jacky asked. "No, he didn't."

That night when I got to my new room, everything I owned was there. I was glad, for I was already getting homesick for Dad, and my own bed. I knew, if I was in that room all the way down the hall, I would have cried myself to sleep.

After I took a hot bath, I came out and Jacky was sitting on my bed. "What's up, Jacky? Can't sleep?"

"No, she replied, "even with Don's picture beside my bed."

I laughed and walked to the closet. I turned back when I heard her sobbing. "Jacky, please don't do this, I'm so close to bawling myself."

"I miss Don, she said. "I wish I could talk to him."

"Sure you do, and I want to be the queen of England, or in this case, the queen of France, if they have a queen."

She laughed when I said that. "You're too much, but I know you better than that. I know you want to be home right now, too."

"Yes, I do, but that's because everything is so new to us." She just sat there. I knew this was going to be one of those nights that we would sit up talking about Don. I stopped, "Look," I said, "let's do what we do best when we can't sleep. You know, because Don didn't call, or one of his girlfriends was at the house."

"Good idea," she said. We jumped up and ran downstairs to the kitchen. There was chocolate cake left over from dinner and it had our names on it.

As we ran, she laughed. I knew that if I could keep her from thinking of Don for the next few days, the change would be easier for her. Not that I didn't feel like crying myself. On the contrary, I wanted to call home and tell Dad to send me a ticket.

When we pulled out the cake, we were surprised to see Jack and Michelle coming through the door. Michelle asked, "Can we join you?"

"Of course," I said and got up to get more plates.

We talked about Jacky and Jazzman; how she won every show we entered, but most of all we talked about Don and the band. I watched Jack looking at her as she talked about Don; he was looking at himself through his own eyes. I could see that Michelle understood what Jacky felt and that she felt sad knowing Jacky would be hurt if Don fell in love with someone while on the road.

It's funny—Jacky had more in common with Michelle and Jack than she thought. Michelle loved Jack so much that she gave up her daughter so she could regain the love she never had. Jack, once and still, loved someone whom he lost, which almost destroyed his life. Looking at them, I knew that only time would tell what their lives would become as a family and Jacky as an adult.

I could see the look in Jack eyes; he was not seeing me, but the reflection of my mother. I reminded him of her. I'd seen the pain in his eyes whenever her name came up. After all these years he was still in love with her. I knew that would never change.

Michelle knew it, too, and had accepted it for a long time. I guess you had to respect her for that. Just like Dad and Jack; they loved the same women, yet the friendship between them all was unbreakable.

The next thing we realized the sun was coming up. "I need to get to the office, and you girls need to check out the school." Jack jumped out of his seat. He kissed Michelle and ran up the stairs, Jacky running behind him.

When I got up to leave, Michelle grabbed my arm. "You were right; all you have to do is listen. Thank you, Vicky."

With Jacky out of the room, I asked her about my mother. "No one ever talks about her at home," I explained.

"Your mother and I became very good friends when we lived next door. She was so happy to find out she was having a baby girl. She couldn't wait to show you off to the whole town. We were all devastated when she died. Do you know that your father, Jack, and your mother were best friends all through college?" She stopped, and then blurted out, "Your mother and Jack were lovers."

I didn't say anything.

She continued, "It wasn't until your mother died that I realized Jack never stop loving her." I could see her pain as she spoke. "I remember the day you were born. Your father and I were with her. Jack was in France. We never expected anything to go wrong. It was your father who called Jack and told him. We didn't hear from him for months, until your father went to France to get him and bring him home. I took you and your brother to my house, and your father and Jack stayed in France for weeks. I think they needed time together. What I understand from Jacky's grandfather was that they went on a drinking binge. When they sobered up, he sent them back to the states.

"As hard as it was for your father, he put his feelings aside and went to France to bring Jack back. He knew Jack still loved your mother, and deep inside he knew your mother held a place in her heart for him. When Jack came back I told him I wanted to come back here. I needed
to be with my family. I understood why we lived in America and just next door, but it was my time to go home and get my husband back. It took a long time, but we made it."

I spoke up. "Michelle, could I ask you why?" She looked at me, puzzled. "What about Jacky, and why didn't you take her with you?"

She sighed. "That's what we regret every day of our lives. I never intended to leave Jacky, but Jack thought she'd be better with your father. I know that was selfish of us, but your father also said she'd be better off with him. He knew Jacky would be shuttled around to boarding schools if she was here. And he knew we needed time to get our lives together. I was so in love with Jack, just like he was so in love with your mother. So, the longer we left Jacky there, the harder it became to take her away from the only home she knew. It hurt so much when we called, and she called Mike, 'Dad' and told us how you and she did everything together. Don't you remember our visits and how she didn't want to leave your father's side? We didn't want to hurt her any more than we already had. I'm hoping we can make it up to her."

I felt the circle that all their lives had taken. They all knew of the love they had for each other and, strange as it may sound, they respected each other for it.

"You will make it up to her," I said. "But you need to tell Jacky what you told me."

"Your father told us about how she feels about Don."

"I'm glad he told you, but Michelle, don't ever try to come between Jacky and Don. I tried, and realized it was not up to me. There's something about the whole thing that seems odd. As long as I can remember, and as young as she was, she always loved him. It was like she knew all her life that he was there for her, and that's how it was meant to be. I hope France will change things, but that will be up to her."

I heard Jacky yelling. "I better get up there before she has a breakdown."

Michelle smiled. "As soon as you girls are ready, we'll head into the city and look around."

"Okay," I said, and ran up the stairs. I passed Jack on the steps; he seemed to be enjoying having us around.

CHAPTER 11

Everything was going great at school and at home. Jacky and I made new friends. And Jacky met a guy. I spotted him the first morning we signed up for classes. He was standing outside the entrance—actually, he was blocking the door with a few of his friends. When I saw him, I thought, *Woo!* But as we got closer to the door I noticed him looking toward Jacky. As he opened the door for us, he said, *"Bon Jour Fillies."* Jacky looked up at him and smiled and kept walking.

After a few days, we saw him again in one of our classes. He made it a point to sit next to us, and of course Jacky was her usual self, quiet and shy. Watching them was like looking at two bookends. Neither one of them said a word; they just smiled back and forth. He was as shy as she was. If not for his friends pushing him to ask her out, he would have waited a few more weeks. And I guess I did the same with her—pushed her, that is.

His name was Jean-Luc Moreau. He had jet-black hair and dark brown eyes. He was slender and taller than Jacky, but not by much. He lived near us and one day, as we were driving home, we passed his house. It seemed that each house you looked at in our neighborhood was bigger than the next, and his house was definitely big. I asked around about him and even Jack and Michelle knew of his family. The Moreaus were from old money and very well-known. According to the people who knew them, Jean-Luc's father had high hopes for son, or I should say, he had his future planned out.

Even though Jean-Luc was good-looking and obviously cared for Jacky, there was something about him that bothered me. I thought maybe I was just being overprotective of her.

After he got his nerve up to ask her out, she finally said yes.

I was sitting in the parlor that night when Rose, the housekeeper, answered the door. It was Jean-Luc. Jacky was still upstairs getting ready, so Rose invited him in. He sat down across from me. Watching him fidgeting in his seat, I thought it was kind of cute; he didn't know where to put his hands, or what to look at next. I remember thinking that for a Frenchman, he was awfully shy.

"Where you guys going tonight?" I asked.

"To the pub," he said quietly.

"That's good."

When Jacky came into the room, she asked, "Would you like to join us?"

But before I could answer, Jean-Luc said, "I think Vicky has other things to do." That stuck in my mind for a long time.

"He's right," I said. "I do have things to do." As they walked out the door I remember thinking, *For someone so shy, he sure is quick to answer when Jacky invited me along.*

I thought about how different Don and Jean-Luc were. They were complete opposites, not just in looks, but in personality. Don was a home-town boy, with that rustic look about him, outspoken and definitely not shy. Don had a boyish charm, but everyone knew not to cross him; even when he was wrong he thought he was right. But maybe I was biased, being his sister.

On the other hand, there was Jean-Luc. I didn't know him that well, but he was definitely not like Don, although, they both saw something special about Jacky. Jean-Luc was shy, but expressed his feelings when it came to Jacky; which became more obvious as I got to know him better. On the other hand, Don made his opinions clear.

One day as we were leaving school, he invited a few of us over to his house. His father was there when we all walked in. The way he was looking at us was as if he was comparing us to Jean-Luc's other friends. Of course, his friends were from well-to-do families. When his father asked Jacky were she lived and who she was, he seemed to be comfortable with it.

"Tell your father I'll be by to see him," he said with a big smile.

When he asked me, I told him I was from a small town in Texas, but before I could say another word, he walked away. He walked over to Jean-Luc and said something. Whatever it was, it resulted in Jean-Luc coming over and telling us it was time to go. I could see that his father controlled him more than we all had thought.

Jean-Luc wasn't one to tell anyone what he wanted, but I knew he was falling in love with Jacky. I think Jacky made a big difference in his life.

At first Jean-Luc felt uncomfortable around our friends, like his father did around me. I think that's why he liked Jacky so much—you know, her being shy and all. I think he thought I controlled her. I didn't find that out until much later. Maybe that's what I felt when I first met him.

One thing I couldn't figure out was what Jacky saw in him. I mean, he was so not Don, but one thing he did do was shower her with the attention she'd craved all her life. Even though she had a mischievous side to her, she needed that attention. He was at her beck and call. Maybe that's how she wished Don would be.

We hung out at a little pub outside the college called The Hangout. Being there was just like being in a bar in America. The bar had a fifties theme. They played all the top hits, and of course, *The Boys of Summer* were on top and one of the best bands all over the world. I remember when Jehane Dupre,' who became a big part of our lives, first found out about us and the band. It was at the pub. Not that we were special, but we had one of the band members as one of the family.

As we sat there, one of the bands songs came on and Jacky shouted, "That's Don."

"No way," Jehane said.

"Tell them, Vicky," Jacky said.

I was in shock, for when it came to Don and the band, Jacky made sure she was the one who bragged about them. This time she put it off on me. I told everyone about them and, as usual, everyone wanted to meet them.

"I hear they're coming to England for a concert," Jehane said.

"When?" Jacky sipped her Coke.

"Don't you know?" came from across the room. We looked back and there were our not-so-girlfriends, as Jacky called them, sitting behind us. They were girls who thought they were too good for anyone who didn't come from money.

When Jacky and I first arrived in France, we couldn't wait to start college. We thought joining a secret society club would give us a new sense of sisterhood. After weeks of looking for the right one, we picked one that had all the really cool girls. We really thought we could make new friends and would be part of the in-crowd, but as it turned out, they believed they were better than us. That's how we met Jehane, she was also trying to join the secret society. Jehane's parents were working-class people. She got into college on a scholarship, so the not-so-girlfriends felt she didn't meet their high standards. .

Jacky was one of the wealthy people, but she never mentioned her money or acted better than anyone. She was good that way. She was raised with me, so she knew how it was to make ends meet. Jacky could never degrade anyone, nor think that money made her a better person.

The day we found out who made it into the society, there was a notice outside their house. I remember seeing Jehane walking in to where all the girls were sitting. Jacky and I were standing at the other side of the room, when our not-so-girlfriends came walking in, then asked all of us to sit down and they would let us know who made it or did not. They called Jehane's name first. Their attitudes were degrading, and that's how they made Jehane feel when they told her why she didn't meet up to their standards.

I knew then, even if I made it, I was not going to join. Jehane looked around the room, feeling ashamed of who she was. She swallowed and got up and walked out, trying to hold back her tears.

Before my name was called I stood up and started to leave, but not before one of the girls asked me where I was going. "You can't leave now," she said.

I knew I hadn't made it, but I was not going to give them the pleasure of degrading me in front of anyone. "Try and stop me," I said, and walked out, leaving Jacky sitting there.

I followed Jehane out the door. She didn't know I was behind her. She sat down on the steps and sobbed.

"They're not worth it," I said.

She started and turned around.

"You don't need them," I said.

This made her feel a little better. "What about you?"

"I think if I spent any more time with them, I might have to put glue in their shampoo."

She laughed.

When Jacky's name was called, Jehane and I ran to the door. Jacky was picked, of course; not for who she was, but for her money. She stood up and very politely said, "I'm happy to have made it."

The girls gave her their secret society look and said congratulations, but before they could get it all out, Jacky stopped them. "You didn't let me finish. I was hoping to be with girls that I'd enjoy being with, but you just turned them down, so I don't think I'd enjoy being with a bunch of nit-wits." She politely walked out of the room.

Jehane and I were laughing so hard they could hear us inside. I don't know where Jacky got backbone to say what she did, but I was proud of her.

When she came outside, she said, "You didn't think I was going to stay if you weren't going to be there, did you?"

I was never as proud of her as I was that day.

A few weeks later all of us were at The Hangout when Jacky dropped all her change into the jukebox. You can guess what she played. As she stood there, our not-so-girlfriends walked up to her. They told her they wanted to play something different, that they were tired of hearing that song and *The Boys of Summer*.

Jacky went off. Normally all you had to do was look at Jacky funny and she'd freeze up. But everyone who knew Jacky knew never to say anything bad about the band.

I walked over to the jukebox where Jacky and the girl were standing. "What's up?" I asked with a smile. "Did you play my songs?" I looked directly at them and asked, "You got change? There's one more song I'd like to hear. You know the one Don sings."

They went back to their friends. Ever since then we'd just say hello or goodbye to them if we saw them anywhere.

Now when one of them would ask, "If you're their sister, why don't you know?" I waited for Jacky to lay into the girl. Jacky looked at Jean-Luc, then at me. I waited for her to open her mouth but she just stared and didn't say a word.

"That's not for sure," I said and added sarcastically, "and when they do, you're not invited backstage with us." Thinking about it now, it was kind of lame.

As the night went on everyone was still talking about the band. It was weird that Jacky was pretty cool about the whole thing. When one guy said something like, "I don't think they're that great," Jacky just went on talking to Jean-Luc without saying a word. I wondered, *is this the real thing? Is she in love with this guy? Or is it because he's becoming so possessive?*

It was getting late and I told Jacky I was going home, that I'd see her later and left. I didn't know what to think about Jacky and Jean-Luc and where their relationship was going. I started to feel uncomfortable around him, and I think he felt the same about me.

The more uncomfortable I felt about Jean-Luc the more homesick I became. I knew if I was home, I could go to Dad and he would make it right. So I went up to my room and wrote him a letter. I missed Dad, and was counting the days till I could see him again.

My letter went on and on, I couldn't concentrate and couldn't seem to finish it. I just wanted to call him. No, I just wanted to hear his voice. Before I could finish, I dropped the pen and started to cry. I was so homesick I couldn't finish the letter. I put my head down on my desk and just let it out. The next thing I felt was a hand on my shoulder.

"Vicky? What's wrong, dear?" Michelle asked in her French accent.

"Oh, nothing," I said.

"Well, nothing is rolling down your face."

"No matter how old I get, I still get homesick for Dad," I sobbed.

She rubbed her hand across my back. "I've being married more than twenty years," she said, "and I still miss my father."

I smiled.

"That's why they invented *le téléphone*, my dear." At that we both burst out laughing. "Get on *le téléphone* and call him. And do us a favor; whenever you feel like this, pick up *le téléphone* and call home. That's why there's *le téléphone* next to your bed."

On her way out of the room, she stopped and turned. "The phone's not going to dial itself."

I ran to the bed and called Dad. The second I heard his voice, I really started to bawl. He must have thought someone died.

"What's wrong, baby?" he asked.

"I just wanted to hear your voice," I cried.

"Oh, Vicky, you scared me. I told you I'm just a phone call away," he said in a soft voice.

"I know, Dad. Now I feel silly."

"That all right baby, I'm glad you called. Are you okay?"

"Yes, but I wish you were here."

"Look, Vick, I wasn't going to tell you this. I wanted to surprise you. Jack sent tickets for the family to come at Christmas."

"They never told Jacky or me!" I said.

"It was going to be a surprise."

"Have you heard from Don? Is he coming, too?"

"Yes, I hope so."

"I can't wait! I'm sorry for scaring you and acting like a baby."

He laughed. "Look, baby, you'll always be my little girl." It felt good to hear that. "Tell Jacky 'hi,' and we'll see everyone on Christmas." Then he hung up.

At that point Michelle walked by and peeked in the room. She didn't have to say anything; she just smiled.

I wanted to thank Jack for inviting everyone for Christmas. As I walked down the hall I thought, *I don't care if I'm a daddy's girl, my father is a man I respect and admire.*

At the end of the hall, I saw Jacky coming toward me. She looked strange. She stopped and looked right at me with a blank stare. Her eyes were as black as coal. She didn't move or say a word. It was that same expression I had come to see more and more lately. I looked in the room, hoping Jack and Michelle didn't come out. I didn't know what to do. When I heard Michelle talking, I looked back at Jacky. I guess the sound of Michelle's voice brought her back from wherever she was. She smiled and asked me what I was doing. I open my mouth and nothing came out.

"Jacky, Vicky is that you?" Jack called out. "Are you girls coming in?" Jacky walked into the room and I followed. She sat beside Jack as if nothing had happened.

"You look like you saw a ghost, Vicky," Michelle said.

I scrambled for words. "I just talked to Dad. He said you invited the family for Christmas."

"I think it would be nice if the family was together for the holiday."

"Is Don coming?" Jacky asked with excitement.

"Sure, baby."

Jacky kissed Jack and ran over to Michelle. "I love you, Mom." It was the first time Jacky ever said that to her. Michelle was speechless.

"Good-night," I said and left the room.

I could hear Michelle sobbing. When I looked back, Jack was holding her in his arms. Jacky had just confirmed what she hoped for a long time. Her daughter did love her.

CHAPTER 12

As the year came to a close no one heard from Don. Dad didn't know what was going on, neither did Glenn's mom. When Don finally called, he told him that they were so busy they didn't know what city they'd be in from one day to the next. They were so big now that it was hard to pinpoint their next move.

Dad knew from the sound of Don's voice the tour was taking a toll on the group. But things were already out of control. All you had to do was pick up a newspaper. I can tell you it wasn't pleasant to read. Besides the tour, it was the partying that when on afterwards.

I remember watching a newscast which said the band sure knew how to have fun. They had started to get a rap for being bad boys wherever they went. During one particular interview, Jacky and I were at The Hangout, and on the television there he was, big as day. Don was sitting between two women and, when asked how the tour was going, he looked over at each one of the girls, "Can't get any better than this."

Thank goodness Jean-Luc wasn't there, when Jacky saw the interview she liked to die. I think, at that second, her heart stopped beating. Trying not to let on how she felt, she got up and walked into the bathroom. "I'll be right back," she said.

I wanted to go after her, but I also wanted to see if Glenn was going to make an appearance. Glenn was not there, but when asked, Don replied, "Follow some guy looking for his girl, and that's where you'll find him." Then he laughed. I wanted to slap that grin right off his face.

When Jacky didn't return, I went looking for her. I knew that this was going to make a big change in how she felt about Jean-Luc. When I got to the bathroom she was staring into the mirror. She took me off guard when I saw that empty look in her eyes, but this time she was seeing herself as I saw her that night on the steps.

Through the mirror, she looked back. She panicked. "What's happening to me, Vicky?" she cried.

I walked towards her. "Jacky!" I yelled.

Suddenly she was herself. She didn't know what to do. "What wrong with me?" she asked and slid to the floor.

I ran to her and put my arms around her. "It's going to be all right. The news was a little too much; you just got light-headed."

That was all I could come up with. I couldn't tell her that this wasn't the first time she zoned out. What else was I going to say? I didn't understand what was going on myself.

That night was the changing point for the events to come. Jacky kept things to herself. She didn't talk about Don, or what was going on with Jean-Luc and how possessive he had become. Though it was obvious to all of us; even Jehane jokingly made a remark to Jacky about it. He didn't want any of us around when they were out, even at the pub. He would make some lame excuse to get her to himself.

One day Jack got a call from Dad, saying that he and Judy were getting married. He asked Jack to be his best man, and Jack said he'd love to.

At dinner Jack told us about the call. And, because the band was so famous, it was going to be a small ceremony. He said the band was going to be the entertainment. I looked at Jacky and was glad to see her smile again. She was so excited that she wanted to go pack right away. We found out later that Dad knew what was going on with the band and if moving the wedding up got Don to come home, so be it.

After dinner, Jacky was in her room looking for the clothes she had bought in France. They were clothes we could never afford at home. They made her look mature. I knew what she was doing; she wanted Don to see her in a different way.

I didn't want to blow her high, but I had to ask her what she was going to tell Jean-Luc. That night I saw her light was still on. I sat up and saw her sitting there looking at the picture of Don that she kept on her nightstand. I got up and jumped in bed with her. "Can't sleep?" I asked.

"I'm so excited about the wedding," she said.

I laughed. "Or are you excited about seeing Don?"

That put a smile on her face. "Did Dad say when we were leaving?"

"No, but he's just as excited as you." As we lay there, thinking about going home, I asked about Jean-Luc.

"What about him?"

"What are you going to tell him? What if he wants to came with us?" She sat up. "He is not coming."

"You know he's not going to take this lying down," I told her.

"I don't care what he thinks, Don's going to be there and that's all that matters."

It hit me. No matter what she had with Jean-Luc, it could never take the place of Don. Jean-Luc was just someone who gave her attention. She couldn't see beyond that. It never occurred to her that Jean-Luc loved her and how possessive he had become. She had us all fooled; she never took him seriously.

But I did. Every day Jacky and Jean-Luc were together, I worried that one day he would do something to her. I knew there would be repercussions.

The next morning, as we were getting into the car, Jack told us that as soon as Dad called with the date, he'd make the reservations. I couldn't wait, Jacky and I were homesick, and we couldn't wait to see Dad and our friends. I needed to see everyone and I wanted to sleep in my own bed. . On Saturday mornings Dad would make his famous pancakes and expected everyone to show up. This was a family tradition. It was a way for Dad to catch up on what was going on in our lives. As he so eloquently put it: "family time."

The next day, I left for my first class. I asked Jacky if she was going to tell Jean-Luc about the wedding, and she said yes. They had a few classes together, and she would see me later.

As the morning passed, I was daydreaming about going home and seeing all my friends, when I happened to look out the widow. Sitting on the grass were Jacky and Jean-Luc. He waved his hands up and down in the air and Jacky looked as if she wasn't too happy about what he was saying. She got up and he grabbed her arm. She pulled away and walked off. He grabbed her again and then she started to yell back. Finally she left and he didn't go after her.

I slipped out of the room without notice. When I got to the door I didn't see either of them. I ran to the car and there she was, just standing there. She didn't seem worried.

"Jacky," I said, "are you okay? I saw what happened from the classroom. Where's Jean-Luc?"

"I don't know. He got upset and I left."

"Are you sure that's all that happened?"

"Yes, let's go home," she snapped.

On the way home she didn't say a word about him or the way she felt, but I knew she didn't care what he thought. Don was the only one in her life, and heaven help the poor soul who stood in her way.

When we got home there was no one there but Rose. I started up the stairs when the phone rang. "I'm not here," Jacky yelled. I knew whom she was talking about.

I picked up the phone. It was Jean-Luc. "Vicky, let me talk to Jacky."

"She's in the shower," I said.

"Vicky, I'm not kidding. Tell her to call me when she gets out."

"Sure," I said and he hung up.

When I started up the stairs Jacky yelled, "Vicky, can you come in here?"

When I got to the room, she was packing. "Are you out of your mind?" I asked, laughing. "We don't even know the dates yet."

"I do. I called Dad when you were on the phone with Jean-Luc. The wedding is the first of the month. That's just three weeks away. So get packing. We're leaving in two days. Jack wants us to get there early so he can spend time with Dad."

I was happy, but she never said anything about Jean-Luc's call. I walked over to her bed and sat down. "We've got to talk. Jean-Luc is not going to take this lying down. He's upset, and he's going to call you back, and you've got to talk to him."

"I don't know what to say to him. Can you tell him I'm not home?"

"You can tell him it's just a family thing and that no one else will be there. That should take care of it till we get back." But I knew that was not going to do it.

Sure thing, the phone rang again. "Hello?"

"Vicky, can you please put Jacky on?"

I handed the phone to her. She hesitated, but when I whispered, "Just tell him what we planned," she grabbed it.

"Hello, Jean-Luc."

"Jacky, what's going on?"

"We're going to America for Vicky's father's wedding."

"Your father wouldn't mind if I tagged along."

"It's just going to be family!" she yelled.

"I think they'll understand if I come along," he insisted. "I don't see where that would be a problem."

"No, Jean-Luc, you can't come. We'll talk when I get back. Don't make it harder than it already is." She hung up on him.

I looked at her. "I told you he wasn't going to take it lying down."

"You're right, but what am I supposed to do?"

"Nothing. Maybe when we get back things will be okay," I said, but

I wasn't at all sure that was going to be the last of it. "Settle down, and you'll be able to talk to him then."

"What if he calls again?"

"I'll talk to him. If he calls downstairs, we'll tell Rose we're not taking any calls for the rest of the night."

A few minutes later the phone rang. I answered. It was Jean-Luc. "Can I talk to Jacky?"

"No, Jean-Luc, she can't talk to you right now." He was silent. "Jean-Luc, right now I think you've got to give her some space. Calling her like this is just going to make things worse, and she'll never talk to you again. Let it be until we get back."

He didn't answer. I felt sorry for him, knowing that when we got back, he would not be so much as a thought in her mind. I asked him if he was going to be all right. He didn't answer. "Jean-Luc, when we get back, I'll make sure she calls you."

Finally he spoke. "Vicky, I don't understand."

"It's just a family thing, Jean-Luc. With the band there, we're just trying to keep it low key." He hung up.

She sat there not saying word.

"Come on, let's go riding."

As we headed down the stairs the phone rang again. Rose answered it. I gave her the "not home" sign and she smiled.

Rose was a great person; she worked for Jack's mother and was kind of a nanny to Jack when he was growing up. She understood how young minds worked. "If you girls want to go riding, I'll handle the phone," she said with a grin.

Just then Michelle walked into the house. "We're going to the States!" Jacky yelled.

"I know, dear, I know. I just got off the phone with your dad. So, are you girls ready?"

"Jacky is," I said, laughing.

"Come on," Michelle said, "let's get dinner ready. Your dad will be home. He's so excited about Mike and Judy, and being the best man. He wants to get there a little early so he can throw Mike a bachelor party. You know how men are."

I smiled. "When are we leaving?"

"In two days," she said.

Jacky was so excited she couldn't control herself. "We have to cancel our classes for the next two days, so we don't run into Jean-Luc."

That night we invited Jehane over to the house. We asked her if she wanted to come with us, but she couldn't tell Jean-Luc.

"As much as I'd love to, I can't. Mother is having a one of her functions and you know how she loves to show her family off. But I'll be there after graduation."

"That's a deal," I said. Jehane was our best friend in France, but I didn't know at the time that she would be a big part of our inner circle.

CHAPTER 13

Waiting to board the plane, I watched Jacky walk over to the gift shop. It was as if she were someone else. She didn't look weird like the day on the steps. On the contrary, she looked like she had it all together; she looked older. The way she carried herself wasn't like a shy insecure little girl, but someone that had all the confidence in the world.

I thought maybe it was me who didn't see Jacky as a woman before. Maybe if she was all grown up, she wouldn't need me like she did all her life.

On the plane she stared out the window. I was happy for her. She looked as if she could handle anything that came her way. I wouldn't worry anymore, I thought.

Then she asked, "Vicky, what do you think?"

"What do you mean?"

"Do you think Don is going to see me differently?"

"Don has always liked you for who you are. If he can't see it now, it's his loss."

She turned back to the window and gradually dozed off. I knew then that inside she would always be a little girl. Watching her, I knew that it had to go the way she wanted. I couldn't see it going any other way. I didn't know what she'd do if it didn't. Being out on the road, Don changed. On TV he seemed out of control. So I didn't have a clue how it was going to turn out. I just prayed that he wouldn't surprise us by bringing home a girl. And if he did, even he couldn't convince Jacky that everything would be all right. Not only would Jacky cut her visit short, so would I. I hoped

Don saw the beautiful young woman she had become. I knew this was everything she had lived for all these years.

As we got off the plane, I saw Dad standing there with Judy. He didn't see me at first. He was holding Judy's hand and they were making faces at each other, like the last time I saw them. I wanted to cry. I missed them so much. Jacky looked at me and started to laugh, like she did when she got me in so much trouble.

Dad turned and saw us standing there. Jacky and I ran to him and tried to jump into his arms. "Okay, girls, you're getting too big for this," he said. He stepped back. "Let me look at you. You're all grown up!"

Jacky looked at me and smiled; I knew that was just what she wanted to hear.

Dad put one arm around each of us and walked over to Jack and Michelle. Judy was bringing up the rear, when Dad turned to her and apologized. As usual, she understood. When we got to Jack, he introduced Judy. "You remember Judy, my bride-to-be."

Jacky looked around to see if Don was anywhere in sight. Dad knew who she was looking for. "He had to go see his agent before he left for New York. He'll see us when we get home."

I walked over to Judy and kissed her and told her congratulations, and that it was about time. She laughed, and so did I.

"Come on," Dad said, "let's get out of here." When we got to the car he said, "I can't believe how much you girls have grown."

Judy turned to him and said, "You're happy now, you've got your girls back home."

Yes, we were Dad's girls, and I hoped that would never change. It felt so good to be home. When we drove up to the house, neither Don nor Glenn was in sight. I walked in the house first, and there they were, coming out of the kitchen. I looked around to see if there were any guests behind them.

I ran to Don and kissed him. I don't know why, but I felt he was looking for Jacky more than for me.

And there, standing in the doorway, was Glenn. "Well," he said, "I guess I can't say you're too young for me anymore."

"I guess you can't," I said, but inside I thought, *I was never too young for you.* I kept a smile on my face. I felt just like that little girl again. It reminded me how it made my heart beat when Glenn did paid attention to me. I stood there, with a big grin on my face at a loss for words.

"Hi, Glenn," I finally said.

"Well," he said, "are you going to give me a hug, too?"

"Sure." I threw my arms around him. *Oh,* I thought, *please don't let this end. Please don't let this end.* Then I got hold of myself. I remember it made me feel all tingly inside. He looked the same, and still to die for.

Then in came Jacky with Dad and her parents. She never expected to see Don, nor did she look around to see if he was there. She thought they were still out of town.

As she stood there in the door, with the light reflecting on her, I saw Don watching her.

He was in a trance. He didn't speak, nor did he go over to her. He was stunned. Everything bad I was anticipating flew out the window. I was relieved.

I called, "Jacky," and she turned and came over. She was light on her feet, and she swayed from side to side, like she was on a runway. Her hair swung back and forth as she walked, gently throwing her arms side to side. She moved with so much grace. There was nothing immature about her.

When she reached us she threw her arms around Don and said, "I missed you."

She stepped back, and he said, "Woo, my little eagle sprouted wings!" The words had been a long time coming, and she smiled. Don continued, "The last time I saw you, you were . . ."

She stopped him. "I know, just a whining little girl."

Don looked at me. "I see Vicky is rubbing off on you." We all laughed.

Glenn just stood there. I watched him from the corner of my eye. He looked so cool, just listening to what was being said, and with that smile that seemed so natural. I walked over to him while Don was making a big fuss over Jacky.

"You seem quiet," I said.

"What am I going to say to you now that you're all grown up?"

Still, I was at a loss for words. Then Dad called Don and Glenn over to introduce them to Michelle. "Don, you remember Michelle."

"Sure I do," he said.

"And Jack, you remember Glenn."

"Oh, yes," Jack said, "the boy who never wanted to go home."

I looked at Glenn and said, "You got that right." He grinned at me.

Then Jack said, "Well, I guess we'll be going to a motel."

"No, you're not," Dad said, "you're going to stay here and that's that." Jacky pleaded with him to stay, too.

Don stepped in. "You're out-voiced." He grabbed their bags and started up the stairs. "I'll show you to your room."

Jacky stared at him. Like always, he had solved the problem. She helped Don with the bags as they showed her parents to the guestroom. As

Jacky started down the hall, she saw Jack and Michelle stop in her room. They were looking at her trophies and the ribbons that she won when she was showing. She stopped in the door without them noticing her. She saw Jack holding Michelle, as she started to cry.

"We lost so much time with her," she said. "Her whole childhood is gone. Oh, Jack, what have we done?"

"Jacky understands," Jack told her, "and she'll never resent us for it."

At that Jacky started to cry, and backed away from the door. She didn't see Don watching her. He walked over to her from behind. "Come, let's go."

As they came down the stairs, she said to him, "Did you hear them?"

"Yes, but I think you need to tell them how you feel, so she doesn't beat herself up about it."

She looked at him with that childlike smile. "You're right, Don. You're always right."

"Jacky," he said suddenly, "I'll always be there for you." Then Dad yelled that lunch was ready.

I asked Glenn. "Are you staying for lunch?"

Don jumped in. "Are you serious? Dad already set a place for him."

I elbowed Glenn. "That's right; we could never get you to go home." We all laughed and walked into the kitchen.

"Dad," I said, "where's Ray?"

"He had to work, but he'll join us for dinner."

I looked around the room. It felt good seeing everyone sitting around the table, talking about whatever came up. I think I missed this more than anything. There were Dad and Jack, talking about old times. Judy and Michelle were getting to know each other better. And across from me were Jacky and Don. Looking at her reminded me of all the heartbreak, and the tears she had shed. And there he was, hanging on her every word.

Then it hit me: she knew this would happen. She had told me over and over again it would happen and I never took her seriously. Yes, I had listened to her, but as much as I wanted to see the two people I loved the most be together, never in my wildest dreams did I think it would actually happen.

I turned to my right and there, with his head leaning on his hand and staring at me, was Glenn. "What are you thinking about?" I asked.

He just looked and never answered.

"Glenn," I said again, "what are you doing?"

Finally he spoke. "I'm just looking at the girl who's going to be my date for the wedding."

"Oh, yes," I said, "you're pretty sure of yourself."

"Well, I think all the years of telling you, 'If you were older' are gone. You are older, and I'm going to keep my promise."

I laughed. But what I though was, *Take me now before I wake up.*

"Okay, Glenn, I'll tell you what I'm going to do. I'll sit with you after you finish singing."

"I guess that's what I've got to do—still the same tough girl. If I'm going to be with you, I guess I'd better get used to it."

"You're full of yourself," I said. This was different than what he was used to. With all the girls chasing him, I don't think he'd ever been turned down before. What girl in her right mind would say no to Glenn of *The Boys of Summer*? I never saw him as the big superstar that he was, for it was like going out with my brother. But don't get me wrong; I wasn't stupid. When he said anything to me, my heart would beat through my chest, just like it did when I was young. Jacky was right—Glenn and I were meant to be together.

After lunch I asked Dad if Jacky and I could take the car to the mall and he said yes. Jack volunteered the limo. . Though it was a rented limo, I would tell my friends it was Don's. Before I could open my mouth, Jacky jumped up and ran toward the door. I noticed Don smiling at her. Everyone laughed. But that was Jacky, always blurting things out. And she was right, I was hoping he'd say to take it.

Don asked, "Do you want me to go with you?"

Before Jacky could answer, I jumped in and said, "NO!" He gave me a look. If looks could kill, I'd be dead.

I grinned at him and started out the door. As I opened it, I saw TV reporters all over the lawn. "Don't go out there!" Don yelled.

Glenn yelled, "They want us!" Then the rest of the band came walking up the drive and into the house. Don told Dad that the reporters wanted an interview, and the rest of the band walked out to meet them.

Don shouted to the crowd of reporters, "If we give you an interview, will you go away and let us have our privacy for my father's wedding?"

One reporter yelled, "Yes!"

Don said, "Thank you," and the questions started.

I grabbed Jacky and started out the door. We slipped behind the group and around to the car, but not before we listened to what was going on. It was so cool, watching them answer the questions. We walked slowly to the limo, so I could see if anyone would notice us. As we got close to the car, one of the reporters ran over to us and snapped our pictures. Don ran over and grabbed Jacky and put his arm around her as if to protect her and a reporter snapped their picture.

"Get in the car!" Don yelled, and told the driver to drive off. I started to laugh; I thought it was kind of cool. Don shouted at me, "Don't do that again!" and looked at Jacky and asked her, "Are you okay?"

Before she could answer I said, "Yes, I'm fine." Glenn laughed and Don slammed the door closed.

On the way to the mall I turned to Jacky. "Since we've been home we haven't had any time to talk."

"I know."

"Well, tell me. I see Don can't stop hanging all over you."

"Well how about you and Glenn?"

"Cool," I laughed. We sat there for a few seconds and then I turned to her. "You were right all those years. You and Don were made for each other. I can see that now. The way he looks, and the way he listens to you. And yes, the way he thought he had to protect you when the reporter came over to you"

"I know," she said, with all the confidence in the world.

"Look at you, all grown up and knowing it."

"Oh, yes," she said airily, waving her hand in the air. Then she turned serious. "Vicky, Don really sees me for who I am." She had tears in her eyes.

"What are the tears for? This has got to be the happiest day in your life."

"That's why I'm crying. I can't believe the time has come. I feel like I'm dreaming."

I reached over and pinched her.

"Hey," she said, "what's that for?"

"Did you feel that?"

"Yes!"

"Then you're not asleep. And you're not in Kansas anymore."

We were still laughing when we got to the mall. All our friends were there. I asked Jacky, "Did you call anyone?"

"Maybe one or two. And I told them maybe Don and Glenn would be with us."

"You didn't!"

"I'll think of something.

As we got out of the car, our friends were waiting for one of the band to get out, too. When they didn't see anyone but us, I told them that, if they wanted to see the group, they had to come to the wedding. The girls were excited and told us they didn't have anything to wear, so we shopped the rest of the day and caught up with everything that was going on in town. When we left to go home, we dropped everyone off at his or her house. Yes, there was a motive—we were showing off.

It was getting late when we got back to the house. Everyone was sitting outside in the yard. I walked over to Dad and sat down. Jacky walked over to Jack and Michelle and told them what we got Dad and Judy for their wedding. Jacky yelled for me to come over so I could hear that Jack got Dad and Judy a round-trip ticket to France for as long as they wanted to stay.

"Dad will like that," I said to Jack. I knew that being there made Jack remember things he had tried to forget. And being with Dad reminded him of the great time they once had. For as long as I knew Jack, I never saw him and Michelle as happy as they were that day. I walked back and sat with Dad.

When Ray and Ruth came in, I ran over and threw my arms around them. Ruth was so happy to see me that she told me after everything calmed down, we'd talk. She said we needed to catch up on what was going on in town. Ray then mentioned to Ruth he wanted to introduce her to Jack. When I turned to say something to Jacky, I noticed her walking over to Michelle, who was sitting all alone. After Jacky sat with her, I walked over to the side of the yard so I could hear what they were saying. I know Jacky wanted to talk to Michelle about Don. Deep down she wanted Michelle's approval. "Mother," she said, "what do you think of Don?"

"He likes you very much."

"Do you think so?"

"Yes, dear, he really does. I think he's a good person. As famous as he is, he's still down-to-earth."

"I do want to be with him," Jacky said sincerely.

"If that's what you want, then don't let anyone tell you differently. You are your father's daughter, and if things are meant to be . . ."

"I know, Mother. I've known for a long time," Jacky said with a smile.

"I know you have, baby." Michelle put her arm around her. "I love you."

"I love you, too, Mother."

Jacky asked, "Can I ask you something?"

"Sure you can."

They sat down. "Mother, I know about Victoria and Dad. I know he loved her."

At that Michelle looked over at me.

"No, Mom, Vicky never said anything to me. She would never do that to you. When were you going to tell me? When we got back home?"

"I've wanted to tell you for a long time," Michelle said, "but I never found the words, or the right time."

"I don't mean to bring this up to hurt you; I just wanted you to know that I understand. I could see that it bothers you more than it does me."

"I guess this is the right time," Michelle said.

"It must have killed you to know he loved Victoria so much, even after you and Dad got married."

"Yes, it did, but I love him more than he can imagine. My love was strong, and it held us together. Just like your love for Don, and how you never gave up on him, and now I see the way he looks at you."

When Jacky looked over at Don, he was looking back. Jacky blushed. He gave her that certain smile that he only had for her. I wanted to cry for her. The way they looked at each other showed that Jacky's dreams were coming true. I could see that he cared for her, not in a sisterly way anymore. Jacky took Michelle's hand. "It must have been hard on you."

"Yes, it was, but I was in it for the long run and I did get what I wanted. Your father is a good man, but the only one who suffered was you. It was so hard after Victoria died that your father had to get away, so he left for France, leaving you and me here. And as hard as Mike took Victoria's death, he put aside his hurt and went to France to help your dad. Till one night I got a call from your grandfather; he told me they were coming home. When they returned, I knew I had to go back home to France if I was going to get your father back. I asked Mike if he'd take care of you until we worked things out. He agreed, and that's how it all started. I longed to have you with me, but I knew without your father I could never go on. We lost many years, and I'm sorry." She started to cry.

I didn't know what to do. I wanted to go to them, but Jacky-being the grown-up now, put her arms around her and said, "It's okay. Mother, this was destiny. I don't think it could have been any different. The best thing that ever happened to me was you leaving me here. I'm so lucky. I have two fathers that I love, and why? Because one woman's love brought them together and gave me a sister that I would never have had, who loves me and has been looking after me my whole life. And two brothers who treat me like their sister, and a man that I've loved for as long as I can remember. Most of all, I got one, and only one, mother, whom I love more than anyone in the world."

At that, Michelle threw her arms around Jacky and they cried together. Don saw them and started over, but caught Dad's eye. Dad shook his head no. Don understood and stopped.

After Michelle and Jacky had had some time together, Dad joined them. "This is my wedding," he joked, "and I don't want to see any tears unless I realize I'm making a big mistake." That broke up the tension and everyone laughed. Judy didn't think it was that funny, but when Dad smiled, she understood.

Sitting there, watching everyone having a good time, I looked over at Don. We had shared a lot growing up, but I felt that over the years we'd grown apart. Don't get me wrong, I was happy for him and Jacky. I guess being around family brings out the child you always want to be. I was feeling sorry for myself and I realized I'd been doing that a lot since I'd returned home.

Don came over and sat down. "You know you can't stay mad at me. I'm sorry I yelled at you, I just didn't want you and Jacky to get hurt. And you're right; you always seem to know how to protect yourself. But I forget that you're still my little sister, and as tough as you seem, there's still that little girl that needs to be reassured. If it wasn't for Glenn reminding me of that, I would have never realized how cruel that was."

I glanced over at Glenn. He did understand me and he cared for me. Don saw me looking at Glenn. "I think he wants to see you more." He kissed me on the forehead. "Sis, you know I love you and, if I don't act like it, I'm sorry." He got up and walked away.

But he was wrong; I needed him to remind me that he did care for me. I know now that Don was not distant; he just had another priority. That was Jacky. And it was one priority I hoped he'd follow through on.

The next morning when I came downstairs, Judy was sitting all by herself. "Judy," I asked, "is anything wrong?"

She broke down crying. I sat beside her. "I don't know," she said, "I just feel like crying."

I realized that with everything going on with Jack, Michelle, Don, and Jacky, and me feeling sorry for myself, nobody had asked Judy how she felt about the wedding. It seemed like she was losing control of it. It was her wedding, her day to tell us what to do and how to do it.

After everyone came in and sat down, I asked for their attention. "I just want to say that today is Judy's wedding, and I think we should be at her beck and call. It's her day." Everyone agreed. I went to the sink and Judy came over to get the coffee to serve everyone. She moved a strand of hair from my face and smiled. She didn't have to say a word, for I knew what she wanted to say.

I gave Jacky a look to take the coffeepot so Judy didn't have to serve anyone. Jacky got up and said, "Sit down, Judy. You don't have to do anything for the rest of the day but get married."

After we all got settled at the kitchen table, Joe, Tim and the rest of the band came in looking for Dad's famous pancakes. "Honey, I'm home,"

Joe called out as he stuck his head in the doorway. Joe was funny that way, always making us laugh. Dad always made extra pancakes. He walked over with two plates and told Joe and Tim to sit down. Everyone that grew up around our house knew there was always enough to go around. Since Dad wanted to speak with all four of them, he was happy they came over. After they ate, Judy told everyone what their jobs were for the day and that after breakfast we should get started. Everyone acknowledged her and that made her feel good.

Jacky and Don strolled out to the garden. I watched them through the window; they were like two lovebirds. The way he held her in his arms and when they looked into each other's eyes, it was like they were seeing each other for the first time. People were in the yard setting up and Jacky and Don walked around like they were the only two people on earth.

Dad joined me at the window. He didn't have to say a thing, for he was thinking the same thing I was. We knew what they were thinking; their eyes did the talking for them. Then Dad went out and told them it was time to get ready. Don and Jacky had lost all track of time. Dad smiled and Jacky blushed and ran into the house.

I sat on the bed as she rushed to get ready. She was the happiest I ever seen her. She wanted to talk about Don, but was waiting for me to bring it up. It was kind of cute to see her rush around so she could get downstairs to be with Don.

"Okay, Jacky, what are you thinking?"

She ran over to the bed and sat down. "I want to stay in the States and not go back to college. I wanted to go on the road with Don."

I didn't know what to say. I tried to find the words to tell her she was out of her mind.

"Don't you think you're moving too fast? You didn't say anything to Don, did you?"

"No, but I will after the wedding." She stood in front of the mirror and put on her lipstick. What was she thinking?

"Are you crazy? What do you think he's going to say? And what about you mother and father? You're moving too fast!"

All of a sudden she looked back at me through the mirror. "There will never be a next time." She turned and looked at me. Her eyes turned black. "Not in this life time." Then she left the room. I couldn't move. *What is going on? Am I imagining all of this?*

Dad called out, "The guests are arriving."

When we came downstairs, the boys stood outside, waiting to escort everyone to their seats. When my friend, Donna arrived, Tim walked her to her seat. She stumbled on the way, because she couldn't keep her eyes off him. I could see Tim trying to flirt with her. Of course Donna was doing the same.

As we walked down the aisle, I saw Don, who was standing beside Dad, looking at Jacky. She looked beautiful. He couldn't keep his eyes off her. Then I looked at Glenn, and thought again, he was to die for. I had to tell him I was going to be his date when the ceremony was over.

Well, looking around at all my friends trying to put the hit on him, I knew I'd better not be sitting on my rear for too long! He looked at me and winked.

Then Judy came down the stairs and she looked fabulous. Dad had tears in his eyes and turned to Jack. Jack put his hand on Dad's shoulder, for it brought back memories of Victoria.

As Judy walked down the aisle, I too wanted to cry after reading what she had written. She told me she and Dad had written their own vows, but hadn't told each other what they wrote. Soon everyone would find out.

When it was time for Dad and Judy to share their vows, the priest asked Judy if she would like to go first, everyone in the room sat up.

She nodded, and began. "Mike, when I first met you, you told me about Victoria. I knew by the way you spoke of her that she was a great woman and how you loved her so much. She gave you three beautiful children that I find fantastic and whom I have come to love very much. As you were lucky, so was I. I too, loved someone that I hold dear to my heart. We both shared loves that we've lost. But I know that as we stand here, they're looking down on us with smiles on their faces. Mike, I love you. I will love you until all the love in the world is gone. And that will never be, for I will hold the love that will hold us together. So will you let me be your wife today, in front of your children and friends?"

Dad answered, "I do."

The priest turned to Dad. "Mike, would you like to read to Judy what you have written?"

Dad spoke clearly. "In my lifetime, I was lucky not once, but twice, to have two women who are the most loving and understanding people that God created. I want you to know that I love you Judy, and I love knowing that every night I will lie beside you, and wake up to your love every morning, and hear you tell me you love me. I know it's not just me that you will be taking into your heart, but the children I love dearly. Judy, I want you to know I will always love you until there is no breath left in my lungs. So will you take me and my four children . . ." He paused and looked over to Glenn, and added, "my five children, to be your husband?"

Judy answered, smiling, "I do."

The priest said, "I now pronounce you husband and wife."

We all ran up to them and congratulated them. They were happy, and Dad couldn't keep from kissing her. As the night went on, Dad was like a kid, or should I say a big rooster. He pranced around the yard like a proud rooster in a hen house. He was proud of who he had on his arm. I've never seen him so happy.

CHAPTER 14

To watch Dad make a fuss over Judy made the celebration all the more wonderful. After the ceremony Dad and Judy carried on like two school kids. As I sat on the side of the stage, I could see Dad and her at their table, holding hands and kissing like there was no one around.

Then I saw Glenn walking towards me, but before he opened his mouth I said, "Yes, I'll be your date tonight."

"Woo," he said, "the wedding got you sentimental?"

I almost fell off the stage. Someone near us started to laugh, as did I. While Glenn was getting me a drink, I looked across the room. The way Don and Jacky were stuck together, you'd think they were the newlyweds. When Don sang, he sang to her. It reminded me of the night of Don's twenty-first birthday. It was so sweet to see her looking at him and not once did he look around the room.

Glenn sang a solo. Don came down and asked Jacky to dance, just like that night. I think at that time, Dad, Judy, Michelle and Jack had tears in their eyes. I know I did. I knew this was the happiest moment in Jacky's life.

When everyone got up to dance, Glenn asked me to take a walk. As we did he put his arm around me. I looked up at him. He was around six feet and I was barely five-foot-two. "This is all right," he said. "You're not going to hit me or break my finger?"

I laughed. "Not tonight."

We stopped and he leaned over to kiss me. I remember thinking,

Legs don't fail me now, for when his lips touched mine, I felt weak in the knees. I felt the sweat roll down my back and goose bumps cover my body.

"Vicky," he whispered, "I want to see you when you get back. What do you think?"

Without hesitation I said, "Yes."

"That's great," he said.

Dad and Judy headed into the house and up to bed. We all waited until the lights went out, and then everyone started to clap. Dad stuck his head out the window. "Go to bed."

The next morning, Jacky got up and started breakfast before anyone came downstairs. I guess she had a motive; she wanted to impress Don. The last time we were all together, Jacky didn't know how to cook. But this time when Don came downstairs he wasn't going to see Jacky sitting at the table in her pajamas, she would be cooking for him. She hoped this was going to show him that she was all grown up.

After I got up I headed down to the kitchen for a cup of coffee and saw her rushing around. Then Don walked in. Jacky was not the little girl who used to run around house in her PJs. He stood in the door smiling as she moved around the way she had practiced in the mirror so many times.

I felt like I was in the way, so I went back upstairs. When I came down again, Glenn was sitting at the table. As I came in he smiled. Jacky cooking away was a sight that no one had ever witnessed. He gave Don the thumbs up. Glenn walked over to me. "I see one of you learned something over there. I looked at him with that bad girl look. "But that's OK with me."

When I sat down, Jacky and Don were talking about The Duke and Jazzman. Jacky was explaining how I missed The Duke, and how I spent so much time down at the barn with him, and that I didn't want to leave him back in France, even if it was just for a few weeks. Glenn asked me what I'd do with The Duke when I came home. I told him I would never leave him, and that I'd bring him home when I finished college. He laughed and said, "So there is a man in your life?"

"Yes, Glenn," I said sarcastically. "I'll never leave that man of mine."

Joe, Tim and Donna came in. Tim was definitely with Donna. It seemed they had hit it off pretty well. Donna whispered, "We've got to talk." I could see she couldn't wait.

Dad, Judy, Jack and Michelle came in the room. "What are you all laughing about?" Dad asked. "Is Glenn being a jokester?"

"Oh, just talking about Vicky's lover that she left in France," Glenn said.

"He's talking about The Duke," I said.

"I'd like to see you compete with that one," Dad told Glenn. "That would be a losing battle."

Dad looked over at Jacky standing at the stove. He smiled and walked over to her. "Why don't you let me take over?" He nodded toward the table where Don was sitting. She smiled, walked over and sat down next to Don. Dad asked Don how it was going on the road, knowing there were problems with the group.

"I wish the tour was over," Glenn said, "it's taking a toll on all of us."

"What seems to be the problem?" Dad asked. "This is what you wanted, and now that you made it to the top you want to quit? That doesn't make any sense." He looked at each one of them. Don just looked back and didn't say a word. "Don," Dad said, "what's going on?"

"Every day and night it's the same thing," Don said, "and everyone's getting tired of it. Tempers are getting short. We never have time for ourselves. We never thought things would get this big."

"No you didn't," Dad shot back. "But that's what you wanted when you started out. Well, it did get big, and now you have an obligation to all the people who come to see you and love you for what you do. He smiled. "You don't think it's the partying." No one said a word. "You started it, and now I think you owe it to your fans to finish it. Soon the tour will be over and you'll be home. So I want you all to just think of what you're doing and go do it. And stop complaining." That was Dad; he told you how it was.

Glenn and Tim started to laugh, and so did Don and Joe. "Well, I guess he's right," Glenn said. "We could have to work for a living." At that they all cracked up.

I could see that Dad's speech did penetrate. And coming home for a few weeks had done a lot of good. All they needed was a break, and maybe a little pep talk from Dad.

After breakfast, as the band put away the equipment, I could see the way Jacky was looking at me. She wanted to talk. She followed me upstairs.

"What going on, Jacky?"

She sat on her bed. "I'm going to ask him to take me with him."

"So you said before."

"I still don't want to go back to France."

"What did Don say? Did you say anything to him?"

"No, but I'm going to; he loves me. I can't be without him, now that I've got him. He loves me, he told me so. And I love him. Help me, Vicky, I know you can."

"How am I going to do that? And what do you think your mother's going to say? You know they're not going to let this happen. Are you ready to break their hearts? And how are you going to break this to Don, since he's the one you've really got to convince?"

"I'm going to say something to him tomorrow. I know Mother will understand. We talked about your mother and Dad. She knows what it feels like to love someone, and so does Dad."

"Okay," I said, "you talk to Don, and if he said yes, then I'll help you."

What was I going to say? This was in Don's hands. I hoped he'd do the right thing. Really, how bad could it be? He loved her, and I knew she surely loved him.

She went down the stairs and outside. Looking out the window, I saw her go up to him. He put his arm around her. As they walked away, he turned and looked up at me. From his expression, I knew he felt there was something wrong.

I watched them and I knew this was meant to be. Why not just go for it? Why did they need to wait, anyway? It wasn't like he couldn't afford to care for her; he had all the money he needed. Then I heard Dad coming up the stairs. I knew if anyone could fix this, it was him.

He peeked in the room. "What's wrong?"

"Do you have a minute?" I asked.

"For you, yes." He sat on the bed. "Is this about Glenn? Don't think I haven't noticed you and him."

"It's more than that. It's about Jacky and Don."

"She finally got what she wanted."

I took a deep breath. "Jacky is going to ask Don to take her with him on the road. He told her he loved her, and now she wants to go with him."

"Did Don ask her?"

"No, but she's going to ask him."

"And you know he's going to tell her no. Not that Don doesn't want be with her, but he knows it's impossible."

"She asked me to help her get Jack and Michelle's okay. But I thought you could talk to Don and let him know what's going on. He'll understand; he understands her better than anyone."

"Okay, I'll talk to him." He kissed me on the head and left the room.

When I looked out the window I knew Dad didn't have to talk to Don, because when he stepped outside I saw Jacky pass him coming in the house. I heard her run up the stairs. She just made it into the room before she broke down in tears.

"He said no!" she cried. "It's not that he doesn't want me with him. He thinks if I go with him, I'll regret not finishing college."

"Jacky," I said, "he's right. You know that. Besides, the tour is almost over. And by then we'll be graduating."

But that didn't seem to help. I looked out the window and Don was there again, looking up. He knew he needed to come up and talk to her. Only Don knew what to say to her to make Jacky understand.

"I'll be right back," I told her. I ran down the stairs and told Don he needed to go to her. He nodded and headed upstairs. I followed him until I got to the top of the stairs and sat down. From there I could see and hear everything that was going on. Did I have to? No. But I know that Jacky could never say no to Don. If he gave her a reason she could not go with him on the road, she would have accepted it. But that didn't mean when he stepped out of the room, she wouldn't cry. And it was me who had to comfort her.

"Jacky," he said, "I didn't mean to hurt you. I just think it's better for you to finish school. It would hurt me if I stopped you from doing that. I could never forgive myself."

That's all he had to say. He put the blame on himself and she couldn't let that happen. "No, Don, you're right, I need to finish school." He smiled at her.

When they came downstairs, Jacky wore a big smile, like the time Don's girlfriend had made a joke about her and Don when she got the news her parents weren't going to make it for her birthday. As usual, Don had made things better.

The rest of the day we all just hung around the house like old times. Dad, Judy, Jack, and Michelle left for town. Tim and Joe went to visit with their families. Jacky, Don, Glenn, and I were the only ones in the house, but this time we were together. We didn't want the day to end. I knew we were going soon, and I wouldn't see Glenn until I graduated. That went for Jacky, too.

Don and Jacky got up and strolled around to the other side of the yard. Later she filled me in on what they talked about. She told him what she would do differently if it had been her wedding. She told him how she and I planned to get married when our time came, and how we were going to have a double wedding, and would wear the same dress.

"You love Vicky, don't you?" he asked.

"If it weren't for her, I don't know what I'd do. She always knew about you, and she promised me she'd help us be together one day. She's been there for me ever since we were young. You know how motherly she is."

"Yes." He grinned. "Even when she tried to treat me like her little brother. When you get out of school I'll come for you and bring you home."

"I'll be waiting." It's funny, whatever Don said, she always felt it was the right thing, and she never questioned him.

Night fell with Don and Jacky trying, in that one night, to make up for the last ten years they'd lost. I, on the other hand, was taking it slow. It was a full moon, and the night felt just as magical as the day. I knew it couldn't last. Glenn and I got to know each other better. Not that I didn't know him already; he was like my brother, but in a romantic way. But this time I got to know him like all the girls he went out with had. Even though we sat in separate chairs, he managed to put his arm around me. Again I felt the goose bumps up and down my spine.

He reminded me of things I did when I was a little girl, and he told me how he knew how Jacky felt about Don even when she was a baby. "I'm going to miss you when I'm on the road." He leaned over and kissed me.

I melted. I don't even know what I was thinking at that moment, but boy, that's how I was going to remember him. All I could do was gaze at him.

"Well, you'll see me when I come back," he said. "Or better than that, if I get some time, can I come to see you in France?"

"Sure you can." I couldn't get the words out fast enough. The rest of the night we just sat around together.

The next morning was Saturday. We all gathered for Dad's family pancakes. That was one of the things I missed, not just the pancakes, but everyone gathered around the table and talking about whatever. I think that's what held the family together, the quality time we spent. The only ones missing were Ray and Glenn. I saw Ruth sitting there talking to Judy and asked her where Ray was.

"I don't know," she said. "He was just here a second ago."

I figured Glenn went home to see his mother, so I went looking for Ray. As I walked closer to the parlor, I heard Ray. "I see the way you look at her, and if you think she's just one of your women you pick up when you're on the road, you've got the wrong girl."

"You got it all wrong," Glenn answered. "You know me better than that."

"I know what goes on when you're on the road," Ray said, "and the women that fall all over you."

Glenn stopped him. "I can't believe you'd think that about me after all these years. She's like my sister! Well, maybe not my sister now, but I would never hurt her. I think I'm in love with her."

My heart stopped. *He thinks he love me.*

Ray just stared at him.

"Well," Glenn said, "are you going to say something, or just stand there?"

"You know how I feel about her, and if you ever hurt her I'll personally take care of you myself."

"Take my word for it, I wouldn't hurt her, no matter what."

I heard them walking towards the door and ran back to my seat. When they came in I saw Glenn looking at me. *Wow*, I thought, *I hope Ray didn't frighten him away.* And then Glenn sat down beside me and kissed me on the forehead. *Okay*, I thought, *that looks good!*

When the day finally came for us to leave, everyone was at the airport to see us off. Don was sick to leave Jacky. She was trying to hold back the tears, but not doing too good. Don was holding her and, as usual, she told him over and over that she didn't want to go. I thought at one point he was going to tell her it was all right for her to stay. He really didn't want her to go, but he could never ask her to give up her college degree to stay with him for the four months left in the semester.

He took her to the airport store and bought a stuffed eagle for the trip home. He told her if she got lonely all she had to do was talk to Mr. Eagle and he'd hear her. Finally, the tears stopped and a smile appeared. Like always, he knew how to comfort her. He treated her like a little girl. To him she would always be someone that would need him.

On the other hand, Glenn was his normal happy-go-lucky self, like always, hiding what he felt by making jokes. I told him, "I going to miss you."

He smiled. "I don't know what to say."

"Cat got your tongue?" I asked only to make conversation. I knew I wasn't going to be able to control myself any longer. Then I felt the tears fill my eyes.

To my surprise, he reached over and kissed me right on the spot. "Look," he said, "we don't have to act this way, you trying to act tough and me making jokes. Let's not do this anymore."

I was relieved to hear him say that. I told him I didn't want to leave. We didn't say anything more until we heard our call to board. He just held me in his arms, which was all I wanted him to do.

Jack and Michelle were saying goodbye to Judy and Dad. I knew Dad didn't want Jack to leave. Being together reminded him of the good old days when Mom was alive. Michelle and Judy had become good friends and promised they'd stay in touch.

"Remember," Michelle said, "we'll see you when you get to France."

"You can count on that," Judy responded.

I told Ruth how lucky Ray was to be with a great person. She kissed me and told me, "We'll become great sisters when you get back from school." Then she went to say goodbye to Jacky.

I looked at Ray and started to cry. "I don't want to leave this time."

"But you will," he said, "and when you finish college you'll come home and the family will be together again. I don't want you to worry about Dad and Don. And I don't want you to worry about Glenn, either. I just want you to enjoy the rest of your time in school and come home to where you belong." He hugged me.

Later, whenever I was scared and couldn't sleep, I'd remember him hugging me at the airport. While I was in his arms I felt that everything was going to be fine. I remember saying to myself, *When you're sad you always look for someone to comfort you, like they did when you were a little girl. No matter how bad things looked, that little bit of comfort made you feel like you could go on.*

Then Ray said, "I think there's someone that could make you feel a lot better than you're feeling right now." He nodded at Glenn, who was standing there watching us. "Go," Ray said.

As I walked over to Glenn, I saw him nod to Ray, like he understood the little talk they'd had before breakfast.

Dad came to me. "I hear Glenn is coming to see you." I smiled. "I knew that would put a smile on your face," he said.

"Glenn's knocking on my door, Dad."

"Well, dear, open it up before he goes to the next house."

I wrapped my arms around him and kissed him goodbye.

I saw Jacky coming and stepped aside. She threw her arms around him. "I don't want to go back," she said. I thought, *Here we go again . . .*

"Jacky, what harm would it do to finish school? You only have nine months left."

"You're right, she said. "I've waited this long, what's nine more months?" At that she ran back to Don. Sure enough, she started to cry. I knew she wasn't going to give up that easy.

"I don't want to go," she sobbed, "don't let me go, Don."

He held her in his arms. "I could never let you quit."

"Please, Don. I don't know why, but I feel like if I go I'll never see you again. You know you want me to stay here, so why don't you just say its okay?"

He pushed her away. "Look at me, Jacky." She lifted her head and looked in his eyes. "I want you to finish," he continued, "and when you do, I'll come for you and bring you home. No matter where I am, I'll be there for you."

I knew he meant what he said. She knew it, too.

"We're meant to be together," he said. "You knew that all the time, didn't you?" She smiled and stopped crying. I think she needed to hear that from him. She had seen too many interviews with Don surrounded by women.

"Baby," he said, "we don't even know were we'll be from one day to the next. Even if I could, I can't take you right now. I'll be there for Christmas and, if you still want to come home, I won't leave without you." Then he smiled that smile he only had for her.

"You're right," she said, "I can't leave like this. I'm glad you're here to tell me what's right and what's wrong." He had done it again; he got her to accept what was going to be.

"Listen," he grabbed the eagle out of her bag. "When you're missing me, just grab this and things will seem better. And if not, call me and tell me, and I'll fix it."

She gave him one of those childlike smiles that could change him from a tiger to a kitten. We all knew what she could do to him, even before we knew he loved her.

He wrote down all the numbers where she could get hold of him. "Any one of these will get me, no matter what time it is." He put his arms around her and held her until we boarded the plane.

Glenn said, "That goes ditto for me. One of those numbers is mine. The rest are Tim's and Joe's, so there's no way you can't get hold of us."

"Yes," I laughed, "and where's my teddy bear?"

"I'll get you one." He ran over to the store.

"Thanks, but no thanks!" I yelled as I ran after him. "Just kidding." But he kept going.

When he got back he had a teddy bear in his hand. "Are you kidding?" I asked. "What does this mean?"

He grabbed my hands and led me aside. "Vicky, you can kid as much as you want and be as tough as you want, but this is me, the person who knew you since you were a kid. I know you better than you know yourself."

By then I was trying to hold back the tears, but it was obvious how I was feeling. He put his arm around me, and I couldn't hold back anymore.

"See," he said, "you're not that tough." He leaned over and held me in his arms and kissed me again. I closed my eyes and my body temperature went sky high. I even felt a bead of sweat roll down my back. "Okay, enough." I stepped back a bit.

He smiled, for he had felt the same way. "You're right; if we keep going you'll never make the plane."

We laughed and walked over to Don and Jacky and sat down. As Don held Jacky and Glenn held me, no one said a word. We all knew what the other was thinking.

Then the call came to board the plane and the goodbyes were emotional. Jacky started to cry again. I took her arm and said, "Come." I kissed Don and told him, "I'll look after her."

"I know you will." He kissed me on the forehead. "Have I told you I love you?"

"All the time," I said through my tears. I grabbed Jacky and walked onto the plane.

What a depressing trip back to France it was. Jacky and I didn't say a word the whole way. When the flight attendant asked if we wanted anything, no one answered until she asked again. I tried to break the ice by asking Jacky if anyone took any pictures before we got on the plane. I just got that look and "No" for an answer.

I looked over at Jack and Michelle. They just sat there holding hands. She gave him a smile and he returned it. I'd never seen them so happy and relaxed. When Jack was with Dad it was like they were teens again. They talked about the past, and sometimes about Mom when Michelle wasn't around. Michelle knew; how could she not?

This was the first time Michelle was on even grounds with Jack. Back in France, she just sat home in a great big house where everyone did everything for her. But at home with Dad and Judy, she seemed like a different person. That made me realize why she'd been so unhappy.

Jacky had the window seat because I was not keen on flying anyway. At one point I asked her again if she wanted to talk, and she snapped, "No." For her to turn down a chance to talk about Don was unbelievable; she'd never done that!

As she looked out the window I saw the reflection of a woman looking back at me. I didn't see the little girl who'd been on the plane on the way to the States; it was the woman Don had fallen in love with when she had walked in the door. She had known all along her love was real, when everyone else thought it was just a childish infatuation.

I realized I was going to miss the shy person I had watched out for all my life. That was the day I understood that Jacky knew what her destiny was going to be.

Later the flight attendant asked me if I wanted a Coke and I said,

"Sure." Jacky was asleep, the eagle clutched in her hand. I knew what I was seeing was what Don saw in her. She was still that little girl who tried to act older than she was. I smiled but it didn't last long.

I became startled when I looked back at the reflection. At first I saw the little girl that showed herself the night on the steps. Then the teenager that saw herself for the first time in the reflection of the mirror at the pub. As each expression changed, it looked as if it was trying to tell me something. I found myself mimicking her lips.

"His love will destroy her." I found myself saying. "His love will destroy her." I didn't know what to think. *No way* I thought, *he loved her too much*. Then all of a sudden I was startled when the flight attendant tapped me on the shoulder.

"Would you like something to drink?"

I smiled and said "No thank you."

CHAPTER 15

When we got back to school and Jack got back to the office, Michelle decided to do something with her life instead of just sitting around the house waiting for Jack to come home. She began exercising and met a few new friends. She kept in touch with Judy; in fact they talked every day. Michelle couldn't wait until Judy and Dad came to visit and she was always out of the house and keeping herself busy. Jack, on the other hand, took a little longer to get back into the swing. I could see how he looked at me and knew that being with Dad had brought back memories of the past.

I hadn't thought about Jean-Luc for sometime and neither had Jacky. We just took it for granted that he had forgotten about Jacky and was getting on with his life, too. When we got back to school, our friends couldn't wait to hear about the trip, but mostly about the band. We told them all about the wedding, and how the band was the entertainment.

One night we all met at The Hangout and Jean-Luc walked in. I wasn't prepared for what happened next. He came over to where we were sitting and asked Jacky if he could talk to her. She looked at me, got up, and they went outside.

We could see through the window that he was upset. Jehane, who was sitting beside me, said he still loved her and couldn't understand what had happened between them. She told me that one night when they were all at The Hangout, he came in with the local paper and showed them a picture of Don holding Jacky in his arms.

"He was so angry he couldn't see straight," she said. "I took him home that night, he was so drunk, and all he talked about was Jacky and how he loved her. I told him Jacky and Don were like brother and sister, but he didn't want to hear it. Then he said he was going to make it up to her when she got back. That picture made him crazy."

"What picture?" I asked.

"You know, the one with them standing beside a limo."

"Oh, NO!" I said, "That was the day the reporters were at the house. He was just trying to keep them away from her."

"I guess you didn't read the paper. It said he had a girlfriend and she was the one. There was a big story about them. And what a story!" She reached in her bag, took it out, and handed it to me.

"Oh, NO!" I said again. As I read it, I had to admit it was a great story. It told how the bad boy of the band had finally found a girl he seemed to care for. It described how she grew up as his sister and how they fell in love after all these years.

I looked out the window at her. This would be something she'd cherish the rest of her life. This was her story, the real story of her and Don, the one she tried to tell us all. She always knew how it would end.

I went outside to see if she was all right. He grabbed her and told her he wanted to get back together. I heard him tell her how much he loved her.

She pulled away and screamed at him, "I don't love you. I'm in love with Don!" She started for the door and he grabbed her again.

I ran towards him and yelled, "Jean-Luc!"

He stopped and she ran inside. He showed me the picture of her and Don. "You knew all about this, didn't you?" he accused.

I didn't know what to say. He seemed out of control. He had a look in his eyes that made me want to back away from him. "Look," I said, "When you calm down we'll talk, but until then go home and get some sleep." He was out of control. I had to get Jacky out of there before anything went wrong.

Back inside, everyone wanted to talk more about the band. Then Jacky started talking. I tried to stop her because I didn't know if Jean-Luc had left, but she was excited, as usual. She told them how Don and she were a couple now, and so were Glenn and I. Everyone wanted to know more, and I started to forget about Jean-Luc. We were so wrapped up talking about the band that I didn't realize Jean-Luc had come back into the bar. We told them the band would be coming to France to see us at Christmas, but we weren't sure if they were going to perform. I

told them that if they did, we'd have a party and invite everyone. They were friends and I didn't think Don would mind, especially if Jacky wanted it.

When I looked up, I saw Jean-Luc sitting on the other side of the room, staring at us. The look in his eyes frightened me. I had to get Jacky out of there. "Well, guys," I said, "It's getting late."

As we passed him on the way out, he grabbed her arm. "Jacky, can I talk to you?" She kept walking. I couldn't get home fast enough.

Jacky drove home. She didn't see Jean-Luc behind us, but he followed us home. As we turned into the drive, I saw him pull up across the street. Thank goodness our drive was a quarter of a mile from the house and there was a gate that would have been closed any other time. When we drove in I told Jacky to hit the button to close the gate.

"What for?" she asked.

"If you have a gate, you should close it," I snapped. It was pretty lame, but it was the only thing I could come up with.

"You're getting weird." She hit the button and the gate closed behind us. I didn't say anything to her about Jean-Luc, and hoped that things would be better the next day.

When we walked into the house, Jack was sitting by the fire. Michelle was sitting beside him. I wanted to tell Jack about what happened, but I thought I might be jumping the gun. I wasn't sure what to think. But I'll never forget the look in Jean-Luc's eyes.

We said good night and went up to our rooms. As we were getting ready for bed, the phone rang. I saw her jump for it, figuring it was Don. It wasn't.

"I don't want to talk to you, Jean-Luc," she said, and hung up.

Ten minutes later the phone rang again. I yelled, "Don't answer it!"

It finally stopped ringing. Then it rang a third time, and this time I was upset. I jumped up and grabbed it. It was Jean-Luc.

I told him not to call again. He didn't want to hear it, so I tried to reason with him just to get him to calm down.

"Maybe if she has a few days, she'll forget about him."

I didn't agree with him, I just said, "Okay." I didn't want to give him any false hope, because that's all it would be.

When I got off the phone I gave her a look. She just shrugged. Funny that she felt that way, she never showed any sympathy for him. Knowing how strong her love was for Don, you'd have thought she'd show some compassion.

I knew Jean-Luc wasn't going to let this go and I needed her to realize it. She went on getting ready for bed. "I hoped Don calls before I fall asleep." At that point I realized I wasn't going to get through to her. But I needed to tell someone who could help. When she went into the shower, I went down to talk to Jack.

Michelle and Jack were still downstairs sitting by the fire. Michelle was holding pictures of the wedding and talking about Dad and the trip when I walked in and asked, "Can we talk?"

"Sure," Jack said.

I didn't know how to begin at first, and then I let it out. I started with how she broke it off with Jean-Luc before we left for the States, and what had happened since we returned. I finished by telling them about Jean-Luc being parked across the street when we came home.

"Did you close the gate?" Jack asked.

"Yes," I said.

"What do you think about it?" Jack was concerned.

"When I looked in his eyes tonight, he scared me. And to find him across the street when we came home . . . I don't know what he might do."

He frowned. "Thanks for telling us, Vicky. I'll take care of it right now. But I want to know where you and Jacky are every minute. And I'd like you and her to come home right after school until things die down."

His phrase "die down" has stuck with me to this day. As I left the room he said, "Don't tell Jacky." I looked back and saw Michelle with a nervous look. Jack said, "Don't worry; I'll call someone right now. He'll watch over the girls when they're out."

I didn't know what to say to Jacky, but I didn't think she cared anyway, so I said nothing.

The next morning, Jacky and I joined Michelle and Jack for coffee before we left for our first class. Jack acted as if nothing was going on, but he was more experienced than I. What really bothered me was not that Jean-Luc was out there looking for Jacky, but that Jacky never gave it a second thought. Maybe I didn't know her as well as I thought I did. Or maybe we just didn't listen to her. She had always told us that she could never love anyone but Don. Thinking about it, I realized her relationship with Jean-Luc was just a friendship that could never be

anything more. He never questioned it when he tried to get intimate with her and she refused him. He just put it off to her being shy and that she wanted to wait until they knew each other better. But inside, Jacky knew there could never be anything more between them than a friendship.

Jack told us to take the limo to school, and that the driver would wait at school to pick us up. "And by the way," he said, "there's a new driver, named Jars."

"I'd rather take my car," Jacky said.

"I'm having the mechanics work on the cars today," Jack answered. I knew what was going down, but Jacky didn't, so she just agreed with him, no questions asked.

We took the limo, and Jars waited for us the rest of the day. After my first my class, Jehane told me that Jean-Luc didn't show up for any of his classes. Then, during my next class, another friend said that Jean-Luc had dropped out of school for the rest of the semester. I felt relieved on one hand, and worried on the other. I'd rather know where he was all the time, until everything was back to normal.

A few weeks passed and we never saw or heard from Jean-Luc. Don called Jacky every other day and when he did I got to talk to Glenn. They were in Germany, and then would be off to Japan. Jacky begged Don to come to England to perform, but he said he didn't think that would be possible right then, that they went wherever they were told.

Even though Don was older than me, when he talked to Jacky it was like he, too, became a child. They were so happy when they talked, and that was for hours sometimes. I remember thinking: *Don better have a lot of money!* She'd fall asleep with the phone in her hand. Don knew when she did, but never said anything about it. He knew hearing from him made her happy, and he did everything he could do to please her.

One night when they were talking, she asked him if he'd come and get her. She reminded him of what he'd said to her before boarding the plane, that if she wasn't happy he'd come and take her home. She was crying when she asked him, and I think that got to him. After a time she fell asleep and when she did I got to the phone before he could hang up.

"What's wrong?" he asked.

I took the phone into my room and told him about the situation with Jean-Luc. He told me Jacky had never said anything about going out with Jean-Luc. I told Don that it was just a friendly relationship, and that Jean-Luc wanted more out of it. I also told him what happened when we came back from the States, and how Jean-Luc had followed us home one night, and that we hadn't heard from or seen him since. "To tell you the truth," I said, "he scares me."

He asked what Jacky thought about the whole thing. I laughed. "All she thinks about is you. I think it gets her through the day."

"As soon as I get a chance I'm coming to France to get her," he said. The thing about Jean-Luc had obviously scared him, too.

"Don't jump the gun," I said, "Jack's taking care of it."

"Maybe you're right. I'll give it a few days. But if he shows up, I'm coming to get her."

I asked him to put Glenn on the phone.

After I told Glenn the whole thing he said he'd watch over Don so he wouldn't do something crazy. "He's so in love with her," he said. "I never saw him like this before. He talks about her day and night and writes songs about her. But enough about them, what about you, what have you been up to?"

'"The same old thing. School, mostly. And you, what's going on in your life?"

"If you mean is there anyone in my life, yes," he said.

I was speechless; he had thrown me for a loop. I felt a hot tingling run though my body and I got a little lightheaded. I sat on the bed and didn't say a word and neither did he. Then he laughed. "And that person is you."

I let go a big sigh and the blood started to rush though my body again. "So you think that's funny?"

"Well, I had you going for a bit there."

"You know, I should hang up on you."

"But you won't, will you?"

"Yes, I will."

"Please," he said, "I'm sorry. I was just kidding with you. Just remember that you don't have to be Miss Toughie around me. You know I love you, and there's no one I'd rather be with."

I didn't say anything and he asked me what I was thinking.

"That's the first time I've ever heard you say you loved me."

Jokingly he said, "Oh, you must have taken me off guard."

"Now who's being the jokester?"

He changed the subject abruptly. "This goes for me, too. If you want to come home, just say the word and I'll come for you."

Just hearing him say that, made my night. "I need to finish here. And you need to finish what you've dreamed about all your life. Then we'll be together."

"You're right. That's what I love about you."

"Well, it's getting late and I have an early class."

"Then I'll talk to you in a few days. I love you and miss you."

"I love you and miss you, too," I said, and we hung up.

The next morning Jacky said, "I did it again?"

"Yes," I said, "but I talked to Glenn after you fell asleep."

"And how is Glenn?"

"F-i-n-n-n-n-e!"

We laughed and started down the stairs. Then the phone rang. I ran back to answer it. It was Jehane, calling to tell me that she had seen Jean-Luc at the coffee shop. She asked him why he hadn't been around. He said his father had taken him to England for a few weeks. Then he asked about Jacky.

"What did you tell him?" I asked.

"I told him to forget about her. He said that she'd come to her senses. Vicky, he's serious."

"I'll see you at school. Don't say anything about this to Jacky."

I ran downstairs and Jacky asked me who it was. "Jehane. She's going to meet us at school."

On the way to school I told her that Jean-Luc was back. "And he thinks you're going to forget about Don."

"I'm not worried about him," she said.

"Well, you better be!" I said loudly. I looked right at her. "Jacky, he scares me."

When I said that, the driver looked back at us. He stopped at Jacky's first class and she ran into the building. When she got to the door, I leaned forward and told the driver what Jehane had said. "Jean-Luc might be back at school today," I finished. "Please, keep an eye on Jacky; he might try to follow her." He nodded in agreement.

I left for my first class. When I met up with Jehane, she told me that Jean-Luc was in class. I knew he'd be seeing Jacky, because they took the same class. I told Jehane I'd be right back, and walked over to Jars in the limo. I told him that Jean-Luc was in school and that he shared the same class with Jacky.

"Go to class," he reassured me. "I have it under control."

I smiled at him and walked away. I knew he knew his job and I shouldn't worry, but I did. As I walked to my class I saw Jean-Luc just entering the building. He saw me but didn't say a word.

I saw Jehane looking at him the same time as I did. "He's freaky," she said. "I think he's lost it."

In class I couldn't help thinking about what was going on in Jean-Luc's mind. Was I letting my imagination run amuck? My gut told me no. When it was time for my next class, Jars

saw me walking towards him. "Stop!" he yelled. "Go to your class and I'll take care of this." I turned and walked away.

When classes were over, Jacky came out and ran toward me. "Vicky," she said, "Jean-Luc was in class and he dropped a letter on my desk before he left. He didn't say anything, just walked out the door." She handed me the letter as Jars came over. Jacky had no idea her dad had hired him as a bodyguard.

"Are we ready to go, girls?" he asked.

We jumped in the car. "Well," Jacky said, "are you going to read the letter?" Jars looked back at me through the mirror, so I decided to read it out loud. It read:

Dear Jacky,

This is my last attempt to talk to you. By the time you finish this letter I hope you come to your senses. I don't know what you were thinking of before you went to the States, for we were in love. I know I said it to you so many times and, even though you never replied, I felt there was something we shared. I never understood why you never wanted me to go with you to the States, but I do now.

When I saw that picture of you and that jerk from the band, I knew there was someone else in your life. But you've got to understand that you are just a fly-by-nighter to him. He has seen many women on his tour and I guarantee you that he has slept with every one of them.

And you're just one more notch in his belt.

After that sentence I looked up and saw Jars looking back at me. He was disturbed by what he had heard so far. "Go on, read the rest," Jacky urged me anxiously.

I forgive you for being with a guy like that. I know you'll come to understand that my love for you is greater than a jerk like him can ever giveyou. I know you more than you know yourself. You need me to show you that you belong to me.

I can never accept not being with you. I know if you give us another chance, you will know that he could never give you what I can and that is love. I know you could never commit to a relationship with him and I understand why, for I am the only one that could ever understand you. I can't imagine you with anyone else and can't imagine me without you. So stop all this childish behavior and come back to me. You will see that I am right in what I say and you will make the right choice.

No one else will ever treat you like you need to be treated. I love you and always did, and always will. I know you love me. You may not realize it now, but I will help you to understand that there is no one but me for you.

Like I said, I could never allow anyone to come between us, and that means Don and Vicky. Again, I love you. Call me after you read this letter. I will be waiting.

Love—Jean-Luc

"P.S. Don't let Vicky influence your decision. She is just jealous that you have a relationship with someone. And someone needs to make her mind her own business.

I looked up at Jars, who nodded that he had heard every word.

Jacky was furious. "I'm going to call him and tell him I could never love anyone like him anyway."

"No Jacky. That's what he wants you to do. He sounds like someone that's not thinking right."

"But he called Don a jerk!"

Jars looked back. "Can I say something, ladies?"

"Sure," I said.

"I think you should forget that he ever sent you that letter for now, and stay out of the guy's way."

Jacky glared at him.

Then he said, "Who in their right mind doesn't love *The Boys of Summer?*"

She could relate to that. The rest of the way home she talked about the band to Jars. She told him that Don and Glenn just might be coming to France.

"I hope so," he said. "I'd love to meet them."

When we got home Jars asked, "Is there anything at all I can do for you ladies?"

"No, thanks," I said, "we're going to stay in for the rest of the day."

"I might take Jazzman for a ride later," Jacky said.

"Okay, Miss. When you're ready, I'll see you at the stable."

"Oh, that's okay. I'll be all right by myself."

"I was heading that way anyway," he said, "so I'll pick you up whenever you're ready." Jars was good at his job.

When we got upstairs Jacky said she wanted to call Don.

"If you do," I said, "tell him I'd like to talk to him, too." I wanted to catch him up on what was happening.

I went to my room to study. With everything going on with Jean-Luc, I was falling behind in my schoolwork.

From my room I heard her talking to Don about Jean-Luc and the letter. She had never told him about Jean-Luc before. I knew he wouldn't tell her I'd already talked to him about the situation.

She said she had just dated him a few times and that it wasn't serious. "You know I could never love anyone but you." There was a pause, and then she said, "Yes, I'm fine. And yes, I'll keep away from him."

They stayed on the phone for a long time telling each other how much they loved one another. I don't know how many times I heard her say, "I love you." Finally she yelled to me, "Don wants to talk to you."

I picked up the extension in my room and waited for Jacky hang up. I asked Don to hang on while I peeked in to see what Jacky was doing.

But before I could put the phone down, Jacky yelled, "I'm going to get a Coke from the kitchen, tell Don I'll call him back." I told Don about the letter, and that Jack had hired a bodyguard for us. "Jacky doesn't know anything about him," I said. "He drives us to school and never lets us out of his sight."

"I'm going to come down at the end of the week," he said. "I'm getting really concerned. I think it's time to bring her home."

"Okay," I said, then asked for Glenn. He said he knew all about what was going on, and asked me if I was okay. I told him yes and that I wished I could see him.

"Don told you we have a few weeks before our next tour, and that we're leaving at the end of the week to come to France."

I didn't say a word, for I didn't want to sound like I couldn't live without him. For a few seconds neither of us said anything, and then he spoke. "Vicky, if you don't want me to come that will be okay."

"Yes, I want you to come!"

"I know." He laughed. "I just wanted to hear it."

We hung up, and I ran into Jacky's room to find out if she knew about them coming. She wasn't anywhere to be found. I glanced out the window. Right in front of me an eagle flew by. *Do they have eagles in France?*

The phone rang and I grabbed it. "Hello." There was no answer. "Hello, is anyone there?" I asked again. There was a moment of silence and then the caller hung up.

I looked all over for Jacky but didn't see her anywhere. I yelled for her, and the phone rang again.

"Hello," I said, very agitated. It was Jean-Luc. "Vicky, you put your two cents in far many times." He hung up.

I ran down the stairs, yelling Jacky's name. Jars came running into the house. "Where's Jacky?" he shouted.

I was frantic. "I don't know, I was on the phone and Jean-Luc called and said I put my two-cents in one too many times."

We ran out to the stable and Jazzman was gone. We jumped in the truck and tried to find her. She was nowhere in sight. I told Jars to drive where Jacky liked to ride when she wanted to be alone.

Looking up as Jars drove, I saw a large bird flying in the same direction. Yes, it was definitely an eagle.

"There!" I yelled.

Jacky was sitting on a rock, just looking out into space. I jumped out of the truck and ran to her. "Why didn't you tell anyone you were going riding?" I yelled.

She looked at me, surprised. "I never knew I had to!"

"Well, now you do."

At that she got angry. "Do you want to explain why?"

"Because you and Jean-Luc broke up!" I shot back at her.

"Give me a break. You're really letting him get to you."

"That's not it. He's crazy. He'll do anything to get you back. You're the only one who can't see that."

"What do you mean by that?"

"Your father and mother feel the same as I do. They think he might do something to you."

She laughed, and reached for Jazzman.

"Jacky," I said, "do you know who just called after I hung up with Glenn?"

"No, but I'm sure you'll tell me."

"Jean-Luc. He said I'd put my two cents in for the last time. He think I'm the one keeping you two apart."

At that she sat down and finally got serious. "Vicky, I never really thought he'd do anything to you or me."

"Look Jacky, he loves you and he can't get it through his head that you're not going back to him."

She looked at me with her big blue eyes. "You were right all along. You knew what he was thinking and you tried to tell me. I'm sorry." She put her arms around me. "How did I ever get by without you, Vicky? I love you too much to see anything happen to you. You're my only sister, and I want to keep it that way. We've come a long way, haven't we?"

I smiled. "Yes, we have."

She stepped back, and frowned. Her eyes turned black. "Vicky, it's the beginning of a new chapter." It was kind of weird, but I wasn't afraid, not like I was before.

Before I could answer, I heard a shot. It seemed to drown out everything, like the whole world stopped, and there was not a sound on earth to be heard but that one shot.

We stood there staring into each other's eyes; her eyes black as if they were an empty shell. It was as if we were lost in time. I didn't know what to do. I wanted to step toward her but my legs seemed to be anchored to the ground.

Suddenly time caught up. She fell toward me and into my arms. Together we fell to the ground. As I was falling my eyes looked up and for a split second I saw an eagle sitting in the tree above us.

I reached up to pull the hair from her face and saw that my hands were covered in her blood. Her breathing became shallow.

"Jacky!" I cried out as Jars came running toward us.

"GO, GO GET HELP NOW!" I yelled. As I watched him drive

away, I heard Jacky trying to utter my name. "Vicky," she whispered as she faded into unconsciousness.

"Try not to speak everything is going to be okay. Just hold onto me," I cried.

"Vicky," she whispered again.

I put my hand on her lips. "Don't talk."

"Vicky, listen to me, there isn't much time. This is the last chapter in my life, but you've got to go on for the both of us. It's okay, we knew this would happen."

What did she mean? I didn't know how to respond, thinking she didn't realize what she was saying.

"It'll be okay," she continued. "If God didn't want me to be with Don, He would never have let us be together in the first place. I'll be with Don, and I'll be at your wedding when you and Glenn get married."

"Jacky . . ."

"No, let me speak," she gasped. "Tell Don I love him and I'll see him again."

"Please, Jacky, save you strength, Jars went to get help."

"Vicky, tell my dads I love them. And tell Mother my life would never have been complete if I hadn't gotten to know her. Tell them I'm half of each of them."

She squeezed my hand. "You and I are one. We know when the other hurts and we know when we're happy. I know you hurt right now, but there will be a time went we'll be happy again." Her voice faded. "Remember what I said. Tell Don he's my soul mate, and that life is not complete until our souls become one. Time will heal all wounds." She smiled and closed her eyes.

As she exhaled, the pressure of her lifeless body rested heavily in my arms, I felt the life she cherished so much escape her. As I looked down at her, it seemed strange. It was as if she were smiling at me. As if she expected things to work out this way. I felt and understood what she had told me. I believed that we were going to see each other again.

Looking out I saw the ambulance in the distance, but it was to late. They couldn't do anything for her now. I leaned over and kissed her on the cheek. "Until then," I whispered. I don't know why I said that but it seemed like the most natural thing to do at the time.

I felt weak. I was in a place where nothing seemed familiar. Everything became black and white, without sound.

The air was still, and everything was frozen in time. I couldn't breathe. I felt like the world was closing in on me. The last thing I remember was the eagle staring down at me.

CHAPTER 16

The next few days were so unbearable that I barely knew what went on. I do remember Glenn walking into my room when I was asleep, taking my hand, and telling me he was there and that everything was going to be alright. It seemed like a dream.

I said, "You're wrong, nothing is going to be the same anymore." Jacky was such a big part of my life I didn't know if I'd ever be able to get along without her.

He held me in his arms and told me he was going to take care of me. I told him I didn't want to wake up.

The next morning when I opened my eyes, there he was, holding me. "I thought it was a dream," I said.

"No, baby," he whispered, "I've been here all night."

"Glenn?"

"Yes, baby?"

"When did you get here?"

"Last night. I came right up to see you."

"I don't remember. Is everyone here?"

"Yes."

"Where's Dad?"

"Downstairs with Jack and Michelle. They sat up all night and talked."

I jumped up. "Where's Don?"

"He's in the next room."

I ran to open the door that joined Jacky's and my room together. There he was, lying on her bed. I walked over and lay down beside him. He cried as I put my arms around him. I looked over at Glenn. He understood Don needed me. He slowly turned and walked away.

I'm not sure, but I think we lay there half the day without saying a word. There were no words that would make everything better. So we just lay there, and hoped by doing so we'd bring some comfort to each other.

I don't know what time it was when Dad came upstairs. Don was asleep. I sat up and grabbed Dad and started to cry.

"I'm here," he said. "I'm not going anywhere until everything is alright."

"I don't know what happened," I sobbed. "One minute she was on the phone with Don and the next minute she was dead. Why?" I cried. "Am I dreaming, Dad?"

He patted me on the back. "There is no why, baby. There is no reason for this, except for the reason in the person who did it. Only he can explain."

From out in the hall we heard, "Mike, Vicky, can you come downstairs?" Dad got up, I looked over at Don.

"Let him sleep, baby."

I followed Dad downstairs where Glenn was standing at the foot of the stairs. "Come," he said. "The police are here."

We followed Glenn into the parlor and standing by the window were two policemen. But before I could ask them any questions, I heard a sobbing from the other side of the room. Looking over, Michelle was sitting on the couch next to the fireplace. Judy was sitting on the arm of the chair trying to comfort her, but there was nothing she could do.

I couldn't help but ask myself how she would ever recover from this. She had just gotten her daughter back. I know she would blame herself for something she had no control of.

Jack asked as his voice cracked, "Can you please speak to the policemen? They would like to ask you a few questions."

He walked over to me and whispered, "We could put this off until tomorrow if you want to, dear." When I looked up into his eyes, it was if I was looking into the eyes of a man who with all his power and wealth had become lifeless.

He had no control of the situation. I recall what Dad told me about Jack when Mother died. How he left Jacky and Michelle in the states and went back to France. Would he do something like that again? Would he leave Michelle until Dad would go looking for him? I had to be strong.

"No Jack, I'm fine. I'll talk to them."

He looked over at Michelle as she sobbed. He tried so hard to be strong, but when he looked back at me he had to excuse himself from the room. My eyes followed him to the front door.

I looked over at Dad and I could see he wanted to go after him. "I'll be fine Dad," I said. Dad didn't say a word. I walked over to the two policemen in their pressed uniforms with pens and note pads in hand waiting to write down every word I said. Jars was standing beside them as they spoke. I could see through the window, Dad and Jack walking down to the stables.

"Sorry *mademoiselle*, but we need to ask this question." I nodded my head and looked over at Glenn. He smiled.

"Do you know if *Mademoiselle* Boilean knew John-Luc was on the hill and was she meeting him there?"

"NO!" I cried out. She didn't want anything to do with him. Michelle let out a scream. I ran over to her. "Michelle, why don't you go lay down," I said. I looked at Judy.

"Come dear," she said. "I'll go with you."

When they left the room, I knew I had to keep control of the situation, not for me but for Michelle and Jack.

"Did you find him?"

"*Wee, mademoiselle.*"

"Where?"

"At his home," one of the policemen answered.

"When you spoke with Jean-Luc, what did he say?"

"He didn't say a word. It was as if he was expecting us. He was just sitting there waiting."

I didn't know why but I asked if Jean-Luc's father was there. I recall the first time I met *Monsieur* Garnier. How he snubbed us. When we arrived Jean-Luc's father knew nothing, only that his son was acting strange.

"Where is he now?"

"We have taken him down to the *mettre en prison*." I didn't know what to say after that. I was mad at Jean-Luc and thought about what I wanted to do to him. But I was at a loss for words.

Jars stepped forward and spoke in French. He must have told them what they wanted to hear because he then walked them to the door.

After they left Jars said that if they needed anything else he would take care of it. Then he walked out the door.

After everyone left the house all I wanted to do is go to my room. I wanted to be alone. When I got to the stairs, Glenn asked me if I alright. "Yes, I just want to go lay down," I said.

He kissed me on the cheek and said "I'll be here if you need me. As

I headed up the stairs I turned and looked down at him. He was standing there looking out the window.

I could see the pain that he was trying to hide. He was being strong for all of us. As I watched him, he looked up at me. I ran back down the stairs and into his arms.

"I'm sorry," I cried. "With everything going on, I never stopped to think about how this must be affecting you."

"Don't be silly," he said with that smile. "I'll be here, I'm not going anywhere. Now go lay down and after you've rested, we'll talk." As I started to walk away I stopped and looked back again. "Go," he laughed. "I'll be right here."

On my way to my room, I peeked in on Don. He was still sleeping so soundly in Jacky's bed. I know if he woke up he would be outraged to know that the police were here and that they found Jean-Luc.

I walked over to the window seat and sat down remembering what Dad said about being strong, and how Jacky expected me to be. But I didn't want to be strong; it was too hard to do anymore. All I wanted to do was to curl up under my bed and wait until all this was over, and get on with my life. It sounds cruel and cowardly, but deep inside I didn't care anymore. I was tired of being the strong one, the one who looked after everyone, the one who held everyone together. And I couldn't even do that right. I wanted to cry and let everyone know that I didn't know what to do. I had lost my best friend, my sister, and I didn't know how I was going to go on without her.

In looking around the room, everything was Jacky, or Jacky and me. I picked up the photo album that she had kept since she was a little girl. There were pictures of her with her mother and father, a picture of her and Don, and of course of Dad sitting with the whole band. Looking over at the night stand, there was that picture of Don at the lake as a little boy that she always carried around with her, no matter where she went.

I got up and went into my room. I had to pull myself together and go see how everyone was doing. I tried to remember the last words she'd said to me, but I couldn't. "Oh, Jacky," I said out loud, and then I lost it. I walked over to my bed and crawled under. I curled up like a little baby and started to cry. It all came out. I didn't care if anyone walked in and saw me. It was about time everyone knew I wasn't as strong as they thought.

I could see Jacky's room from where I was, and that made it worse. I lay there and just cried for what seemed like hours.

I must have fallen asleep. I awoke when I felt a hand, then an arm wrapping around me. I opened my eyes and there was Glenn, under the bed with me.

"Don't say a word," he whispered, "just let it be. I'm going to be strong for the both of us."

I opened my mouth to speak, but he said, "Hush, don't say a word."

We lay there together until the sun went down. Then we heard, "Vicky, Glenn, dinner is ready." Not that anyone was hungry, but that was Dad's way of dealing.

We came out from under the bed, and I smiled at him. He put his arm around me and we started down the stairs. He squeezed my hand, reassuring me.

When we got to the dining room I could hear Judy coming down the stairs. When she came into the doorway I noticed she was alone. "Where's Michelle, is she sleeping?"

"No baby, but maybe you can get her to come down," she said.

I ran up the stairs and peeked into her room, "Michelle," I whispered. "Are you awake?" She rolled over and looked at me. I knew there was nothing I could do to make her feel better but if there was one thing that all of us learned from Dad growing up was sometimes listening was much more powerful than any words.

I sat down beside her. "Michelle, is there anything I can do?" She started to cry. I looked over at her night stand and saw a bottle of pills. "Michelle, where did you get these?"

"Dr. Toucherbien was here this afternoon," she said.

"Dad made dinner and everyone is downstairs. Would you like to come down? It will help being around family." She smiled and didn't say a word.

I don't know how long I sat there when she finally said, "Yes, we are family."

"Yes we are, and we will always be."

She sat up, "Maybe you're right, I think I'll come down."

As I helped her to her feet she stopped and looked at me. "How about you, how are you doing?"

I smiled and chuckled a little. "Just fine," I said.

She looked up, "Sure," she said, "sure."

As we walked down the hall she said to me, "If you need to talk I'm here for you."

Funny, everyone was in pain, but we all thought we needed to be strong for each other, some more than others.

After I helped Michelle to her seat, Jack walked in and sat down. I noticed he smiled at Michelle, and for that matter, all of us. As I watched, I never heard him ask Michelle how she was feeling or show any affection toward her.

Maybe it was because I was thinking about the last time he lost someone close to him. Or maybe it was my imagination running away with me.

I was thinking the worst. I looked over at Glenn and he smiled. I put my hand on his leg just to reassure him that I didn't forget about him. Since Glenn came we didn't speak about anything. He just held me when I needed him and all the time he just gave me that smile which assured me everything was okay.

As I looked around the table I didn't see Don. "Where's Don?" I asked. "I better go see where he is."

Glenn said, "No, I'll go."

I wondered if that was the way Glenn dealt with all of this. He never talked about Jacky, but listened to what we all had to say. I walked over to Dad.

"I'm worried about Glenn. He never stops helping everyone and I never hear him talk about her, not to me, nor to Don."

"Yes, he listens, but that's Glenn. Maybe this is how he's dealing with it. For now, just let him be."

I sat down as Glenn and Don walked in. Don didn't speak all through dinner. I don't recall anyone striking up much conversation that night. I guess Dad figured just sitting together made it better.

When dinner was over, Don and Glenn walked down to the stables. He had always enjoyed watching Jacky ride, and I think he felt closer to her there. Glenn, the friend that he was, stayed with him, hoping that he'd talk, hoping that it would help him get through the next few days.

I stood on the porch and watched them. Michelle came out. She passed right by me and headed straight to one of the paddocks were Jazzman was. Jacky loved that horse. She had made sure her father had it sent to France so it could be there with her, along with The Duke. Jacky had given Jazzman the name because Don loved Jazz.

I walked up behind Michelle and tapped her on the shoulder. "Like some company?"

"Yes," she said quietly.

We just stood there watching for a glimpse of Jazzman. Michelle said, "She really loved that horse." I could see the tears filling her eyes. I couldn't find the right words to say to make her feel better. I don't think there is a right thing when you lose someone you love. Sometimes it's better not to say anything.

Jazzman came running and stopped in front of Michelle. She laid her hands on his head. It was as though the horse knew the pain she was going through. He dropped his head and sided. It was comforting to her.

Then Jazzman looked her in the eyes and stood real still. He blinked, it was his way of telling her he, too, missed Jacky. Michelle looked up at him. "You miss her, boy, don't you?" With that Jazzman reared up, turned, and ran off, as if he knew she understood.

Michelle broke down. She turned to me and cried out, "Why, why? Can you tell me why this happened?"

Still I didn't have the words to comfort her. We sat down on the grass as she cried out "why" over and over again. All I could do was hold her, like Glenn had held me earlier. Just being there made me feel better, and I hoped I was doing the same for her.

We sat there late into the night. Then she said, "We hope we never lose you."

I took her hand. "You'll always be a mother to me, no matter where I am or what I do in life. I hope you'll always be there for me too."

I think she needed to hear that. Wiping the tears from her eyes she said. "I understand why Jacky loved you so much."

"Before we go back into the house," I said, "I want to tell you I'll never be far from you, even when I go back to the States. I promise."

She smiled. "We better get into the house before they wonder where we are."

At the front door she kissed me and told me she loved me, we then went inside. Glenn was right; words don't have to be said all the time, our actions speak for us. I knew she felt better, just as I did when Glenn held me that afternoon.

Inside the house, I stopped at Glenn's room. He wasn't there, nor was Don. I hadn't seen either of the guys walking back from the barn, so I decided to go down and see where they were.

When I got to the barn, I could see they'd been drinking; in fact, they were intoxicated. I stayed outside, not letting them know I was there. Don paced back and forth, saying how much he loved her and that he'd never forget how she had asked him to come and get her. "I'll regret it for the rest of my life," he said. "I want to kill him for what he did," he sobbed.

Glenn said, "No, you're not going to do anything; he'll get what he deserves." Don glared at him. "Here have another." Glenn tossed him a beer.

Don caught the beer and sat down. Glenn continued, "I know you're not going to remember this in the morning, but I want you to know that I loved her, too. She was my sister in more ways than you can imagine. Just like you felt for her when she was growing up, so did I. That goes for Vicky, too. I never knew I'd fall in love with her, but I did and if anything happened to her I don't know what I'd do."

Don lifted his head and said, "I knew how you felt about Jacky." When he said that I felt the tears well up in my eyes. It felt so good to hear those words come from his mouth. "You were more like a brother to us all. I couldn't imagine not growing up with you or Jacky," Glenn put an arm around Don's shoulder. "Let's go, I think we've had enough, don't you?"

I ran before they saw me. As I dashed into the house, I heard the door slam behind me. I raced up to my room and made like I was just lying there.

After Glenn put Don in Jacky's bed, he passed my room to get to his. He stopped, looked in, and smiled. "Just getting to bed?" He laughed.

"Yes."

"Well, Miss, you better take your shoes off." He winked at me and continued down the hall.

I ran out the door and whispered, "Good night." I heard him laughing. I hoped he'd come back to my room, but maybe he needed time to be alone, too.

CHAPTER 17

During the next few days I realized things were beginning to happen. It all started at the funeral. We all felt uneasy and I never gave it another thought. While I was sitting there I looked up and sitting in the tree was an eagle. Maybe my mind was playing tricks on me or maybe I wanted to see it. I swore it was the same bird I'd seen the day Jacky died.

Oh God, I prayed, *help me get control, I'm losing it.*

I don't know how any of us kept control that day, but something was happening that I couldn't explain. I think Don felt it too, although he never said anything. With everyone in the frame of mind we were in, I suppose what we were going though was normal.

I sat alone beside the grave and watched everyone walk up the cemetery hill back to their cars. I needed a few minutes to personally say good-bye to Jacky. When Glenn approached me I told him I needed a few minutes, and without a word he walked off, he stopped at the nearest tree and sat down.

I didn't have anything to say to Jacky, but I felt just by sitting there I could make everything right. Of course I couldn't, but I felt that if I walked up the hill I'd be deserting her.

I felt a cool breeze pass over my body. I felt something pulling my eyes up. There he was, sitting right above me looking down—that eagle. He just sat there still as could be, as if he was guarding her grave. I didn't feel bad when I thought about it that way. Something so strong and free spirited, that was Jacky.

I heard Dad and Jack talking a few feet away. They were seated under a tree. Jack was having a rough time. He said, "Why, Mike? Why did this happen to my little girl? What did I do to deserve this?"

Dad replied, "You're a good man, Jack, you can't do this to yourself."

"So tell me why, Mike? First Victoria and, now my little girl. Was I never meant to be happy?"

"Jack," Dad said, "look up. What do you see?"

Right up the hill was Michelle, sitting all alone in the car with the door open, trying to understand the whole thing.

"Tell me, Jack," Dad asked again, "what do you see?"

"Michelle," he said.

"Yes, Michelle. Through all this you haven't turned to her for comfort, nor have you tried to comfort her. She's all alone, and she needs you."

Jack cut Dad short. "She's not alone."

"Yes she is. We've been down this road before. Not once did you go to her and listen to her, or even ask her how she feels. I don't recall you doing that, Jack. Never once since I've been here, have I seen you hold her and let her knew you're there for her. She's going through the same thing we all are. This time, comfort her. Don't cut her out."

Jack looked up at Michelle, then back at Dad.

"Yes, Jack," Dad continued, "remember Victoria. I remember you left for France to get away from the pain you felt when she died. And I also remember you leaving Michelle all alone so you could get away from it all. Even though I was grieving for my wife, I never had a chance to grieve for her like I wanted to because I was so worried about you and what you were doing there without your wife and child. I left my children and came to get you. Michelle was grieving for the friend she loved, knowing you'd been in love with her all your life. Jack, don't let this happen again. Don't do this to her. She needs you more now than ever. I'm going to tell you like I told you before. Victoria would not accept your behavior. Go to her, and tell her you love her and that you're here for her. You're both in pain, share it together."

Jack looked up at Michelle. "What would I do without you? I'm sorry for pulling you away from your family in your time of grief to come and pull me out of the fire."

"If I hadn't dragged you back to the States, maybe I would have never dragged myself out of my own sorrow. Your little diversion made me forget the pain I was going though. I thank you for that."

"You're a true friend. All these years you were there for Jacky and I never saw her grow up. I can never forgive myself for that."

"For what it's worth, my friend, Jacky called me a few weeks back and told me how she was so like you, and how much she loved you and

Michelle, and how lucky she was to have not one, but two fathers, and a mother she loved so much. You know, all the years watching her grow up, it was like seeing you when we were young. The way she talked and walked and even the way she ate. And the way she hurt, it was like looking at you. I felt good having her with me, for I saw my best friend grow up again."

Jack wiped away the tears. "It's funny how things go around. When we came to see you and we were sitting at the table and Vicky walked in, I was at a loss for words. I thought Victoria walked in the room."

Both men sat for a few minutes staring into space. Then Dad said, "When I came for you I knew that's what Victoria would have wanted me to do. She would have wanted me to make sure you were all right. So I did it for her. You know, she never stopped loving you."

Jack stood up. "No, you were the one she loved and you were the one she deserved." Then he walked up the hill to Michelle.

She threw her arms around him and started to cry. She'd been waiting for this ever since Jacky died. She could finally really cry for Jacky—Jack was there for her.

Dad sat there looking over at Jacky's grave, and then he lowered his head and cried. He put his head in his hands so no one could see how emotional he was. I didn't go over to him, I felt that he wanted to be alone. Maybe I wasn't thinking clearly, or maybe I didn't know what to say to him.

Judy came down the hill to him and sat beside him. He put his head on her lap and sobbed. She rubbed his back and sat, listening. I was sad, but in a way I felt happy for him for having a great person in his life.

I looked up. Glenn was still sitting there under the tree waiting for me, but I was not ready to leave. I was so busy watching my parents that I hadn't said goodbye to her.

I walked over to the casket, leaned over, kissed it. "You see, Jacky, they're all here to see you off. You never knew there were so many people that loved you. I'm going to miss you, and I'm going to have to learn to live without you, and I don't know how I can. We've never been apart." I forced out a laugh. "I even had to come to France with you to go to college, but I couldn't see it any other way. You've been a part of us all, and now we have to learn to go about our lives without you. I love you, girl."

I turned and walked away.

All of a sudden a cool breeze felt like it went right through me again. I looked up into the trees but didn't see any leaves blowing in the wind, and that eagle was still sitting there. I don't know why, but I turned and looked back at the casket. What was I thinking?

As I walked up the hill where Glenn was sitting, a breeze blew past me. At the same moment so did the eagle. But this time I felt the wind go right though my body, almost knocking me down. Glenn saw me jump when it happened. "Did you see that? I said. "It almost blew me over!"

"That was weird." He took my hand and we walked to the car where Don was sitting. I leaned over and hugged him. He said he'd be right back, that there was something he had to do.

As Glenn and I watched him walk down the hill, he told me that Don was really taking it hard. "Maybe getting back on the road would be the best thing."

"All the time growing up he was always there for her," I said. "I wonder if he knows, just as Jacky knew, that they were meant to be together."

As we watched Don in front of the casket, a funny thing happened. It was like something went though him, just as it did me. It was like he was jolted back, and then forward. "Did you see that?" I yelled to Glenn.

"Yes."

"What was that all about?"

Then it happened again.

Glenn stepped out of the car. "That's weird."

Don was talking; I guess he was saying good-by. Glenn started to walk down, and then stopped when he saw Don walking back. He had a smile on his face when he reached us. Glenn asked, "Are you all right?"

"Yes, buddy," Don smiled, and went to the other side of the car and stepped in. Glenn and I stood there, wondering what had happened. We got in the car and waited for Dad and Judy. When they arrived, we headed back to the house, where the rest of Jack and Michelle's family were gathered.

Don was silent on the ride home, but when we got there he said, "I need to do something very important."

In the car I'd sensed something about him I couldn't explain and I knew Glenn felt it too. Don didn't seem sad, or mad, anymore. He looked satisfied, a big change from when he woke up that morning. He'd been full of anger toward Jean-Luc, and himself for not taking Jacky back home.

When we got out of the car we all went in different directions. In the house, Judy asked me how I was holding up. I smiled and looked at Glenn sitting in the other room. She knew that without him I would have been a basket case. I asked her how Dad was doing.

"He's dealing, one minute at a time," she said.

I didn't see Jack anywhere, so I asked Dad were he was.

"I don't know, baby. You might try the barn."

I walked down to the barn and there he was, sitting outside Jazzman's stall.

"Can I sit with you?" I asked.

"Sure you can." He forced a smile. When I did, he put his arm around me, pulling me close. "I came here hoping that Jazzman could solve my problem; she loved him so much. Being close to something she loved gives me peace. How you holding up?"

I shrugged.

"Well, my dear, you're the only one we have left. I hope you're not going to go home. I love having you here."

"I'm not going anywhere," I said. "I'm going to stay, if you'll let me."

"If I let you? I hope you never have to ask that question again. You're always welcome here. You were like a sister to her and that makes you our daughter."

I stood up and threw my arms around him, and told him how much I loved him and Michelle.

He got up and rubbed his eyes. "I'm going to the house. Would you like to join me?"

"If you don't mind I think I'll stay here for a bit." Before he got to the door, I asked him if he'd talk to Dad. The two of them had lost someone they could never replace, just like so many years ago. As he left the barn, I heard the door latch catch as the door closed.

I noticed Jazzman throwing his head up and down, so I walked over to him. "What's wrong, boy?" I asked. He turned his head to his side, as if he was looking at something. *Maybe it's a fly or something irritating him,* I thought. I looked around to see what I could do, but there was nothing there.

Suddenly a breeze flowed through the barn. Never thinking anything about it, I went on petting Jazzman. "I'll be back to see you later boy," I said. Then I headed for the door. Half way through the barn I felt a chill, but this time it seemed to go right through me. The hair on my arms stood up as I turned back toward Jazzman. He was throwing his head up and down. It felt weird, as if someone were there.

I rubbed my arms together and headed for the door. As I reached my hand out to open the door, it opened on its own. "This is strange," I thought to myself. Something was going on that I couldn't explain. But before anything else could happen, I ran out the door. Once outside, I stopped and looked back. I chuckled, feeling kind of silly about the whole experience. "Get a grip," I said to myself, shaking my head as I walked toward the house.

As I entered the house I asked Glenn where Don was. Before he could answer I saw Don headed for the barn.

"Come on, babe," Glenn said, "let's go down with him."

When we got inside there was Don, sitting beside Jazzman's stall, like Jack had been. We sat with him and Glenn said, "We'll be going in a few days. Maybe we can put all this behind us."

Don looked up. "Before we go, there's something I have to do."

"Does this have anything to do with how you felt when you were down at the grave?" Glenn asked.

"Yes, but I don't want to talk about it."

I should have realized then that Glenn knew something strange was going on, too.

Don got up and headed out the door. "You mean now?" Glenn asked.

"Yes," Don said, "right now."

We didn't try to talk him out of it; we just followed. When we got in the car Don drove.

"Where are we going?" Glenn asked.

"You'll see." We pulled up in front of the jail. Don rushed out of the car so fast that we didn't know what to think.

Glenn and I quickly followed him inside.

Don asked the guard at the front desk if he could see Jean-Luc. The guard left then returned and said that Jean-Luc was ready to see us.

When we walked into the room, Jean-Luc was sitting at the table, his hands and feet in shackles. He looked dark and full of remorse. . He had lost weight and you could see in his eyes the pain he was suffering. I felt sorry for him, even though he had killed my sister and best friend. I hoped the reason why we were here was not to get all over him. He was wrong and he knew it. He knew he had to pay for what he did. He knew that she loved Don, and that he could never live without her no matter what the circumstances were.

I walked to the other side of the room and stood against the wall. Don sat across from Jean-Luc and they just stared into each other's eyes. Maybe they were trying to see what Jacky saw in the other. I couldn't tell you. But, watching them stare at each other, I could see none of the anger each of them had before they met. I knew Jean-Luc wanted to say something, but could not find the words. Then he looked at me. When he did I felt someone reach out and pull the life out of me. I felt my heart beating right thought my chest. I don't know why I did it, but I put my hand on his.

The chain on his wrist felt cool. Why did I do it? It was like someone else made me.

A tear rolled down his face. How could I feel sorry for someone like him? On the other hand, he had seen the innocence in Jacky and he loved her for it. He knew I understood what he was going through.

Then Don and I looked at each other and I think, just for a split second, he knew it, too.

I walked back to where Glenn was standing. A few seconds passed and Don said, "All I could think of was how I wanted to kill you for what you've done and for all the lives you have destroyed, but I'm not here for that."

Jean-Luc said, "I know."

Glenn and I didn't know what he meant by that, but I think Don did. He said, "You must have loved her so much. And it didn't take you fifteen years to find out. You saw her for what she was and loved her for that." He lowered his head. The room was completely still.

Then Jean-Luc said, "So you're Don. You know she belonged to you from the first day she could understand what life was all about." Don just stared at him. "I knew her love for you was strong, but every day I thought I could convince her that you would never see her for who she was. I came to hate you. In the long run, I lost her to you. You, who could have had any woman, in the world. You don't know how she admired and worshiped you. She believed in her heart that you and she would be together one day. I couldn't accept that.

"You waited too long to show your feelings for her. If you had told her earlier, this would never have happened."

Don lowered his head "I should have told her a long time ago how I felt for her. But I never realized it until I went on tour and saw all the women out there that I could have. I knew they could never hold a candle to her. I miss her. I miss the way she came to me to solve her problems. And when she cried, no matter what it was, I could always make her forget what made her sad in the first place. I had so much control over her. That's why I never told her how I felt about her."

Oh, my, I thought. I looked at Glenn. He smiled. He knew all along how Don felt about her. That's when I understood how strong the bond was between Don and Glenn.

Suddenly Don jumped out of his chair and his voice got loud. The guard in the room took two steps towards the table. "If I had told her how much I loved her," Don yelled, "she would never have gone to college and went out on her own and made her own decisions. Sure, I could have stopped her from coming to France, but unlike you, I wanted her to be her own person. But you made sure that would never happen. I have so much hate for you right now, I could kill you." The guard walked up and stood behind Jean-Luc.

I looked at Glenn, but he was silent. He just stood there. I guess he was there for Don if he needed him.

Suddenly Don sat back down and told Jean-Luc, "I'm not here to judge you."

"I know that." Jean-Luc looked up at us and then turned back to Don, leaned over, and whispered to him, "She came to you."

"Why do you say that?" Don asked.

"Because, being the person she was, she forgave me. And you know it. That's why you're here now." Then in a whisper, hoping that Glenn and I could not hear, Jean-Luc said, "She came to me and told me she forgave me." He sat back and smiled at us. "Now I know I can face anything that comes my way. I know I have to pay for what I did. She knows I couldn't get through it unless she forgave me." He sat there for a moment, and then went on. "You know what I admired about her? She understood what love was all about. No matter how she felt about me, she knew what it was to love someone."

Don looked down at the table again. Jean-Luc leaned closer, and in a low voice said, "She'll be back. She never gave up on you. Her death will never stop her. She loved you too much for that." He said it as he believed it was the truth.

Don got up and started to walk away, then stopped and turned back to Jean-Luc. "Do you need anything?" Glenn and I looked at each other.

"I now have everything I need."

Don seemed to know what he meant. He turned and walked out the door. Glenn followed, with me right behind.

Vicky," Jean-Luc stopped me before I could walk out the door. "She will come to him, and to you. This is not over. You know I'm right. You can feel her." When he said that, he looked towards the window. I followed his gaze, and there, sitting in a tree, as if it were listening to our every word, was an eagle.

There were so many questions I wanted to ask Jean-Luc, but I felt he believed what he was saying. As we stared into each other eyes, I too, believed it in my heart or maybe I just wanted to.

I opened my mouth to speak but he stopped me. "This is no time for words. She'll make it right, Vicky, you'll see."

I didn't answer. I left the room. I had to stop and lean against the wall. I couldn't believe what had just happened, but I knew for sure that Don and Jean-Luc believed, or we would not have been here in the first place.

On the way home no one said anything about the events in the jail.

When we got there, Don went directly to Jacky's room. I sat out on the porch with Glenn until everyone had left.

"Glenn," I said, "are we going to talk about it, or just act like nothing ever happened?"

"Maybe it's better if we just let it go. Maybe this is how it's supposed to be. When we get back on the road, he won't have time to think about it too much, anyway. But for now I don't want to talk about it."

I thought his reaction was sort of strange, but I dropped the subject and we didn't talk about it any more that night. In fact, we didn't talk about it for a long time.

On the day Don and Glenn were leaving France, it was leaked to the press. I volunteered to accompany them to the airport. They suggested that everyone stay home, since with all the reporters and fans it would be a mess. I wanted to be with Glenn, not because I would miss him, but because, ever since we left Jean-Luc, he didn't have much to say at all.

I also hoped Don would have something to say about what happened.

The goodbyes were emotional. When Don approached Jack and Michelle the tears rolled down his face. "I should have come for her when she wanted me to," Don said.

Jack took him by the hand and said, "If you did I would never have let her go, so if there's anyone to blame, let it be me." I knew he was just saying that for Don's peace of mind.

On the drive to the airport we made small talk, avoiding the subject of that day at the jail.

CHAPTER 18

I stayed in France to finish school, but most of all I couldn't have left Jack and Michelle, not then. Though I didn't know how to tell them that I planned to go back to the States after graduation. I needed to go home, it wouldn't the same anymore without Jacky. I had to learn how to live without her and I didn't know how.

I kept busy at school and did a lot of riding. Being with The Duke and Jazzman made me feel closer to Jacky, but that still wasn't enough. Lying in bed at night, I found myself looking into her room, the door which I always kept open, just like it had always been when she was alive. I often cried myself to sleep and, when I couldn't get hold of Glenn, things got even worse. It was tearing me apart. I knew I had to be with Dad if I was going to get past this. Even though Jack and Michelle were doing everything they could to help me, they were going through their own pain. When I was in their company I acted like nothing was bothering me. Knowing that I could not help anyway made it harder for me to cope. I was helpless and I had never felt that way before. I'd always been there for everyone growing up, especially for Jacky, but now I was lost. This time I needed someone to be there for me. I was losing control.

I guess I could have dealt with it better if things weren't strange. I thought it was my imagination, a way of coping, or my mind playing tricks on me. I was trying to forget to soon, but inside I didn't want to.

I remember one night in particular. I had an uneasy feeling, like something was pulling me down to the barn. Maybe something was wrong with The Duke or Jazzman. I knew he'd been getting plenty of company lately, but not the one person he wanted to see. Funny, the people closest to Jacky were the ones who made the trip down to see him and all they did was just sit there, hoping for some answers from him. Maybe he did give them an answer just by being there. I knew Jazzman had run a close second to Don in Jacky's eyes.

Even though there was a night watchman on the grounds, I'd never walked down to the barn at night, not even with Jacky. It was kind of dark and a ways from the house. You had to walk down a small road where the trees formed a canopy. During the day it looked nice and cool, but at night you couldn't even see the stars it was so black. Jacky would say, "Freaky." So why was I walking down there now, especially when I was waiting for a call from Glenn? I couldn't answer that.

When I got to the barn and opened the door, I felt a breeze flow through. I didn't recall the wind blowing when I walked down. As I entered the barn, The Duke was in the first stall and Jazzman was in the stall beside him. I headed over to see The Duke, but Jazzman nickered, so I walked over to him first. "What's up, boy, are you lonely? You miss her, don't you?" He rubbed his head on me and I patted him on the neck. "Things will get better." I wondered if he understood me, I didn't believe what I just told him myself. Again I felt a breeze, but this time it was chilly. I looked back at the door and remembered closing it when I walked in. I patted Jazzman's head and he nickered. "You and she made a good pair in the ring," I told him. He nickered again, like he knew what I was saying.

Then I walked over to The Duke and hugged him. What Jacky felt for Jazzman was what I felt for The Duke. He was the only one that gave me comfort. As I put my head on his neck I felt that breeze again, but this time it made a sound. I looked over at Jazzman, and the strangest thing happened.

He started to paw the ground, and look to his side. He was counting to ten with his hoof.

Jacky had taught him that. She'd stand at his side where he could see her. She'd tap on his shoulder and with each tap he pawed the floor once. Then she'd reward him with a handful of sugar.

I walked over to him and stood in front of him. "Jazzman, what's up?" Funny, he didn't even acknowledge me; he was still looking at his side, as if he was looking at something. Then he tapped the ground again, like he was trying to count. In between each pat, he hesitated, like he was waiting for someone to reward him.

I backed away a few steps when I saw him licking his lips. Then I heard tap, tap, tap, ten times.

I walked back to The Duke and just stared at Jazzman. I knew he would never count without being rewarded. I remember Jacky would get so mad with him. She'd say, "He knows what to do, but if you're not there giving him sugar he'll never do it."

This was getting too weird. I decided to walk back to the house. As I stepped through the door, I heard tap, tap, tap, ten times again. I looked back, and again he was licking his lips.

I ran to the house and sat on the step. "What's going on?" I asked aloud. I tried to collect myself before entering the house. I knew Jack and Michelle would be sitting in the parlor and I didn't want them to think I was losing it. Then I heard the phone ring and ran inside. It was Glenn, and I felt better.

"Hello, Glenn. I miss you."

"I miss you, too, babe. You sound out of breath."

"I just ran up the steps. I'm glad you called, the weirdest thing just happened to me down at the barn."

"What? Are you all right?"

"Yes, but it was the strangest thing." I went on to tell him about Jazzman.

"You know," he said, "things have been a little strange around here, too, and it always happens when Don's around. I can't explain it, but he seems like he's getting on with his life. But let's not talk about Don. I want to talk about you. What did you do today? And how's your horse? And do you love me?"

I laughed. "Good one, Glenn. You slipped that in."

"Well, babe, a man needs to know."

"Then I'll tell you all the time."

"I just miss you so much that I need to hear it."

"Hear what?" I laughed.

"You know."

We went on talking for hours, until late into the night. I enjoyed talking to Glenn; he made me forget whatever was bothering me. He was able to make me imagine myself in his arms, doing all the things you were told not to do until you got married. All I wanted to do was to jump through the phone, like you see in a cartoon, and come out the other end and right into his arms, then lie beside him and feel the warmth that comes with all the kissing and hugging and whatever follows. You know what I mean. I just wanted everything that comes with being in love. And, not to sound selfish, I just wanted to forget about Jack and Michelle, Don and Dad, and even Jacky, and run away. Not that I didn't owe it to Jacky to look after Jack and Michelle. I loved them as much as I loved Dad and Don. I guess when you're in love with someone you kind of get selfish and only think about what you want. And that's what I was doing. At least that's how I was thinking as I was listening to Glenn.

The more I talked to him the more relaxed I became. I forgot about what happened down at the barn; maybe it was just my imagination anyway. I thought, *Jazzman did that trick so many times before, and he hasn't seen Jacky in so long, maybe he was just lonesome too.*

"You know I love you," Glenn said. That's when I came back down to earth. I do that a lot when I'm on the phone with him—I kind of go into a trance. As he talks I imagine myself with him. But when he says, "I love you," I tend to come back down to earth.

"When you come home," he said, "I'm going to take time off. You'll see; it'll get better. Right now you're all alone and so far away."

He was right. Everything here reminded me of Jacky and, with the trial going on, I couldn't forget about her even if I wanted to.

He was ending the call. "Vicky, if you can't get hold of me, call your dad."

I stopped him. "I don't have to call Dad, I forgot about everything already."

He laughed. "That's my girl. Just think about me. Okay, baby, got to go, I'll talk to you in a few days. But remember if you need me, just dial."

After getting off the phone with Glenn, I did feel better. He always knew the right thing to say to cheer me up, much like Don when he talked to Jacky. Now that I was off the phone, I was worried I might have sounded like a big baby. But Glenn never seemed to mind.

As I got ready for bed, I couldn't help thinking about what had happened in the barn. I sat there for what seemed to be hours, combing my hair. I just couldn't figure out a logical reason for what I had seen. But I soon turned my thoughts to Glenn and everything felt better.

When I was finished with my hair, I reached for the lamp to turn it off, but suddenly felt drawn to look one more time in the mirror. And again I was freaked.

I saw Jacky's face on my body.

I jumped back from the mirror and looked again and this time it was my face looking back at me. "Holy smokes!" I said out loud. I waited for something else to happen, but saw nothing. Again I made excuses for what was happening. I seemed to be doing a lot of that lately. I turned out the light, and ran to my bed.

I continued to think about the strange occurrences and my connection to Jacky. At that moment I realized my only chance for a normal life was to put Jacky's memory behind me.

Was that even possible? Jacky had been such a major part of my life. She was family, and I wondered if it would be a show of disrespect towards her. Everything reminded me of her. She was still in my head and in every memory concerning my life. I decided to clear my head and only think of Glenn. As long as I had Glenn, everything would be all right.

I rolled over to turn out the light and remembered how she always said good night to me before going to sleep. I looked toward her room. "Good night," I whispered, and turned the light off. Immediately the room became unbelievably cold. I looked around, but couldn't see anything except the window opened a crack. That could explain the chill that came through the room. I also felt heaviness on my bed, like someone sat down. But nothing was there. Could my mind still be playing tricks on me? I reached down to pull the covers up over my head and curled up in a ball. I repeatedly told myself it was only my imagination, and that I had to return home. I wasn't able to handle living in France anymore. Finally I fell asleep.

After a few months had passed, I decided it was time to tell Jack and Michelle I was going back to the States after graduation. I wanted to tell them when they were together, and hoped they'd understand.

The night I decided to tell them, Jack was out of town, leaving Michelle and me alone. Michelle asked if I wanted to go out for dinner, but it was only an excuse to get out of the house.

"Sure," I said, "That would be great."

She couldn't wait to go, and even insisted on rushing me. When we got into the car she seemed to relax.

"Are you okay, Michelle?"

"Why do you ask?"

"Just a feeling," I said. But she didn't answer.

We didn't talk much on the way, but I knew there was more on her mind, something she wanted to tell me.

We went to her favorite restaurant. After we ordered she just continued to look at me silently. "What wrong, Michelle?" I demanded. "I know there's something on your mind that you're not saying."

She started to speak, but the words wouldn't come out.

"Has this anything to do with you rushing me out of the house?" I asked.

"Yes," she said, looking up and finally beginning to speak. "This is going to sound ridiculous."

I sat there smiling, "Try me."

"Don't say I didn't warn you," she said as she looked around the room. "Two nights ago," she whispered, "the night Jack went out of town, I awoke with an eerie feeling that someone was in the room with me. I thought Jack decide to cancel his trip and come home. When I opened my eyes, no one was there. I tried to go back to sleep, but I couldn't get rid of the feeling that someone was there. I got up and walked around and saw nothing. I went downstairs, made a cup of tea, and just sat there, reading. I felt a breeze on my neck, like when someone walks by you. When I turned around, no one was there. I don't know why I decided to go for a walk, especially the way I was feeling, but I walked down to the barn. I thought I was losing my mind."

She never looked up. I knew that ever since Jacky's death, Michelle hadn't been the same. I didn't say a word; she went on.

"When I passed the barn, I thought I saw the figure of a girl run inside. When I looked back, no one was there. I thought my eyes were playing tricks on me. I continued my walk to the front gate, never giving it a second thought. When I got to the gate, I remember thinking the walk was just what I needed. I felt better and started to walk back to the house.

"As I passed the barn again, the girl was standing in front of the barn door. I stopped and stared, not knowing what to do next. I should have walked down to the barn and confronted her, but I saw the night watchman making his rounds, so I thought he'd take care of it. It was a strange feeling that came over me when I saw her the second time. I'd been thinking of Jacky earlier and then thought my imagination was playing tricks. I hurried back to the house.

"When I walked into the house, I looked up and saw the girl running up the stairs. For a minute I assumed it was you, but her hair was lighter. I ran up to see where or what it was. I stopped at Jacky's room and opened her door. There was no one there. I walked into your room to check on you, but you were sleeping. I knew there was no explanation, but I couldn't help thinking of her."

I reached over and grabbed her hand. She had tears in her eyes as she spoke. "Today, I walked out to see Jazzman. As I stood in front of his stall, I heard someone giggling. I turned around and followed the laughter into the house. It was coming from upstairs. When I reached the top of the steps, I heard a door slam. It was Jacky's room. I ran over and opened it; no one was there. I sat on her bed and then I heard the girl laugh again."

She looked up, waiting for a response, but I didn't have one. Heck, strange things had been happening to me too. "I don't know what that means, Michelle," I said, "but it's only been a few months since Jacky's been gone and, with the trial coming up, it gets harder to forget. In the early hours of morning, when everything is still, your mind tends to play tricks on you. We all know Jacky spent a lot of time down at the barn, and deep inside you'd like to think she's still there."

We were quiet for a minute, then I said, with a chuckle, "Knowing Jacky, the jokester that she was, she was amusing herself." That made Michelle laugh. I reached out to her.

"I think Jacky was a happy girl. I don't think she would've lived her life any other way. She lived for love. For being so young, Jacky had a kind of wisdom you never expect to achieve until you reach maturity. Don't ever feel that you made the wrong choice to leave Jacky with us. If it were up to Jacky, she would never have wanted it any other way. Would it be a bad thing if she came back to us? She enjoyed life."

She looked at me as though I believed Jacky could come back. "Look Michelle, everything reminds us of her. But Jacky's gone, and if strange things are happening around here, it's only that we want them to."

On the drive home, I wanted to tell her that I had seen weird things lately, too, but I couldn't. Still, I think she believed that she saw Jacky.

When we got to the house we stepped out of the car, Michelle hesitated. She looked up toward Jacky's room. "If Jacky came back would you be afraid of her?"

"No. I would enjoy it." I could tell she felt good when I said that. There was nothing to be afraid of. We said good night and, as I watched her walk up the stairs. I thought, *How can I leave, knowing how she feels?* I just hoped that in time everything would work out.

CHAPTER 19

I began counting the days until I could go home. I still needed to tell Jack and Michelle and hoped they wouldn't take it too hard. Some of my friends had planned to go into town to celebrate one of our friend's birthdays. A week or so had passed. Everything seemed to be getting back to normal; I hadn't even seen the eagle in a long time. It felt great to get out. I had spent so much time in the house lately, or down at the barn with The Duke, that I had started to feel like a hermit.

We were having a good time when someone asked me about the band. They wanted to know when they were coming to France. I knew they were still planning to go to England, but wasn't sure about France. When Jacky was alive we talked about the band constantly. Now they didn't seem as important. Even when I spoke with Glenn we never talked about the band, only us. Then Jehane came running in the door. "Are you ready for this?" She dropped the paper on the table. "Read!"

The article gave the dates the band was coming to England. I was shocked that I didn't even know they were coming. Jehane said, "Don't feel bad, they probably don't know themselves." I couldn't wait to go home and call Glenn.

On the way home I thought about Jack and Michelle going through all this, knowing it would have been the biggest day of Jacky's life. When I came into the house, they were sitting in the living room in front of the fire. I hesitated, wondering whether or not to disturb then. I stood in the doorway watching them. They looked so peaceful. I knew then they'd be all right. Jack had his arm around her, as he did every time they sat in front of the fire. It gave Michelle a real sense of security.

As I walked into the room I made a little sound so I wouldn't catch them by surprise. Jack turned around. "Glenn called. He wants you to call him whenever you get in."

I decided to sit with them for a moment, so I took a seat in a chair across from them. "I have wonderful news," he went on, smiling. I looked up at them, not knowing what they were going to say. I hoped it had something to do with Glenn, considering his recent call. "The band is coming to England for the final leg of their tour," Jack said. "I believe Glenn said two weeks after your graduation."

I acted like it was the first time I'd heard about it. I could see Jack and Michelle were happy the band was coming and were looking forward to seeing them, too. Maybe they knew Dad and Judy would be there. Then I thought of Jacky's feelings about the band. It saddened me, knowing she wouldn't see them with me. I sat back in my chair.

"Please don't hide your feelings," Jack said. "You have every right to be happy. We know that both you and Jacky looked forward to seeing the band for a long time and even though Jacky isn't here, she'd want you to enjoy this moment." He made me feel better.

Jack continued. "Michelle and I spoke with Don and Glenn tonight. In a special way they were able to come to grips with her death. We both feel she was happy with her life and believed she wouldn't have lived it any other way." I remembered telling Michelle the same words that night at dinner.

Jack squeezed Michelle's hand and she gave him one of her trademark smiles. Looking at them made me so happy, I felt better about telling them I'd be going home after graduation.

But before I could open my mouth Jack began talking again. "Victoria, for your graduation, Michelle and I had planned to give both you and Jacky a huge party. We thought we'd have the band play especially for you girls. Even though Jacky isn't here, we'd like to do this for you. You know we think of you as our daughter. But it's impossible for them, because they're due to be in England the same day for a press conference. We feel so terrible not being able to have them, but if you'd like to give us the name of your favorite group, we'd be happy to get them for you."

Michelle added, "We think Jacky would have wanted it that way."

I didn't know how to respond, so I just got up and gave them each a kiss. I told them that I loved them both, and that they would always be a part of my life. Then I said, "I need to tell you something, but I'm not sure how."

"You know you can always tell us anything that's on your mind," Jack said.

Once again I took a seat in front of them, "After graduation I'll be returning home."

I think Michelle knew I was a little wary about sharing that news. I could only wonder what they were thinking.

Michelle sat on the arm of my chair and put her arm around me. I couldn't speak. "Don't feel bad," she said. "We've always known you couldn't stay here forever. We've known for a long time. We just want you to know you've been a god-send. Even though Jacky hasn't been here physically, she's here emotionally and spiritually through you. I think that's what helped get Jack and me through the rough times. Whether you realize all you've done for us or not, you are an amazing woman."

"Thank you," I replied. Everything she said meant so much. "I hope both you and Jack will come visit me and Dad in the States after I return." I reminded both of them just how much of a family we'd become, and that Jacky would always be there for them through me.

Michelle giggled. "Just try and stop us from not remaining a part of your life."

I went over to Jack, kissed him, and whispered into his ear, "I know why Mother loved you so much."

Jack smiled. "Well, you better get upstairs and call Glenn."

I ran up the stairs. I couldn't wait to get in my room, close the door, and let all the excitement out.

When I called Glenn, Don answered. He sounded great. "Well, sis, I'm sorry we can't be there for your graduation, but we'll be there a week later. Are you going to catch us in England?"

"I sure will. Jack and Michelle are looking forward to seeing everyone, too." As I listened to him talk, it was as if the last few months had never happened.

"Everything is going to be okay, sis, you don't have to worry anymore," he said enthusiastically. I didn't know what he meant by that, but still I could never forget that day at the jail. "I'll see you in England. I can't wait until the next time I see you. I need to go, so here's Glenn."

"Hi, baby," Glenn said. I loved the way he began every phone conversation by saying those words. It made me feel as though I belonged to only one person and not a whole family. I wanted Glenn all to myself.

"Hi Glenn, I really miss you."

"Sorry we won't be able to play for you at your graduation party. You know, I would have enjoyed playing for my girl," he said in a sly voice.

I couldn't help but laugh. "It's okay. But when everything's over, I want to go home."

"Sure. England will be our last gig; we're cutting the tour short. The guys are tired; they want to be with their families. Honestly, even I can't wait to see Mom."

I remembered his mother always telling him how she was in labor with him for a long time and how she'd wait up for him until he came home at night when he was growing up. She'd go on to tell how she walked him, Don, Jacky, and me to school every day so nothing would happen to us. She was like a surrogate mother. Glenn would just laugh when she'd say things in front of his friends.

"Don sounded as if he's doing better than I've heard him in a long time," I said.

"That's another thing, we're all so burned out, and all of a sudden, he's been running around like a chicken with his head cut off. He acts like nothing ever happened. From someone who was so depressed all the time, he's changed into someone who doesn't have a care in the world. It's really strange; you'd have to see it to believe it. When we all decided to cut the tour short, he went ballistic. You know how he can get. I guess it all started when he wrote his last song. He's been on a high ever since. He can't wait to get to England to perform it. A few months ago he was looking forward to going home, but to see him now, well, you'll see when we get there. I called Mike and told him what was going on. He said to just come home. We've been on tour too long. It's gotten crazy, there are so many people screaming at us every night, trying to get into our rooms. Can you believe we haven't been able to go out? We've spent most of the days on tour just like prisoners locked in our rooms. We can't even go out to get our meals. Personally, I think it's time we came home. We did what we set out to do, never really thinking we'd get this far, or so huge."

"You guys have become the greatest band out there," I said.

He laughed. "You're a little biased, don't you think?"

"No, I'm just telling the truth."

"Well, baby, sorry to talk your ear off, but we've got a big day tomorrow. I miss you so much," he whispered.

I had always thought being a couple in love, meant never having to apologize for the little things, but it was cute how he always made a point to do so. Then he said, "I also want to apologize for not asking how you are."

He was just too cute. "That's okay. I'm fine now that I talked to you."

"In few weeks we'll be together and I'll take you home. That's a promise. I have to go now, but I'm counting the days until we see each other. I love you."

"I love you too!" I yelled as he hung up.

After I got off the phone my normal thing would've been to think about Glenn, but I couldn't stop thinking about Don. I wondered why he was acting as if nothing had happened. Maybe we all just needed to go home. I also thought Don was blowing up because the band was going home. I had so many questions and no answers. One thing was for certain about Don, he could really be thickheaded sometimes. He was never much for words, but he always told you what he thought. If you were in his way, it usually meant big trouble for you. I knew what a pain he could be. I had been around him a few times and saw how he reacted with Glenn or someone who tried to change his mind about something that he really believed in. Even when he wasn't, Don always felt he was right. You really had to understand him to know what kind of guy he was. But once you did, you had to love him.

CHAPTER 20

Jack and Michelle were planning the graduation party. Actually, Michelle did all the work, but she did come to me for ideas before following through with them. They repeatedly told me it was my party and all the decisions were mine. I told Jack about the local band that played at The Hangout. We had gotten to know them pretty well since we'd been in France and all my friends liked them, too. I told everyone, they were just as excited as I was. I think, when I mentioned my family coming to the party, they just assumed the band would be there as well. Everyone was looking forward to the party so much that I couldn't tell them the guys weren't going to be there.

As the party quickly approached, I spoke to Dad on a daily basis. I couldn't wait to see him. He wouldn't tell me when he and Judy would arrive; he wanted to surprise me. When I talked to him, I could hear Judy yelling, "Hi, Vicky!" in the background. I thought it was cute how he always had to tell her to settle down. I remember time and time again Dad telling Jacky and me to settle down when we waited to talk with Don; it was like old times. I think that's what Dad liked about Judy—she had a childlike way about her.

Jack also looked forward to seeing Dad. Ever since he'd come back from his trip he'd been acting strange. Maybe strange wasn't the right word, but he wasn't acting like himself. He seemed withdrawn, just like I felt the first time I saw Jacky's reflection in the mirror.

Come to find out much later, he too, had experienced what Michelle and I had. It was two in the morning and he was riding back from his trip, when he saw the figure of a girl standing in the middle of the road. The driver kept going. It seemed that he couldn't see her and drove right over her. Jack yelled, "Stop!" He jumped out and walked to the front of the car, but no one was there.

The driver asked, "Are you all right, sir?" Jack walked back to the car and never said anything.

When Michelle brought it up, he would just say it was because he was tired. I didn't bother to ask; I just waited to see Dad. Jack was a secretive person when it came to opening up about what was on his mind, but with Dad he was always able to let his guard down. It was funny how, when they got together, they were like two young men still in college. My only wish was that they could spend more time together. There were just too many memories of Jacky for me to remain here.

The only request I remember Jack and Michelle making about the party was that it take place outside, under a tent down by the stable. Being closer to Jazzman just seemed to be an appropriate place. I wouldn't have it any other way.

As the party drew near, I couldn't help thinking more about Jacky. When we had first arrived in France we had started talking about this day. It was as if we knew it would open up a new chapter for us both. Jacky even believed she knew what was going to happen next in her life. She thought we'd go home and marry the men of our dreams. Given the insight she had on life, why should we go to college? I looked at college as an adventure, because you never knew when life was going to throw you a curve. Look what happened to her. Here was a girl who had a vision of what her future would be. She didn't have to go to college because she knew, or thought she knew what her destiny was. Who'd have thought she'd get shot by a guy who loved her? From the time she understood what marriage was, she always knew who her husband would be, and he was nothing like the man who killed her.

Every time I thought things were getting back to normal, all heck would break loose. I thought about her every waking minute the last week before graduation, even crying myself to sleep at night. I didn't want to walk up and receive my diploma without seeing Jacky walking ahead of me, getting hers.

The day before graduation I visited her grave. When I got out of my car and walked down the hill, I heard something screeching as it flew by my head. I ducked, but it flew back towards me, screeching as if it was in pain. Then it landed in the tree right above me. It looked down on me as though trying to tell me something. It was an eagle. I felt it was the same one I'd seen before.

As I looked down at her gravestone, it hit me. It was the first time I'd seen her name in big bold letters:

JACQUELINE BOILEAN, DAUGHTER TO MICHELLE AND
JACQUES BOILEAN. BORN 1951—DIED 1973.

I looked up again, and the eagle was gone. I stood there frozen, not knowing what to say or think. I don't know how long I stood there, but when I came to, I got in my car and drove home. I guess it didn't hit me until I walked in her room. Looking at all the things that meant something to her, I felt the tears roll down my face. I walked over to the bed where we had sat many times as she cried for Don. How she had missed him and cried for him to come and take her home. When she was lonely we'd never get to sleep until two in the morning. But that was okay because the time we spent talking was helpful to us both.

On the nightstand was the photo of Don down by the lake. I remembered how she kept one photo back home and one here in France to remind her of Don. She said that no matter where she fell asleep, Don would be looking over her. I picked up the picture and held it to my chest, and cried. "Jacky, why didn't you wait for me, why did you go riding that day?"

I lay back and curled up in a ball and sobbed. Why is it when we feel helpless we roll up in a fetal position and cry? Maybe it's because we feel safe, the way we curled up in our mother's arms as she protected us from the world. All I knew was that I was doing it more and more those days. Going to her grave and seeing her name carved in stone had made me realize she was really gone. I guess that's why I never went to her grave; I didn't want to accept it. I thought about all the strange things that were going on. Maybe she was still here somewhere in another dimension, but watching over me. I cried out, "Jacky, I miss you. Wherever you are, please take me with you. I don't know if I can live without you."

I must have fallen asleep. In a dream I saw Jacky and me playing in our yard back home. I didn't think much of it at the time, knowing I was dreaming, but I remember what she was saying. "We'll be together," she said, over and over again.

"Why do you keep repeating that?" I asked her.

"So you'll know everything will be fine."

"How can you be sure?"

"Because I never lied to you before."

Then she was gone. I started to cry, and yelled, "Don't go!"

A soft touch on my shoulder awakened me. I sat up in the bed, surprised to see Don standing in front of me. I was still half-asleep, and it didn't seem odd that he was there. I jumped up and threw my arms around him. "Are you all right, sis?" he asked.

"Yes, I must have been dreaming."

As we sat there on the bed, it began to feel like home again. "Everything's going to be fine," he said.

That's what Jacky had just told me. "I miss her, Don," I cried. "I try getting along without her, but she's all around me. Tomorrow we were supposed to graduate together."

A tear rolled down his face, he was having trouble himself dealing with the graduation, or so it seemed. I pulled him closer to me, laying his head in my lap.

"Vicky," he whispered, "Who am I to tell you everything's going to be fine, when I don't even know myself?"

I pushed the hair away from his face and lay my head down on a pillow, looking at him. We lay there for a bit, and he closed his eyes and fell asleep. I felt as though he wanted to tell me something, but wasn't sure of his self.

I looked up and Ray was standing there. He put his finger to his lips as if to say not to speak. Then he sat on the bed. I put my head in his lap and cried. "Okay, Little Miss," he whispered. "Don't say a word."

Words couldn't express how I was feeling then, but his words always seemed to settle me.

Dad and Glenn came into the room, although I didn't see Glenn at first. Dad walked over to the bed and knelt beside me, smiling. I smiled back at him, I was so happy to see him. Then he said, "We can talk later." Dad tapped Don on the shoulder and nodded for him to come with him. Don got up and kissed me on the check, and then Ray got up and followed.

Glenn took Ray's place and that's when I started to cry. Don, Ray, and Dad had left the room and, when I looked up at Glenn, he said, "You don't have to say a word." I thought it was cute how we didn't need words to share our feelings. I fell asleep, only to be awakened by Glenn, letting me know everyone was waiting for us downstairs.

Dad yelled, "Dinner's ready!" I smiled; that was Dad for you.

Then it hit me. I was awake; this wasn't part of my dream! "What are you doing here?" I asked Glenn. "I thought you guys weren't coming until next week."

"Vicky, you knew we had to be here for your graduation. We were just an hour away when Jack asked the band to stay here. Jack planned all this with Mike. When we called Mike a while back he told us when he was coming, so we planned to be at the airport on the same day. That's where

Jack and Michelle were today, picking up the family." He frowned. "What's upsetting you?"

I told him that I went to Jacky's grave, and before I knew it I was in her room lying on the bed with Don's picture. With his arms around me, he said, "Let's go downstairs. Everyone is here just for you."

As we started down the stairs, I saw Jack and Michelle standing at the bottom of the stairs looking up. I ran down to them, thanking them both for all they had done.

"Are you all right?" Michelle asked.

"Now I am," I replied. I hugged her and told her how thankful I was. I turned to my right and saw Dad and Judy standing there. I ran over to them and again started to cry. I remember thinking I had never cried so much before in my life.

"Now it's time for all of us to enjoy your graduation," Judy said. Sitting behind them were Tim, Joe, and Donna, my best friends from back home. I'd been so wrapped up in my own life that I'd lost contact with Donna during the past year, but I was happy to see her again. "I'm glad you're here! There's so much to talk about. I've needed a friend who knew Jacky and me."

I kissed Tim and Joe and thanked them for being there; we'd all been like family growing up. Glenn sat down beside me and put his arm around me. Then the doorbell rang.

It was Jehane. She wanted to see if I was going to The Hangout. As she walked in the room, I introduced her to everyone and she sat down beside me, across from Joe. She'd been waiting for this day for a long time. I saw Joe looking at her off and on, not once cracking a joke.

Judy went into the kitchen to get a cup of coffee. I followed and stopped behind her as she stood at the sink. She turned and said, "There's nothing to say, Vicky, I understand what you're feeling, but you have to put all that behind you now and get on with your life." I went to open my mouth when she said, "Not a word. Remember, you can't keep crying or you won't look good for your graduation. Now go and call everyone and tell them everything is ready."

The rest of the night we all sat in the kitchen talking and remembering little things about our childhood, more about Jacky than anyone. It was the first time we all talked about her without feeling like we had to hide our feelings. Throughout the night I noticed Don looking at me as if he wanted to tell me something, but then he'd turn to Glenn. I thought Glenn already knew what he wanted to say.

Dad, Jack, and Michelle all went to bed, and slowly the kitchen started to empty out until Glenn and I were left. Don went up to Jacky's room and fell asleep. When Glenn and I went to bed, we decided to stay in my room.

As we passed Jacky's room, Glenn stopped. "Ha," he said, "that's strange."

"What?"

"That's the first time I've seen Don sleeping so soundly in a long time."

I guess being in her bed made him feel as though he was closer to her. Little did I know what an understatement that was?

Early that morning I couldn't sleep. I looked up, rolled over and noticed the clock. It was three a.m. I don't know why I couldn't sleep.

Don and Glenn were still asleep. I sat by the window, looking out at the barn. I thought about The Duke and how I was going to ship him to the States when I got home. He was my friend, being there when I needed someone to talk to. Then I thought, *what about Jazzman?* He meant so much to Jacky, and I couldn't leave him behind.

With the windows open, I could feel the warm morning breeze on my face. It was so quiet, and the trees were gently swaying back and forth. A few birds chirped as the sky lightened a bit. What a good day for a graduation. I thought about everything, from how Jacky would have looked in her robe to how excited she would've been seeing Don there to see her, having twenty-four years of dreams coming true. I thought about how she would have gone home with Don to start a new chapter in her life, and how of all the people in the world who ever deserved a new start, it was her.

Then all of a sudden, a fast breeze blew in. I looked over to the other side of the room. It seemed to make a turn, and went into Jacky's room. I thought, *how strange.*

I heard Don moving around and went in to see if he was awake. His hair moved as the end of the sheet blew in the breeze. The new morning light shone on his face. He was so peaceful. Then again a breeze came by, but it was going in a different direction than his hair. I leaned over him and I was freaked, remembering earlier that day when he was lying on my lap, and how I had rubbed the hair out of his face. With every stroke, I had moved more hair. The same thing was happening now, but there was no one there.

Then he moved his face toward me, smiling in his sleep.

Still freaked, I ran back to my room and right into Glenn. "Sorry," I said, out of breath. "I didn't see you standing there."

He looked at me with disappointment. I jumped back into bed and closed my eyes. Glenn turned and left the room. I could hear him walking down the hall to his room. I called his name, but he never answered. He couldn't be upset, I thought.

Eventually he came back to my room. When I rolled over and looked at the clock, it was five a.m. and Glenn was asleep. I got up and tiptoed over to Jacky's room and looked in on Don. He was still asleep.

It was dawn. I headed downstairs and out the door, walking down to the barn. I heard a screech. Looking up, I saw the eagle flying in the same direction I was going. I looked back at the house to see if any lights were on. There weren't.

As I approached the barn, I saw the eagle, sitting on the roof, looking down. Chills ran down my spine. I opened the door and walked over to The Duke. Jazzman started to paw the ground, like he had the last time I came to see him.

I didn't respond. Then he did it again and I snapped. "Stop!" I yelled. "If you're here, why don't you show yourself?"

Then a strong wind blew into the barn, so strong that it blew the rakes and forks off the walls.

"Stop playing games!" I yelled. "This it not a prank you played when we were kids. Why don't you show yourself? As much as I try not to believe, I know you're here. Is that eagle part of your games?"

Everything went still, and a weary feeling came through the barn. The wind picked up again, but this time it was a gentle breeze and I wasn't scared. I turned and started to walk out—again, right into Glenn.

"Did you feel that?" I asked.

"Feel what? What are you talking about?" His voice shook. He grabbed me. "You've got to get a grip."

I didn't know what to think. Why was he acting so strange? "You had to have heard that!" I yelled.

"I didn't hear anything."

"Did you hear Jazzman banging the ground?"

"No, I didn't hear anything! There's nothing here!" he said. .

"Glenn, you have to believe me! There's something strange going on."

"Look," he said sarcastically, "it's getting ready to rain. That's what comes with rain, wind! You have to stop this, or else. I'm not going through this anymore. First Don and now you!" he yelled.

He had never told me anything about what was going on with Don. Then we saw Don, walking towards us. "What about Don?" I asked.

"Ask him yourself," he murmured and headed for the house.

When Don approached me, I asked him what was going on. I told him the strange things that happened in his room.

"Funny, Glenn asked me the same thing. I knew you were there."

"How could you?"

"Didn't you see me smile? Look, you have to get yourself together and stop doing this to yourself. You need to let this go, or you're going to lose Glenn."

"Let what go?" I yelled.

He grabbed me. "Sis, Jacky's back."

"But you knew that?" Even though I had felt her, I needed to hear it from him.

"She came back for me," he said.

"I don't want to hear this."

"Look, Vicky, you know it's true. I've been a fool for a long time, and now we're together, and I'm not going to let her go again."

"I can't listen to this; this can't be happening," I said. "And what about Glenn? Does he know? Has he seen her?"

"No," Don mumbled.

"What was I thinking? You got me believing in all this. She never came to me, and how do I knew that you're not going crazy?"

"Vicky, you can't talk about this to anyone, especially Glenn. Even if you don't believe me, Glenn thinks there's something going on.

"And why is that?"

"When Jacky first came to me, it was when we got back on the road. I've being spending so much time in my hotel room that Glenn thinks I cracked up, especially when he walks in on me and I'm talking to her. What's he going to think?"

"Maybe he thinks you're going crazy."

I started for the house; I didn't want to talk about this anymore. I knew he was right. I saw it all. Even before she died, I knew something wasn't right. I knew what I saw when I looked in her eyes and looking back was a big black hole.

I didn't know how to deal with it, especially without Glenn. I had to convince Glenn, but before I did, I had to convince myself. Until I was able to see her myself, I wouldn't say a word. I had to go to Glenn; he was upset with me. I was afraid I was going to lose him. From now on, I decided, whatever happened, I'd never say anything to Glenn about it. Not now.

As I watched Don disappear into the barn, I was surprised to see him look up and smile at the eagle that I thought I was the only one seeing. Don had always been aware of the world around him, noticing things down to the littlest detail.

It's been said that before a child is born, God separates their soul into two halves, giving the other half to another unborn child. Then, as the children grow, they unknowingly spend their lives looking for their other half, their soul mate.

It's only when they find each other that they begin to make sense, realizing they were meant to be, unable to live without the other. Thinking about Don and Jacky, I realized they were two lost souls, needing the other not only to live, but to survive.

At the house I didn't see anyone around, so I asked Rosie where everyone was. She said, "They left a few minutes ago, but Mr. Glenn is in the kitchen having coffee."

As I walked in, Glenn looked away from me. I stopped, hoping he would say something to me, but he just went on writing on a piece of music paper. This was the first time that Glenn was upset with me. It was also the first time I was at a loss for words. I sat down beside him

"I'm sorry. I don't know what I was saying." Tears began rolling down my face.

He reached out and pulled me to him. "No, baby, I'm sorry. I should never have acted that way. Please don't cry."

I put my arms around him. "It's this graduation thing that's got me thinking of Jacky. When I get away from here, I'll be all right. I love you and never want to lose you."

"I love you too, baby. When this is all over were going home."

He pulled me toward him. "I love you," he said. "And soon this will all be behind us," as we started toward the stairs.

At the graduation, my whole family, including the band, sat in the back row. It was bad enough that The Boys of Summer were getting all the attention. People I didn't know were coming over wanting to meet them, even kids that never bothered with Jacky and me. My friends couldn't wait until graduation was over, so they could hear the band sing. I didn't have the heart to tell them they weren't the entertainment. Still, I was sure they'd sing something for me; I knew all I had to do was ask.

I sat in the second row, Jehane beside me. I looked back to see if Glenn was looking, and there he was. He smiled as I waved. I was happy. I knew what I had to do to keep him. As much as I loved Jacky and missed her, Glenn was my main concern.

As Jehane and I sat waiting for the dean to come out and make his speech, our not-so-girlfriends made it a point to sit in the row in front of us. They tried so hard to make conversation with us, playing up to us because they wanted to come to the party. Jehane was just as surprised as I was. She thought I was going to invite them. But remembering the look on her face when they told her she didn't measure up to their social standards, I decided to let her have the last laugh.

When the dean came to the podium everyone became quite. A gust of wind blew by us, and although it didn't feel like a strong wind, our not-so-girlfriends' caps blew off. We really didn't think about it until it happened a second time. They turned around and looked at us as if it was our fault. When they did, off went their caps again!

Having a sense of who was behind the cap blowing, after the ceremony I told the girls they were invited to the party. Jehane wanted to drop dead when I told them what time to be there, but she didn't count on Jacky being there. I knew Jacky would be ready for them.

As the dean made his speech, mentioning the numerous accomplishments made by our graduating class, I could see how proud my father was. Looking over at Jack and Michelle, I could tell they were thinking the same thing I was. We were all thinking about Jacky. I know it must have been tough on them seeing me shine. They wanted what we all did, to see Jacky up there, too.

I looked over at Don. He smiled one of those smiles that Jacky loved so much. I knew Jacky was on his mind, too. I just hoped, after all this was over, everything would go back to normal.

As the dean read down the docket of names I waited for mine to be called, knowing if Jacky were here, she'd be going up before me.

Then I heard the name, "Jacqueline Boilean."

My heart dropped and everything went still. I was frozen to my seat, knowing every eye was on me. I looked back, and all of our friends had shock on their faces. Jehane looked at me, hoping for a reaction, but I had nothing. I wondered what Jacky would've done if she were in my place.

Then all of a sudden I felt her presence more than I had ever felt it before. My legs pulled my body forward and up out of my chair. The more I tried to resist, the more control she had over me. Jacky was inside me and I knew what she wanted me to do.

As I approached the stage I noticed I was even walking like her, in her lady-like manner. I even had her smile on my face, the one she had after pulling a prank. I looked back at Don; he was smiling one of those smiles that he had just for her.

I knew what I was doing, and I fought her every step of the way, but I had no control over anything. But I could read her mind as if it were my own. Looking at Dons' face, I knew now that she had been with Don. I also felt Don knew what was going on. I was in her mind, feeling and knowing all she thought. I knew he was keeping his promise to her by taking her on tour with him. I knew she'd been with him the last few months, in mind and body. And now we were one in mind and body, too.

When I got to the podium, I saw Don getting ready to take "our" picture. He was the happiest he'd been in a long time. I reached out as the dean handed me Jacky's diploma.

He was startled. Covering the mike with his hand he said "I'm sorry for the mistake," he whispered.

I clutched her diploma firmly; I wasn't giving it up. "I'm not," I said with a smile.

As I was walking away from the podium I turned and waved to Don, or should I say, Jacky did. Walking down the steps, I felt this overwhelming pressure lift from my shoulders, as though I had finished what I was meant to do. I stepped to the side to get myself together, as someone came over to see if I was all right. I felt drained and weak. When I finally got myself together and back to my seat, Jehane asked if I was okay. .

"Yes," I said, "I was just in shock when they called her name." I thought about what I had done and how it felt when she took me over. Now it was clear that she was here and how much she'd been waiting for this day. She always told me she was meant to be with Don. And if she couldn't be with him in life, she'd be with him in death. I didn't know at the time what she meant by that, but I was finding out.

Jehane whispered, "You know, when you were up there and you turned away from us, for a minute I thought you were Jacky."

Then I heard my name. The whole back row stood up and started to take pictures. I never felt so embarrassed. I went to the podium and turned to look at them. *Oh my*, I said to myself. I grabbed my diploma and ran back to my seat. The dean said over the microphone, in a joking way, "There's someone who made her family proud." I wanted to die.

After the ceremony, the first ones who came over to congratulate me were Jack and Michelle. I handed her Jacky's diploma and she started to cry. I told her not to cry, and that I knew that Jacky would not have it any other way. I sensed that Jacky would want Michelle to have it.

Then Don came over. As I was going to say something to him, the dean appeared and again apologized for the mix-up. I told him it was okay, and that Jacky would have been happy it worked out this way.

"Yes," he said, "but we took her name off the docket yesterday. I don't understand how it got back on." Then he walked to Jack and Michelle and began apologizing to them.

I was just staring at Don when Glenn came over and asked, "What was wrong?"

"Nothing, I was just shaking when they called Jacky's name."

Don whispered to me, "Good save."

I knew Glenn was picking up on the little things that were happening, but he remained quiet. This thing with Jacky and Don must have been going on for some time. I'd had no idea. Don never spoke of it. It hurt me to no end that he couldn't come to me about it.

On the way home, Jehane rode back to the house with us. I had introduced her to Joe, but I never thought they'd hit it off this fast. When we passed our not-so-girlfriends, we stuck our

heads out the window, giving them the evilest look. As we sped past, their robes blew up over their heads. We laughed so hard that Glenn pulled us back in the window. As we sat back into our seat, Glenn and Joe just shook their heads and laughed with us.

I looked over towards Don; he just sat there smiling. It seemed as though Don knew why we did what we did. Ever since Jacky became one with me, I was able to communicate with Don without speaking. At that moment our minds were one, and the things that were going through them were things that Jacky and I did. I couldn't explain how we could do this, but I could clearly understand that he knew what Jacky felt when she tried to join the secret society.

Glenn stared at Don, and then turned away.

The party was fantastic. Judy and Michelle had a chance to catch up on things. Jehane, Ruth, and Donna continued to hit it off. Jehane mentioned she was coming to the States after I got home. I invited her to stay with me for as long as she wanted. Jack and Dad talked about old times, as usual. Dad told Jack about their old house being for sale. Jack told Dad to go ahead and buy the house and that he would give the money to him. He said he wanted to spend more time with the family. I was happy to hear that. All my friends from college were there and having a good time, too.

When the band took a break Glenn talked with them, then motioned for Don, Tim, and Joe to come up on stage. Everyone was eager to hear them sing. Ray was sitting all alone, so I went over to sit with him.

Before they started to sing, I was shocked by Glenn's speech. "This is for all the graduating class, but most importantly for my girl."

They began to play, then all of a sudden, they stopped. Glenn walked over to Don. When he resumed his spot he grabbed the microphone. "I was going to wait until after the party, but the suspense is killing me."

The crowd became quiet.

"If it's all right with Mike," Glenn said, smiling at Dad, "I'd like to ask Vicky to marry me."

"Oh, no!" I said. I was in shock and didn't know what to say.

Then, just when I thought things couldn't get any worse, he called me up to the stage. "I want everyone to hear her say yes—I hope," said Glenn.

I couldn't believe how silent the crowd became and all eyes were on me. It was as though everyone was hanging on my answer. I couldn't move out of my chair. Ray got up and helped me out of my chair and walked me to the stage.

"I better watch myself," Glenn said, "here comes her big brother." Everyone laughed.

I did my best to hold back my tears, but it was hard. As I came to the stage, looking out at everyone was like standing in the middle of a football stadium with a thousand eyes staring at me.

"Before she answers," Glenn said, "I'd like her to stand up here and let me sing her favorite song, 'Within You Is Me.'" It was the first song Don and Glenn wrote when they were just starting out and I used to sing it around the house. It always stuck in my mind.

As he sang, I felt like the happiest girl alive. I knew he loved me and wanted to spend the rest of his life with me.

When he finished, he asked everyone for silence. I could see every eye looking at him. "Before you answer," Glenn said as he knelt down on one knee. He reached in his shirt pocket and pulled out a blue velvet box and opened it. I put my hand to my mouth and gasped.

"Oh, Glenn, it's beautiful." I couldn't move.

"We're all waiting," he said.

I couldn't speak.

"She's speechless!" Glenn said. "Now here's a first."

As I searched for the words, I felt a gust of wind come out of nowhere. It was the same feeling I felt that afternoon. Jacky was in my mind again. I tried telling her in my head, *not now*, but she wouldn't leave.

Don was laughing; he knew she was there. He came over to me and said, "You know Jacky would approve."

I yelled, "Yes!"

Everyone applauded. Glenn kissed me and then we headed down to Dad and Judy. I turned back and saw Don standing on stage, smiling. I knew he was happy for me, but I knew he was hurting at the same time. I think he had planned to ask Jacky the same way. After making my rounds with all the guests, I returned to Don, who was alone. "Can we walk?" I asked him. I didn't want anyone to hear us or see us. I couldn't find the words to help soothe the pain he was feeling. I turned back and saw Glenn looking at us. He nodded and gave me a smile. That let me know he understood.

When we got to the far end of the barn, Don and I sat down. I didn't know how to start at first. I finally said, "Don, she's here."

"I know. This was going to be her day."

I felt her step inside me. "I feel her love for you. I never realized how much. I hoped I could find the love she had for you, and give it to Glenn. I love Glenn with all my heart, but when I felt her love for you, I realized it came from all those years of waiting."

"I knew she loved me a long time ago," he said, "but I never thought it was so strong. I knew she wanted to come with me, and I should have just told her how I felt."

"I don't know if we'll ever know what the right thing was. You can't blame yourself for her death. You know you did the right thing. Did you want to be like Jean-Luc, demanding too much from her? And if she had gone with you, how would it have been when she regretted not finishing college? Would you have been able to answer that for her?" I put my hand on his shoulder. "Don't you think we should get back to the party?"

Just then Glenn showed up. He gave me a look that said he wanted to be alone with Don, so I left. As I stood some distance away, I saw Glenn put his arm on Don's shoulder; they were the best of friends. I felt good knowing they had each other.

Back at the party, I saw Dad and Jack together and remembered the day Jack came to the house for the first time. They reminded me so much of Don and Glenn. I noticed Dad putting his arm on Jack's shoulder to comfort him. I knew then their friendship could never be broken.

You can imagine my surprise when I saw who was walking up the hill from the house. Yes, our not-so-girlfriends. I couldn't imagine the nerve they had showing up, but I was glad they did. I was on top of the world; maybe I felt there was nothing anyone could do or say that could make me feel I was not in control. This was my party, and I had Glenn right there beside me.

Just then Glenn came walking over to me. "Behave, you." He grinned.

"I certainly will," I said with a smirk. I knew, before the night was out, our surprise guests would wish they'd never come. Besides, it was impossible to ruin this night. Or so I thought. I went and sat with Jehane and Donna, my best friend from home. Jehane had become my closest and best friend in France. I loved them both very much, and they seemed to get along great.

Glenn and Don walked over to join Tim and Joe at the table. They were all listening to the band from The Hangout. As the band finished playing, they headed over to where The Boys of Summer were sitting. The band couldn't help but give them the royal treatment. It was kind of silly, if you ask me. I couldn't understand what made them so different from the rest of us. No matter how big they got, they always remained grounded and remembered who they were. But that was me talking.

The band from The Hangout asked the same questions our boys

heard time and time again. "How does it feel being on top of the world, and achieving your dreams?" They were so excited to meet them; it wasn't every day they found themselves within reach of the No. 1 band in the world. Listing to them talk and remembering what Glenn had told Dad about how hard it was being on top, I wondered what advice they could give them.

Suddenly Jehane nudged me. Four of our not-so-girlfriends, Clarice, Theresa, Tatienne and Brigette were making their way over to Don's table. We thought it was funny the way they carried themselves, all high and mighty. When they reached the table, the guys hung on their every word. Jehane, Donna and I couldn't help laughing and I could feel the tension starting to lift.

Ruth came to where I was sitting. She sat down and said, "I hope you're not planning to say anything, Vicky." Why was everyone telling me that?

I couldn't imagine what brought that on until I looked over at Glenn. I was surprised to see the girls throwing themselves at the guys. I always knew what kind of girls they were, but I never thought they'd be so open in front of me. But they always thought they were better than anyone.

I had two choices. I could go over and knock one of them out, or I could just let Jacky do it for me. I choose the second. Having Jacky around seemed to be working out pretty well, I didn't have to lift a finger. I could see how Donna kept her eyes on Tim. I think she was looking for him to somehow signal her for help, but he never looked her way. Joe was a different story. His eyes never left Jehane; he did everything he could think of to get her attention.

Donna said, "That's how the guys always act. They're just playing with those girls. They do that type of thing on the road all the time." After Tim and Donna met, she went on tour with him, so she knew first hand how the boys carried on. She went on to say that the guys enjoyed all that attention. The girls who were throwing themselves at them now were the same type of girls they dated on the road. This was all new to me. I saw the guys as normal guys at home waiting to become big, not knowing how they were on tour.

Suddenly I felt kind of funny. I tried closing my eyes to clear my head. As the sounds of the party faded I began hearing a buzzing noise. I didn't think anything of it because no one else seemed to hear it. I noticed Don looking at me. Apparently, Don knew, but it was only when our eyes met that we realized Jacky must be near. Suddenly the sound was gone, as quickly as it had come.

I continued to watch the guys; you could smell the testosterone.

Tara threw her arms around Don in a playful way. You know how girls act when they're trying to impress a guy, all touchy-feely.

Then it happened again. I felt this overwhelming presence enter my body. I knew it was Jacky and tried to resist, but she was too powerful for me. I felt the increasing anger within her. I knew what was going to happen, and I didn't like it. Within what seemed to be the blink of an eye, I was out of my seat and walking over to Don. It was all happening so fast, I felt like I was airborne.

I pushed Tara across the tent and into the lake. It was as if I had the strength of ten men. I turned to Don and he was smiling; he knew it was Jacky in control.

Glenn was outraged. He yelled, "Are you insane?" and walked away.

I just stood there, Jacky was still in control. I looked towards Don, more for support than anything, but he just sat there. In my mind I heard him say, *Don't try to explain. Just let it be.* He knew I was concerned about Glenn.

"Where did he go?" I thought.

Jacky must have given us something the first time she entered my body. It gave Don and me a way to communicate with each other without speaking.

Let it go, sis, he said. Then all of a sudden I felt free to move on my own.

If I had any remaining doubt about telling Glenn about Jacky, I knew now it was out of the question. He had to know.

The party had become surprisingly quiet, except for Donna and Jehane, who couldn't stop laughing. Glenn was still nowhere in sight, but I remembered the look on his face. It was as though he was seeing me for the first time. But that wasn't it. He grew up with me, he knew of the fights I got in at school when I was young. He knew every time Dad or Ray had to come to school because of my temper. I couldn't figure him out since he had come to France. One minute he asked me to marry him, the next minute he was upset with me for talking about Jacky. I didn't know where to turn.

I saw him leaving the tent and called his name, but he kept going. I ran after him and yelled, "It wasn't me!" but he never stopped.

I noticed Don going down to the barn, so I followed him. I was going to tell him he had to tell Glenn just what was going on. As I entered the barn, I saw Don sitting next to Jazzman. I took a seat across from him. We sat for several minutes before either of us spoke. Don got up and took a seat next to me, and put his arms around me.

We had no idea Glenn had seen us both heading to the barn and decided to follow. If Glenn had had trouble dealing with things before, he was in for the ride of his life.

All of a sudden I felt that same sensation come over me, the difference was a warm feeling. It was exactly like when Glenn held me in his arms for the first time. I couldn't stop myself. I put my arms around Don and kissed him on the lips. He whispered, "I love you." For a moment I thought he was talking to me. I then heard myself reply, "I miss you and want to be with you always." I felt myself grabbing him tighter. It was at that moment I knew Jacky had never left; she was still using my body.

I used all my strength to try and fight her off, but I was losing the battle. I tried everything to get away, and then finally I begged Don, "Help me!"

Don yelled, "Jacky, let her go, now!"

I fell to the ground. Jacky was gone. But this time I felt even weaker than I did at graduation.

Looking up at Don, I yelled, "You can't ever let her do that again! How could you? Promise me you'll never let that happen again."

He reached out to help me up. "I'm sorry, Sis. I'll never let her do that again."

I felt so weak that I grabbed the stall door. I had to sit down, he sat beside me. I didn't say anything until he started to laugh.

"What's so funny?" I said. "You had to see the look on Tara's face," he said.

At that we both cracked up.

"You really put her in her place," he said.

"Not really," I pointed out, "Jacky put her in her place. "We better get back to the party and make sure everyone's okay."

"You go on ahead; I'll be up in a minute."

As I started out of the barn I encountered Glenn. He acted like he had just shown up. "I was just coming to see where you were," he said, with a strange look on his face. "We should go back to the party." I thought, *He saw everything.*

Don came from the barn, and we all went back together. As we walked, Don looked up and made a remark about the eagle sitting in a tree. He acted like he was glad to see it. Glenn just continued to look at Don curiously. Maybe he wanted to say something, I don't know. Looking back on it, I wish I had said something. Maybe things would have turned out a little better for us. But who was I to say anything? I wasn't sure about anything anymore.

After that night it was some time before I heard or felt Jacky's presence. Glenn never spoke of the night he saw us in the barn. I guess, in his own way, he needed time to sort things out. What would you think if you saw your girlfriend holding her brother whispering, "I love you" in his ear? The only thing I knew for sure was that, whenever he saw Don and I together, he had a look of distaste. He never knew what to expect or how to react with either Don or me. The whole situation was beginning to make me sick. I tried to understand why Glenn was behaving that way. I guess if I'd seen my best friend caressing his sister while they both confessed their love, it would've pushed me over the edge too. But if that was the case, why didn't he bring it up so we could talk about it? If I'd known for sure he saw us, I would have immediately.

However, now I was free of Jacky. Or so I thought. I needed to try and put the pieces back together, but how?

Even though I hadn't felt Jacky's presence for a few days, Jacky kept visiting Don. I didn't know how often, but I knew it was happening.

Rehearsing at the house made it easier for the band, as opposed to going back to England. The concert wasn't for another three weeks. They didn't have to worry about reporters or fans jumping them whenever they went out.

Don would quietly eat his dinner and retreat to Jacky's room, just like Glenn said he did when they were on the road. That went on until it was time to go back to the States. Nobody ever said anything; they all thought that all the rehearsing took its toll on them. However, I knew better.

One evening after everyone had gone out, I ran upstairs to get a sweater. It was the first time Glenn agreed to go riding with me. Even though his feeling towards me seemed strange, I hoped that being out in the woods would change things. But, by that time I was willing to do anything that would get us back to where we were before the party. So I ran upstairs to get my jacket before he could change his mind.

When I walked in my room, Don was in Jacky's room with the door closed. I heard his voice. It sounded as though he was having a conversation. "I wrote it for you," I heard him say.

I didn't know whether I should knock, so I just grabbed my jacket. I sat on my bed, wanting to say something. But what?

I heard him again. "No, I haven't sung it yet. Of course, I'll sing it tomorrow night. I can't wait for you to hear it. I'm looking forward to singing it for you. I wish you'd join me on stage." Then he laughed and said, "I know, I love you, too."

She was there with him.

I couldn't bear to listen anymore. I made a noise so he'd hear me and stop talking. Then I turned away, humming to myself, so he wouldn't think I was eavesdropping.

Jacky's door opened. "Hey, what's up, sis?" Don asked.

"Nothing, I just needed to get my jacket. Glenn is going riding with me. You want to come?"

He laughed. "No, I think I'm going to turn in early, we have a big day tomorrow." He closed the door.

I had to admit I was a little jealous of Don. He got to speak and share things with Jacky one-on-one. I wondered why things weren't the same with me. I knew her just as well, even better than most, I thought. Instead, the only way I knew she was ever around was when she took control of me. As much as I loved Jacky, I hated that. It was getting harder and harder to keep control of myself.

I wanted to tell Glenn. I wanted his support, just as he'd given it to me so often before. But not knowing how he would react frightened me. Still, to go on facing this alone was ludicrous. Sure, Don knew, but his emotions and judgment were so clouded that I needed more. He was happy to just go on the way he'd been going for the last year.

I'll never forget the following day. That was the day of the concert. I stayed up all night making a decision about telling Glenn about Jacky, and how she'd been with Don all year. I had myself convinced that Glenn would understand. Why wouldn't he? He'd always been there for me, why wouldn't he be there for me now? It was about time I started taking my own advice. If Glenn couldn't handle it, then fine. I'd stay in France until I got over him.

It was so hectic with everyone excited about the concert. Glenn, Don, and the rest of the band left earlier in the morning, so they'd get to England with enough time to rehearse. They'd already arranged backstage passes for everyone, so we could all meet up before things got crazy.

Before Glenn left the house I told him that I wanted to talk with him, but he said he wouldn't have time until after we got to the States. That bothered me. For a minute I thought he was giving me the brush-off, so I didn't want to make matters worse. He was already upset because the band's agent had ordered everyone back to the States after the concert that night.

He knew I was upset and apologized. "It couldn't be helped."

I bit my tongue and said, "That's okay. I'll see you in two days."

I guess he was able to see the sadness in my eyes, because he said, "Baby, if it's really important, tell me."

"No, that's okay. It can wait until we get home."

I don't know if he believed me, but he gave me a kiss goodbye. It wasn't like any other time he kissed me; it was on the forehead, which I thought was strange. Then he left for England.

I didn't get a chance to see Don, except for him walking past my room when Glenn was leaving. He said, "See you tonight," and was gone.

At that point all my plans of telling Glenn blew out the window. After the way he kissed me, I felt like I had lost him already. I felt like he couldn't wait to get back to the States. Maybe it was all too much for him.

As I dressed, I noticed the door to Jacky's room was still closed. I wasn't comfortable seeing it closed so I opened it.

When I pushed the door open, I felt a rush of cool air unlike anything I felt before. I walked farther into the room and sat on the bed. Chills ran down my arm as I sat there, looking out the closed window. I turned to look at Don's picture still sitting on the table and was abruptly pushed forward, then back.

I was really getting tired of how I was being treated; it was time to confront her. I got up from the bed and stood in front of the mirror. I could feel her enter my body, as I did before, but this time there was a major difference. As I stared into the mirror looking for a reaction, I could see her reflection looking back at me. I was well aware it was my body in front of the mirror, but it was her reflection.

"Why are you doing this to me?" I demanded.

She whispered, "It's because of our special connection. You're the only one I can become one with."

"Well, I want you to stop it! You have to move on."

"No, I'll never leave without him."

"Jacky, if you truly love him, you need to let him go."

"I'll never do that."

"Don't do anything tonight," I pleaded. "It's a special night for everyone. If you care for Glenn and me, let me be."

"If I care for Glenn? He doesn't even care enough to listen to you. Or should I say he doesn't believe you? Maybe I was wrong about you and Glenn."

"Don't even say that!" I yelled.

All of a sudden she started to fade. I repeatedly asked her to stay, but she was gone.

I didn't know what to think. I couldn't figure her out. This encounter was unlike any of the others. I was unable to read her mind this time; it was as though she was purposely blocking me out. It gave me an uncomfortable feeling, not knowing what to expect. I ran out of the room.

I ran until I reached the stairs. Dad was on his way up. "What's wrong?"

I didn't think he'd believe me, so I responded, "Nothing, I'm just very excited about tonight."

I don't think he believed that either, though. He asked me to sit with him for a moment. We took a seat on the steps. Taking my hand, he began telling me how happy he was for me, and how he wished my mother was here to see me. "She'd be so proud of you." I did everything to keep from crying, but the tears began to flow.

Without thinking I blurted out, "Dad, do you believe in ghosts?"

"It all depends on who it is." He smiled and I knew it wasn't the right conversation to be having with him.

He got up and headed down the hall while I remained seated. I couldn't help worrying about Glenn. I didn't want to lose him, but if I told him the complete truth, I risked doing just that. It was killing me not knowing what to do. I knew if I couldn't tell him what was bothering me, it would forever damage our relationship. But I needed someone to tell.

Before I knew it, it was time to get going to the concert. We all decided to drive in the limousine. Dad, Judy, Jack, Michelle, Ray, and Ruth took their seats in the back, while Jehane, Donna, and I sat up front. We had no trouble getting backstage where the band was with Jack in the car. He had enough wealth and power to get in anywhere he wanted.

When we got out of the car, we all headed for the dressing rooms. I could see Glenn standing in the doorway. I didn't know how to react, or what to feel. I loved him, but given the events of the past few days, I didn't know where our relationship was heading. I made sure to put a smile on my face when he saw me, but I think he knew there was still something going on.

He walked towards me. "Hey, baby, I missed you," he said. "Let's go see the rest of the guys."

We entered the room where everyone was sitting watching the band get ready. "Well, sis, are you ready?" Don asked.

"Yes, I am."

"You don't look it. In fact, you don't look happy at all."

Glenn looked at me and I smiled, but he could see it was an act. Part of me wanted to tell him everything, right there and then, but he was getting ready to go on. I wasn't going to ruin this night for him or anyone.

"Come on, let's take a walk," he said.

I followed him out the door, but before I left Don murmured, "Don't tell him."

We were going down the hall when he said softly, "I know there's something bothering you."

"No, there really isn't anything wrong."

"Does any of this have to do with Jacky?"

"No, Glenn! I just wish we were going home tonight, but one more day won't matter."

I don't think he believed me, but he said, "Okay. I love you, Vicky."

"I know," I replied. He looked at me when I didn't reply with "I love you, too." But I did love him. Then we kissed, this time on the lips.

When we got back to the room, the band was already heading out the door. Don was smiling because it was once again a time to make history.

The rest of us took our seats in the front row, where we could witness all the action. It was great. I couldn't help but think about everything. Glenn was looking right at me. He could tell I was still bothered. I think he was more upset than I was. I was just glad that after the concert we'd all be heading home. Then, just maybe, things would return to normal. I hoped Jacky's spirit would remain in France. I couldn't have been more wrong.

I turned and saw so many different faces. There were so many fans sitting on the edge of their seats. As the band went from one song to the next everyone in the stadium was jumping and cheering, clapping and singing along with them. Watching the guys playing, I could see their emotions change, as if they were feeding off the crowd. I could see their energy as they went from one song to the next. You could feel the adrenaline in the air. The more the crowd cheered, the better the guys played. It was a real feeding frenzy. I got a rush just watching. I'd never seen the guys in concert before. It wasn't at all like Don's twenty-first birthday party.

I said to myself, *My brother and boyfriend are in one of the hottest bands ever, and I've never been to a concert in my life. What a sheltered life I've led, I've missed so much.*

Clapping my hands and jumping out of my seat, I sang along with crowd. I was on a high. I could see Glenn laughing as he pointed at me; getting the attention of the band to look over. They knew I was caught up in the whole thing.

Then all of a sudden the crowd got quiet and the lights dimmed. Glenn began singing my favorite song, while looking right at me. The crowd was looking around to see whom he was singing to. I chose not to turn around and let the crowd know where I was. Jehane, on the other hand, said, "Unbelievable!"

I looked up at Glenn and smiled, forgetting about everything that had happened over the past few days. No matter how things seemed, I knew Glenn loved me, and if our relationship ended, it would only be because of him not understanding or accepting what was going on with Jacky.

Tim sang a solo, followed by Joe. Donna and Jehane were on cloud nine. Jehane was especially happy because Joe never took his eyes off her as he sang. It was even more impressive when the crowd joined in.

Suddenly the air around me became cold. I looked at Jehane and saw beads of sweat rolling down her face. I seemed to be moving slower than the rest of the crowd, as if I was trapped in time. When I looked up at the band, I saw Don getting ready to sing. As the crowd jumped up and down and yelled hysterically, I couldn't hear a thing. It was so silent I felt as though I could hear a pin drop, but I knew it was impossible.

Jehane gave me a nudge. Looking over at her I could see her lips move, but I didn't hear a word.

Then Don started to sing. It was as if his voice was the only one I could hear. He said, "This song is for my girl. I wrote it just for her, for this day. The only thing that would make this better would be to have her standing here with me as I sing it for the first time."

I could see this was unexpected by the other band members. Then, before I knew it, I was losing control of my legs. I could hear the whispering, *There's Don's girlfriend.* Some cheered me on, some booed me.

I was as mad as I have ever been and tried to fight her off, but like always, she got the better of me. "Stop!" I yelled, "Please don't do this." I could see Jehane looking at me as if I was talking to her.

Then Don said, "Will my best girl come up here, so I can sing her this song?"

As I stood, I knew what I was doing, but I didn't have any control over my actions. Jacky was also attempting to take over my mind, causing me to drift in and out of consciousness. The next thing I remembered was standing next to Don on stage. I could see her reflection in the mirrors on the wall behind him. I mean, she was standing there, her face on my body.

I tried to get Glenn's attention with my eyes. I wanted him to see what I was looking at. He looked back at me, so I turned toward the mirrors, hoping his eyes would follow, but he just looked to his side. I had to try one more time, but before I could, my mind blacked out again.

I remember standing beside Don as he started to sing. He sang a song called "Miss Ghost." It was about a girl who had died and later returned to her true love. The extended version of the song included how he loved her, and how he chose the remaining days only loving her. I could feel a lump in my throat, and tears in my eyes, so I stopped fighting her.

Tears rushed down my face, and I felt her love. How could I fight something so pure and good? I looked back at the mirrors to see if she was still there. She was, and smiling back at me, too. In the reflection I saw Don. He saw the same thing I did. I turned, smiling at him. I nodded yes in recognition. He knew what I was saying. He finished singing, and I felt Jacky exit my body. Don knew she was gone; the smile left his face.

I sensed that Jacky was really gone this time. I never fully understood why or where she went, but I now understood her feelings. Each time she entered my body, she never exited without leaving a little piece of herself behind. I wanted to believe she did that on purpose, so that I always had a better understanding of how and why she loved Don.

I felt her wanting to run to him as he finished his song. She wanted him to know she loved him. I believe she also knew how that would look and she didn't want to hurt me. I was glad she chose not to run to him, but at the same time I really didn't care. Jacky reminded me of the innocence that love has to offer and how it affected both my love for Glenn and her love for Don. I thought about all those years I'd spent watching out for her, while all along she was teaching me what love was all about. I wanted that same kind of love for Glenn and me.

When I turned my attention back to Glenn, I heard the crowd cheering and yelling for more. Time returned to normal. Glenn looked as if he saw a ghost and I hoped he had.

Don put his microphone down and escorted me off the stage. When we reached the end of the stage I asked softly, "Where is she?"

"I don't know; she was gone so fast."

"You have to go to her, she needs you right now."

He looked back at the band. "After the concert," he said.

I was glad they were playing the last song of the night. Then Don could wrap up everything and go to her.

As he walked back on stage, everyone gave him a standing ovation and The Boys of Summer began playing their last song. I never went back to my seat; I just found my way to the dressing room. I didn't know what to expect when Glenn came back, but I was ready for anything. I spent time alone trying to think of what to say, but kept coming back to the decision I had made that morning. I thought about Jacky's last words to me when I saw her in the mirror the night before. I came to the conclusion that she must have been trying to tell me to explain everything to Glenn.

I thought it ironic that she was telling me the same things I had told her years before about her and Don. "If Don doesn't understand you, then he doesn't love or deserve you," I used to say. Now it was my turn to test the waters with Glenn. I was going to tell him everything, and if he didn't understand, it meant he didn't love me enough to care. I was going to tell him, but not until we returned to the States.

The next thing I knew, everyone was coming into the room, except for Glenn. I wondered why he didn't come right back. I stood at the door thinking he'd come any minute, but still he never came.

Donna and Tim caught my eye. They were sitting side by side on the sofa. I couldn't remember ever seeing them so happy. A year ago she wouldn't have been able to imagine sitting next to him, let alone dating him. Joe and Jehane were hanging all over each other, and Dad, Judy, Jack, and Michelle were acting like teenagers. It was great seeing everyone having so much fun. Ruth and Ray were sitting beside Jehane and Joe, laughing at Joe's jokes.

Don was suddenly next to me. "Well, what did you think?" he asked.

"It was great Don, but where's Jacky?" I asked in a low voice.

"Don't worry, I'll see her later, but never mind that. You'd better focus on Glenn. After the last set, he was the first one off stage."

"Where did he go? You have to help me find him."

Suddenly there he was, standing in the doorway. Don whispered, "You better talk to him before we have to leave."

As Glenn and I walked down the hall together, I could tell he was nervous; he kept looking around, as if expecting to see something. I grabbed his hand tightly. To be honest, I didn't know where to begin. "Glenn," I said.

He didn't answer.

I stepped in front of him, forcing him to stop. "Why are you not talking to me?"

Still no response. I felt the tears welling up in my eyes. "Glenn, what can I say?"

Without warning the tears came. I didn't want him to see me cry. I didn't need him feeling sorry for me in any way, so I turned and left. As I walked, I was able to get control of myself, although I did feel a few tears run down my face.

I was halfway down the hall when Glenn called me back. I didn't want to stop because I was afraid of losing control. I didn't want him to see what a mess I was.

"Vicky, stop!" he yelled. I stopped but didn't turn around.

He came up from behind and grabbed me by the arm. "Please stop," he begged, pulling me toward him. I began to cry uncontrollably as I hugged him. "Don't cry," he said.

"There's something I need to tell you and I know this isn't the time. But I want you to know I've wanted to talk with you for a long time. I just didn't know how to begin. You don't understand how difficult it's been for me lately. I didn't feel I could tell you because I thought you'd get upset with me. But I need to talk with someone and there isn't anyone but you."

He put his arms around me. "I'm sorry. I never meant to give you the impression you couldn't talk with me about what's bothering you."

"But you didn't want to hear about Jacky anymore, so I didn't know what to do."

"I'm so sorry; I've been acting like a real jerk lately. You know you can come to me about anything. When we get home, I promise we'll talk. But for right now I don't want to leave you, considering I'm partly responsible for making your life what it is."

I smiled and leaned my head on his shoulder.

"Listen, no matter what's going on in your life, no matter how silly or unimportant it might be, I want you to come to me. I never want you to feel you can't trust or rely on me. I'll never let this happen again." He kissed me. "I love you, no matter how things look."

I felt he was trying to tell me something more, but just then we heard Don yell down the hall, "Tell her you love her, we have to get to the airport!"

He squeezed me hard. "Baby, I'm sorry. I have to go, but I'll see you in two days."

The band was heading down the hall and Don yelled again, "Come on, Glenn, the limo's waiting."

I couldn't keep my tears from falling, as he yelled, "Goodbye, baby."

I went back to the dressing room. I was hurting so bad that I wanted to cut loose again with the tears. There was no one in the room so I sat down and cried into the arm of the chair. Then a voice said, "Come on, baby, walk me to the car. Stop crying. I never want to make you cry again."

I opened my eyes to find Glenn standing in front of me. I threw my arms around him and we kissed. With my arms around him, he lifted me off the chair and carried me to the limo. As we went down the hall, I told him I wasn't ever going to let him go.

"Baby, if you don't, it'll be weeks before I see you, instead of just a few days."

I jumped out of his arms. "Well then, get in the car."

I stuck my head in the limo and gave him one last goodbye kiss. I felt good as the car pulled away. Jacky was right about Glenn, I needed to confront him, and now that I had, I was at ease. As good as I felt at that moment, though, I realized how life could throw you a curve.

I wished I could see Jacky when I got home. This wasn't just her night, but it was ours to share. When we finally got back to the house I ran up to Jacky's room. I called her name, but there was no response. I walked over to the mirror and called and call again, but there was still no reply. As I stood there thinking of where she could be, I realized the only place she could be was with him. I looked into the mirror and smiled. "Stay with him," I said. "I'll see you soon."

CHAPTER 21

Being back in the States for a few days really felt great, I hadn't been so relaxed in a long time. Of course, there were memories of Jacky as soon as I walked in the house, but it was still great to be home. Don and Glenn had expected to be home before me, but due to business restraints they were delayed in Los Angeles for a few weeks. Apparently they had decided to wrap up any and all business there so they wouldn't have to return.

Dad and Judy were excited about Jack and Michelle buying their old house back. That meant we'd be seeing more of them. As soon as we got home, Dad contacted the realtor to get the ball rolling. It was cute to see how excited he was. Even though there were three acres between us, he was discussing putting a walkway in between our homes. It made me feel good inside hearing him talking about hanging out with Jack again. Hearing Dad talk about old times made me miss Jack and Michelle even more. It felt as though I'd left them behind. I knew I'd see them soon, so I quickly directed my mind to other thoughts. I'd become good at that.

I wasn't surprised that I hadn't heard from Don. I mean, why should I? He had accepted his new way of life with Jacky; there was no changing that. I felt better that they were finally together, it was what life intended. I was even happier knowing she no longer would be taking over my body to get what she wanted.

The first few nights back in the old house were full of nostalgia for the old times. That quickly turned to concern. I wondered how things would be once everyone returned home. I heard from Glenn infrequently; I'd talked to him more when I was in France. I always made it a point to ask about Don. Glenn said Don never made it out with the band; after all, responsibilities were done for the day, he'd retreat back to his room. I worried that he'd spend the rest of his life in that state. Glenn told me it was almost like Don didn't want to be around anyone else. He constantly stayed to himself.

Glenn would always remind me about our talk. It seemed he was worried about something, which at the time I didn't understand. Or maybe he was hoping there would be no talk when he came home. I think deep inside he knew what was going on with Don and it was getting to be too strange for him.

Glenn would ask if our talk would have something to do with the way Don was acting. I think if I told him yes, he'd feel that he'd not only have to put up with Don, he'd have to put up with me, too. And I didn't think he was ready for it. I just told him he'd understand after we had a chance to talk. At that he stopped asking.

As we talked, the possibility crossed my mind that he'd never understand, or that he simply wouldn't accept the truth. It was still hard to accept, even for me.

CHAPTER 22

I decided to surprise Glenn and Don at the airport the day they arrived. Of course, so did our entire town. There was a mad rush of newspaper reporters and television news crews waiting for them to walk through the gates. I didn't know what to expect. Dad and Judy thought it was a bad idea to meet them, and besides, a limo was waiting to bring them home. But I was so excited to see Glenn that I decided to go anyway.

I was sitting outside in my car when it came over the loudspeaker that their plane was arriving at Gate 9. I knew people would be mobbing the gate and probably following the band outside. I hoped I wouldn't be passed by in all the excitement. I was standing against my car right in front of the door they'd be coming through. I was so excited, waiting to see the look on Glenn's face when he saw me.

I started to walk toward the gate, when I saw Glenn. He was escorting a long-legged blonde. I immediately turned back toward my car. I didn't want to let on I'd seen him.

I took note how unconcerned Glenn was to be with someone else. He never even looked around to see if someone would notice.

They were shuffled quickly into a limo that had pulled up in front of them. As they drove by me, I could see her sitting between Don and Glenn. I didn't know what to think, I was in a state of shock, unable to reach for my car door to open it. I felt as if I was going to throw up.

Once I got in my car I wanted to cry. I couldn't even start the car. At least, until a cop tapped on the window and asked me to move along. As I pulled away, I kept telling myself, *There has to be some sort of explanation, Glenn wouldn't do this to me*. I didn't want to be like every other girl, who would quickly assume the wrong thing. I was going to find out the truth before I proceeded with my nervous breakdown. At least, that's what I told myself. Why hadn't I taken Dad's advice and stayed home? I tried to convince myself that Glenn was just being Glenn.

I drove straight home, wondering if they were going to be there when I arrived. When I pulled into the driveway, I only saw Dad's car. Ray was there to greet me at the door. "I thought you were Don," he said. "Where are the guys?"

"I didn't pick them up." I ran upstairs.

"What's wrong? Is everything okay?"

"I'm fine. I just want to be left alone for a bit."

In my room I just looked around. It was so quiet and surreal. It was painfully clear I had no one to talk to. Then I took a seat in front of my mirror. I didn't know what to think, everything was a complete blank. I repeatedly asked myself whether this was for real. I just couldn't believe the possibility that it was.

As I stared into the mirror, my thoughts turned to Jacky. I watched the tears roll down my face, thinking the worst. Was she the only one destined for happiness? I used to tell her to play the field, that she was too young to settle down. I should've taken my own advice, because the first time I got seriously involved, I was getting played. What was I going to do? The only person I'd ever been able to really talk to was Glenn, but he was no longer the solution, he was the problem. I didn't want anyone to think anything was wrong. I locked the door, so I wouldn't be bothered.

I'd spent my entire life worrying about other people. Why didn't I take the time to think about myself? Then without warning a chill ran through my body. I looked up into the mirror to see Jacky looking back at me.

"Why are you crying?" she asked.

"You know why, you saw them at the airport. Does Don know I was there?"

"He didn't until I told him."

"Well then, since you were there, tell me what that was all about!"

She smirked. "You know what a ladies' man Glenn is."

"What are you trying to say? Get to the point!" I snapped.

"Since I've been with the guys, Glenn has been totally loyal to you."

Had he? I had trouble believing her. "Then explain the girl I saw getting into the limo with them, she was hanging all over Glenn."

"She was only an old friend they met on the plane. She talked them into giving her a ride home. And you know how Glenn is around the ladies."

I sat there for a moment, not knowing how to respond. Jacky spoke again. "C'mon, Vicky, don't let that kind of thing get to you. Glenn is a great guy. You know he loves you."

"And what about you? How do I explain you to him?"

"I've been here all along. I tried a few times to let you know I was here, but I couldn't control it. I know what you've been going through. I'm sorry for what I said the last time I came to you. I've been so confused, not knowing were I was, or how I was going to cope being who I am now. Just follow your own advice. You used to tell me, if he doesn't understand you he doesn't deserve you."

Then just as quickly as she had appeared, she was gone. I screamed for her to return, but she didn't answer.

I lay on the bed, not knowing what to do next. I hoped Jacky was right, but why did he have to be a ladies' man? I thought, *He has me, he shouldn't need another girl. Maybe I can't make him happy.* I must have spent hours just playing the events over and over in my head, trying to understand why, when I heard a knock on my door. It was Dad letting me know Don and Glenn would be late getting back to the house. They were on the other side of town.

Without turning to acknowledge him I said, "Okay, Dad. Thanks."

"Are you all right?" he asked.

"Yes, Dad, don't worry."

"Dinner will be ready in an hour."

"That's okay, I'm not really hungry. I think I'm just going to go to bed early."

I'm not sure how much time passed, but before I knew it Ray was knocking on the door. "Little Miss, are you okay?"

I almost broke into tears when he called me Little Miss.

"Vicky, what happened today? Did you go to the airport?"

"Yes."

"So why didn't you pick the guys up?"

"I couldn't get to them in time. By the time I did they were gone, so I just came home." I'm not sure if he believed what I was saying, but I really didn't care. "Can we talk about this in the morning?"

He tapped on the door and said, "Okay."

As I heard Ray walking down the hall, Judy knocked.

"Come in," I said.

She sat on the bed. "What's going on?"

I told her what had happened at the airport. I'm not really sure why it was different talking with her. Maybe because Judy was like a mother to me. I knew I could talk to her without worrying about anyone knowing what we talked about. It was never easy talking to the males in my family, especially about boys.

"Vicky," she said, "as long as you've known Glenn he's been considered a lady killer. Women find him so delicious." She laughed. "I think, deep inside, Glenn knows he doesn't want a girl simply to hang on his every word, but like every guy he enjoys the attention. Glenn loves you, and would never do anything to jeopardize that. If you want my opinion, men are all the same, they enjoy the things they can never have. Sweetheart, you just need to be smarter than they are." Then she leaned down and whispered in my ear, "Besides, you'll be lucky to find a man with half a brain when it comes to women."

As always, she knew how to make me feel better. I'm not sure how long we sat there laughing, when Dad came in the room.

"Hey, girls, what's so funny?" he asked.

Judy winked at me, and then looked at Dad. "Am I right, Mike?"

You could see he was puzzled by the question, but he responded, "Yes, dear." At that, Judy and I started laughing.

"I know when I'm not wanted." He grinned and left the room. Judy and I laughed so hard we almost rolled off the bed.

"Well, I better get going," she said. "You know, when they do something you like, you should reward them." That brought a fresh burst of laughter.

I thought, she must've been a hot cookie in her day. I loved talking with her about anything. She always had a wonderful outlook. Judy had a unique and special way of making me feel better, not to mention being right about Glenn. But regardless of what Judy had said, I couldn't help feeling a little insecure, especially now that I planned to tell Glenn about Jacky. I thought if I could only get Jacky to appear, he'd understand.

Eventually Glenn and Don came home. Ray asked them why they were delayed and why hadn't they come home from the airport with me. Glenn was shocked to hear I had gone to the airport to pick them up.

"Tell me what happened," Ray said again. "When Vicky came home she didn't say a word and went upstairs to bed."

Don said, "She must have seen Sherry."

Glenn turned and headed for the door.

"Where do you think you're going?" Ray asked.

"Home," Glenn replied.

Don followed him out the door. "You've got to go up and talk to her," he said. Glenn kept walking toward his car. Don closed the door so Ray and Ruth couldn't hear. "What's your problem?" he asked.

"You know what the problem is. It's all this weird crap! If you'd come out of your room now and then, you'd know what I've been going through. Between you and her, I think I'm going crazy! You stay in your room, not saying a word for days, acting as if you want to be alone all the time. And when you talk, all I hear you talk about is a mysterious eagle. It's like you've never seen an eagle before. Then there's Vicky; she thinks she sees Jacky!"

"Hold on!" Don yelled. "Did you ever ask her what was bothering her? All you ever do is think of yourself. Vicky's been trying to talk with you for a long time, but you keep putting her off. If things don't go smoothly or go your way; you don't want to hear about it."

"Well, I'm listening now," Glenn, replied.

Don lowered his voice. "Do you really want to know what's going on?"

Glenn stood there without speaking. Don told him about all the strange things that had been happening. "But because you're the kind of person you are," he said, "you chose not to listen. Or maybe it's just that you can't deal with the possibilities."

"What are you talking about?"

"Remember that night at the barn when Vicky threw her arms around me, telling me she loved me? You were outside watching everything."

"How did you know?"

Don didn't answer, but went on. "Remember when she pulled away from me and fell to the ground?"

"Yes. How sick was that, her kissing you? You're her brother."

"But when she yelled at me, 'Don't ever let her do that again,' you never said anything," Don replied.

Glenn didn't know what to say. He stepped back, trying to figure out how Don knew he was watching.

Don wouldn't let up; it was as if he'd been waiting to vent his frustrations and Glenn was his target. "Remember Vicky's graduation party? The way she seemed to float across the tables, and the way she threw Tara through the air? Don't tell me you thought that was normal. And don't tell me you missed what was in the mirror at the concert. When Vicky was standing on stage, I saw you looking back into the mirrors. I know what you saw, Glenn. And how about the way Vicky came up on stage when I said I wrote 'Miss Ghost' for the one I love? You should've seen your face, you couldn't believe it."

Glenn stared at him. "What are you trying to say? It's Jacky?" He didn't wait for an answer, but walked away laughing. "You're crazy, and she's beginning to act just like you. I'm getting out of here."

As he open the car door, an eagle swooped down and flew by his head. Glenn ducked.

Don laughed out loud. "She should have landed on your skull!"

"You know, this is all you fault," Glenn yelled back. "You're sick, and now you have her believing you!

Glenn sat in his car and watched; it seem as Don was talking to someone. Then Don's face filled with anger, and he shouted at Glenn, "You fool, you saw Vicky at the airport as we were leaving the plane. That's why you were falling all over Sherry, helping her into the car! You're the jerk, you wanted Vicky to see you!"

Glenn drove off.

Don yelled, "Go home, you don't deserve her."

When I awoke the next morning, I grabbed my robe and made a mad dash downstairs to Glenn's room. I opened the door to find he wasn't there.

Don popped his head out from his room. "Have you seen Glenn?" I asked.

"Not since last night. We stopped at Joe's and I walked home."

"Was Glenn with you?"

"Of course he was. I just said I saw him, didn't I? All the guys were there." He slammed the door. Don was never a morning person. .

Where is he? I wondered.

Dad came down the stairs. "Hello, baby, you're up early this morning. Want some breakfast?"

"Of course. I'm going to get dressed first." My mind was telling me just to get dressed, but my heart was telling me to call Glenn. I had no idea what I was going to do. I thought about the girl I'd seen him with at the airport. If he wasn't with her, where was he?

At breakfast, I continued to press Don for information. I asked him whether he knew if Glenn was coming over today, but he said he didn't know. I tried to put all the pieces together. I was going to call him, but I didn't want to let on I was concerned.

Ray and Ruth came in. I'd forgotten about our Saturday ritual of getting together for Dad's pancakes. I wasn't complaining, though. It took my mind off Glenn, if only briefly.

Ray asked Don if Glenn came back. I looked at Don without saying a word. He couldn't even look me in the eye. He knew I was mad because I had caught him in a lie. "He went home," Don muttered back.

I decided that Glenn was not going to ruin my breakfast. I spent most of the time catching up with Judy and Ruth. When the phone rang, I jumped up to answer it. Don beat me to it, grabbing it out of my hand.

"Okay, I'll be there," he said, then hung up and returned to the table.

"Who was that?" I asked.

"Glenn," he replied.

I couldn't believe it. Was that all he was going to say? I was really starting to get irritated. "And he wanted?"

"Nothing, he just let me know he moved into his mother's pool house. He wants me to stop by when I can. Apparently, his mother wasn't able to handle all the noise he makes with his guitar."

"He could've moved back into his old room here," Dad said.

"He didn't want to," Don murmured. "He didn't want to be too far from his mother, I guess."

I could tell he was lying again, but pretended I didn't notice. I got up from the table and began helping clean up the dishes.

"That's okay, sweetheart," Judy said. "I got this mess. Don't you have something better to do?"

I left the room and ran into Don. "Do you have a minute?" I asked.

"Sure," he said, but you could tell he didn't want to hear my questions. He tried to act as if nothing was wrong as we walked into the parlor, but we both knew better.

"What's going on, Don?" I asked.

There was hesitation in his voice. "Sis, he knows all about the crazy stuff that's been going on about Jacky."

"And just how did he find out? Did you tell him?"

"As a matter of fact, I mentioned it to him last night, but to tell you the truth he already knew."

"Tell me what he said!" I shouted.

"Will you relax?" He grabbed my arm. "The last thing you want to do is let others know what's been going on. Look, he can't deal with it. Nothing you can do will change his mind. I tried to explain everything to him last night, but he just didn't want to listen. Can you blame him? I also told him you saw him at the airport. That's when he left."

"I need to call him and try to explain," I said, following him out the room.

"No, you don't," he replied.

I heard his words, but I didn't want to listen. I ran up the stairs and immediately called Glenn's house. As the phone rang, I tried to find words to say to him.

His mother answered. "Hello, is Glenn there?" I asked.

"Oh! Hi, Victoria. Hold on, let me go check."

I could hear her in the background telling Glenn he had to talk to me, but she was the one who returned to the phone. I could hear the hesitation in her voice as she began to speak.

"He's at the pool house, dear, and his phone isn't in yet."

I knew she was only covering for him, but I didn't want to make a scene. "Okay, can you please tell him I called?"

"I sure will, honey, don't worry," she said, and hung up.

I didn't know what to do next. Should I go all the way over there or should I wait and see if he came here?

Don came in my room. "You called, didn't you?"

"I did. I think he owes me some sort of explanation, don't you?"

"You're right, he does. But in his own time."

I knew what he meant by that; it was a lot for anyone to take in. I wasn't going to let this get me down. I'd go out and make an afternoon of it. I figured if Don wasn't stressed over the past month's events, then I wasn't going to be either. But he had Jacky and it seemed I was losing Glenn.

I went downstairs and told Dad I was going to the mall. Remember, this is a small town and the band was there hometown boys who had made is good, so when I walked in there were posters of them all over the walls. I guess you could say I was a glutton for punishment. As I passed the music store, I saw a large poster of them on the wall. I stopped and stared at Glenn's face, then reached up and touched it. I had to get out of there. I needed to talk to someone. If I was in France, I could go down to the barn and talk to The Duke, but he was still in France.

I couldn't help thinking how alone I was. I mean, let's be honest, you couldn't blame me for feeling that way. My best friend was gone and now my fiancée was gone. You might think I was making a big deal out of nothing. Maybe Glenn had a reason for not coming by last night. But inside I knew there was more to it. Come on, we were in love. I couldn't even call Jehane. I guess I could have called her and told her I needed to talk, but I didn't want Joe saying anything to Glenn. But there was no one I could talk to. This was all about Jacky coming back as a spirit; who would believe me? Yes, I could go to Don, but he already knew. There was nothing he could do. I had to deal with this on my own. How, I didn't know.

The only thing that was left was to go to Glenn and find out where we stood. If he couldn't deal with it, I could understand. I had hoped that we would always be able to remain friends. I decided not to phone him anymore, it would only make matters worse. He needed time to think. I'd been naive to expect him to instantly accept the situation, as it really was bizarre.

I was in such a state of concentration that without notice, fourteen days passed. I guess I was handling the situation better than expected. I'm not saying I wasn't hurting. I'd never felt anything like it before. It was as if my heart had been run over by a Mack truck at full speed. It felt as though my stomach dropped into my gut so bad that it hurt to stand up. I was really putting myself emotionally through the wringer; my head, heart, and body weren't communicating with each other at all. I couldn't eat or sleep. If I tried to do either, my mind drifted to thoughts of Glenn. My mind was like a freight train moving at full speed. I was dealing with everything, but if I had someone to talk with maybe I would have felt better about myself.

I couldn't believe that not once did Jacky show up. But I was convinced she had something to do with the eagle I kept seeing. The whole mess was actually her fault. Sometimes I even wondered whether she was jealous of Glenn and me, although I knew better.

I'm not sure how many hours I spent crying in my room. I was doing that a lot lately. I'd wet my face and head downstairs, and if I passed Dad and Judy on the way Dad would yell, "Hey, where's Glenn been?"

"He had a few things to do tonight," I'd say, or words to that effect, and leave. I knew Dad knew something was wrong, he just wasn't sure what. Plus, Glenn hadn't been around in weeks.

One night, I saw Don sitting on the porch and I went to sit with him. He was looking at the house across the street. Funny, he too was intrigued with the young couple who lived there when we were growing up. When I was a child and didn't really know better, I would laugh whenever I saw them holding hands and kissing.

The couple was oblivious to the world and the people around them. Sometimes you could even hear them telling each other, "I love you." It was cute. But that was a long time ago. They had both since passed away. The man died first, and was followed shortly by his wife. Everyone said she died of a broken heart.

As Don and I sat there on the porch we talked about them. I couldn't help but think about Don and Jacky and wondered if he'd fall to the same fate. He turned to me as if he knew my thoughts, and said, "Don't worry, Vicky, Jacky's here with me." I could only smile at him.

Then out of the blue he said, "I'd like to buy that house."

"For you and Jacky?" I asked.

He nodded.

"I'm glad to see you and she are happy in your own way."

He took my hand. "You should call Glenn," he whispered.

"Why? He's made it perfectly clear he can't deal with this. There's nothing I can do to change that."

"Sis, there's always something you can do."

I started to cry. "He never even told me it was over."

He didn't answer.

"There's something wrong here!" I cried out. "I'm supposed to call him?"

Don looked pained. "I know he still loves you."

By this time, I couldn't help but be a little irritated. "What am I, some sort of basket case? I don't need a relationship like that!"

"You know he's going to come over eventually. What are you going to say to him then?"

I got up and turned toward the door. "I'm not going to even speak to him and give him the satisfaction."

I knew Don meant well, but I was really hurt by what he had said. It wasn't exactly easy for me to deal with.

Just as I closed the door, I saw Glenn's car pull into the drive. I looked back but couldn't see him.

"Hey, honey," Dad said, "was that Glenn's car I heard?"

"Yes," I said, "he's here to see Don." I shut the door, said, "Goodnight," and ran upstairs to my room. When I got there, I ran to the window. I was satisfied only seeing his car. I had hoped to see his face, but seeing his car was good enough. I couldn't help smiling. Oh, how I missed him. I remembered telling him I would never date another as long as I was alive.

I hoped he'd say what he needed to and go, so I could catch a glimpse of him leaving. But he stayed long after I fell asleep.

The following morning I knew that if I missed breakfast Dad would really start asking questions. I didn't feel like eating, I hadn't been able to eat much since this whole thing began. I had lost a total of twenty-one pounds, but wore baggy clothes so as not to draw attention to myself. I knew Dad realized something was wrong with me, he just wasn't sure what.

Dad knocked on my door. "Breakfast's ready."

"Coming, Dad," I shouted.

As I passed my window, I could see Glenn's car still there. "Oh, no!" I said aloud, "I can't go down there and sit beside him." Just thinking about food made me sick. Before I knew it, I began writhing in pain.

Don came rushing in. "You better get downstairs before Dad blows his stack," he said. "A stack of pancakes." At that he started to laugh. I couldn't believe he was joking at a time like this.

"How can you laugh?" I asked. "And when were you going to tell me Glenn is still here?"

"Don't get upset. It was late after we finished, so he stayed in his room."

"Don, please, you need to make an excuse for me. I can't go down there," I said nervously.

"You can't stay in your room forever. Have you seen yourself lately? How much weight have you lost? I hope you don't think those clothes are hiding anything."

I was hurt. "I thought if anyone would understand it would be you."

"Dad even mentioned to Glenn about how rundown he's been looking lately. Glenn just blamed it on the tour. What's your excuse?"

"Please, just go tell Dad I don't feel well," I begged.

After a little hesitation, he agreed. I lay back down on the bed. I really wasn't feeling well, but I wasn't going to let anyone know.

Again there was a knock on my door. *Doesn't anyone realize I want to be left alone?* I thought, but hoped it was Glenn.

It was Dad. "Honey, can I come in?"

"Yes," I said. I prayed he wouldn't ask me to come downstairs. I thought I'd surely get sick.

He came in and took a seat on the corner of my bed, like he always did. "What's the matter, honey?"

"Nothing really, I think I'm coming down with the flu or something," I mumbled.

I wasn't sure if he believed me, but he said, "Okay." As he got up to leave, he turned to me. "Look, honey, I know something's going on between you and Glenn."

At that point, I lost control. I started to cry uncontrollably. As Dad sat back down, I reached up and put both my arms around him. "Oh, Dad, Glenn called everything off. I would've been okay, except he told Don and not me. When I went to the airport to pick up the guys he was there with another girl."

"Oh, baby, you don't know the whole story. The girl you saw was Sherry. Don't you remember? She was at his twenty-first birthday party." I nodded, but knew it was no excuse. Dad went on, "Sherry was simply on the plane and the guys gave her a ride home." He paused. "Let me tell you something I've never shared with anyone, not even Judy. When I was dating your mother, I did the same thing, but it was a mistake. I knew she'd never stop loving Jack, so it drove me away. I didn't know if I could go on with our relationship, or hurt my best friend. It was only after some time I realized what had happened. I've regretted that ever since." I could only look at him in amazement. "Yes, that's right, dear. Your mother forgave me, knowing the love she had for us both.

"What I'm trying to say is, if you keep ignoring Glenn and this problem, of course he'll find another woman. Sweetheart, your relationship could always be rebuilt, but don't lose what you've always had. What you need to remember is a good friendship is the foundation for all relationships. Without friendship, you have nothing to build on. Your mother and I had a great relationship, and that's what made our marriage as strong as it was."

I don't know how long we sat there hugging each other, but I didn't want it to end, I felt so secure in his arms.

He pulled back and looked at me with surprise and concern. "Baby, you're losing too much weight."

Again I started to cry. "I love him so much it hurts," I whispered. "I can't eat or sleep. All I think about is him. I don't know how I'm going to go on. I wish you could fix it like you did when we were young."

He smiled. "That's why you'll always need your father. I'm going to help you through this. First, you need to march downstairs and put something in your stomach. Then let him know you don't care. That you're going to be fine. Don't give him a chance to know something's wrong. This will be our secret."

I couldn't help but feel better. I changed and as I reached the steps I saw Glenn getting ready to leave.

"No, don't go, she's on her way down," I heard Dad tell him.

As I started down the stairs, Glenn said, "That's okay, Mike, I better go. It's better for everyone." I could see Dad trying to keep him from leaving, but there was nothing he could do. Glenn walked out.

Dad saw me standing on the stairs. I started crying again. "Baby, come down here, everything will be okay," he said.

"If you don't mind, I don't really feel like eating," I said, and returned to my room.

Again, I looked out the window. This time I could see Glenn in the car. I could tell he, too, was bothered. His head leaning against the steering wheel, he was looking up at me. Our eyes met. Then he started the car. I could tell what he was thinking and he couldn't deal with it either. As much as I ached inside for him, I understood. Not just anyone could handle what was happening. It was getting harder and harder for me to cope, too.

At that moment, I knew what I had to do. I left window and sat in front of the dresser. I was hoping to see Jacky. I called out to her, "If you don't come now, I'll never talk to you again."

Suddenly she appeared, but not in the mirror. "Over here," I heard from the other side of the room.

I turned and there she was, sitting on my bed.

"What's going on?" I asked.

"What you are seeing is my powers at full strength," she replied. "I'm getting stronger everyday. I want to apologize for all the pain and suffering I caused you over the past months. I hoped when you saw the eagle you'd know I was trying to contact you."

I was confused. "What are you talking about?"

"I'm trying to tell you that now I can appear to anyone I choose and soon I'll be with you all the time. Vicky, it took this long for me to get where I am. I tried so many times. I heard you calling me, but I couldn't appear. Like I told you before, I only had the power to go to Don, but it wasn't like I am now. Now he can hold me and feel me as I was in life, not the empty shell that he came to be with since I died. Now he can touch me and feel my love." She hesitated. "But there are a few things I cannot do."

I walked over to the bed where she was sitting and she looked up at me with tears in her eyes. She said, "I can never feel his love, the warmth you feel when Glenn touches you. At least, not until he's ready to join me."

She saw the look of shock on my face, and said, "No, Vicky, I'd never do that to him. What I'm saying is, when I take over your body it's to feel Don. Unlike you, I can't feel the warmth of his love. Sometimes I can't control myself, the craving is too strong for me to resist, and you're the only one who can help." She laughed. "It's the nature of the beast, it comes with the territory. I give up the warmth of the flesh to be with him."

I was overwhelmed with sadness for her. "Jacky, I'm sorry."

She smiled one of those smiles that made you want to help her. "It's not that bad."

I threw my arms around her. "I'm so happy to see you, I missed you so much. But I have to tell you, when you use my body it's as though you're draining the life from me. It's really painful."

"I know. That's why you need to go to Glenn. I know Glenn loves you just as much as you love him. Your spirit is craving him, and you won't know happiness until you have him."

It was beginning to make sense. I was allowing her to enter and control my body because I, too, craved and needed the same things. I realized that Jacky had been hurting just as much over this past year as I had.

"Vicky, you need to go to him and explain everything to him. Reassure him of your love."

"But what if he can't handle it? He doesn't seem to be able to."

"I know you and Glenn are one soul," she whispered. "And if not in this lifetime, there will always be the next. Now, I must go. If you need me just call my name and I will be here."

Then she was gone. I thought about what she'd said. I knew I couldn't wait for my next life to be with Glenn. I really didn't know what to think. What if I couldn't be with Glenn in this life? I lay down on the bed.

Maybe Jacky didn't have it so bad. Don was happy knowing Jacky would always be with him. Maybe that's how life was supposed to be. He did seem to love his life even more now. Jacky even seemed happier knowing that Don loved her. That's all she needed. Nothing would ever take him away from her. I thought about Jacky taking over my body, and what it did to me. I knew if I let her keep on doing it, I could really endanger my life. I fell asleep, thinking. When I awoke it was clear what I had to do: I had to find and talk to Glenn.

I went downstairs looking for Don. He was alone in the kitchen. "Don," I asked bluntly, "do you know where I can find Glenn?"

I took him off guard. He hesitated, then said, "He's home, we've been practicing all day. I'm sure he's still there. Why?"

"I've decided I'm going to talk. I need to know once and for all."

He was happy about that. He'd been trying to get me to talk with Glenn for a while. "Do you want me to go with you?"

"No, I need to do this by myself. But you need to talk with Jacky."

"Why?"

"Don't worry," I said jokingly. "She'll explain."

"Are you going to be all right?"

"Yes, Don," I said, smiling. "I just needed to make up my mind and decide what I want out of life."

It was pouring rain so I ran up to my room to get my raincoat. Don eventually made his way back to his room, where he could talk to Jacky. I later learned Jacky had discussed with Don how weak I was getting and why.

As I was about to leave the house, Don came running after me. "Vicky, what are you thinking?" he asked.

"You and Jacky are both happy. It's really not that bad a life, is it?"

"Victoria . . ." he started, in a broken voice.

I stopped him before he could finish. "The only time you ever call me Victoria is when you're getting sentimental. Go back to Jacky," I whispered. "I'll be all right." I got into my car and headed over to Glenn's house. As I pulled away, I could see Don in the rearview mirror, still standing on the porch. I didn't know it at the time, but he had asked Jacky to follow me and let him know what was going on.

In a way, I felt good going to Glenn. Maybe if I just confronted him and took him off guard, he'd know that I loved him more than I ever loved him before.

When I got to Glenn's I parked away from the pool house and walked the rest of the way, giving me time to think about what I was going to say. The rain cane down so hard that before I got to the front of the house I was drenched. I didn't care. As I reached the pool house, I could see Glenn's silhouette in the window. Just seeing him put a smile on my face. I wanted to rush in and tell him I forgave him.

I stood in the rain, my eyes following him from room to room. When he entered the bedroom, I could see he wasn't alone.

Sherry was there, standing in the window, removing her robe.

As the lightning lit the sky, I couldn't move. My heart started beating though my chest. He walked over to her. As one arm fell out of the sleeve, she wrapped it around him until her robe fell to the floor.

I stepped back against the tree for support. *Oh, no, this can't be happening.* The rain felt heavy on my body. I couldn't move. I tried to, but my legs felt like they were stuck in the mud.

I don't know how long I stood there, but a crash shook the sky, and in the following flash I saw Glenn looking out the window. He saw me standing there. I ran to my car. I was in such a state; my mind was a complete blank. I jumped in the car.

Later I learned that Glenn ran outside to stop me. He chased me down the driveway, but I was gone before he could reach me. After he returned to the house, he asked Sherry to leave, telling her that having her there was a huge mistake. Sherry put her arms around him, "I can make you forget all about her if you let me. Vicky's not your kind of girl."

Glenn snapped, "Don't say another word. She means more to me than anyone will ever realize. Now, grab your things and go."

I don't know if I would have felt any better knowing the outcome between them, I just wished I never went to see him. On the way home, I cried so hard that, between the tears and the rain, I had difficulty seeing the road. I was in such a terrible state of mind that I wish the car would go off the road. I thought it was the only way I could be with Glenn forever. I pulled over to the side of the road, hitting my fist again the wheel. "Why? I don't understand!" I cried out. One minute we were happy in love and waiting to get home so we could get married; the next minute he didn't want to see me anymore. How could this be happening? This was Glenn, the guy I had grown up with. He was part of the family.

I couldn't go on like this. I looked up through the windshield. All I could see was the rain. I tried to look down at the road, but all I could see was the water on the window. I closed my eyes and grabbed onto the steering wheel. I looked back into my mirror and was ready to pull out, when I heard a voice behind me say, "No! Vicky, don't do it!"

I looked in the rearview mirror and saw Jacky looking back at me. "You can't do this!" Jacky yelled.

"Were you with me the whole time?" I muttered.

"Yes, and if you want my opinion . . ."

"If I want your opinion?" I yelled.

She stopped me. "I'm going to give it to you anyway. I don't think he knows what he's doing. I know for a fact he still loves you very much. Do you know he chased you down the drive?"

"Well, he wasn't fast enough," I snarled. I started the car, turned the windshield wipers off, and started to drive.

Jacky tried to get me to stop. "Vicky, what are you thinking? Stop the car!" she yelled.

By this time, I was even mad at her. "What nerve you have, popping up at your own leisure! Whenever I call you, it takes you forever to show yourself." I stepped down on the gas.

I wasn't going to give her the satisfaction, but she kept persisting. "Vicky, listen. Remember the advice you used to give me about Don? You said if he didn't see me for me and who I was, he didn't deserve me?" I knew where she was going, but still I kept driving. "Did you really mean those things you said to me back then? I love you, Vick. Please, if you do this you may never see him again, not in this lifetime or the next."

At that I hit the brakes; the car spun into the rail. I looked back at her. "You know I meant that," I said in a low voice. "I never told you anything I didn't mean."

"Believe me, I know just what you're going through. I've felt that way ever since I first came to live with you. You know how I've always loved Don. You felt it every time I entered your body. You not only felt the love we shared together, but you also felt the enormous pain of not knowing whether I was going to be with him."

"I know what you're trying to say, Jacky. I know how happy you both are. I've never known two people who loved each other as much as the both of you. Maybe you had to die to reach that point." I lowered my head into the steering wheel.

"No, you have to listen to me, when I tell you that you and Glenn will be together. Maybe not now, but I know that you and Glenn are soul mates."

When I looked up she was gone. I started the car and headed home. I knew what I had to do. Jacky was wrong. If she could be with Don, why couldn't I be with Glenn? When I pulled into the driveway, I could see Don standing on the porch, waiting for me to get out of the car. I figured she had filled him in on what had happened. I didn't feel like being around anyone right then, let alone Don. I knew what he was going to say and I was not up to hearing it.

As I passed him on the steps he started to read me the big brother act, but I stopped him. "Please, Don, not right now." I walked into the house. Knowing how I felt, he just stepped aside and let me go by without a word.

I returned to my room and lay down on my bed. As I lay there, soaking wet, I had a feeling I wasn't alone. "Jacky, I know you're here," I said aloud. I turned to look across the room and saw nothing.

Then I felt her enter my body. We were once again as one. I could feel her strength, and her craving for the flesh. I could feel the love she had for Don, and the will to be with him. I knew she was able to read my thoughts, as I was able to read hers. *Jacky, your thoughts on love and life are so innocent.*

Yes Vicky, you taught me such things, but now I feel your heartache as well as your pain. Your soul is crying out.

My heart's broken Jacky, and there's no reason to go on. You of all people know what a broken heart can do.

I know where you're going with this. You should never think such horrible things, life's too precious.

Don't worry Jacky, I wasn't thinking of anything drastic. I hoped she believed me so she wouldn't leave my body.

I felt her relief, and her thought, *You are a kind and loving spirit, with a pure heart. Your living life is a privilege. Be grateful. Glenn loves you so much.*

"Well, you could fool me!" I yelled aloud. "He has a strange way of showing it!"

I tried to keep her from leaving my body. She didn't, and the thought came, *Vicky, you've changed. You were always the strong one. I depended on you for everything. But now I see that your body is weak and frail. I'm aware of what you're planning to do and I will never allow such a thing.*

"Jacky," I said calmly, "try to go to Don. If you can."

Suddenly she screamed inside my mind, *Let me go!*

"This time you underestimated me!" I shouted. I had learned to control her, due to all the times she had entered my body. I had distracted her long enough for her to remain in my body, so that she would drain the life from me.

I could feel myself weakening rapidly. "Relax, Jacky," I whispered, "soon everything will be just as it used to be. I'll be with you forever."

But my attempt at self-sacrifice was short-lived. Jacky had summoned Don to help her. How she contacted him, and how he heard her, is still a mystery to me. Just as I felt my life coming to a close, Don ran into my room. He repeatedly pushed me against the wall until Jacky was free. I felt her go. But the damage was already done; my body was already suffering.

"What happened here?" he yelled.

I turned away from him, weak and upset because he ruined my plan.

Don was shaking. "I know what you were trying to do!"

"Did she tell you I found Glenn alone with Sherry?"

"Yes, but you don't know the whole story. After you left, Glenn asked Sherry to leave."

"I don't care anymore, Don, I just want to sleep." I was suddenly exhausted, barely able to stand. I made it to my bed and lay down.

Don and Jacky were still in the room. "Do you need an invitation to leave?" I said sarcastically.

As they left, I heard Don ask Jacky if she was all right. He was so afraid of losing her. He and Jacky never realized that my plan was working. Weak and disoriented, I fell into a deep sleep.

Later I learned that Don returned to the kitchen, where Jacky filled him in. "She wanted to die," she said. "She wants the kind of life you and I have, she doesn't think she'll ever find

happiness. She figured out that the longer we stayed as one, the weaker she gets. I couldn't believe the amount of control she had over me. She stayed focused and wouldn't release me."

"Why did you enter her body in the first place?"

"The way she was talking, I needed to know for sure. I was right, but by that time she wouldn't let me go."

Don checked on me frequently while I slept. I guess he was worried I'd hurt myself.

Sometime later, the phone rang, awakening me. I managed to walk to the top of the stairs to see who it was, hoping it was Glenn asking to talk to me. Don said, "Is there any way to get out of it? Okay then, I'll get the guys together." He turned to find me standing there. "We have to leave in a few days. The band has a benefit in Los Angeles."

I could see he was hesitant about going. "That's wonderful," I replied.

"Do you want to come?"

"No, actually I was thinking about going back to France."

I could tell my words caught him off guard. I don't know why I said that, but lately I didn't know if I was coming or going anyway. He just stood there staring without saying a word.

"What's wrong?" I asked. "You should be happy for me."

He turned and headed for the kitchen.

I knew what was wrong. But it was my problem. I didn't want to burden him any longer. I thought about how happy he was. Now, after so long, I wasn't going to ruin that for him.

I walked downstairs and into the kitchen, where Jacky was sitting. It was good to see her with all her power, glowing like angel. I said, "I'm sorry for what I did to you, and that will never happen again. You know I would never want to hurt you."

"I can never be mad at you," she smiled. "I, of all people, know what love can do."

All of a sudden we heard a loud bang, and the sky lit up like a Christmas tree, and the rain just let go. Jacky jumped halfway out of her chair. I laughed.

"What's so funny?" she said, like she used to when we were kids. She'd always been afraid of lighting.

"But you're a ghost!" I said.

Don ran to her side. "Are you all right?"

I stopped laughing. Watching them, it wasn't funny anymore. It was kind of cute how he still looked after her. That made me think about Glenn. Don looked at her with a gentle smile. I knew he loved her more now than life itself. Then he said, laughing, "We are a mess. If this wasn't happening to us, I'd never believe it."

As Don and I sat drinking tea, the phone rang. Don answered it. It was Glenn, letting him know he'd contacted the rest of the guys. Don turned to me. "Glenn and the guys are coming over."

"Great." I got up and placed my cup in the sink. Walking past him I said with a smile, "Look, I'll be okay. I'll just have to get on with my life."

I left the kitchen, passing Dad on his way in. I told him I was taking the car. "Be careful," he said. "It looks real bad out there."

As I was exiting the driveway, Glenn pulled in. We sat there, wondering who was going to back up first. Through the wipers I managed to see his face. My heart stopped, as did time. It was like everything slowed down as each drop hit the windshield. Each one sounded like a big splash. He looked as though he wanted to say something to me, but then maybe he was just being careful not to run into me.

I pulled out around him. It was raining heavily, but I kept going. It was the last time I saw him until they returned from Los Angeles.

CHAPTER 23

When they left for L.A., I thought things would get better. Boy was I wrong.

They were booked for two benefits. One was televised. I didn't watch it with the family, but I did see it at Joe's. Jehane and Donna invited me to hang out with them for the night, and with Joe being a great fan of Don and Glenn, he agreed to hold a special evening at his place. It was the first time I'd really been out of the house since I'd been back from France. I thought that if I started to get out more I could keep myself busy enough to forget about Glenn, but that turned out to the biggest mistake I ever made.

At first it felt good to get out of the house, especially when I got to Joe's and saw all our friends that I grew up with. Joe turned the TV on and there they were, big as life. Don started out with "Miss Ghost." I knew who he was singing it to. As he sang, he'd look to his left every once in a while and smile. I could see that Jacky was standing there. I smiled, thinking that's where she belonged.

I felt that Glenn, too, knew she was there. He looked over and stared at Don as he sang, then all of a sudden I saw a smile on his face. Maybe I was trying to convince myself that he understood. My mind was in such a state that every move Glenn made I assumed a reasonable answer for.

When Glenn walked over to the band, they looked surprised. He took them off guard. He had changed the next song. I didn't know what to think as he started to sing. It was my song, the one everyone got a kick out of when I sang it around the house when I was growing up. You know, when you get a tune in your head and you can't get it out, and you don't remember all the words but you hum the tune all day.

Now for sure my mind was running amuck. Was he trying to tell me something, or was I still reading into it something that was not there? I just stared at the television. And to make things worse, everyone began singing along. It wasn't even a hit song.

Don looked kind of surprised to hear him sing it. It hadn't been placed on their play list for the evening. He looked over at Glenn and smiled and sang along.

I had to get up and get out of there before I broke down. When Jehane asked me where I was going I said to get a breath of fresh air, but the real reason was that I couldn't hold back my tears any longer. She asked if I needed some company. "No, I'll be fine," I said. She understood.

I was reading too much into everything Glenn did, and interpreting it for my own benefit. Then I thought what a loser I had become. I knew I'd hit rock bottom.

Donna came out and asked if I was all right. She knew the situation with Glenn and me. This was the first time she hadn't gone with Tim.

"I'm okay," I said. "I just had to get out of there."

"Are you going to be all right?"

"Yes, go on back inside." Although she cared, I knew she wanted to see the rest of the concert. Her being Tim's girl, this time she was the queen of the party. But that was okay, I was happy for her.

After a few minutes I decided to walk home. I just couldn't watch it anymore. It had been two months, and nothing I did to keep myself occupied seemed to help. As I walked, I lost control and bawled.

I came to a dark alley and looked down. It was so dark I couldn't see the other end. I thought about going in, to where no would ever find me, and without realizing it I found myself doing just that. As I walked I saw a broken bottle lying on the ground. Without any conscious thought, I leaned over and picked it up.

As I stood there with the bottle in my hand, Jacky appeared. She had felt what I was thinking.

When she told Don what was going on, he had stopped singing. It seemed as if Don was concentrating on someone beside him. But as usual, no one knew, except this time, Glenn. He walked over to Don while the rest of the band went on singing. "What's going on?" he yelled over the loud crowd.

"What do you care?" Don yelled back, and then turned to Jacky. All Glenn heard was "Go now."

Glenn walked back to his spot, but before he did he said, "We have to talk."

Don smiled, "It's about time."

Back in the alley, I told Jacky, "Don't worry; I'm not going to do it. But it was a thought. Do me a favor. Go back to Don and tell him I'm okay."

"No, I'm going to stay here with you."

"No, you're not. Funny as it may sound, I'd feel better if you were with Don and Glenn. I'm going home."

She stood there.

"Jacky, go do this for me, I need to be alone." As I walked away I turned back and laughed. "You'll know if I'm going to do something. You'll know before anyone." I dropped the bottle and headed home.

When I got home Dad asked, "Do you want anything to eat?" It was his way of reminding me how much weight I'd lost.

"No, Dad, I had something at Joe's," I lied. "I'm just going to bed. I'll see you in the morning."

When I was in my room, Dad came to the foot of the stairs and yelled up, "Something must have happened, Don just stopped singing." He paused, watching the television. "Glenn walked over to him to see if he's all right. I wonder if everything's okay."

"They've been changing the order of songs all night," I yelled down. "Don must have taken everyone off guard." But I knew better.

"Do you want to watch the rest of the concert with Judy and me?" Dad asked.

"No." I heard him leave the stairs. I guess he was trying to make heads or tails about how I was.

The remainder of the months drew out. Still I couldn't wait to see Glenn drive up and drop Don off. I missed him even more.

At the end of three months they returned home. As usual, they were a big hit. I had lost so much weight that I scared myself. Even when Dad got me to eat something, I'd get sick and excuse myself from the table, run to the bathroom, and throw up. When I looked in the mirror I was shocked. I knew I had to try to eat, but it seemed so hard. I was never hungry. I just ate for Dad, knowing he was worried about me. Judy knew what I was doing when I'd leave the table right after I ate. It's not that I wanted to what I did, but I just couldn't keep anything down.

The night the boys were to come home, I met some friends at Joe's. I didn't want to be at the house when they arrived. If Glenn was to stay there, I didn't know if I could look him in the eye, knowing what I looked like. I really didn't want to go out. All I wanted to do was sleep all the time, but I went anyway. I think I was the only one having a terrible time, thinking that when I got home Glenn would be sitting in the parlor.

Suddenly, taking me off guard, they came walking into Joe's. I didn't see them at first until Don came over and sat beside me. He smiled. "Hi sis, how you doing?"

If I ever wanted to die, that was the time. I never looked back to see if anyone else, like Glenn, was there. It wasn't until I saw Donna run over to Tim and Jehane that I knew the whole band was there.

"Nothing much," I said to Don. "As usual, you guys killed."

Just then Glenn came over. I wanted to drop dead, but I smiled at him, trying not to let on how I was. I couldn't believe he took a seat across from me, as if nothing had ever happened. It was like I was in the twilight zone. It was killing me. I wanted to leap over the table and put my arms around him and cry out, "I'M SORRY, I'M SORRY!" I had to get out of there before I made a fool of myself. I had trouble remembering things. I felt weak. When I lifted my legs to move, they shook. All I wanted to do was go home and hope I could make it without passing out.

I looked over at Jehane; she knew that I had to get out of there. She got up and asked me to go with her to the bathroom.

As I got up from the table I turned to Don. "I'll see you at home, and see the rest of you guys later."

"Okay, babe," Joe said.

As I left, Glenn said, "See you."

I didn't respond, except to tell Don, "I'll let Dad know you're home."

After I left, Glenn told Don how bad I looked. "Has she been sick?" he asked.

"No, but look at yourself; you're not the picture of health, either. I think you can answer that for yourself."

When I got outside, I thanked Jehane for getting me out of there.

"Why don't you let me drive you home?"

"No, I can use the fresh air."

"Okay, sweetie," she said. "Give me a call in the morning."

When Jehane went back into Joe's, Glenn asked where I was. She told him I had decided to walk home. As I walked I saw a car in the distance. As it got closer, I realized it was Don and Glenn. I thought, *Maybe they won't see me here in the dark.*

They pulled up beside me. "Hold up, sis," Don said, leaning over Glenn. "Jump in."

I could see Tim and Joe in the back seat. I knew, if I did get in, I'd have to sit in the front between Don and Glenn and that was not going to happen.

My stomach turned and it hurt to keep my body straight. I remembered how I used to sit beside him, and he'd say, "If only you were five years older."

He was so close, but so far away. I was doing everything I could do to hold back my tears. It was bad enough that he had sat across from me at Joe's, even though I made it out okay. I didn't want to get too close to the car; they would see I was crying.

"Come on, sis," Don said again, puzzled.

"That's okay," I said, "I have to stop at Jehane's."

Joe stared at me. He knew I was lying; Jehane had driven Donna home. "I'll see you at the house," I said.

Before Don drove off Glenn turned, and our eyes met. I took a deep breath and whispered to myself, "Please keep driving." He looked tired. It looked like the last few months had taken a toll on him, too.

As they drove away I could see Glenn's face in his mirror, looking back at me. The tears started again. Doubled over, I cried out, "What wrong with me?"

I stood up. I knew now what I had to do.

When I reached the driveway I saw the car parked outside. I stopped to get a grip, hoping that when I walked in the house I'd have complete control of my emotions. The feeling I got from Glenn at Joe's was that he wanted to be friends, and that I could not do. I opened the door, and everyone was in the kitchen. Dad yelled, "In here, Vicky." I heard Judy walking around upstairs. If she'd been in the kitchen I might have gone in and sat down, knowing I could talk to her.

"That's okay, Dad." I said. "I had something at Joe's. I'm going to bed. Goodnight, everyone."

I heard Don say, "Goodnight."

"See you in the morning," Dad yelled.

As I started for the steps I heard, in a low drawn-out voice, "Goodnight, Vicky."

I stopped. It was Glenn. I buckled over as I took the next step. "Goodnight, Glenn," I said. My stomach cramped up on me as I struggled up the stairs to my room. I just made it to my bed.

As I lay there, dizzy and disoriented, I ran over everything in my mind. It was hard to accept that it was over. My mind was running amuck. Could it be that I was just another one of those girls he picked up at his concerts? I could not accept it. I would not accept it. I thought for sure when he left for Los Angeles he wasn't coming back. Maybe it would have been better if he hadn't. But regardless of our current situation, he was a friend to Don and a very important part of our family. I knew I couldn't return to being his friend, or, as Dad put it, "Just a sister to him." Granted, we had known each other most of our lives, but now we were so much more. In my mind there was no going back after we'd grown so far apart.

I spent the rest of the night wondering if he'd ever accept Jacky. I knew she was the whole problem. But Jacky was here to stay as long as Don was here. Her happiness was more important to me than my own life.

I couldn't go on thinking that each time the phone rang it was going to be Glenn. It was funny, really. I found myself praying that it was, but I couldn't pick up the phone. And when everyone said it wasn't healthy to sit around waiting, I ignored them. But I wanted to. I wanted to because it left me time to think about him. I didn't want the thought of him to leave my mind, for if I did I would lose him forever. Just the sound of his voice on the phone when he called for Don, or just the fact that he came to pick him up or even walk though the house, made me feel closer to him. I could never really explain to others how I felt, but it was like not wanting the memory of him ever to leave my head.

I went through my days with blinders on. All I could see or think about was Glenn. Sometimes it was a miracle I was able to get through at all. I would pass my friends and family, oblivious to what was going on. They would talk and ask me questions, and somehow I was still able to answer. I was afraid to take my blinders off for fear of losing him.

I'd sit on the porch at night while Don and Glenn practiced. I lived for the moments when he dropped Don off after a long day, or when he spent the night at our house. I couldn't explain it, but just knowing he was in the same house gave me relief. At times I was so mesmerized by him that I was able to pick up his scent, regardless of the other smells in the house. My stomach

would get weak and my eyes would fill up with the thought of him, but I didn't care about the pain. It kept me going. When I fell asleep I thought that when I awoke the next day it would be the day we were going to be together. I would tell myself it was just a simple dream.

But finally my mind was made up. I couldn't go on like that. I knew that my body couldn't take any more, and neither could my mind. I knew what I had to do.

CHAPTER 24

Glenn and Don were sitting in the kitchen when Dad decided he needed to hear from Glenn what was going on. "Glenn," he said, "can I have a word with you?"

When Glenn sat down Dad asked Don to leave the room. Don knew Dad was upset about what was going on between Glenn and me, especially with me floating around in the ozone all the time.

When Don left Dad just let it out. "What is going on with you and Vicky? A few months ago you and she were inseparable and now you can't be in the same room together."

"I didn't think I was ready to settle down, Mike," Glenn mumbled.

"Don't tell me that, a few months doesn't change a person."

Glenn put his head in his hand. "I screwed up, Mike. I know that now." His voice cracked. "I saw Vicky at the airport and she saw Sherry with us. We were just driving her

home, but I thought that if Vicky saw us together, she'd think something was going on. But there was nothing going on at the time."

Dad looked at him, until Glenn said, "But after a few nights I did stay with her. I realized I'd made a mistake and it just snowballed from there. Ever since then I've been going through misery. I do love her, Mike, and I don't know how to make it right."

"I'm disappointed in you, Glenn. You're a part of this family and I never expected this from you. And for heaven's sake, she's like a sister to you." Dad paced back and forth. "I'm not going to tell you what you should do. I think you know what you have to do." He paused. "But I'd like to know the real reason that brought this all on in the first place."

Glenn didn't know what to say. How could he tell him? *Oh, by the way, Mike, Jacky returned from the dead?* He just sat there.

"You were never at a loss for words before," Dad said.

Glenn looked up. "I do love her. I can't sleep. I stay awake just thinking of her."

Don came in the room in time to hear Glenn say, "I try to blame everything on different reasons, but I know I just had cold feet. I'm sorry for what I did and how I treated her; she meant so much to me."

The phone rang and Judy answered it. "Mike, Jack is on the phone."

As Dad left the room he looked back at Glenn. He smiled as if to say, *You know what to do.*

Judy came in. She had heard the whole conversation and said, "There's no time like the present."

Sarcastically Don said, "You had to make sure you fully understood that the problem is still here and it's not going away."

"I know what you're saying, you don't have to be a jerk about it," Glenn said. Then he noticed that Don seemed preoccupied.

Suddenly Don jumped up and said, "It's Vicky. Something's wrong." They both ran for the stairs.

"Dad! It's Vicky," Don yelled, "There's something wrong!" Dad dropped the phone and rushed upstairs too.

When Glenn got to my room, the door was locked and there was no answer. Don yelled, "Break it down," and together they smashed the door in.

Glenn got to me first and yelled, "Call 9–1–1." Don did just that. Dad came in and started CPR. Judy was right there, calling my name. Glenn slowly backed away from the bed until he hit the wall.

I felt my body float across the room, over to where he was standing. I could see Dad and Judy trying to bring me back. I looked over and saw Glenn. I could see the look on his face. I heard him repeatedly say, "I'm sorry . . . I'm sorry."

As I watched everyone trying to bring me back, Jacky appeared next to me. "Vicky, what did you do?" she asked.

I smiled at her. "I miss you. Things just haven't been the same without you here. I've been so lost and confused. When Glenn stopped loving me I didn't want to go on any longer."

"Vicky, you don't know what you've done. Glenn never stopped loving you, he just didn't understand. Look at him and tell me he doesn't love you anymore."

All I wanted to do was reach out and touch him; to let him knew I was there. Jacky gave me a nod as if to say it was okay. I placed my hand on his face as though to caress it.

Then a soft glow appeared around me, and he was able to see me standing beside him. It was as though time stopped.

Glenn looked at Don and saw Jacky standing beside him. The look in his face showed he accepted the way things were. Glenn reached up and placed his hand on my face. "Baby, I am so sorry. I love you so much. You'll never realize."

I whispered into his ear, "I'm here now and I will never leave you." I placed my hand on his face. I wanted to feel his warmth, but I couldn't. I looked at Jacky, but she only smiled. She knew what I was thinking. I finally understood what she meant when she spoke of craving Don's flesh. And like her, I didn't care. Glenn was able to see, feel, and hear me. He was satisfied. What could be better?

"I'm here, Glenn," I whispered. "I will never leave you again."

"No!" Jacky yelled, "It's not your time." She turned to Glenn. "Only you can bring her back. If you really love her, bring her back now." Then she turned toward me. "Vicky, you have so much to live for, not only for yourself, but for me." Glenn was listening closely to her. "Don't let her do this!" she yelled at him. "Only you can bring her back."

I saw Glenn looking towards the bed. He could see the paramedics trying their hardest to bring me back. He approached the bed, sat down, and started to shake me, every time looking back at me. "Don't leave me," he commanded. "I love you!"

I stood behind him, with my hand on his shoulder, and I cried out, "No, Glenn, please!" I fought him with all my strength. "Please, Glenn."

Without warning I felt breath fill my lungs. I was back in my body, gasping for air. I turned to Jacky. *It was his love that brought you back.*

"I have a pulse," the paramedic said. "She's back!"

I dimly remember them putting me on a stretcher and rolling me out of my room. At the hospital the doctor told Dad I was in a coma and I was too weak to fight much. "It's up to her," he said.

I heard Glenn say, "She's a tough girl."

He was wrong. I was not going to fight, not anymore. Like Jacky was with Don, I was going to be with Glenn forever.

CHAPTER 25

While in a coma I could see Jacky in the distance, sitting high up on a hill. I yelled out her name. Funny, as far away as she was, she heard me calling. She turned and looked at me, but she never tried to answer or come towards me. Then in a flash, I was sitting beside her.

She looked sad and when I asked her why she replied, "I'm disappointed in you."

"Why?"

"You're not the girl I knew when we were young. You're not the one who helped me though all the hard times. I don't know who you are anymore."

I waved my hand at our surroundings. "Jacky, would it be so bad for me to have all of this, too? Why can't I have the same things you have? Look around you. How can you deprive me of this?"

If this was the place Jacky was trapped in, between two worlds, heaven and earth, then this was the place I wanted to be. I can't explain how beautiful it was. It was everything you could imagine.

In a soft voice she said, "Do you know that I'd kill to be with Don in the flesh for just one night? Look how I took over your body to be with him. I had no control. You don't understand, you will never understand, how the craving for the flesh can destroy you. Sure, you see all of this, but this is not a fairy tale. When the first time you lay beside him and he puts his arms around you, you want to yell out and beg God just for one night with him, to feel the warmth, the comfort that comes with love.

"Glenn loves you. You have to go back. Did it ever occur to you that

Don wishes I were alive? He'll never say it, but I know deep inside that's what he craves.

"It was my time to go, and that couldn't be helped. I'm making the best of a bad situation. This is the only way I can be with Don. I've accepted that. I have no choice other than to be with him in this way. I know I'll never be with him in the flesh. If I was never meant to be with him when I was alive, then I'm happy just to be with him now, this way. Do you understand? You need to live, not just for you, but for me, too. You'll have all the happiness you seek, if you only go back."

I looked down at my hand. Jacky smiled. It was Glenn squeezing my hand. "That's what it's all about."

I heard Glenn's voice and I wanted to tell him I was okay. I was not feeling any pain and I was happy. His voice became clearer. As I listened to him talk about his feelings, my confidence increased.

When the doctor arrived, he informed Glenn that I wasn't getting any stronger. "She's going to have to fight harder to come back," he said. I looked down at my hand. Glenn began to cry. A warm teardrop appeared on my hand. Looking at it made me feel like I wanted to cry, not for me but for him. Then Jacky and I both heard him whisper, "Jacky, please help me. I love her." There was despair in his voice.

When I heard him call out to her, I knew he had finally accepted her. I asked Jacky to do something for me that would convince me that he did understand. I knew I could not go back if he didn't really understand that Jacky existed.

"What do you want me to do?" she asked.

"I don't know. Do something a ghost would do." I laughed.

At that, she was gone.

The room was dark, and everyone had gone home but Glenn. As he sat on the bed beside me, Jacky appeared as an eagle at the head of my bed.

"I know who you are," he said. "I want her back and you're the only one who can bring her to me." I guess he did accept her.

"No Glenn," a voice came from the eagle. "Only you can do that." Then she was gone.

Don came into the room. "Vicky can hear you, but you need to convince her of your love for her. Go ahead, she can hear you. Only you can bring her back." He took a seat on the other side of the bed.

"Don," Glenn said, "I want you to know I'm sorry for not believing what you were going though."

"I think you did believe it on some level, but I also understand how hard it must have been to accept. One of us had to keep things together. I should be apologizing to you."

"When I saw all that weird stuff going on, I just didn't want to accept it. I thought, if I ended my relationship with Vicky, I wouldn't have to face it and look at what happened. I was a fool. Why didn't you come to me?" he demanded. "You're supposed to be my friend."

"I am your friend," Don replied, "but think about what you'd have said if I told you. You would've thought I was crazy. Besides, I didn't feel it was my place. Vicky wanted to tell you before we left for the States, but by that time you were already having difficulty dealing with it."

Glenn was silent for a minute as he sought for words. "You're right," he said finally, "I knew she wanted to tell me when we all arrived home. That's why I did what I did. I was afraid."

"Well, you're here now," Don whispered.

"I must have put her through."

"You sure did, buddy. It got to the point she didn't know who to turn to. It was as if she didn't have anyone."

Glenn sighed. "Please, don't make me feel any worse."

"I don't have to; you're doing a good job by yourself. Besides, I wasn't much help to her either. I was so happy to see Jacky again that I never gave a thought to Vicky."

I think Glenn was still finding things hard to believe, but he was willing to accept them now.

Don went on to explain, "All I wanted to do was be with Jacky. Nothing else mattered. I still can't fully explain it, except to say her love was overpowering. Whenever I'm with her it's like we're the only two in existence, with the whole world's beauty belonging to us. It's like being on stage, surrounded by all the craziness and noise and then when she appears, the only thing I can see is her. Jacky allows me to see and feel love the way only she can."

I could see Jacky's tears as she listened to Don's words. It was as though she had waited so long to hear them. "Why are you crying?" I asked her.

Tears rolled down her checks. "My time is running out, Vicky. I have to leave everyone and move on."

"What are you saying?"

"All my life I've wanted one thing, and that was to be with Don. It was the only way I thought my life could be complete. I believed if only I could return and marry Don, I'd be able to stay forever. But I don't really know what I was thinking. My spirit's getting weak. It cries for him. Things weren't supposed to turn out this way. I even considered asking Don to return with me, but again I just don't know anymore. That's why every minute together with him is important."

"Have you told him?" I asked.

"No, I could never bring myself to hurt him and take him from what he knows and loves. You must tell him before its too late. "I can't," she said. "His love for me is so strong that I can't even imagine the outcome."

At that moment I knew what I had to do, not only for Glenn, but for Don and Jacky as well. There had to be a way she could complete her dream and stay with Don forever.

Glenn told Don, "Go and be with her."

I believe Don was finally happy hearing Glenn's acceptance of Jacky's being there. "You sure?"

"Go," Glenn said. "I'll see you in the morning."

As Don left the room Glenn walked over to the corner to grab his guitar. He took a seat next to me on the bed. "Vicky, if you don't come back to me I don't know what I'll do. I'm not sure I could go on without you." A tear rolled down his face.

He began singing my favorite song. It brought back memories of how the guys would kick Jacky and me out each time their dates came over to the house. I began to cry. I felt the tears roll down my face.

"Baby, I know you can hear me." He wiped the tears from my cheek and took my hand. I felt the warmth from his lips as he kissed me. "Vicky, I love you. Come back to me. I want to take you home where I can care for you the rest of your life. I guess I haven't said it enough, but I'm saying it now. I love you." He leaned over and whispered in my ear. "Can you hear me? I love you."

I dimly heard Jacky telling me to go. "He needs you. It's time for you to live and be happy."

"Will I see you again?" I asked her.

"Sure you will. You and I are closer now than we ever were."

We both heard Don calling her. I felt myself returning as she began to fade away. Glenn's words were getting clearer. I felt a tear hit my hand. As I opened my eyes I felt Glenn squeezing it. "Think you can get a better grip?" I joked.

"I missed you so much." He leaned over me. He held me in his arms. I remember thinking that this was what I needed.

Shortly the doctor came in and Glenn yelled, "She's back!" He was crying and laughing at the same time.

In no time, my whole family was in the room. It was great to see them all.

"I'll give you a moment to visit," the doctor said as he passed Glenn. "I don't know what you did, but she's very lucky." Everyone gathered around me. I could see a mixture of relief and concern from everyone. As Ray and

Judy came over to the bed, Glenn left the room, with Dad right behind him.

In the hall Glenn broke down. Dad placed his hand on his shoulder. Glenn immediately rose and went into his arms. As always, Dad was there, like a father for his son.

"I love her, Mike," Glenn said.

"I know, son. I've always known. It was your doing that brought her back to us. I always knew you'd do the right thing. We should get back in there before we're missed."

Glenn walked over to me and took my hand. "Where are my clothes?" I asked.

"Going somewhere?" He smiled. Everyone laughed.

"I'm going home," I replied, and tried to sit up. I immediately fell back. I felt like I'd been hit with a bat on the back of my head.

"You better just stay in bed and let me worry about taking care of you," Glenn said. "You'll be home in no time."

I lowered my head back onto the pillow. It felt so good hearing those words. In some way I always knew when I awoke I'd be back with Glenn. Well, I can say that now.

Dad spoke up. "I think we should get out of here and let her sleep." Everyone started to say their goodbyes.

I was surprised to see Jack and Michelle. Michelle came over and took my hand. "Jacky's okay," I whispered to her, "and she promised to see you before she goes."

Surprised, Michelle looked at Jack. I guess Jack still thought I didn't know what I was saying. He said, "Good night, sweetheart."

As Michelle kissed me, a tear rolled down her face. "See you in the morning."

I felt I'd done the right think by telling them about Jacky. I was tired and felt like I could sleep for a year.

"You better get some sleep, I'll be here when you get up," Glenn said.

"Glenn," I told him, "go on home and get some rest. You no longer need to worry." I closed my eyes, I felt him lie down beside me. I hadn't felt so secure in a long time, not having to curl up with my pillow in a fetal position like I'd been doing the last few months. This time I wrapped my arm around him and fell asleep.

In the hall, Jack placed his hand on Dad's shoulder. "Everything will be okay," he said. The two men walked down the hall, Judy and Michelle following. Michelle was crying over my words. Dad told Jack, "I don't know what I would've done without you being here."

Jack smiled. "Because we are family."

As Glenn and I lay together, holding each other tight, I opened my eyes to find Don and Jacky at the foot of the bed. Glenn opened his eyes too, and whispered, "Thank you, Jacky."

Don and Jacky left the room. Before they got to the door, Jacky disappeared.

Looking back over those months, I was glad not to dismiss the pain and discomfort I'd been feeling. In so many ways it had been the driving force bringing me to this point. As I lay there with my arm around Glenn and a smile on my face, I realized everything was worth the pain.

About 2:00 a.m. I woke up. Glenn was sitting in the chair next to my bed, holding my hand. He looked so tired I wanted to tell him to go home and get some sleep. I knew that he had been at my side for the last ten days.

I sat up and watched him. I knew he'd also had a rough time dealing with the last few months. I believe it took an equal toll on him as it did me. I didn't feel that bad physically, for someone who'd been lying in a coma for ten days.

I must have made a little noise because Glenn opened his eyes and said nervously, "Are you all right?"

"Yes," I said, smiling. It was a great feeling knowing that he'd been there all this time with me. I'd never felt more secure. "You should go home, you look awful."

He placed his hand over my mouth. "It looks like you're back, Miss Bad Thing."

"You have me all wrong. The last few months should have proved that."

"I love you," he whispered. "And I'm sorry for the pain I caused you." He reached over and kissed me.

I held my nose. "You've been here for too long. I think it's time for you to go home. And shower."

He laughed. "That's what I missed about you, babe. But you're right; I need to get a change of clothes and a good night's sleep."

"I'll be all right," I said. "Today is Saturday. Dad will be making his special pancakes this morning and I know he'll be happy to see you there."

I asked him to close the door. He grinned and came back to the bed. I did all I could to keep from cracking up. He sat on the bed and put his arm around me, and I burst out laughing.

"Do I smell that bad?" he asked.

"You're not the reason I was laughing," I said, looking at the foot of the bed. We both glanced there and Jacky suddenly appeared.

"Okay, girls, I know when I'm not wanted." He kissed me on the forehead and headed for the door. As he walked past Jacky, he stopped for a moment. They just looked at each other, and Glenn shook his head. When he closed the door behind him, Jacky and I started laughing.

Jacky got serious quickly. "What's wrong?" I asked.

"Do you remember when you came out of your coma? You told my mother and father I was here. Vicky, my mother is so unhappy. Dad is doing everything he can to comfort her, but nothing seems to help. She's acting as if my passing was only yesterday."

Seeing she was a little uncomfortable I took her hand. This was the first time I understood what she'd been going through. Her hand was cool as ice. I could understand how she needed me to be with Don.

"Does this have anything to do with what you told me when I was in a coma?"

"Yes."

"What do you want me to do?"

She squeezed my hand. "I want to tell them everything. I owe them that much."

There was an eerie silence as she waited for me to answer. I have to admit I wasn't too eager about that idea. I was skeptical about how everyone would handle the news. "Did you talk to Don about what you want to do?" I asked.

"Not yet. I was afraid of what he might say."

Even though I wasn't enthusiastic about the whole thing, I was ready to stand behind her and her decision. "Whatever you decide. I'm here for you. Just remember what happened to me. Be ready. I don't want either of our families to go though what Glenn and I did."

I could see she was really listening to me. Finally she said, "You know this is something I need to do."

"Okay, I understand and I'm with you, whatever you decide. Just be sure."

She frowned. "Remember when I told you my spirit was getting weak?"

I looked closely at her. I could see a change in her and the way she was trying to keep going. Even in life she could never hide anything from me.

Then she said, "When I first realized the power that brought me here was getting weak, I knew that I wasn't fulfilling my dream. In order for me to stay, I must do what I came for. I realized that it might never happen."

She waited for an answer. I knew what she was saying, but I needed to hear more.

"Do you know what I'm talking about?" she asked.

"Of course I know, but there's got to be a way to make it happen. I'll talk to Glenn to see if he can talk Don into it. Don't worry, whatever needs to be done, Glenn will do it."

Jacky and I passed the rest of the night talking about everyone and everything, just like we used to do when we were growing up. It was good for me to have her back, and this time I'd be there for her, just like always.

We spoke about what it was like for her to be stuck between two worlds, one being earth, the other heaven. We also spoke about the advantages and disadvantages she gained and lost as a result of her being dead. She was happy where she was, for she wanted to be there for Don and Don alone. Sure she liked seeing me and being with me, but that's not what had brought her back. Don had. And now she wanted Don to change all that and share what he had with everyone who made a difference in her life. She would have loved her life as a rock and roll wife. She had lived for that alone. The band was like her family, anyway, just as Dad, Judy, Jack, and Michelle were, along with Ray and Ruth. And her friends Jehane and Donna, who were so much more like her than she knew. She wanted them all to know what it was all about. She wanted them to know that there was nothing to be afraid of.

The time seemed to go by so fast. Before I knew it, it was 6:00 a.m. and my doctor came in the room. Of course, he couldn't see her. But it wasn't long before she started pulling her pranks.

"How are you feeling?" He took a seat on the edge of my bed. As he sat down, the bed began to rise, then when he stood up it began to lower. I couldn't help but laugh aloud; it was so funny to see his reaction. He looked at me, surprised and confused, then sat down again. This time the bed went down. He jumped off. I didn't know what to say, but I knew I had to say something. I didn't want him to burst a blood vessel, so I peered under the blanket as if I was looking for an answer. "Sorry," I said, "I think I'm lying on the controls."

He laughed and sat back down. I found it hard to keep a straight face. He explained he was going to give me a brief looking-over, and pulled a stethoscope from his pocket. Just as he put it to my chest I felt Jacky enter my body. I felt the doctor place and replace the stethoscope in his search to find a heartbeat. Of course there was none now. He tried again and again before he said, "I think I need to invest in a new one of these. I'll be right back." I couldn't remember seeing the doctor move as quickly as he did leaving the room.

As he left, the lab nurse came in. "I need to get some blood from you, sweetie," she said, smiling. She was perky and had a smile from ear to ear. "If everything comes out okay with these tests you should be able to go home soon."

Oh boy, I thought. I really hated needles. Then I heard Jacky whisper, "It will be okay." I have to admit, her words didn't reassure me, considering she followed them with a laugh. I braced myself for the unexpected. I wasn't sure what Jacky was going to do. "I promise you're not going to feel a thing," she said.

Just then the needle went into my arm. She was right. I didn't feel anything.

I was surprised to see the blood crystallize in the syringe. So surprised that I never noticed Glenn and Don enter the room.

The nurse was puzzled. "Hmm," she said, "let's try that again."

I lost count of the number of times she tried to take my blood. Each time, the blood crystallized. Thankfully, Jacky made it painless. If she hadn't, I'd have had to kill her again.

Finally the nurse gave up. "I don't understand," she said. "I'm going to get the doctor." As she left the room, we could see how shaken she was. Still, it was funny.

Jacky appeared and I turned around laughing. Don and Glenn were standing by the door looking on. They couldn't help but see humor in what they'd witnessed. "Okay, girls," Don said, "What's going on?"

Jacky disappeared and I threw the covers over my head. Glenn pulled them away. "Would you care to tell us what's going on?" he insisted.

Still laughing, I said, "It was Jacky. She's up to her old tricks."

Before the guys had a chance to respond, the doctor and nurse came back in the room. "Let's try this again," the doctor said.

"Don't worry," Glenn snickered, "I think things will be okay now."

The doctor reached for the needle and the blood vial. I readied myself for the unexpected. "Jacky," I whispered. I was still hoping for Jacky to enter my body, so I didn't have to feel the pain.

Don laughed. "Oh, by the way, Jacky popped out for a minute." Like that was going to make things better.

"Are you ready?" asked the doctor. I grabbed Glenn's hand, and I think I hurt it squeezing so hard. I was a chicken when it came to needles.

This time everything went smoothly. "If everything looks good I think we can let you go home soon," the doctor said again. That was the best news I'd heard recently. "But you have to promise me you're going to keep your strength up," he said.

The doctor and nurse left, and I asked Don, "Can you close the curtains?"

Jacky appeared, and seeing the three of them, all in one room made me feel so good.

"We better get going before everyone starts showing up," Don said.

"Okay, see you guys later," Glenn replied. "I'm going to stay until Jacky comes back tonight." At that they left.

Glenn and I talked about what Jacky and I had discussed. I told him why she came back and why she wanted everyone to see her now. I told him that she felt like she owed everyone that much. But I also told him the real reason she was here.

"What did Don say about all of this?" Glenn asked.

"He doesn't know. Jacky wanted you to talk to him. I told him that Don might not go for the idea. He wanted to keep Jacky for himself. He wouldn't want anything to come between their love.

"I'll talk to him tonight," he responded. "Right now all I want you to do is hold you." He sat on the edge of the bed, put his arm around me, and pulled me close. Thankfully the doctor didn't come in to take my blood pressure; I could feel it rising.

"I love you," I whispered.

"I love you too, babe."

I don't know how long we sat there, but it seemed like forever. Then out of nowhere he said, "They seem to have a very strong bond."

I didn't know what he meant.

"You know Jacky and Don."

"Yes, they do. In fact, she's felt that way about him ever since she was a little girl. Maybe that's why she's been able to return."

"Maybe." Glenn nodded.

CHAPTER 26

It was my last night in the hospital and I couldn't wait to get home. Jacky stayed the whole night with me. Glenn and Don's agent flew into town to discuss their new album, so they didn't visit. It's funny, that night I learned to appreciate having a ghost around and other reasons why she was here. Some people would have felt she was an angel. I came to understand why that night.

When Don and Glenn left that day, Don told me to behave myself. "And that goes for you, too." He pointed at Jacky.

Glenn added, "There's still going to be a hospital in the morning, I assume." He smirked.

"Go home," I said. "What could happen in a hospital?"

"That's what I'm afraid of," he said, and left.

Around six in the evening the nurse came in with my food tray. One look at it made me decide to head down to the cafeteria for a big cheeseburger. As Jacky and I walked down the hall, the nurse at the deck asked me where I was going.

"Down for a cheeseburger," I said.

"Great," she said, knowing that not eating had put me there in the first place.

On the elevator Jacky seemed preoccupied. I asked her if everything was all right; she didn't answer. Then the elevator stopped. "This isn't our floor."

Jacky never said a word, she just got off. It seemed something was drawing her to wherever she was going. I followed her.

The sign on the wall read:

PEDIATRIC WARD FOR THE TERMINALLY ILL.

Most of the patients had cancer and had no chance for life, but they all believed in miracles. Jacky stopped outside the first room on her right and looked in. Lying in a bed was a child about seven-years-old. It was hard to tell she was a girl, as she was bald. Jacky walked in. I stood outside, never moving from that spot.

Jacky sat on the side of the bed. I saw with amazement that she had a glow about her. It tock me off guard when the little girl opened her eyes and plainly saw Jacky sitting there. I didn't know what to think.

It was if the girl had seen a ghost, but not quite. Her face showed that whatever she was seeing was good; something pure, something innocent. She raised her arms to touch Jacky's face.

Jacky reached down and took her hands. The little girl smiled, as though her pain was gone. I felt like I was going to lose it right there on the spot. This was a side of Jacky I hadn't seen before. I just wished Don were there to see it too.

Jacky looked over at me as though she knew what I was thinking. Then in my mind I heard the girl say, *My name is Myra. My mother told me you'd come soon. No, they can't do anything anymore, but Mommy tells me everything's going to be all right. I want to tell her I understand so she doesn't have to be afraid. Will you tell her I'm going to be all right, now that you're here?* Jacky smiled at her.

I turned to see a woman coming down the hall. As she stopped at the desk to talk to the floor nurse, the doctor asked if he could have a word with her. I couldn't hear what was said, but I knew that Myra was the woman's daughter.

Whatever the doctor said to her made her fall forward as though she didn't have the strength to stand up. The doctor and nurse helped her to a chair and sat with her. I walked over to the water fountain so I could hear more clearly.

"What I am going to tell her?" the woman cried.

The nurse rubbed her hand. "The truth."

"I don't know if I can," the mother sobbed. "I promised her everything would be all right. How do I tell her I lied?"

"I've worked here for a long time," the nurse said, "and I've found that they already know. They just need to hear you won't be mad. Let her know it's okay to let go. Help her take the next step."

I walked back to the room and stood across the hall. The women came my way. She stopped to look at a picture on the wall, to check her face in the reflection and wipe her eyes. She put on some lipstick and a smile. Then, with a hitch in her walk, she went into the room.

Jacky stepped away from the bed. Looking at the little girl, she put a finger to her lips. The little girl smiled, and then hugged her mother.

"How are you feeling, baby?" the mother asked.

I never saw a little girl as strong as Myra. As hard as it was for her to sit up, she pulled herself up, as though to tell her mother that everything was going to be okay. I could see her mother trying to keep control, but even to Myra it was obvious that she wanted to cry.

Jacky nodded.

"Mother," Myra said, "I need to tell you something."

Her mother couldn't speak, but nodded yes.

"Remember when Daddy died and you said an angel came to take him to heaven?"

Her mother nodded.

"Well, the angel's here."

Her mother broke down.

"That's okay, Mommy. It's all right to cry because you're going to miss me, but I'll always be here with you. Just like Daddy is." Myra looked towards Jacky. Standing beside her was Myra's father.

Her mother didn't know what to say. She couldn't see Jacky or her husband.

Just then the nurse came down the hall and saw me standing there. "Is there anything I can help you with?" she asked. That's when she heard Myra tell her mother that the angel was there to take her to see her Daddy. Her mother couldn't answer.

"Mommy, I love you. I don't want you to be sad."

"I'll be okay, baby, knowing that you'll be with Daddy."

Her father walked over to the bed and sat beside her. "She'll be all right dear," he whispered in her ear.

It was as if she heard him, for a look of relief came to her face. Jacky looked at me and smiled. Myra looked at her father with the biggest smile I'd ever seen. She leaned over to hug her mother. "I love you, Mommy," she said, and closed her eyes.

When her mother said, "I love you," she didn't get a response. She lay Myra back on to her pillow.

When I looked at Jacky and the man, Myra was standing between them. She looked like she'd never been sick. She had long brown hair and the biggest brown eyes. The nurse was right, she was happy now.

Myra took her father's hand and smiled at Jacky. Jacky nodded and they were gone.

Still standing beside me was the nurse. We watched the woman as she cried over her baby. Then I saw Jacky standing behind her. Jacky put her hand on the woman's shoulder, and the most amazing thing happened. The woman lifted her head and smiled.

I asked her, "How could you see that day after day?"

She brushed the hair from my face. "Because I believe when they go, an angel is there to meet them."

I never asked Jacky what she said to the woman that day. But the nurse and I both knew that the woman understood her baby was finally happy.

And I never forgot what the nurse said to me when we saw the woman smile. "When the angel comes, it's the child that helps the mother carry on."

"Her angel did come for her," I said.

"You do understand," the nurse responded, and walked away.

Jacky was gone. Maybe she was with Myra. I don't know. But wherever she was, I knew she was doing something great. I wasn't hungry anymore. I felt fulfilled. I'd never forget that night for as long as I lived. I wished Don had been there to see what I'd always known—that Jacky was, and always had been, an angel.

I went back to my room and sat in the dark. I was glad no one was there, not even Glenn. I knew what I'd seen that night would always be between Jacky and me. I didn't realize that the next time I'd encounter an experience like that would be with my family and friends, or as we would come to call it, our "inner circle."

Jacky woke me at 3:00 a.m. "Are you going to sleep all night?"

"Don't ghosts sleep?" I mumbled.

"Well, no. Come on, let's get you something to eat."

I sat up in bed. She had that look in her eyes. "Jacky, what are you up to?"

"I'm just worried about you." She grinned.

"Sure you are." I knew that whatever she was up to, I'd be left holding the bag before the night was over. But after what she had given me that night, I guessed I could let her have a little fun, even though it would be at my expense. "I don't think I can experience any more of your new life tonight," I said.

"Don't worry," she laughed. "I made my quota for the night." I looked puzzled. "Just kidding," she said. "Let's get you something to eat."

In the cafeteria, while we ate, we watched a couple sitting together in the corner. They had just gotten off duty. They were our age and you could tell they were in love. He couldn't keep his hands off her.

"Let's go to my place," he said.

"I can't," she said, "I volunteered to work the next shift." From the look on his face you could tell he wanted something else.

Jacky and I laughed. When they turned to see who was laughing, all they could see was me. They must have thought I was crazy. Then he said, "I know where we can go before you have to get back on the floor."

When they left they passed by me. "You okay?" the guy asked.

I tried not to laugh, but it was hard. I smiled and nodded.

When they went out the door Jacky jumped up and yelled, "Follow me!"

"No," I whispered, "I've got to get back to the room."

"Come on, we have time."

We followed the couple as they made a right down the hall. I kept looking back to see if anyone was behind us. Then I saw the sign ahead. It read, in big bold letters, MORGUE.

"No way," I said. I was not going in there.

"Come on, you don't want me to make you"

I sighed. "Okay, I'm right behind you."

We crept in and then crawled on the floor behind the couple. It didn't matter that the room was cool, for what we were witnessing made the whole place warm up. We couldn't move; we didn't want to get caught.

I quietly asked Jacky what time it was and she said she didn't know. I should have known better when she said that. Of course she knew. "I'll go find out," she whispered. And before I could stop her, she was gone. I had to wait until the couple left so I could get out of there.

I felt like a jerk, remembering that every time Jacky made one of her moves, I got the shaft. I sat there quietly trying not to hear what was being said. I don't know how long it took, but when I heard the door open and close, I said, "Thank goodness." I crawled out and headed for the door, hoping no one else was around.

As I was leaving I ran right into Glenn.

"I'm not even going to ask," he said, then started to laugh.

"It was Jacky," I said.

He wrapped his jacket around me and smiled. "Here, put this on. I guess I have to keep you and Jacky apart." Then he kissed me. "That's what I love about you. You're always going to need me to watch over you."

When we got to the room, Don was sitting there with Jacky. "Tell me," I asked her, "how do you kill a ghost?" She jumped up and started to explain what happened. I told Don and Glenn. We all laughed.

Later that morning the doctor returned. He informed me the blood work was fine, and that it was safe for me to return home. Without a word or a thank you, I ran to the bathroom to change into my clothes. Glenn asked if I was going to be all right, and the doctor reassured him that things were fine now. "She's a tough girl," the doctor said.

"Yes, doc, she sure is . . . she sure is," Glenn agreed.

Dad and Judy came in, asking where I was. "The doctor said she could leave, so she's getting dressed," Glenn replied.

"Just remember," the doctor said, "she has to eat; she's still not out of the woods."

Dad told Glenn, "I guess you've got your hands full."

Laughing, Judy walked over to me as I was coming out of the bathroom. "Are you ready?" she asked.

"You bet," I replied. Just as we were walking out, a nurse stopped me. "Here you go, young lady, its hospital policy."

She had a wheelchair. I wasn't about to argue. I jumped into the chair and we headed for the exit. It felt as though my life was starting over, but this time I was in control. It was clearer to me now that I had to help Jacky complete her quest. It was the only way to help her reach a goal that she'd been seeking ever since I could remember. But this time I had Glenn to help.

CHAPTER 27

I'd only been out of the hospital a few days, and it seemed like the last few months had never taken place. Glenn even moved back into his old room. He was becoming more and more protective of me with each passing day. Deep inside I didn't think he was able to forgive himself for what happened. He became overprotective, making sure I ate and that I got enough rest. There were times when I thought he was a bit too protective, but I had taken care of my family for so long that it felt good to have someone finally looking after me.

I never did put the weight back on that everyone expected me to. I wasn't that crazy. I never forgot that Glenn was, and always would be, a ladies' man and I knew the types of girls he was attracted to. I do learn from my experiences.

Don bought the house across the street and fixed it up just like Jacky wanted it, all the way down to the garden in the backyard. As changes took place I remembered Jacky speaking about the way she wanted everything to be when she and Don finally got together. It was truly

amazing seeing her dreams coming true. I was also reminded of how history repeated itself, with the house again occupied by a couple who knew the real meaning of love.

Jack and Michelle moved back from France, once again occupying their old house. They were so happy. It didn't compare to the mansion they had in France, still they had all the comforts of home. But now they seemed more relaxed. As a result, they spent more time together and they seemed to fall in love all over again. Jack still made trips to France, but never without Michelle.

Let's not forget about Dad and Judy. What can I say about them? Not a day went by that they didn't act like newlyweds. I was beginning to see Glenn more and more in Dad and, because of that, I knew I didn't have to wish about finding love any more. I still thought about my mother whenever I saw Judy and Dad together. Knowing Dad, I knew that Judy was just like her.

One morning Judy was in the kitchen with Dad, helping him cook his famous pancakes. I walked in to pour myself a cup of coffee, but before I could get to the pot Judy told me to sit down, she'd get it for me. You might be saying to yourself, that's not so unusual, but without thinking I said, "Thanks, Mom."

Judy surprisingly dropped the pot, sat down, and started to cry. I had to say something fast, so I put my hand on her shoulder. "Judy, I'm sorry, I never . . ."

She stopped me. "There's nothing for you to be sorry about. Those are the nicest words I've heard in a long time."

Dad cleared his throat. I tried not to laugh, but couldn't resist.

"I've wanted to say those words for a long time," I replied, "but you never looked like you were old enough to be a mother."

Judy laughed and stood up. "The compliments just keep coming," she said, and we hugged. "You'd be surprised how young I feel hearing you say that."

Dad had to add his two cents. "And just how young is that?" It was cute how she ran over to him and punched him in the arm. He responded by grabbing her closely and telling her how much he loved her. I caught his eye as he winked at me. They began kissing as though they were two young lovers who had been apart for a long time.

Then I heard laughing in the background. When I turned, right in front of me was Jacky.

"What?" I whispered.

"Don't worry, no one can see me," she said. Then she went to where Dad and Judy were standing and blew in Dad's ear.

Dad pulled away from Judy and turned around. Then Jacky did the same thing to Judy, laughing as she did. I couldn't help laughing myself.

Judy looked around to see who or what was there. Of course, she didn't see anything.

"Are you all right?" I asked Dad.

"There must be some kind of draft in here." He pulled Judy close to him.

Glenn came into the room. "Oh, my goodness. Get a room, you

two." That was the same remark Dad always made whenever he caught Glenn and me kissing.

"Sit down and shove some food in your mouth," Dad told Glenn.

Don walked in. "Did Glenn say something he shouldn't have?" He looked at me and Jacky.

Once again she walked around the table. She didn't do anything just then, but when she got to Glenn she seemed to appear out of nowhere. Glenn still wasn't used to her popping in unexpectedly, and she knew that. She got a kick out his reaction.

He choked on his pancake and Don patted him on the back. Then Glenn said, unexpectedly, "Did you see that?"

Don and I acted like we didn't know what he was talking about.

Dad turned around. "See what?"

"I didn't see anything," Don said.

"What was that, Glenn?" I asked.

Glenn shook his head and went on eating.

"You better get some sleep," Dad said.

Then Jacky was gone. Don and I continued laughing.

Looking over my family, I couldn't help but feel something was missing. Then Ruth and Ray came in. *That's it,* I thought, *I missed Ray.*

He kissed me. "How you feeling, Little Miss?"

"Good." I smiled. I hadn't seen him since I'd come home from the hospital. He'd been out of town on business.

As everyone took their seats around the table, we were all surprised when Jack and Michelle came through the door. "Okay, where are the pancakes?" Jack demanded.

"Sit down, you goof," Dad said, laughing.

Later, I saw Don looking at me. "What're you thinking about?" he asked.

"I was thinking I hope Jacky doesn't show up," I muttered quietly.

And there she was, standing behind Dad. She had that look. You know by now what I'm talking about. When Don saw her, he knew we were in for a morning prank. He gave her his look, the one he'd give us when he wanted us out of the room when their girlfriends came over. When was he going to realize that didn't work anymore?

Jacky laughed, and as a matter of fact, so did I. She shook her head and grinned from ear to ear. Don went on eating, trying not to look at her. On the other hand, I tried to encourage her. I nudged Glenn under the table and when he looked up to see Jacky standing there, he choked again. That got Don laughing, all the time keeping his eyes from making contact with her. I heard him say, "Oh, boy."

Dad asked Judy if she'd get the OJ out of the fridge. Don, Glenn, and I watched to see if she was going to make it back to her seat without Jacky's interference.

When Judy opened the fridge, there was Jacky inside, in a ball with her arms wrapped around her legs. We laughed so hard and so loudly that everyone stopped eating.

"Like to share it with us?" Ray asked.

"We're all listening," Jack said.

Just as Don was going to explain, a sound came from Glenn that got us all laughing, except for Glenn. You know the sound that comes from a whoopee cushion? Glenn looked at the
ceiling. I leaned over and kissed him. He smiled and went on eating. He'd managed to divert everyone's attention.

Jacky was back in the room, making her way around the table, looking for her next victim. I heard Glenn mumble, "She-e-e's ba-a-a-ck," without looking up.

She stopped and sat in the center chair, between Dad and Michelle. Dad was talking to Don. I don't know what about, but Dad had a habit of talking with his hands. They would go up and down, side to side, and that's all Jacky had to see. She started mocking him, imitating his hand movements. We tried like not to laugh.

When she got through with Dad she turned to Michelle.

To picture Michelle, think of a complete lady. If anyone went to a school for the prim and proper, it was her. She was a beautiful lady, one to be admired. When she picked up her napkin, Jacky imitated her and picked up an imaginary one and patted her lips delicately, just like Michelle did. When Michelle picked up her glass, Jacky made believe she picked up one, too. You know, with the pinky standing out in the air. It was all we could do to keep from roaring, but we held it back.

When Michelle put down her glass, Jacky stopped and just stared at her. Michelle went on eating, but Jacky's face went from happy to sad. It wasn't hard to figure out what she was thinking. She knew Michelle couldn't forgive herself for all the years she'd been without Jacky.

Jacky looked over at Don, and I saw a tear roll down her cheek. It was time to make things better.

Don got up. "I have to make a call," he said and left the room. Jacky faded out. I knew Don was going to make it right.

After a few minutes Don returned. When he sat down I told him that we needed to talk.

"I know," he said. "I've already spoken to Glenn. Maybe they're all ready for her. I know Jacky needs this, too."

After breakfast we were all clearing the table when Dad said, "Don't forget to tell the boys about tonight." I'd forgotten Dad was planning a coming home party for me. As much as Dad enjoyed cooking, he enjoyed having all our friends and family around more. Our inner circle.

Before Jack and Michelle left, they asked Don and Glenn to stop by their house to help them with something. Jack was going to show Dad his new boat.

"Sure," Glenn replied, "we'll be over in a bit."

"Great, see you soon," Jack said as he left.

"Babe, why don't you come with us?" Glenn asked me. "We'll only be a few minutes and then we'll have the whole day together."

Of course I agreed to that.

Rushing up the stairs to change, I grabbed Glenn and motioned for him to follow. After Jacky's little joke on him, I felt bad about what she'd done. Before he could speak I kissed him.

"What's that's for?" he asked.

"Nothing, really, it's just my way of saying thanks and for talking to Don about Jacky."

"I'd do anything for you, babe, you're my girl. Who else can be the brunt of Jacky's jokes?"

I had to ask him, "Are you okay with the whole Jacky thing?"

"Not only am I all right with everything, I'm a little excited to see how things turn out tonight."

I couldn't believe how things were coming together. I'd never been happier in my life than I was at that moment. It was like old times.

Dad yelled, "I'll meet you guys over at Jack's." He and Judy liked to walk over ever since he and Jack had had the walkway put in. It was about a half a mile between their homes, but they enjoyed it and made it a regular ritual to walk over to Jack's house. The distance and time never seemed to be an issue. They welcomed their private time together. It was cute seeing them holding hands and enjoying their walk.

Before heading to Jack's we stopped to pick Don up. By the time the three of us arrived, everyone was at the barn. "What's going on?" I asked. There were no horses, so I didn't understand why everyone was hanging out at the barn. I had a feeling, because Don and Glenn were being so quiet, that something was up.

When we reached the side of the barn I heard neighing. "Come on in!" Jack yelled. As we piled into the barn I heard the loud sneeze of a horse. I was getting excited. I turned to my left and there was The Duke.

"You got to be kidding," I screamed. With everything going on in my life I'd almost forgotten about him. I couldn't hold the tears back as I ran to him. I threw my arms around him and knew he recognized me. I immediately stepped into his stall and began having a conversation with him. I remembered the long talks we used to have. He never said much, but he was a really good listener.

Glenn leaned against the stall door. "If I only had four legs and a tail," he said. Everyone laughed.

I thought, *Now my family is complete.* I started to thank Jack, but he stopped me before I could speak. "Don't look at me. This was all Glenn's idea. He couldn't wait until we got the barn together. He just sent for your horse."

I thanked both Glenn and Jack with a kiss.

Even though this was another happy day in my life, there still was something missing. I turned to the stall next to The Duke, like I had so many times when I was in France, and couldn't help feeling sad. Then I felt an arm on my shoulder.

"It's all right, Vicky, she knows," Don said. He nodded to me to follow him outside. And there he was—Jazzman, running free. I couldn't believe my eyes. I ran to him and called his name. He heard me, and immediately headed right for us. I turned to find Don and Glenn looking right at Jazzman and I knew they were seeing what I was—Jacky, riding like the wind on his back. She looked so enchanting. Don seemed to be spellbound by her. I, too, felt there was something different about her. Maybe she knew that today was not just for me, but for her as well.

I turned to Glenn with open arms. "Thank you, sweetheart. You don't know how this makes me feel. And Don, she's so happy."

I saw Michelle standing by the fence watching Jazzman running in the distance. I'm sure seeing Jazzman reminded her of Jacky.

I wasn't the only one who noticed Michelle. Don nudged my shoulder to go over and speak with her. As I headed toward her, it was like history rewinding. I was reminded of the day Jacky died and how Michelle stood by the fence watching the horses run.

"It's difficult to put into words," she told me, "but it's beginning to feel as though Jacky passed away only yesterday."

I looked to my side and there was Jacky, standing beside me. I didn't react to her. As I placed my hand upon Michelle's shoulder, Jacky put her hand in mine. With the three of us connected, I could see Jacky was feeling Michelle's emotions.

Tears fell from Michelle eyes. "I still haven't gotten over her," she said. "I miss her so much. Seeing Jazzman just reminds me again."

As I struggled to find words I saw Jacky had tears rolling down her face too. Then she was gone.

"Michelle," I said, "consider yourself lucky, as I do, that you were touched by her love. She may only have been with us a short time, but her impact will outlast our lives. God has a plan for each of us and I believe in her own way she will accomplish His wishes."

Michelle placed her hand on my face. "The day you came out of the coma you told me Jacky was there. Do you remember?"

Before I had a chance to answer, Don and Glenn came over. They had heard her ask me the question. The three of us stood there searching for words. None of us knew what to say, but she did deserve an honest answer.

"Michelle," I started, "when I was in the coma I had a dream about Jacky. I wanted so much to be with her. It was she who insisted that I come back to where I belong. Jacky told me she'd always be looking out for me, and I, too, would find happiness."

I didn't know what else to say. Glenn took my hand, but even with his reassurances I felt nervous. I stood in silence, awaiting Michelle's response.

"You and Jacky share a bond that has no boundaries," she replied. "I'm grateful she found in you a friend and a sister who helped her through her troubled times."

I hugged her. "Everything will be fine," I whispered.

Then Jack shouted for Michelle to walk with him. I wondered if he knew how troubled she was. As I watched Michelle walk away with Jack, Dad, and Judy, I could only hope that tonight would bring her peace.

CHAPTER 28

The rest of the day Glenn and I hung around the house.

I was sitting in the kitchen when Glenn leaned down to kiss me. "What was that for?" I asked.

"No special reason. Just for being you."

I felt the warmth of his body all over, as though I was melting into his arms. It almost felt like when Jacky entered my body and we became one. As I sat there feeling lost in his arms, he held me close. Maybe he thought I would escape. With my head on his chest, still feeling the warmth from his body, I couldn't help thinking how deprived Jacky must feel, never being able to experience this.

I had to tell Glenn the whole story. Not just that Jacky needed to get married to stay here with Don, but to feel the warmth that lovers feel when their souls become one. But how could I tell Glenn that she needed to be with Don in the flesh, and the only way for that to ever happen was through me? I knew Glenn was fine with everything that was going on with Jacky so far, but I'd have to be out of my mind to tell him this one. I'd lost him before and I vowed I'd never lose him again. Still, I had hoped we could find a way for Don and Jacky to be one. I owed her that much. I refused to think it was impossible.

"Glenn, I need to tell you something."

"Sure, baby, go ahead. What's on your mind?"

I told him about how when I was in a coma I learned of Jacky's spirit getting weak. "The reason for her returning was to marry Don, like it should have been. And if she doesn't accomplish that, it will destroy her." I stopped, unable to find the words to tell him the rest.

"Is that all? Vicky, is there anything you're not telling me?"

I sighed and lied. "No, that's all."

But he knew. "Let's get through tonight first, and then we'll work out whatever it is you're not telling me."

I felt bad not telling him the whole thing, but until I found the words, I needed to let it go at that.

As the friends arrived I remember thinking that they'd never forget this night, and probably never be able to explain it, either. Jacky was so excited about telling her mother and father that she was here, and about her life after her death. Don, however, was still skeptical about the whole thing. Of course you couldn't blame him. He didn't want anything to interfere with the way things were going. Theirs was a relationship like no other. Even I felt jealous of the special bond they had.

Dad and Judy were preparing the food while Jack and Michelle helped set up the table, when Joe and Jehane came stumbling into the house, laughing. If you knew Joe, you'd understand. Everyone knew what a prankster he was, and you could depend on him to get a party started. As Joe talked to Glenn I was able to get Jehane alone. She told me that she and Joe were planning to get married.

"Joe will make you happy," I said.

"And I'll make him happy, too." She winked.

I laughed. "Girl, you and Joe make a good pair."

We heard, "What's so funny?" and turned to see Donna and Tim coming in the front door.

"We were just wondering when the two of you were going to tie the knot," I said

At that, Tim walked over to Glenn and Joe.

"What's up with him?" Jehane asked Donna.

"We're not sure yet. Everything is so perfect, and we've talked about it, but he's afraid of change," she replied.

"Well, whatever works for you," I said.

Ray and Ruth finally walked in. I was glad to see him. I turned to look for Jehane and Donna, sitting between them was Jacky, just like old times. Her eyes caught mine and all we could do was grin.

Glenn and Don, too, were watching Jacky. She waved at the three of us. She seemed so happy among her friends and family, and you could see the anticipation on her face. She wanted everyone to know about her.

The evening was going well. It was a perfect night to introduce a ghost. Everyone was sitting around, talking among themselves. It was cool; the sun had just gone down. A full moon lit up the yard. Don was still hesitating over whether it was the right decision to tell everyone about Jacky. I couldn't blame him, I was a little nervous myself.

I saw him arguing with her. She was insisting he tell everyone now, before it was too late. "What are you not saying?" he asked. Jacky vanished.

Glenn walked over, "She means you'll never get another chance to get everyone together."

"Why's that?" Don asked.

"Cause we're going on tour to promote the new album. I got the call from L.A. today."

I knew that wasn't true, but he had to come up with something fast. After thinking about it for a moment, Don agreed. They headed over to where our parents were sitting.

"Don, sit down. You look like you've seen a ghost," Dad said. Glenn and I couldn't help smiling at each other—if they only knew.

We watched as Don decided whether to sit or stand. He stood. Then he said loudly, "Okay. I need to talk to all of you."

All talking stopped, and all heads turned his way. He glanced at Michelle. What he was going to say would affect her deeply, if things didn't work out as we hoped. He took a deep breath and started. "Michelle, Jack, what I'm about to say may seem strange." Everybody waited expectantly. He had their full attention, for sure. "When Jacky passed away, I know all of you thought I was acting strangely. What I'm about to say will explain all that." You could cut the tension in the yard with a knife as he fought for the words. Then he blurted it out. "Jacky is here now."

Michelle's head fell into her hands and she began to cry. Jack became angry. "Don, why would you say something like that?"

"Jack," Don pleaded, "before you blow your top, let me finish."

But it was too late. The yard roared with comments. Dad was also obviously upset and unsure why Don had made such a remark. Don sat down; he couldn't gain control. A few minutes passed. Then Glenn, Don, and I saw Jacky walk into the center of the yard. At that moment she appeared.

There was dead silence. It reminded me of when she was at the shows and she and Jazzman became one, and the spectators gasped when they made that last perfect jump.

Everyone stared at her with expressions of amazement. They were all speechless. I smiled at Glenn. She looked so beautiful, even Don couldn't take his eyes off her. However, I was concerned. She looked a little different than she had all those other times. Maybe it was the reflection from the moon, or maybe it was the love that surrounded her, but she was definitely different than I'd seen her before.

Michelle kept looking back and forth between Jacky and me. I smiled as if to tell her everything was okay. Then she stood up and walked over to her. Jack stood up and walked towards Jacky. As he reached them he opened his arms, and Jacky fell into them. He pulled Michelle toward them and they all hugged one another. It was like time stood still. Her glow consumed them and they became one. I tried to remember the last time the three of them had been together. This moment was a long time coming. Not only did her family need her, Jacky now needed them more than ever. You could tell she was happy because the glow around her got brighter. She said, "Don't cry, Mother, I've always been here with you. I always wanted to tell you not to cry for me. I had to wait till the time was right, but I'm here now."

Dad watched with amazement. Then a tear rolled down his face, maybe because his daughter had returned. Or maybe he felt left out. Judy tried to comfort him by rubbing her hand on his leg, but that didn't seem to help.

I went over to him and knelt down in front of him. "Dad," I said. He didn't answer. I felt tears roll down my face. Maybe, for a split second, I felt jealous of the way he was looking at

her. Then I remembered I'd never had my father to myself growing up. Sure it bothered me, especially when I came downstairs late at night and peeked through the crack in the door so they couldn't see me. He'd be holding Jacky in his arms, sitting in front of the fire across from Mother's picture. It was like Mother was watching over the two of them. I remember thinking it should have been me he was holding. She was my mother, not Jacky's, and he never held me like that.

"Dad," I said, "can you hear me?" Still I did not get an answer. At that moment I felt someone watching me. I rolled my eyes left and there was Ray, as always. No matter how old I got, he always had that expression for me, the one that told me everything was all right. As always, he was there for me when I didn't expect it. He smiled and then winked. Everything was all right.

"Dad," I said again, "it's Vicky."

Finally he took his eyes off Jacky and looked at me. He rubbed his hand across my face, as if to see if I was real. "Are you all right, babe?" he asked.

I smiled. "Sure, Daddy." Then I felt ashamed that I'd thought what I had. I knew Dad loved us both. He knew I was the strong one and that we had different needs. He knew how Mother felt about Jack, and I think, because of Mother, he did what he did for Jacky. Mom knew that Jack loved her until the day she died, so you could say that Dad did it for her. Then I realized how the little girl inside me would act if her daddy held another member of the family. That was how Jacky and I acted when Dad held one of us. It was just sibling rivalry.

I stood up beside Dad as Jacky walked over to us. Everyone was still astonished. I stepped aside when Jacky stopped in front of me. She put her hand on my shoulder and I knew what had to be done. I looked at Glenn. He nodded.

Simultaneously we took one step toward each other, and we became one. She wanted to feel the warmth that she had missed and craved. She wanted to sit on Dad's lap, like she had so many times as a young girl. She needed Dad to tell her everything was going to be all right.

We sat down, and Dad put his arms around us. We rested our head on his chest and felt him squeeze us tight, but this was Jacky's night so I faded out. When I did, every eye was watching. Sure, I was still there, but just in spirit.

Being one with Jacky made me feel how Dad had been feeling for a long time. I realized that he hurt, knowing he couldn't be there for Jacky when her life had been taken from us. Now she made him complete.

Inside, I heard her say, *Thank you for sharing Dad.* I don't know if she picked up on what I was thinking, but I wanted to cry more now than ever for feeling jealous of her.

Then Dad said, "Now I have my two girls back again."

As we faded in and out, everyone was more amazed and still couldn't find the words to talk. But it was good that now everyone knew what Don and I had been going through for the last year.

After we got up from Dad's lap we walked over to Don. He could only see Jacky. We sat down on his lap and he told her he loved her. I could feel now more than ever that she craved his flesh. The warmth of his body was what she missed, even though she had never felt it before. It was what kept her there. When she made contact with Don, the cravings that she longed for were all so real. Even though she spent all her nights with him, this was her first.

Don kissed her on the forehead. Being the jokester she was, she took me off guard and left my body. She appeared standing behind me. I never realized it until everyone started to laugh, that she had left me, in my form, sitting on my brother's lap. I jumped up as fast as I could and we laughed together. But it was okay; it kind of brought everyone back to earth.

The rest of the night brought all the questions: "What's it like?" "How does it feel?" "Did you know you were coming back?" and "Did you see a light?" I sat on the side with Don and Glenn, watching her. She had a smile that I hadn't seen in a long time. She was the center of attention. Every once in a while she looked over at us. We'd smile and she'd go on to answer more questions.

I went into the house, not knowing that Michelle followed me. I turned to see her standing there. Jacky had told her about Don and all the things they'd been through. She hugged me. "What you must have being going through the last two years," she said. "And, as always, you thought of her first."

"To know her was a joy," I said, "and to leave her is so hard. I miss her so much." I started to cry. "Maybe her coming back was her way of saying goodbye and letting us get on with our lives."

She put her arm around me. "Remember the day you said to me that, once I got to know her, I'd love her?"

"Yes, clearly."

"Well, the next day, Jacky came to me and said the same of you."

We smiled. There was no need to speak. As she left the room I knew that if Jacky didn't fulfill her quest, Michelle would be prepared when Jacky had to leave. That's why I said what I did. I hoped that if Jacky did have to leave, Michelle would get on with her life, too.

I sat down and poured myself a cup of coffee. I needed a few minutes alone. It had been so long since Jacky had taken over my body that I'd forgotten how weak I became when it happened. Plus, I was so worried about Jacky's coming out that I never stopped to think about Glenn asking me to marry him. I never told anyone. Not that I didn't want to, I just didn't have the time to think about it. I was worried about this night and the repercussions of it, if it didn't work out as we hoped. But I knew that, regardless of the outcome, they'd all be leaving with something they wouldn't be able to explain in ten lifetimes.

Glenn came in. "What's wrong, baby?" He knew that when Jacky took over my body it left me weak.

I smiled. "I was thinking about how great everything turned out."

"It sure did. She's so happy." He reached for my hand. "Baby," he whispered, "we have that kind of love, don't we?"

My eyes filled. "Yes, we do, but I think all of us realize tonight what love is all about."

"I'll never let anything come between us again." He pulled me toward him. I put my arms around him and we kissed. I had to stand on my toes; he was so much taller than I. I always loved hugging him.

I started to cry.

"What's wrong?" he asked.

"With everything going on, I haven't told anyone about us."

He laughed. "That's what I love about you. You act so tough, but you're still my little girl."

Then I heard in my head, *Vicky*.

"Yes," I said out loud.

Glenn asked, "Jacky?"

I nodded. "She wants us to come outside."

He put me down and we headed for the yard. It was getting late, but I could see Jacky didn't want the night to end. Don walked over to her. He felt her sadness more than any of us. I think he knew there was more going on than Jacky was admitting to. I could also see she knew just how Don was feeling.

Jacky, what's going on? I asked silently.

If you can hear me, Vick . . . she began. At that Don looked over at me.

What's going on? I thought. *Can Don hear me, too?*

Yes, he can hear you. Tonight was the first step. The beginning of Don and I becoming one. Don is able to hear my thoughts, but it's still too early for him to fully understand.

I was never fully able to understand what was going on either, but I did feel that I was not going to see her anymore.

"Oh, no!" I said out loud.

"What wrong"? Don asked.

I didn't answer him but said silently to Jacky, *He doesn't know, does he?*

No, Vicky, I can't think about it, it would be better if you didn't either.

I didn't communicate with her the rest of the night.

"Vicky," I heard Glenn say, "What's going on?"

"I can't tell you now. Not until everyone goes home."

He nodded.

Until she was gone I tried avoiding Don so I didn't have to say anything to him about her. As long as I didn't communicate with Jacky, he wouldn't know. I kept the thought, *how wonderful that Don and Jacky are becoming soul mates*, in my mind for the rest of the night.

As the night was coming to end, Jacky walked into the middle of the yard. She lit up like the moon. Everyone stopped what they were doing and turned to look at her.

"I have to go," she announced. "This is a night that I hope will help me to go on and do what I have to do. I was able to come to all of you this evening, for this is one step on my journey. I need to fulfill my journey in order to stay with you. Please always remember, I'll be here in spirit, but you won't see me again until, or if, I'm able to complete my quest. You gave me the strength to carry on. I want all of you to know that without you I could never have come back."

Don had the same sad expression on his face as everyone else. Even I hadn't known that she wasn't going to be here with us. Jacky hadn't told me that Don wasn't going to see her, either.

Jacky concluded, "I missed all of you so much and I hope one day I'm able to be with you again."

The glow around her was fading. "No!" Don screamed as he ran to her. When they met, they became one. Then she was gone.

CHAPTER 29

Don fell to his knees and Jacky said silently to me, *that's why I never told you what I had to do. But it doesn't mean I won't be here. It has to be this way.*

Everything went silent and for a moment no one moved. Don said, "I can't feel her, where is she?"

I didn't know what to say. I couldn't tell him, for I didn't know what she had to do.

"Come, Don," Glenn said, "time to go home."

Don remained on his knees. "She's gone. I can't feel her."

Glenn put his hand on Don's shoulder. I walked back to where everyone was standing. I could see this night had changed the way they looked at things.

Everyone wanted an answer. "Where is she?" Michelle cried.

"Jacky's still here," I said. "All I know is she's going through a test and we're part of it. Tonight was a part of that test. She needed to let all of us know the love she carries with her.

Jacky needed to know she could touch your lives, because if she didn't, her quest would stop here."

The women had tears in their eyes and the men did their best to hold back their emotions. Joe, the jokester, for once was quiet. I could see Jacky had touched all their lives deeply. I knew she'd fulfilled the first part of her journey.

Everyone left quietly. Joe put his arm around Jehane and in a soft voice said, "Come, time to go home." She took his hand and they left silently.

Tim, who could not commit to Donna, responded by saying, "Let's go. There's so much we need to talk about." They left the yard together.

Jack had his arm around Michelle, rubbing her shoulder. I had to say something to them, but what? They were waiting for some kind of answer.

"You can talk to her whenever you want," I told them, "and when she completes her journey she'll be back. I'm sure of that."

"Are you really sure?" Michelle asked. Then she whispered, "Good night, Jacky, I believe in you. I know you're right."

Taking her hand Jack said, "Let's go, love, time to go home." They said good night to Dad and Judy and left their car and took the path. They seemed closer than in a long time. He held her tightly as they walked off.

Ray and Ruth, who eloped about a year ago, were also touched. . After that night Ray limited his work and even refused any more long trips for the firm. Soon Ruth got pregnant. They'd always been in love, but after that night they seemed to take their love to the next level.

I thought it funny that Dad hadn't seemed that surprised. I opened my mouth to tell him about Jacky, but he put his finger on my lips. "Its okay, Vicky, I understand. When she was sitting on my lap she told me she had to do something before she could return and, if she didn't complete it, she'd see me when I crossed over."

I was glad Jacky had confided in Dad. I wished she'd told him the rest. Maybe it was a bit selfish of me, but I didn't want to be the only person who held the answers—what few I did have. I also believed that in order to help her complete her journey, I needed to confide in Glenn.

Dad and Judy headed towards Don and Glenn. "No, Dad," I said, "let Glenn help him. Glenn also understands."

He smiled and they said, "Goodnight."

When the light went out I knew they'd gone to bed. Now I had to go to Don. He was sitting on the ground now. He looked up at me, his face full of sorrow. "Why didn't she tell me?"

"I didn't know and I have no answers. I knew she was going on a journey, but I didn't know that this night was the beginning of her quest."

Don got up, grabbed a bottle of whiskey, and walked across the street. Glenn followed him, but when they got to the street Don told him he wanted to be alone.

Glenn stopped and watched Don enter the house. Don never turned the light on and Glenn finally came back to the house.

I was lost. I had no answers, and I couldn't tell anyone what I knew for fear of it getting back to Don. He had to prove his devotion for Jacky; only that would change everything. I didn't know then what Don had to give up, besides Jacky, for her to return. But I did know that this time I needed Glenn to be with me. There had to be a way for Don not to lose her again.

The rest of that night Glenn and I sat thinking of what came out of this night. He never asked me any questions and I never brought it up. I needed time to figure it out. He knew when I was ready I'd tell him, but right now I needed to be alone.

For the next few days everyone went about their daily routine, but you could see that Jacky had affected them in different ways. No one spoke about that night, even though we were all there. It was a strange feeling. Let's face it, it wasn't every day your best friend came back from the dead and sat down with you at a party. That alone was hard, but there was something else.

A few weeks passed and still Don didn't come out of the house. Glenn went over to check on him every day, but they never spoke. Don always had the same answer; either he was not feeling so good or he was still working on the new album. There was always an excuse for him not wanting to see anyone. You couldn't blame him, really. It was easy to see that he believed Jacky was never coming back. You could tell he hadn't been sleeping. He looked like crap.

Glenn tried talking to their agent, hoping he could send the group out of town. Unfortunately, it didn't work that way. Glenn even spoke with Joe and Tim about cutting their new album sooner, instead of waiting until spring. But when they confronted Don, it was always the same excuse—the songs needed more work. There was never any discussion after that, simply because we all knew what a perfectionist Don was. Not even Glenn would open his mouth.

There was just no getting through to Don. I was glad they didn't go out of town. I didn't want to be away from Glenn any more than I had to, nor from Don, for the matter. I wished Jacky would contact with me, just once, to let me know if she'd come up with any ideas. But that didn't happen either.

One day when Glenn made his daily run over to see his mother while Dad and Judy were out shopping, I decided to visit Don alone. When I reached for the door, it was locked. That was unusual; I couldn't remember anyone in town ever locking their doors. I was going to yell, but then I remembered I could get in through the back window.

When I walked around the back of the house, I could see he was sitting in that same old chair. He must have heard me, for when I opened the window to climb in, he was standing there. He waited for me to climb halfway before he asked, "What are you doing?"

I laughed, hoping he'd think it was funny, too. Fat chance. I climbed in the rest of the way. Standing in front of me was half a man. He seemed like he didn't care about anything anymore. He looked like he hadn't been to bed in days. The house looked like he'd held his own private concert. When he finished drinking a bottle of scotch or vodka, he just left it there. I walked into the kitchen and realized he hadn't been eating. It was the only room still clean.

"What are you doing here?" he demanded.

Jokingly I said, "If Mohammed couldn't come to the mountain, the mountain must come to Mohammed." Original, don't you think?

He didn't think it was funny. "Go home, Vicky," he said, with that look in his eyes.

"Oh, no, this time that's not going to work."

"Go home."

I sat down. "Not until we talk," I said, without making eye contact.

"There's nothing we need to talk about." He walked over to the door and opened it. "Here's the door. Or would you like to go out the same way you came in?"

"Now that's funny. But not until we talk."

"Sis, you're going, one way or the other."

"Not until we talk. Don, talk to me. Please don't let this go on."

He sat down across from me.

"How can you think she'd leave you? She loves you so much, and in my heart I know she'll come back. And when she does, what would she think about all of this?" I waved my hand at the mess around me.

"Why didn't she tell me?" he asked.

"Do you not believe there's a power higher than you?"

"What are you saying?"

"All I know is what she told all of us; that she had to complete her journey, and if she does, she'll be back."

"And if she can't?"

"Well, Don, then we are blessed with the time we have. She's left us with an experience that no one could ever imagine." I reached for his hand. "Look, how many girls come back to see the one they love from the other side? Consider yourself one of the lucky ones. I do. We share something. Not everyone has that opportunity. Acting like this will not help. And if she doesn't come back, you know she did everything she could. Remember what she said before she left? Being here and touching all of us was part of her quest."

I could see he was thinking about my words. I walked over to the window. "I'm leaving now," I said, and started to climb out. And finally, he smiled.

When I got outside I poked my head back in the window. "If I have anything to do with it, she'll be back."

As I walked across the street, I saw Glenn pull into the driveway.

Glenn got out of the car and stood beside it watching me approach. Before I got to him he said, "We need to talk." He knew I'd been acting kind of strange the last few weeks, I'm sure he was wondering if I was going to explain things. I'd been avoiding him until I could come up the right way to tell him.

I kissed him. "Yes, we do."

In the house I sat down at the table and he grabbed a Coke from the fridge. "Glenn, remember when I told you that Jacky needed to accomplish something so she could stay here with Don?"

"Yes, of course I remember. She needed to get married."

"Right. But I didn't tell you the whole story. Remember when I stopped breathing, and my spirit came to you? I told you I would've stayed there if I couldn't remain with you always."

"I remember."

"Well, what I didn't tell you was that I couldn't feel you that night. Sure, I felt your body, but I couldn't feel the warmth of your skin."

"I don't understand. What do you mean?" he asked.

"It's different being on the other side. Jacky said that people like her, who never had the chance to love, crave the flesh. That's why she takes over my body. She can't control herself. I don't know how to explain it. It's like when I touched you that night. I felt your body, and it was cool. It's like lying beside you and not feeling the warmth that comes from your love. You feel like you exist, but there's no one there to notice you. I would have accepted it, knowing that I'd be with you forever, but I was lucky to know what it was like for you to hold me and to feel the warmth that comes with the love we share.

"And now Jacky has a chance to feel Don for the first time. Glenn, I know what is it to be with you, to touch you and feel you hold me, but Jacky has never felt that. She was taken from Don before they ever were together. And to complete her quest, she has to find a way to feel what she had never felt in life.

"She made me promise never to tell Don what it's like for her on the other side. That's why I feel like I owe it to her. Sure, Don feels her, like you feel me, but she'll never know what we feel. She deserves to experience what it's like to be loved. If anyone ever deserved it, Jacky sure does. You know that."

He sighed. "I'm sorry, baby, I can't imagine not being without you and I know Don would never give her up. He'll wait forever for her to come back to him." He paused. "If she ever comes back."

"If she doesn't fulfill her quest, she won't."

"Just tell me what we have to do to make it right."

"This is going to sound weird but when I said Jacky craved the flesh; it means that she needs my body to be with Don."

The way he looked at me, I knew that he finally understood. "This has to be your decision, babe."

I felt really good that Glenn and I could talk about it. Sharing all of this with him made it easier for me to get on with the wedding. It made our love and trust even stronger. I knew that to do what I had to do would mean Glenn would have to live with it for the rest of his life. I said, "I love you."

"Babe, I told you I'd always be here for you, no matter how bizarre it might be. And this is bizarre." He shook his head.

We heard a car pull up the drive. I ran to the window and saw it was Dad. As always, he slammed his car door loud enough for us to hear him. He stopped and showed Judy the roses that had bloomed the night before. He always gave Glenn and I time to get ourselves together, so we could be sitting in front of the television or at the kitchen table before he came inside. Dad was pretty cool about Glenn and me. He of all people knew what it was to love again. And all who had come in contact with Jacky were blessed by knowing what real love was.

When Dad would first walk into the room it was cute how he always said something to Glenn. He'd give him a look that let Glenn know he wasn't born yesterday. Glenn was standing at the window when Dad came in. "You can sit down now," Dad said as he put the groceries on the table. Glenn smiled and took the bag out of Judy's arm.

This was Dad's house and, as much as Dad understood what love was, he was still old-fashioned and I was still his little girl. I guess it would be hard for a father to let that go on in his own house. He'd be the first person who'd encourage us, knowing that Glenn and I were meant to be together.

Glenn looked out the window and saw Don sitting on his front porch. "Whatever you said to Don today got him out of the house."

I looked out at Don, then back at Glenn, silently indicating he should go talk to Don. "Yes, dear," he said sweetly, "I'll go." He kissed me on the lips. "See you later."

Dad told Glenn to tell Don he'd better be here for dinner, or he was going over to get him himself. Glenn laughed and walked out. I sat there with a grin on my face.

Judy sat down beside me. "Well, are you going to tell me?"

I was so excited I jumped up from my seat and yelled out the date of the wedding. As always, Judy was just as excited as I was. We hugged each other and jumped up and down. I looked over at Dad. Judy nodded to go over to him. When I did, he kissed me and told me he was happy for me. I saw that one tear I always see, the one he could never hold back, roll down his face.

"Dad," I said, "now I know I don't have to answer that knock on the door, for I answered it all ready." He knew what I was talking about.

I looked toward the window and saw Glenn heading back our way. I pushed away from Dad. "Glenn wanted to be the one to tell everyone, so please don't let him know I told you."

We ran to make like we were putting away the groceries when he walked in. "I'm calling the guys," he said. "We're going to practice over at Don's today. I guess that talk worked." Then he looked at Dad. "Yes, he'll be here tonight."

"Well," Dad said, "tell all the guys to come over, there's plenty of food. Seeing Don out of the house is something to celebrate." But I knew it wasn't for Don, it was for Glenn and me.

Glenn laughed. He knew Dad didn't need a celebration to cook for everyone; he just enjoyed having everyone around.

"I'll call the girls," I said. Judy offered to call Jack and Michelle.

"I'm out of here," Glenn said. "See you all later." I knew he knew now, for when he passed me, he shook his finger at me, smiling.

Dad yelled to Judy, "Don't forget to call Ray and Ruth!"

I ran upstairs to tell Jacky. Even if I couldn't see her, I could tell her about our wedding.

When I got my room, I tried calling out to her and, as usual, there was no answer. Sitting on her bed, I couldn't help looking at all the things she had accumulated over the years. I realized that everything that meant something to her was still there, sitting right were she put it. Even things Don had thrown away were sitting up there.

I laughed; there was that ugly little eagle that looked like something a cat dragged in. She'd slept with it until he gave her something new. Then she put it up on the shelf to sit with the rest of the things he had given her.

As I walked towards the bed, I grabbed a teddy bear that Don gave her when he first left for college. I could smell the shampoo that she washed it with.

Dad yelled up that he and Judy were going to the store.

"Okay, Dad." I yelled. Since everyone was out, I decide to go riding. I threw the teddy on the bed and walked over to the closet to get my jacket. As I started to walk out, I looked towards the bed and the teddy was gone. *What?* I thought. I turned and there it was, sitting on the shelf, just were she had put it. I knew I threw it on the bed. I walked over and pulled the teddy off the shelf and threw it on the bed and stepped out of the room. I gave it a few seconds and walked back in. It was on the shelf again. *That's it,* I thought. *That's it.* I grabbed the teddy and headed for Don's house. What I had to show him would convince him that she'd be back.

As I crossed the street I saw the eagle flying above me. Now I knew I was right. Glenn and Don were sitting on the porch, waiting for Tim and Joe. I stopped when I reached the porch and looked up.

Don and Glenn stepped down from the pouch and looked up to see the eagle sitting right above us. Don smiled. He knew it was Jacky.

I showed him the teddy. "Do you remember this?"

"Yes, I sent it to her when I left for college."

"Come with me," I said. "I just figured something out."

Glenn and Don followed me across the road, into the house, and up to Jacky's room. There were all the things that Don had bought her in the last year. I put the teddy on the bed, and we left the room.

"What's going on?" Don asked.

"Come with me and I'll show you."

We went back in and there was the teddy, back up on the shelf where she'd put it, with the rest of the things she cherished. Glenn and Don couldn't believe their eyes.

As Don walked around the room, he was surprised at all the little things he'd won or given her throughout the years. They were all sitting right in front of him. Even things that he didn't have any value for were there. She had taken them out of the trash, cleaned them up, and kept them.

He laughed. "Look at this." He grabbed some old drumsticks off the shelf. "She wasn't even here when I threw these out. She must have grabbed them before the trash man showed up."

Sitting on her nightstand was the picture of us that Dad had taken at the lake. Don picked it up.

I sat beside him. "We were so young in the picture. She knew then she loved you. And that's why she never changed anything in this room. She knew she'd be going on a journey and,

if she didn't complete her quest, it would be as if she'd never come back in the first place. Even if we wanted to change this room it would always be the same until she returned. Not even Jacky can change it. She knew all along, and that's why I know she will be back."

"What makes you so sure, Vick?" Glenn asked.

I got up and walked over to the shelf. "When people die everyone packs all of their things and put them away, or they throw them out." Showing them again, I grabbed the teddy and threw it on the trash. Again we stepped out of the room and, when we returned, it was on the shelf.

"See, you can't change something that was never meant to be changed in the first place. It's like time is standing still for her, until whoever it is decides Jacky's fate. If she is meant to come back, then no matter what we do to change the teddy, it will stay as it was meant to be. If Jacky wasn't coming back, we could pack everything and time would move on.

The expression on Don's face changed from what it had looked like the last few months.

"We need to tell the others," Don said. "Michelle would want to know."

"And we will," I said, "tonight, when everyone's here." As we left the room I threw the teddy on the bed again. Don looked hesitant. I grinned. "Don't worry. She'll put it back."

I knew what Don had just seen gave him hope about Jacky. And I needed to talk to her and hoped that what I told him wouldn't backfire on me.

Don and Glenn left to meet the guys to go over the album and I went down to the barn to see The Duke.

That night at the table, Glenn got up to tell everyone about our engagement. He had rehearsed what he was going to say and, when he finished, no one made a sound. But then everybody already knew. Glenn's announcement was no surprise. Glenn stood there silent, waiting for a reaction, and everyone tried to hold back their laughter, because Glenn was never short for words.

He turned to me and said, "You told them." At that everyone cracked up.

When he sat down, I put my arms around him. "You looked so serious." He couldn't help joining the laughter.

Dad reached over and put his arms around him. "Is it a go this time?"

Glenn grinned. "It's a go."

Before dinner was over I told everyone about Jacky and took everyone up to my room to show them what was going on, and why. When they saw the teddy bear appear, and understood the reason for it, they all felt convinced that Jacky was coming back. I think Glenn and I were the only ones who weren't so sure. We knew it was up to us to make it right.

CHAPTER 30

Everything was going so great that night, we told everyone about the wedding and about Jacky. After dinner we all headed outside. The cool air felt good, considering the how hot it was during the day. What happened next threw us all for a loop. I'll never forget that night, not because of my engagement, but because of a letter that was waiting for me.

On the way out, Dad picked up the mail and brought it with him. As I sat there, a cool breeze blew by. It felt good against my face. I leaned my head back and closed my eyes to take it in. When I opened them, I noticed the eagle, sitting quietly just above us. Funny, no one else seemed to notice it, and, of course, didn't call any attention to it. Seeing it, I felt I was in for a long night.

"Vicky, there's a letter for you from someone in France," Dad said.

"Where in France?" Jack asked. Dad handed him the letter. By the look on Jack's face, it wasn't good. "It's from the prison where Jean-Luc is," he said sadly.

Glenn came over and sat beside me as I opened it. I started to read the first few lines, and then I checked the date on the envelope.

It was a letter from the priest of the prison, along with a letter from Jean-Luc, written before he had been put to death. I didn't know if I wanted to read it or just hand it over to Glenn, but I tried. The letter read

> Dear Victoria,
> My name is Father Patrick O'Donnell, the pastor of the correctional facility where I had the pleasure to spend the final days with Jean-Luc Moreau, whom I understand you knew quite well.

I couldn't go on, knowing that Jean-Luc had died for a special person. I handed the letter to Glenn. As I did, Don went to the end of the yard and stared up at the bird. Knowing it was her, I nodded to Glenn to read on.

During his final days of life, Jean-Luc told me something that was hard to believe. What he had to tell me is hard to explain, but when we took our last walk to where he would go to meet our Lord, he had a smile on his face, as though there was a higher power guiding him. Never once did I see any fright in his eyes. I don't know how to explain it, but he seemed anxious to be going. As he took his last breath, he looked to his side and lifted his hand, as though someone was there comforting him. He smiled, and with a sigh of relief, he stopped breathing. I believe, in my heart, what he told me was the truth. I, being a religious man and a human being, do have some doubt as to what is true or not, but now I can put my doubt aside. No matter how wrong what he did he was, and the hardship he caused, deep in his heart he was sorry. I have never experienced anything like this in all my years as a priest. As hard as it is to accept, I felt that you needed to know. He told me to tell you that he was entering a new chapter in his life. Thank you for your time and understanding. I hope this make some sense. God bless you all.

Sincerely, Father Patrick O'Donnell

P.S. I sent you a letter from Jean-Luc, which he wrote the morning of his death.

When Glenn read that Jean-Luc was starting a new chapter in his life, I knew that Jacky had been there at the end.

Don's eyes were fixed on the eagle. I didn't know if he was mad or sad. This person had taken Jacky away from him. He wanted revenge, but on the other hand, he felt what was in his heart. If he had been in Jean-Luc's shoes, what would he have done?

It was quiet until Michelle said, "Read it." She wanted to hear the letter from Jean-Luc. Glenn looked at me, and I nodded.

"Read it, son," Jack said. He too wanted to hear what Jean-Luc had to say.

Glenn read:

This is to all who knew her. I can't say enough how sorry I am.

I'm sorry for all the pain I caused. I know I took a perfect human being,who had so much to give, and so much forgiveness in her heart for all who came in contact with her. What hurts more than what I'm going to face in a few hours is that she forgave me for what I have done.

Michelle let out a cry. Glenn continued:

> She knew what love was, and how love could destroy your hope
> of ever getting what you want. She knew all her life she had to
> fight for the one she loved. Even now she continues to fight for
> him.

Glenn looked up at the eagle in the tree, then at Don. He knew
now more than ever that Jacky would do anything to be with Don. Glenn
went on to read:

> I loved her and always will. Vicky, you told me once how her
> love for Don could never be changed, and that it would destroy me. If
> I lived for a hundred years I would never meet anyone like her, so with
> that I look forward, as Jacky said, to the next chapter. As she sits here
> waiting to lead me to a beautiful place, I know that God forgives me,
> for Jacky forgave me a long time ago. She leads me to heaven because
> of who she is, and her understanding for love. The only thing I regret,
> Don, is not being you. I look up and see her smiling as I write. Just the
> mention of your name puts a smile on her face. I can never imagine a
> love so strong. When you came to see me after her death, you wanted
> some kind of revenge, a way to hurt me. I saw all the anger in your
> eyes. You knew then that Jacky was here, just as she was with you at
> the cemetery, but when our eyes met you knew that Jacky would never
> allow you to do anything you would regret in the long run. I don't have
> much time left. I want all of you to know she made it easier for me to
> cross over. Vicky, you were right when you said that she will never let
> me down. The guard has entered the room, and the look in his eyes tells
> me it is time. She reached for my hand when he walked over to me. I'm
> not afraid anymore. I will keep my eyes on her until I'm gone. I'm not
> afraid. I'm sorry.

After Glenn said that last word there was a silence. Don and I made
eye contact. He wasn't hurting, he was proud of her for what she had done
for Jean-Luc.

At that time I hoped Joe would come up with one of his mood-
breakers, but he was at a loss for words. Until Jacky's death, none of us
believed that this sort of thing was possible.

Ray broke the silence. "Jacky touched all our lives, and I know she
wouldn't want us to just sit here. She'd want us to celebrate Vicky and
Glenn's engagement."

Thank goodness he said that. It made us all get on with the evening.
We all felt what Jean-Luc had said. Funny, although he took Jacky from us,
we all felt sorry for him and were happy Jacky had been there all along.

I asked everyone for a minute of their time. When all eyes were on me I explained, "Jacky taught us to forgive and forget, no matter what the circumstances were. Maybe that's what she was trying to tell us that night she came back. We needed to forgive, and that's just what we did tonight."

Don walked over to the tree and looked up. The eagle didn't fly away—it vanished.

After everyone went home, Dad and Judy left with Jack and Michelle. Dad knew the letter had thrown Michelle for a loop. I think it did the same to all of us.

Glenn talked to Joe and Tim and Don sat on the steps with me. "How do you feel?" I asked him.

"I remember when I wanted to kill him. Now I don't know what to think. But I'm glad Jacky was there for him."

"Maybe this was part of Jacky's quest."

"You're probably right, sis. I'm going home. See you in the morning."

After everyone had gone I needed to tell Glenn how much he meant to me. Maybe I was a little jealous of how the letter sounded. My love for Glenn was just as strong as Jacky's love

was for Don. Maybe I'm not the kind of person that shows it as much, but I know what I'd gone through. I could never live without him.

"Something wrong, babe?" Glenn asked as we started up the stairs.

We sat on my bed, and I said, "I know this is going to sound silly, but I just want you to know I love you."

He smiled. "What's this all about?"

"I want you to know that I love you more than life itself and our love is just as strong as Jacky and Don's."

He squeezed me. "I know that. I've known that for a long time. That's what I love about you and when we get married everything will be okay. You know, babe, I knew this isn't the kind of wedding you wanted, and that you're just doing this for her, but I want you to know I understand you more than anyone here."

"I can't wait until we get married."

"Me too, babe."

We lay on the bed and he held me in his arms. We didn't do anything; it just felt good lying in his arms. Maybe that's what Glenn understood about me, just holding me made me feel wanted. I said, "Jacky, if you can hear me, I never meant anything to hurt you. But you not being here is making it hard for me to help you."

The next morning the phone rang. Glenn ran to answer it as I sat there, thinking about the night before. To us it was a normal night in our circle, but to anyone else, well, I'll let you answer that.

It was his mother, telling him his agent had called. Glenn said, "Okay, Mom, love you," and hung up. As he called his agent, I knew he'd be going out of town and with everything going on I'd have to stay.

I walked out of the room as he hung up. "You're going out of town?"

"Sorry, babe, I hate to dump all this on you, but there's no way out of it."

"That's fine. I'll handle it." I asked him if he talked to his mother about the wedding.

"No," he said, "that's been on my mind for days now."

"We need to think about that. We don't want her to see Jacky for the first time at the wedding. If she does show up there." I visualized it in my head, and laughed.

"What's so funny?" Glenn asked.

"Just thinking how your mother will respond when she sees Jacky for the first time."

"I'm glad you find that amusing."

"Sorry." I turned and left the room.

"Okay, babe, that's my mother you're talking about!" he yelled to me from the other room. With my back to him I didn't see him creep up on me. I turned and was startled into laughter.

He joined me. "That would be a sight for sore eyes," he admitted.

We were kissing when Dad and Judy came in. Glenn motioned to me that he was leaving and out the door he went before Dad had any wise remarks. "I'll be back!" he yelled from outside. "Have to tell Don about the benefit."

I was still laughing when Dad asked me what was going on. "Nothing," I said. Even Dad didn't know about our plans for Jacky.

I went outside and sat on the steps, remembering how Glenn's mother had been a big part of us as we were growing up. I remember her always being there, making sure we had breakfast, and she often walked us to school. I knew that she had to be there on the day her son got married.

At the end of the day, Glenn told me that the group was leaving in two days. The bad news was that it was going to take longer than they thought.

"Like how long?" I asked.

"We'll be back a week before the wedding."

Just then Judy came out of the kitchen. She'd heard everything. "Well, that will give us a chance to get everything finished. Not to hurt your feelings, Glenn, but you guys can't keep your hands off each other long enough for us to get the wedding organized."

I knew she just said that to make Glenn feel better about going.

After Judy left us Glenn said, "Let's take a walk." As we walked he said, "I want you to make me a promise before I go."

"Sure."

"Don was so happy about us getting married that he wanted us to do it at his house. We've been working day and night trying to get everything ready for the wedding."

I got excited. "Can I see it?"

"Not until the wedding."

I was so excited that I jumped in his arms and told him, "I wouldn't have it any other way. You know, this will be perfect for us and Jacky."

He smiled. "I thought it would. Remember, I don't want you to go over there at all. Don wants to surprise you."

"What happens if we need to get in the yard to set up?"

"I'll be home by then."

"Okay, I won't go over there."

For the next two days the band got ready to leave. I knew I'd be too busy to miss Glenn, but once again I missed out on going with him. Out of all the girlfriends of the band members, I was the only one who'd never made it on the road with the boys. Even Jacky made it, and she was dead.

CHAPTER 31

While the band was out of town, Judy, Michelle, and I did all the last minute arrangements for the wedding. I guess I could consider myself lucky for someone who hadn't had a mother growing up—I had two now. Funny, they knew more about me than I thought. When Glenn said he was sorry for leaving me stuck with all the work, he shouldn't have felt bad. I never had to lift a finger the whole time he was gone. Judy and Michelle were so excited they did everything that had to be done. Not that I dumped everything on them, but they looked forward to doing it.

They were more excited about the wedding than I was. Judy had become a big part of my life. She felt it was her responsibility to do what she did. She started planning it as soon as Glenn and I got back together again.

Then there was Michelle. She had become so much a part of my life that I could never think of doing anything without her. And deep inside, she thought Jacky would be coming back to us. All the time we were out shopping, you could tell that Jacky was on her mind. You could almost hear her say, "This would be something Jacky would wear," or "This would look good on her."

I remember the day we shopped for my dress. As I tried on one after another, I could see in Michelle's face which ones she didn't like. As I stood looking in the mirror at her, I could see she was imagining what Jacky would look like in each dress. Judy picked up on it, too.

Then I came out in a dress that I loved. When I stood in front of Michelle, I saw by her expression that she loved it, too. I turned around and looked in the mirror. I could see her behind me, watching. Her eyes filled and I knew that this dress was the one. I knew she was imagining Jacky standing in that spot.

I didn't even stop to ask her. I said, "This is it. I love it and I have to have it."

You should have seen the expression on her face. She smiled and stood up and said, "Then you shall have it."

At the counter she told the woman to put it on her charge card. All I could say was, "Thank you," and I barely got that out.

She really caught me off guard when she said, "There's nothing too good for my daughters."

My eyes filled with tears. "I think this dress would be the one she would have wanted."

As we left the store, Judy pulled me to the side. "That was a nice thing you said." I just smiled, knowing that Jacky was going to wear this dress, too. I hoped.

Then Judy said to Michelle, "Let's get something to eat." They were like two kids in a candy store, wanting to buy me the world. I looked up and whispered, "Jacky, I hope you're seeing this." I knew she did, for when I was getting in the car I saw the eagle fly by.

When we got to the restaurant I felt I had to say something about Jacky. But what? It's funny, after the night she'd appeared to us all, no one had spoken a word about her. I believed from the bottom of my heart that Jacky would be back, that she'd complete her quest and come back to us. And, if everything worked out, she'd be at the wedding as we planned. She'd come so far, and I couldn't see anything that would stop her from being with Don.

As we waited for the waiter, Michelle brought up the evening wedding. "I have to say, Vicky, that sounds so romantic. Did you and Glenn decide on that?"

"As a matter of fact, it was Jacky's and my dream to have a double wedding. We talked about how romantic it would be to have it as the sun went down and the stars came out. We also imagined just what we were going to wear."

Michelle looked up. "And the dress?"

"Yes, we planned on wearing the same dress on the same day. That's why I decided on the one we just got. She also knew just who we were both going to marry. She always said Glenn was the man for me."

"Well, she was right," Michelle said.

"That's why I think she'll be back." I think that's what Michelle needed to hear. She wanted to be reassured that I believed Jacky would come back one day. It made it easier for her to get through the days.

I still hadn't heard from Jacky. Every night I called her name before I fell asleep, hoping she'd give me a sign that she was definitely going to be there, as we planned. When the boys came home, Glenn asked me if I'd heard from her. I told him no, but I was sure that somehow she'd be there.

Dad and Jack threw Glenn a bachelor party, to be held at Jack's house. Joe had a surprise for Glenn, as I found out that night. Of course, we women were not invited.

That night I stayed home, hoping to hear from Jacky. Judy, Michelle, and Ruth did last minute shopping. I don't know why I didn't hear from Donna or Jehane. Maybe they were all shopping too. It was about seven and I was making sure I had everything I needed for the next day. I didn't want to be running around like a chicken with its head cut off. Afterwards I took a long hot shower, threw a movie on, and was ready to just relax. As Judy would say, get my beauty rest. I did want to look great for my wedding.

I turned off the lights and got comfortable on the couch, knowing that if I fell asleep, Dad would throw a blanket over me and let me sleep till morning. The house seemed so quiet and the only light came from the television.

As I was getting into the mood, I felt a breeze. I thought it was just my imagination, considering the window was open and the movie I had on. I didn't give it a second thought. I should have known better.

Just as I covered my eyes, knowing what was going to happen in the next scene, in a flash of light, she appeared right in front of the TV. I screamed and jumped about three feet off the couch, my heart beating like a drum. "What?" I yelled, as loud as I could. "Jacky, you scared the crap out of me!" She laughed. As the blood started to circulate thought my body again I joined her.

"You should have seen you face," she said.

"Could you have made a better entry?" I yelled.

"Just looking at your face made it worth it."

I sat there for a bit trying to get my heart to slow down, when Jacky said, "Let's have some fun." I knew by the way she'd made her entrance that she was up to her old tricks.

"Not until I know if you'll be staying this time. And if so, we need to know what to do before the night is over."

"I'm going to fulfill my dream and be here for Don forever," she told me. She sat there for about an hour, telling me how strong her powers were now. Then we came up with a plan and how we were going to carry it out. She said, "If the guys can have fun, why can't we? Why are you sitting all alone?"

I could see our talk was over. When she got mischievous there was no way she'd sit still until she did something that got me in trouble. "Okay, Jacky, what do you want to do?" I asked. My plans to get my beauty sleep had flown out the window.

"Let's call Jehane and Donna."

By that time I, too, was ready to go and, as usual, felt like doing something crazy. I called Jehane first and told her to come over and to stop and pick up Donna. Jacky was in the background, whispering for me not to tell them she was there.

"Be there in a few minutes," Jehane said.

I hung up and told Jacky that when they got there I didn't want her scaring them like she had scared me. She laughed and said she wouldn't, but I knew better.

When they got there, Jehane had a bag in her hand. "If they're going to "paaarrrty," so are we." She walked in the kitchen and pulled out a bottle of rum and two bottles of Pina Colada mix. Even though she went to the best school in France, she always talked about how she wanted to be a bartender in the States. Go figure. She knew that Pina Coladas were my drink of choice. I wasn't a drinker, but I could suck that drink down in a heartbeat. It was like drinking ice cream floats, at least until I tried to get up from the chair.

I sat down at the table and Donna decided to make popcorn. I don't know why, but she loved that stuff. She put the corn in the microwave and turned back to me. Then all of a sudden, BANG! The popcorn exploded. She jumped from one end of the room to the other. "How did that happen?" she gasped, as she held her chest.

When Jehane grabbed the blender and turned it on, it stopped. She opened the lid to see what the problem was. SPLASH! On it went. Donna and I laughed. Jehane was a mess and I knew who was behind it.

I ran down the hall to the bathroom, went inside, and closed the door. I turned around, and there was Jacky, sitting on the throne.

"How do you kill a ghost?" I asked.

"Why?" She snickered.

"Because when she finds out, you're going to die."

Suddenly the door was pushed open and standing there were Jehane and Donna. This time Jacky was caught off guard. "You little witch!" Jehane yelled and ran toward her; but Jacky was gone. I couldn't get off the floor I was laughing so hard.

Then we heard a voice coming from the kitchen. "In here!" we heard Jacky yell.

We ran down the hall and, sitting at the table with a Pina Colada in her hand, was Jacky. "Well, are you going to join me?"

Jehane walked behind Jacky and said, "I better clean this up, before Judy comes home." Taking Jacky off guard again, she grabbed the blender off the counter and poured it on top of Jacky's head. At the same time Donna started to throw popcorn at us.

"Now that's funny!" Jehane yelled. We all laughed, until right in front of us, we saw Jacky's hair and clothes starting to dry. We stopped laughing and watched. When it was dry, Jacky reappeared fully. Jokingly she said, "Being a ghost has its advantages."

As she was telling us what went on the doorbell rang. Jehane had ordered a pizza while Jacky was gone, and we all ran for our money.

We watched from the window. She never opened the door, but appeared behind the deliveryman. She tapped him on the shoulder and snuck some money into his pocket without him seeing. When he turned around she was all in white, like a typical ghost. Well, she was! He dropped the pizza, ran to his car, and drove off.

Before the pizza hit the ground Jacky grabbed it, yelling, "Pizza's here!"

We all went into the kitchen and ate and drank ourselves into a coma. I wondered if Jacky could get drunk, but I'm sure just being there was enough to make her feel as if she did.

CHAPTER 32

I don't know what time it was or how much we drank. . When I opened my eyes, Glenn and Dad were looking down at me. I couldn't lift my head. It felt like someone had hit me in the back of the head with a bat. I looked to my side without moving my head, and there were Donna and Jehane lying on the other side of the room on the floor. Judy told them to go upstairs and get some sleep.

Jehane asked, "What happened?"

I wondered if I looked as bad as they did. Then slowly I got up and leaned against the chair. The room started to spin. "Oh, no," I moaned, holding my head, "I don't feel too good." Glenn was grinning from ear to ear. "What's so funny?" I whispered.

He leaned over me as if he was going to whisper. Then loud and clear he yelled, "For someone who's getting married today you don't look so good!" Dad smiled and left. "I see you guys had a great time last night," Glenn said.

Judy came back in the room. "Glenn, you've got to go. You're not supposed to see the bride before the wedding."

In a loud voice he yelled, "I wouldn't have missed this for the world!"

"Please, don't yell," I begged.

Judy told him to go home. As he left the room he yelled back, "I'll see you later!" I remember thinking how I could kill him in his sleep.

Judy helped me upstairs to my room. "Get some sleep," she said, "you need all the rest you can get." I was glad we'd planned the wedding for late in the day. If I'd had to get ready right then, believe me, I would have called it off.

As soon as my head hit the pillow I was out like a light. I was at that place I loved so much. I loved being there, especially now; I felt great, no hangover, no motion sickness. As always, time stood still.

She was sitting in a field near a pond. "Jacky," I said. When I spoke her name, in a flash I was right beside her.

She was looking down. "What's wrong?" I asked. She looked up, and there were tears in her eyes. "Talk to me," I said. "Why are you so sad, especially on a day we've been looking forward to for such a long time?"

"That's it, Vicky," she said. "I'm so happy, I can't believe it's finally happening."

I put my arm around her and we just sat there not speaking. A few minutes passed, when we must have thought of the same thing at the same time. "Are you thinking what I'm thinking?" she asked.

"Don doesn't have a clue what to expect tonight," I said. "For that matter, neither does Glenn. I never told him." We laughed.

I got up. "I better get back, or I'll never be ready for tonight. Jacky, is this the last of your quest?"

She smiled. "Yes. If tonight goes well and Don is ready to give up his way of life as he lives it now, then my quest will be completed and I'll be with you and Don again."

"Look, Don is happy to just be with you. I know he'd never want to spend his life any other way. Of that I'm sure." I leaned over her and kissed her.

"What's that for?" she asked.

"Just for being who you are."

As I went down the hill she yelled, "Are you ready for the next chapter in our lives?"

"What do you think?" I yelled back.

I awoke to Judy shaking me. "Time to get ready," she said.

I felt good for some reason. I didn't feel like I'd been run over by a train. I jumped up out of bed and ran into the bathroom and took a hot shower. I was so excited about tonight, more for Jacky than myself. It was Don and Jacky's turn to be happy.

Jehane and Donna came in the room when I came out of the shower. I prepared them for what was going to happen. I told them all about how Jacky was going to be there, and that she was going to complete her quest. I told them how she was going to marry Don at the same time that Glenn and I were being married.

They had a lot of questions, and I had to answer them all. They seemed so happy, and couldn't wait till they saw Jacky again.

"Just remember, girls," I warned them, "Don doesn't know."

Judy and Michelle were there to help me get ready. I felt like a princess, with everyone at my beck and call. I could have never done it without them. The men across the street were helping Don, checking on the last details. Glenn called a few times, but no one would let me talk to him. They didn't understand why, only that the groom could not see or talk to the bride before the wedding.

I kept looking across the street, hoping there were no reporters hanging around. We had gotten this far without letting anyone know what the band was up to. Doing the benefit had helped keep the press at bay; for all they knew the band had just got back and were resting. But you can never tell with a small town like ours.

When everyone left to go over to Don's house, Jehane and Donna and I waited for Judy to call. That would be our cue that everything was ready.

We were standing by the phone, when Jehane looked like she had seen a ghost. Donna and I turned around and Jacky was standing there in a dress exactly like mine. She looked divine, her long hair flowing down her back, with a wreath of flowers on the crown of her head. It was like Jehane and Donna were seeing the dress for the first time. "Okay, guys," I said, "I have the same dress on."

Jehane pointed at the mirror. "LOOK! Turn around and LOOK! Jacky and I turned around and stood side by side. "You guys look just like real sisters," Jehane said.

There was nothing to say. We did look just like real sisters. You could never tell that we had different parents. I guess the truth is, we did have the same parents. The phone rang and Jehane answered it. "We'll be right over."

I turned to Jacky. "Are you ready?"

She hesitated. "Before we go, I need to tell you something."

I really didn't want to hear what she was going to say, afraid it might be that if things didn't work out I would never see her again. I'd forgotten that she knew what I was thinking.   "No, Vicky," she said, "I just want to tell you that all my life you've been there for me. When I was sad, you cheered me up, when I needed something you got it for me; and when I missed Don, you talked to me till I fell asleep. I could never imagine you not being there for me. Even in death you're here."

"Jacky . . ."

She stopped me. "This is your wedding day and still you put aside your needs for me, so I can complete my quest."

I took her hand, knowing she could not feel my flesh. "We share something no one could ever understand. If you weren't here, I know I could have never gotten on with my life. So when you say I put aside my life for you, you're wrong. After your death I didn't want to go on. You helped me when I needed you the most. You have a wisdom that no one could ever experience. That's what you gave all of us."

Donna and Jehane came over to Jacky and me, and we all hugged. Jacky had tears in her eyes.

I took a deep breath. "Are you ready, Jacky?" She nodded. We took two steps toward each other and became one.

Jehane gasped. "That is so cool!"

We left the house, and I could feel Jacky getting excited. In my mind I heard her say, *This is it, this is it!*

"If you don't settle down," I said out loud, "we'll never get through this."

When we got to the front steps Dad was there to meet us. "Are you ready?"

"Dad," I whispered, "Jacky is here with me." He looked puzzled. "I can't explain it right now," I said, "but can you ask Jack if he'd walk down with us?"

"Of course." He motioned to Jack to come outside.

I could see Jack wanted an explanation.

"Jack," I said, "I'd like to have both my fathers with me when I walk down that aisle." He was so emotional he couldn't speak. I took his hand and Dad's hand and we walked together.

I could see Glenn and Don standing there. They were so handsome, not in their usual rock-band blue jeans and T-shirts, but in tuxedos. They were to die for.

You can say that again, Jacky said. *Thank goodness none of their fans are here.*

When we got to altar Jack kissed me. "Thank you," he said, then went to his seat.

Dad leaned over to kiss me, and whispered, "I don't know what you girls are up to, but I guess I'll know soon."

I looked around the yard. There weren't any words to describe it. I don't know if the word beautiful was close.

"Do you like it?" Don asked.

"It's like you reached inside my dreams."

"Between Glenn and me, we thought of all the things we heard

Jacky and you talk about when you were kids. As funny as it was at the time, we never knew it would come in handy one day."

Of course Jacky could hear Don talking, and she couldn't wait to come out and let him know she was there.

I didn't hear the priest ask if I was ready. Then I heard Glenn say, "Can you give us a minute?"

The smell coming from the flowers was so intoxicating. I closed my eyes and remembered the flowers that Jacky would bring in the house in the spring, when everything was in bloom. The house would smell just like it did right now. She loved roses and there were over a thousand roses here, in every color. My favorites were the white ones. The color seemed innocent. Without thinking I said aloud, "Jacky, can you believe this? I don't know where they got them all; there was only one flower shop in town."

I didn't think there were that many flowers in the world, she said in my mind and I laughed.

"What's so funny?" Don asked.

"I'll tell you later."

"Now, are you ready?" the priest asked again.

I asked Glenn to have Don stand on the other side of me. The priest must have thought I was just as crazy as the band's reputation. When Don stood beside me I took his hand, and told the priest, "We're ready."

As he opened his book he was looking at my hands, wondering why I was holding Don's. I smiled at him. I felt a light squeeze from Glenn. He looked down at me and I knew he knew that Jacky was one with me.

Feed off my power, she said, *you did it before and you can do it again. I'll help you.*

All of a sudden I felt energy flow though my body. She was right; her powers were as strong as they'd ever been. *It's time to let everyone see you*, I told her. Of course, I meant just our inner circle.

I stepped aside, and she appeared. First she turned to Don. He was so mesmerized he was at a loss for words.

As the priest talked I could hear the whispering behind us. I looked around. I saw from their faces that they were entranced by her, too. I heard a faint cry from Michelle. I felt the love the two of them had come to share. They smiled at each other. Jack was trying to hold his emotions, like all the guys in the yard.

Then the priest said, "Glenn, would you like to say your vows to Victoria?"

I knew he was nervous, the way he was squeezing my hand. As he started to speak I thought, *Here's a man who can stand in a stadium in front of thousands and sing his heart out, but now he's holding on to me for support.*

His voice, which sounded so confident when he sang, cracked as he spoke. Feeling him squeeze my hand made me realize that he needed me and loved me. "I thought I had it all," he said, "but all the fame and all the money could never give me the happiness that we have. And when I almost lost that, I knew my life was not worth living without you. We experience the kind of love that could never be explained in this lifetime. So, Vicky, will you stay with me now and into eternity?"

I opened my mouth, but nothing came out. I didn't need words to let him know I loved him. I tried again and again but nothing came out. He put his finger on my lips like he always did, telling me he didn't need words to let him know that I loved him and would be his wife. I smiled. Jacky was crying tears of joy for us.

"Well," the priest said, "I'll take that as a yes."

Everyone laughed. Then he said, "Victoria, would you like to say something to Glenn?"

Holding on to Glenn, I started to cry. *Oh,* I thought, *I'm a blubbering idiot.*

I felt a hand on my shoulder. It was Jacky, reassuring me that she was there. At that, the words came. "Glenn, I don't know what to say, but I know that I love you. When I came back that night, I knew I'd be with you no matter what I had to give up. When I listened to your vows, you said it for both of us. So will you marry me?"

He answered immediately, "Yes." Then he looked back at his mother, and they smiled at each other. I knew she was proud of him; she had always been. I also knew Glenn was feeling bad that she could not be a part of our inner circle.

But Jacky knew what to do. She stopped time as we know it. Glenn's mother had a tear on her cheek, and it stopped rolling down her face. There was a bird flying just above her, and it seemed to be frozen in the air. The crowd never stirred. It was like seconds were minutes. But some things were moving, and our inner circle saw everything.

Don's face split in a wide grin; he always got a kick out of the things Jacky could do. I nodded to let her know it was time for her to read her vows, or tell Don what he needed to know.

She turned to our inner circle, and said, "The night I came to you I was on a journey. I had to prove that being here made a difference in your lives. By the looks on all your faces I know I've completed my journey to this point."

She turned back to Don. "You are my quest. My love for you is what made it possible for me to come back after I died." She hesitated and looked at me for reassurance. *Go ahead*, I told her in my mind, *you've come this far.*

"Jacky," Don urged, "go ahead, tell me what you have to say."

She forgot he was able to read her mind, and blurted out, "Don, will you marry me?"

All you could hear was the gasp that came from behind us, and the faint sob coming from Michelle.

"Yes," he said. "Did you think I was going to say no?"

But she still had to tell him more and he sensed it. "What's wrong? What do you have to say?"

"Don, it's not that easy."

He took her hand. "Now it's easy."

She tried to smile, but she knew what Don had to give up to stay with her.

"Jacky," he insisted.

"Don, if you do marry me, it will be you who gives up so much. Before you answer, I need to tell you that I don't know how long I have to spend with you, or how short our time together will be. But if you say yes, you will never have a chance to marry anyone else, if I have to leave." She paused for a second. "You will never be able to marry or have children to make you happy and I will never be able to show myself to anyone other than our friends and families. So before you say anything, realize that, if you say no, I will understand. I would never do anything that would deprive you of having a happy life."

Don looked at Glenn, then at Dad, as if he wanted someone to reassure him that if he didn't marry Jacky it would be okay. But only he could make that decision.

There was a moment of silence. I remember thinking that Dad would never have a grandchild from Don, nor could he or anyone here tell anyone about his daughter-in law.

Everyone stared at Don, waiting for an answer. The look on Jacky's face was the same one she had when she was a little girl, waiting for Don to say something that was going to make everything all better.

All eyes were on Don. He took a deep breath and said, "Jacky, no matter how long we have to share together, it will be enough time to make me happy. Knowing you and the love you have is enough to hold me through thousands of lifetimes. If you have to go, all of us here know that it will be just for a short time, for when it's my time to go, I know you'll be there when I arrive. And we'll start our lives all over again, knowing that there will never be anyone who

could come between us." He grinned. "And for the children . . ." He chuckled and looked at Glenn and me. Everyone laughed. Then he took Jacky in his arms and said, "I will marry you."

She cried in his arms and told him that she felt like she'd never died, that life with him made everything that happened to her go away.

Glenn nodded to Don to tell her his vows, which he longed to say. He released her from his arms and said, "Jacky, you are my angel. Until now I never realized that you were always here beside me, all my life. Being with you makes up for all the things that anyone could want. Like all people, we never know what we have until it is gone, but God gave us a second chance. For however long we have to be together, we will be as one. So yes, I will marry you."

In the blink of an eye, time started again. Jacky was gone, and we heard the priest say, "I now pronounce you husband and wife. You may kiss the bride."

Everyone ran up to congratulate us. The priest told Dad he was sorry he couldn't stay around, but he had another engagement. That's when Jacky appeared right in front of Jack.

"Daddy," she said. That was the first time I heard her call him Daddy.

"My little girl is married," he said.

"Yes, Daddy, your little girl is married." She walked over to Michelle and said, "Mother, I'm home and I will always be with you."

Michelle hugged her and they cried together. Dad walked over, and she threw her arms around him.

Dad had tears in his eyes. "I love you," he said.

She returned by saying, "I missed you, Daddy."

All our friends gathered around us to congratulate us. As the night began, Glenn and I noticed Jacky walking over to Glenn's mother. With everything going on, it kind of slipped our minds that Glenn's mother was still in the dark about her.

The yard became silent as all eyes turned toward her. Before anyone could stop Jacky, she was standing beside her. Glenn and I ran over, knowing that Jacky would never hurt her by showing herself. She looked down at her and sat down. I looked over at Glenn, but it was as if he hoped that his mother could see her.

All of a sudden his mother turned and in a calm voice said to her, "That was a beautiful wedding, dear."

"I had my fingers crossed, you know," she continued. Then she leaned over and kissed Jacky on the cheek. "You know, dear, I'm still up at night if you need to come and talk. I'll always have your favorite cookie waiting."

We were all startled. Glenn's mother knew more than we thought. Glenn knelt in front of her. "Fine son you are," she said.

"I was afraid to tell you, Mom."

"I know, dear. Jacky filled me in on everything. But you've got to admit, it is kind of weird."

Jacky smiled at Glenn and said, "You didn't think that the cookies were for you, did you?" Everyone laughed. He reached up and kissed her. She whispered, "She's been a mother to all of us, you know." Our inner circle was complete.

CHAPTER 33

Sitting there in the yard, looking up at the sky, I felt that among all the stars shining, Jacky and I were the brightest of all. All my friends would remember this day, not just because of the wedding, but also because of how our lives had changed. If not for a freak accident we'd never have known what life was truly about.

As I watched everyone enjoying this special day, I saw more evidence of how much our lives had changed since Jacky's return. She was right when she spoke of the differences she made in our lives, as we continued to learn from one another. We knew, no matter where our paths might lead, we'd always be part of each other. We'd been through so many changes together.

Tim and Donna were no longer afraid to commit to one another. Seeing Ray and Ruth taught us it's possible to grow more in love with each passing day. Then there was Jack and

Michelle. From them we learned that time does control everything. We also found that, if we believed in one another, we could all get through life.

Suddenly I heard a loud laugh where Joe and Jehane were standing. I knew laughter was part of growing, and that without it we could never get over the hardships that might cross our paths in everyday life. Joe reminded us of that important fact every moment he was around. And what can I say about Dad and Judy? Both of them showed Jacky and me that you never have to grow old and that you're just as young as you let yourself be. And let's not forget Glenn, the man I love more than life itself. He found out that if you think you have it all, love can always make life better.

Lastly, there was Don. He learned that getting to the top didn't mean forgetting to stop and smell the roses. I think inside he always felt there was something special about Jacky. He always cared for her more than he probably should have, or than anyone might have thought. He taught us all that taking the straight and narrow path would always get you where you wanted to go, but it didn't hurt to take a few curves along the way to enjoy the little things in life.

As for me, I learned the most. I learned from an insecure little girl how to never give up trying to obtain what you want out of life. I guess we could look at it as if Jacky was a guardian angel for all of us.

I felt a tap on my shoulder and when I turned around Don sat down. "Are you happy, sis?" he asked.

"Yes, and you?"

"I've never been as happy as I am right now. I want you to know that without you none of this could have been possible. I don't say it enough, but thank you."

I started to cry, and threw my arms around him. "Don, you don't know how long I've waited to hear that. I've missed you so much. I thought I lost you a long time ago."

He patted me on the back. "Look, sis," he whispered, "I know I've been a jerk for a long time. I know I haven't acted like a brother. But you have to know that I love you very much. I promise I'm going to start acting like a big brother, instead of the other way around."

He looked over at Jacky. "I love her so much," he said.

"I know. I think you always did." When I said that, his face lit up. "Go over and be with your wife."

As he walked away he had the look a child gets when he first opens his presents on Christmas Day, receiving all he wished for. I knew he'd always be my big brother, and that I'd always be there for him, at least until the day he joined Jacky in the next life.

When he finally got to Jacky it was as if they were seeing each other for the first time. He put his arms around her and held her as if she were a rare rose, being careful to not squeeze too hard so as not to damage it.

As the evening came to a close, Joe yelled, "Can I get everyone's attention? I think the last dance should be for the newlyweds." Jacky and I looked at each other at the same time when he said "newlyweds."

Glenn took my hand and Don took Jacky's. We walked to the middle of the yard. As Glenn held me, it was like the moon eclipsing the sun. He told me he loved me over and over again, wrapping his arms around me, holding me tight. He reassured me that whatever I decided he'd be there for me. It went without saying I needed that right then. As always, Glenn knew what I needed.

Seeing Don and Jacky so happy, I knew that no matter what I was feeling, I owed it to them. I closed my eyes and let Glenn take control. Suddenly I heard whispering from everyone. They were looking at Jacky and Don.

Being the jokester she was, she had levitated herself and Don. I looked down and they were floating a few inches off the ground. Don didn't realize it until he saw us staring at him. He smiled like he always did at Jacky's tricks.

Then Jacky looked at Glenn and me and suddenly we were off the ground, too.

I didn't realize everyone was leaving until I saw Dad walking Glenn's mother into the house. He nodded and whispered, "Good night." It was funny how our inner circle seemed to know what we wanted without any questions or explanations. Maybe everything we learned made us more receptive to one another.

It seemed that we danced the night away. We didn't want the night to end.

Finally I felt my feet touch the ground, and heard Jacky reaching inside my head. *Vicky, are you ready?"*

Don knew what was going on. He reassured me with a smile. Glenn and I went into the house. We never said good night. It was like we were all in a trance, knowing what the other was thinking. I thought I'd be nervous, but I wasn't. I can't explain why, but we could hear each other's thoughts.

As we went down the hall to our room I was not apprehensive about it being our first time as man and wife. It seemed time had slowed down; with each step evenly place. It was as if we were going though the motions. I remember walking down the hall, into the bedroom. I remember walking into the bathroom to change; pulling off my dress and placing it on a hanger, then on the hook above the door, noticing every detail. I noticed the stain that came from the grass when I walked in the yard. I noticed the tile on the bathroom floor was cracked. As I grabbed my brush to comb my hair, with each stroke I could feel the bristles as it combed from my head down to my waist. In the mirror I saw Jacky looking back at me. "Everything is going to be fine," she whispered. Then she was gone.

I put the brush down and stood there, knowing what I had to do. I was not afraid, nor did I feel uncomfortable about it. I walked out of the bathroom, Glenn was sitting up in bed. As I slowly approached he reached over and turned out the light. As I laid there waiting to what was to come,

I felt my soul slowly become one with his, as my body became one with her. Jacky was with Don.

When Glenn and my soul became on, we felt something that no one would never feel in there live time. We felt what love was all about from deep down inside of our souls. It made me feel warm, soothing, and secure. But most of all, I felt loved.

It was 4 in the morning when I looked up to see Jacky standing at the foot of the bed. It was time. I felt myself leaving Glenn body, and just before we separated I told him "I will never forget this night."

"Neither will I," he reply. "I love you, babe."

I was fully back in my body when I heard myself say, "I love you, too." Jacky was gone, and Glenn rolled over and wrapped his arms around me, then closed his eyes.

I don't know why, but as I lay there I felt everything that Jacky had felt being with Don. When I was one with Glenn, Jacky was completing her quest. She has stopped time, like always. This time, however, she made it seem like a lifetime. She was able to feel Don's flesh, and the warmth that came with being in love.

I vaguely recall how Don apologized over and over again that she wasn't able to feel the warmth of his flesh, but he was going to make sure that this night would last a lifetime, until they were able to join each other in the next life. Again he was her teacher.

The next morning, I could hear Jacky calling out to me. I closed my eyes and saw her sitting beside Don as he slept. *Meet me outside,* she said.

Reaching for my robe, I leaned over Glenn and kissed him on the lips, knowing I'd be waking up to him the rest of my life. My dream had come true. He mumbled, "I love you," as he fell back to sleep.

The birds were singing as the sun try to break through the sky. It was going to a wonderful day. Jacky was still running and jumping around the yard like a little girl. She yelled, "Oh, my goodness, I never knew this would even be a possibility."

"Jacky, keep it down," I said.

We both laughed. When she died, no one expected her to return, but we were certainly not your typical family. We'd been thriving on the extraordinary, so whatever she experienced, we were happy for her. I yelled to her, "Come in the house, Jacky."

"You're a party pooper," she yelled. Her laugh told me she was up to no good. I was getting better at reading her. It must have been an effect from allowing her to join my body so many times.

"Jacky!" I yelled, but before I could react, the sprinklers came on in the yard while I was standing right in the middle. "Turn them off now!" I screamed. I looked up to see Don and Glenn standing in the doorway, and across the street, standing in the yard, were Judy and Dad. They were all laughing uncontrollably. Don wiped tears from his eyes as I walked past him. "Do you need a towel?" he said with a grin.

"Ha, ha, we'll see who laughs at breakfast."

He yelled for Jacky to come in the house. As she passed us with a smirk on her face, you could see she was drying off.

"Real funny," I said.

We heard Dad yell, "You coming over for breakfast?"

"Be right there!" Don shouted.

As I was changing, Jacky appeared in my room. Now I was feeling mischievous myself. "Jacky," I said, "I was thinking, maybe you should tell everyone about last night at breakfast. I'm sure everyone would love to know everything." She was so excited that she wanted to run over and tell Dad and Judy first. "Oh, no," I said, "Dad is making his famous pancakes. Besides, why not wait for everyone to arrive?"

"Speaking of the devil," she said. I could see Judy and Dad going in the house. We ran across the street, yelling to Don that we'd meet them there. Jacky was so excited she couldn't wait to get there. Entering the house we ran into the kitchen, tripping over ourselves.

"You could never tell you two just got married," Jack said.

We sat down at the table waiting for everyone to get there. Tim came in first with Donna and right behind them were Joe and Jehane. "Honey, I'm home," Joe said as he walked into the kitchen. We all got a kick out of it. And behind him came Don and Glenn.

"Hurry up, Don," Jacky yelled from the kitchen. "I've got something to tell everyone." She fidgeted in her seat like a child that couldn't keep a secret.

As Don came in, I pointed to the seat next to me. "Sit here," I said. "Jacky has some wonderful news to tell everyone." I turned to her. "We're all here, Jacky, go ahead and tell everyone what you want to share."

Don was smiling, excited to hear what Jacky had to say. "Oh, Don, wait until Jacky tells everyone the good news," I said. He had no idea what was coming. The look on his face was priceless.

She began explaining what Don and she had done the night before, blurting out intimate detail after intimate detail, never stopping to take a breath. Everyone's eyes were glued to her as she spoke. Don, completely red-faced by now, was unable to stop her.

I said, "Don, that's funny, don't you think?" I tried not to laugh. He rose to his feet and sternly asked Jacky to come in the other room so he could talk to her.

We all tried to hold back the laughter until they left and as soon as they went through the door everyone broke loose. Of course we were all were glad that Jacky had been able to experience love, no matter how awkward it was for us to hear the details.

Glenn grinned at me. "He's going to kill you."

"Yes," I said primly, "but it was worth it."

I'll never forget that day. It was as if last two years of pain never existed.

CHAPTER 34

As time passed, we all got on with our lives. Glenn and I live in Dad's house. Jacky had fulfilled her quest, and got to stay. She and Don set up house across the street. After a few months, Jehane and Joe got married and not long after that Tim and Donna did the same. Maybe we started a trend, or maybe they saw how happy we were.

After a few months passed, I got the shock of my life. With all I'd been through, I still wasn't prepared for what was ahead.

When everything settled down, I got back to riding again. The Duke was getting old, and I tried to spend more time down at the barn. I was so wrapped up in everybody's weddings and Jacky that I hadn't seen The Duke in weeks. But one day stood out in my mind.

The group was rehearsing at Don's. Jacky didn't come with me that day, but I knew what she was doing. Every few days she'd go off on her own. We all knew she was visiting the hospitals on errands like she'd done that day with Myra. Don or I would go with her sometimes, but on this day she asked to go alone. We understood.

As I was driving home from the barn, and before I turned into the drive, I saw Jacky leaving the house. She was visiting Dad. This was normal enough. But the expression on her face got me worried.

That night we were having dinner with Jacky and Don, which we did often. Jacky didn't cook, she never learned. But, like Dad, Don enjoyed cooking. Like Dad with his famous pancakes, Dad was getting good about cooking chili.

After dinner we sat outside on the porch and just enjoyed the quiet of the night. Then I took, not only Jacky, but Glenn and Don, off guard. I asked her if I could become one with her. She jumped at the chance. This was one more chance for her to feel Don's touch, even if it was just sitting beside him. Don was excited, too.

As we stood and took one step together, our bodies became one. She took me to that place I enjoyed, where there was no time. I asked her about the expression she'd had on her face earlier that day, when she was coming out of the house.

She looked at me with that look in her eyes, the one she had when she didn't want to tell you something she knew could hurt you.

Jacky, I insisted, *you have to tell me what's wrong.*

She blinked. *Dad is dying.*

I wanted to cry. Jacky went on, *When he went to the doctor for his yearly check-up, he found out he had cancer. He told me he knew I'd find out about his illness sooner or later. He said, "This time you're here to comfort me." I didn't cry, because I know he's going to a good place. I'm happy for him; he'll be with Mother. When I told him about Mother you could see the expression on his face change, he was excited about going, and he knew he'd never be alone. He told me, 'You're always being my little angel.'"*

I started to cry, and that's when she left my body. I was back on the porch standing there crying.

"What wrong?" Glenn asked, putting his arm around me and looking at Jacky. She didn't say anything, just smiled at him.

"Jacky," Don said in a low voice, "What's going on?" It wasn't like Don not to know, but this time she'd held it from him.

I watched her look at him, and then he sat down heavily. From the look on his face, he now knew.

"What's going on?" Glenn demanded. Jacky, still standing at the end of the porch, came to Glenn and stood beside him, still not speaking.

"Jacky," Don said firmly. He wanted to hear from her own mouth that everything was going to be okay.

Finally she said, "Dad has cancer. He's dying."

Glenn was stunned. "How long does he have?"

"In one year he will die." She smiled.

"How can you smile?" Don asked angrily.

"Because your mother told me." We all looked at each other.

She walked to the middle of the porch and asked us all to stand together. She took Glenn and Don's hands, and I reached out and took their hands too, and instantly we were standing in my favorite place again.

Don had been there many times, but Glenn was amazed. "So this is the place where you and Jacky come in your dreams." He turned to me.

"Yes, Vicky, I know where you are when you're asleep and you smile. When you talk about your favorite place I know you and Jacky are here."

As we stood there a woman appeared. I was stunned. I looked just like her. She was beautiful, my age, with dark brown hair down her back. Her skin was olive and her smile . . . I don't know, but when I looked at her, I wanted to run to her and let her hold me. I knew who she was. I looked at Jacky and she smiled. It was Mother.

She was far from me, but like always, all I had to do was to imagine myself beside her, and there I was. She sat down and I leaned over her. She wrapped her arms around me. All the pain of the last few years was gone. All I remembered were the happy things that had happened in my life. She made me feel wanted and safe. She made me feel like no matter what I did or will do, there was someone there to tell me she was behind me all the way. She made me feel that special kind of love a mother and child receive when she carries that child for nine months. I felt the bond you receive when you enter world, and the love that can never be broken, no matter what obstacles.

"You remember the bond we had when I carried you in my body?" she asked.

"Yes, Mother, I do."

"As time went by it was harder for you to remember. Victoria, never grow up, always be a child at heart." She turned to look at Jacky. I followed her gaze and saw that she was right. Jacky had remained a little girl at heart, and that's why she was able to come back to us.

I started to cry.

"Why are you crying when you should be happy?" Mother asked.

"Dad is dying," I sobbed.

"Yes, baby, and when he does he'll come here to this special place and I'll be waiting for him. There will be no more pain." When she said that, my tears stopped. "That's what I want to see," she said. I smiled, and she said, "See, Victoria, you remember."

Don appeared beside us. She reached out her arms to him. He stepped toward her, and they became one. "My little boy is a man now," she said.

He cried just like he did when he was a little boy. "I miss you so much."

"I know Donny, but I'm always there with you. I'm happy you've finally realized that you always loved Jacky, even when you were young. You just needed a little push."

He looked at her. "You mean?"

"You and Jacky were meant to be together from the day you were born. You never realized it until she died, and yes, that's why she died. You two had a love that had to be fulfilled. She always knew what her life would be, and when she cried at night and you went to her, she could never tell you. But you made her forget for a bit."

Suddenly he was standing besides Jacky, holding her hand.

Mother waved at Glenn to come over and he was instantly standing beside me. "Mother," I said shyly, "this is Glenn."

She smiled. "He's so much like your father. He, too, never knew." She turned to Glenn. "I can remember you telling Victoria that one day she'd be old enough for you. You never realized she was your destiny. And with a little push you realized she was your soul mate." She put her arm around him. "You have a good heart, Glenn. Mike always knew that one day you'd be walking our little girl down the aisle. You were always a son to him."

She started to fade. "Take care of my baby."

I yelled, "Don't go, Mother!"

"Victoria," she said faintly, "remember that bond, the one between a mother and her unborn child. One day you'll understand." Then she was gone.

We all stood silently beside each other. We knew that Dad would be with Mother one day and that he'd be happy. We were not sad anymore. Like always, Jacky showed us that dying was nothing to be afraid of.

We all grabbed hands and opened our eyes. And we were back. We weren't sad anymore, but overwhelmed, knowing how happy Dad would be when his time came.

Glenn took my hand and we left to go home. I knew I didn't have to worry about Dad. Sure, we were going to miss him, but we knew he was going to be with Mother.

In be that night, I recalled what Mother said before she left: "Remember the bond between a mother and her unborn child." It hit me. I put my hand on my stomach. "Glenn," I yelled. "Glenn!"

Glenn jumped up out of bed, startled awake. "What's wrong, what's wrong?" he yelled.

"I'm pregnant!"

"How do you know?"

"I just do."

"I'm not going to ask," he said. We hugged each other happily for a while, and then he kissed my belly. "Go to sleep, Vick."

I lay back down and then I heard Jacky. *Congratulations!* Smiling, I closed my eyes. I though of Mother, and realized that's what she had been trying to tell me. In a soft voice I whispered, "I love you Mother."

CHAPTER 35

The next few months went by so slo-o-o-o-owly. Well, that's how it seemed to me. Everyone enjoyed me being pregnant, especially Glenn. He'd wait on me hand and foot, knowing what a big baby I was. You know, the morning sickness, the bloating, the weight gain. It was everything I said I would never do. It was Jacky who wanted all of this. She wanted as many kids as it was possible for one person to have. Don's kids, that is. I just wanted the good husband without all the extras. She was going to be the good mother and I was going to be the cool aunt that let them get away with murder, but as we all know, life can throw you a curve.

So I was pregnant and getting ready to give birth to my first child. I was scared, and Glenn knew it. Whenever he knew I was thinking about the day to come he'd wrap his arms around me and tell me how much he loved me. When I felt the baby move, it scared me. I told you before what a chicken I am.

When the time came, I remember that night as if it was yesterday. It takes top priority on my forget list, but I can't forget. I wasn't one of those mothers who cherished the moment. I'm going to be honest with you; there wasn't anything romantic about it. Whoever said that a woman is sexy when she's pregnant had to be wrong.

It was around 8:30 p.m. Judy, Michelle, Jacky, and I was sitting in the kitchen. It was a warm night, and the men were sitting out on the porch talking about whatever men talk about when they're together. I felt a cramp. I ignored it. From the time you get pregnant you go though torture.

A few minutes passed and I felt it again, but this time Jacky said, "He's coming."

Now I was scared. Judy yelled for Glenn, and they came running in the room. By this time I was really worried. "I don't know if I can do this," I told Glenn, and started to cry.

Then the cramp came again, but this time it felt worse. "They're getting close," I heard Judy say. "I think it's time."

I cried out to Jacky to take over my body. "No!" Glenn yelled. "You don't know what could happen!"

Jacky knew Glenn was afraid something would go wrong. You know, with me getting weak whenever she took over my body. She knew it wouldn't harm me, but she respected Glenn's wishes. But we did keep our minds open so we could talk to each other without Glenn worrying.

Jacky, don't leave me, I said.

I'll be right beside you all the way, she promised.

When we got to the hospital there were reporters and a television crew waiting for us. Don told us to go in, that he'd take care of it.

As I lay in my room the nurse came in. I could still feel Jacky's presence. As the nurse checked me over she chuckled. "New mom? You have a long way to go."

She finished and started to leave. I grabbed her arm before she could take one step away from the bed. "Get me something for the pain!" I yelled.

She raised her eyebrows; I must have sounded desperate because she said, without hesitation, "Okay."

When she was gone Jacky appeared. "Jacky!" I screamed, "I wish Mother were here."

"Vicky, there's nothing to be afraid of." I laid back on my pillow and felt another contraction. Jacky knew what I was feeling. "Close your eyes," she said.

I didn't even realize that Glenn and Don had come in the room, because she took me to that place. I felt no pain.

As we sat there she told me that she had something for me. Then Mother appeared.

"Everything is going to be fine," she said.

The sight of her relaxed me, and I was filled with calm. "Mother, I don't know if I can do this."

"We never think we can, but we do," she assured me. "But I think you should go now." She and Jacky looked down at my belly. The look on their faces said it all; this little kid was not going to wait for anyone.

"Oh, no!" I yelled. I was back in my hospital room, and holding onto Glenn's hand.

"It's going to be all right," he said, "you're tough."

"If I hear you say that one more time," I gasped as another contraction gripped me, "I'm going to stick something up in you and see how tough you are."

I heard Jacky laughing, and Don joined her. I was mad. "You can both kiss my. . . ."

Then the doctor yelled, "Push!"

It was like Chinese torture, and I was on the rack.

"Push, push," the doctor kept saying.

Each time I did, I yelled out, "Mother, help me!"

Then all of a sudden, out it came—this tiny little thing!

Glenn laughed. "How could this tiny thing cause so much trouble? He takes after his mother." Then he kissed me and the baby.

After they took care of the baby and I was back in my room, I guess everyone was out making calls and Glenn and Don were talking to the reporter. I opened my eyes to see Dad sitting there, all alone.

"Dad, are you all right?"

He had that single tear in his eye, the same tear I'd seen so many times before. "You called out for your mother," he said.

I could feel Jacky in the room, but she didn't appear. She knew, like we always knew, when one of us needed to be alone with him. She knew Dad needed to talk.

"I saw her, Dad," I said. "Jacky took me to that place where we go, and Mother was there." He squeezed my hand. "She's so beautiful, Dad. She knows everything, and she misses you so much."

For the first time, the tear he always kept under control rolled down his face.

"She loves you, Dad, and she knows. She knows you'll be with her soon."

Then Jacky appeared and went to the door and locked it. I knew what she was going to do. I placed my hand on Dad's, and the next thing I knew we were in that place. He looked so frail. I knew he'd been trying to hide his pain from us all. But he felt no pain here. Dad was so strong for us when we were growing up and he was trying to keep it from us now. I knew I had to be strong for him. He just sat there and stared out. I wished I could be one with him to know what he was feeling, but he was a proud man, and out of respect for him, I'd never invade his privacy.

"Now I know why you love this place," he said.

And then, right in front of us, Mother appeared. He cried out, "Victoria!" I'd never seen Dad like that before.

He walked over to her, and she consumed him in a white light. She felt his pain. "Mike, I know what you're going through, and one day soon

I'll come for you. I never left you or the children, and soon you'll be here with me. We'll be together."

A tear rolled down his face. "I miss you, Victoria." He cried in her arms.

"I know, my love, and soon we'll be together. Our girls wanted you to see your grandson before you had to leave. Jacky is my connection to you all." She wrapped herself around him again. We couldn't hear what they were saying; it was something only between them.

I think now Dad knew it was all right to leave us. He came away from that place more ready to be with Mother. He knew he had to make sure Judy would be fine before he left, and for that matter, all of us.

"It's time for you to go," Mother said. Dad didn't want to leave. "But you must," she said. "You have to take care of our family before we can be together."

He smiled at her and told her he loved her. Then he looked at Jacky and said, "Thank you."

I took Dad's hand again, and we were back in my room. Jacky unlocked the door and everyone came in. Dad was at a loss for words, but one thing we'd all learned in the past few years was that we didn't always need words to let someone know what we felt.

Our whole inner circle was there to see me. Then the nurse came in to give me the shot I'd asked for hours ago. I should have figured it out when Jacky disappeared. "Oh, crap," I said, but this time Jacky was inside me and I didn't feel a thing.

When the nurse left Don said, "You can come out now."

"How did you know?" I asked him.

"You never moved."

Glenn cracked up. Then Jacky appeared. "I think I could get used to that stuff," she said. That's when it hit me—I was in the twilight zone. It didn't matter anyway, everyone was enjoying themselves, and that's all I could remember.

I don't know what time it was, but when I opened my eyes, I saw Glenn in the chair next to my bed holding our son. He opened his eyes and smiled. It felt good to be alone, just the three of us.

"He looks just like you, Glenn." Glenn smiled, then laid his head on my pillow. He said he loved me, and closed his eyes.

Now there was one more person in my life, and I'd have to share my love with him, but I would never deprive Glenn of my attention. I would never change anything in my life that would come between my love for him and my love for my son. I think that's when I realized that I was finally growing up. I guess you could say I was starting another chapter in my life.

CHAPTER 36

As time went on our inner circle started to grow. With every child that was born to any of us, he or she knew from the very start that we shared a secret that could never be shared with anyone outside our circle. It was hard to wander out, not that we would ever want to. We could never tell anyone outside about Jacky. But we were happy just the way things were. We experienced life more fully than anyone we could ever come in contact with, and we wouldn't want it any other way.

Jehane and Joe had a baby boy, who was named after Joe. He was a chip off the old block, the funniest kid and a pleasure to be around. And you'll never believe it, Tim was so into married life that Donna became pregnant a few months after they said "I do." We were happy for her, and it didn't matter if she was or not. Jacky knew all along, but never mentioned it to anyone but me. It was funny how Donna would insist she wasn't pregnant and we'd let it go, unless we were trying to bust on her.

It wasn't long after she gave birth that she announced she was pregnant again. She turned out to be a heck of a broodmare. They have five children, and she's expecting her sixth.

Dad passed away, but we were all glad that he was around to see all our children. We made sure that we all came to Saturday morning breakfasts, and with all the kids Dad was in his glory. Jacky was there for Dad when he passed on, and so was Mother.

We all look at death differently than others outside our inner circle do. We didn't cry or mourn. Instead we celebrated his passing to a better place, knowing Mom was there to meet him. Jacky told us he was the young man who held her when she couldn't sleep. She told us how Mother and he would be there when it was our time to pass on, too. Jacky told Judy how Mother admired her for being who she was, and that one day they would be able to sit down and get to know each other better.

Jacky told Ray and Ruth that Mother was glad he had given her a granddaughter. Mother was happy that the woman in Don's life was the one she'd wanted him to be with all along. Lastly, Mother wanted me to know that she never thought I'd find a man out there just like my father. Of course, she didn't forget Jack. She told him she never stopped loving him. Jacky also told Michelle that Mother missed her and couldn't wait to see her again.

So no, we didn't cry the day Dad died. We were happy for him, and we all knew one day we'd be sitting together again. I guess we took it so well that others at the funeral were disappointed in the way we behaved. We all knew that, if we needed Dad, all we had to do was ask Jacky. For example, Judy didn't know where Dad put the cookbook (yes, the cookbook). Dad was glad she asked. Even though he was with Mother, he worried and loved Judy.

He'd also leave messages through Jacky for me not to be so stern with the children. One thing I can say is, unlike us, our children will know from an early age that if you keep love in your heart only good will come out of it.

On special occasions Jacky would take us all to that place, where we could all be together.

It's been a long time since The Boys of Summer performed in the States, but I think you'll be hearing from them quite soon. And don't be surprised if you see them out on tour again. As usual, I'm going to be left at home with the kids. Glenn says no, but we'll see.

I find myself sitting on my porch more and more these days, watching Jacky and Don in the yard, playing with our kids. I always wondered what kind of mother she'd be, and now I know. I guess I always knew. She has a way of asking them to do something, and they're pleased to do it. She's a child at heart, and it's easy for her to relate to them. We all know that if anything should ever happen to any one of us, Jacky would be there for the children. Watching her, I know she was never left out of the joys of life. We all make sure of that. She has Don, and she has all the love of our kids. Heck, they never want to leave her house.

One day, as I watched Jacky in the yard playing with little Glenn, I knew that all she ever missed out on was giving birth to a child of her own. She would get so excited when she'd find out one of our inner circle was expecting, but that all changed the day I returned from the doctor. She broke the news that I was pregnant again. Believe me, I didn't jump up and down for joy. I wasn't looking forward to going through the agony of giving birth again. Don't get me wrong, I

love my son and I could never see myself ever being without him. But giving birth again? Please!

I didn't say anything to anyone about it for a few days. I needed time for it to sink in. That day I watched Jacky and Don in the yard playing with children. I decided that Jacky and Don would be part of it, all the way down to giving birth.

Eight months later when we had all our friends and family over for the Fourth of July, I broke the news to Glenn what I wanted to do. I could see Jacky staring at me. I knew what she wanted. Glenn smiled, for he even knew. Even Don wanted to know how it felt, being a father. That's when I told Jacky and Don what I wanted to do.

Jacky walked up and stood in front of me. She had that childlike look on her face, and I knew what she wanted to do. Glenn nodded. We took one step toward each other and became one. Jack and Michelle watched as I faded out and saw Jacky eight months pregnant. She walked over to Don and sat on his lap. He placed his hand on her belly, then rubbed it up and down and all around, hoping to feel the baby kicking. Jacky make it possible for Don to see and feel the baby as it started to form into what it would be.

Of course I saw the whole thing too; it was my body she was using. Even with little Glenn I had never experienced what I was experiencing then.

She got up and walked over to Glenn, sat down, and took his hand, and he, too, felt what Don felt. He could feel his little child form into something that he would be able to hold in his arms.

Then Jacky faded out, leaving me sitting there. Glenn was so overwhelmed that I could see the tears filling his eyes. I leaned over and kissed him.

Together we looked at Jacky and Don, and the realization came to me that this would be the last thing I could ever do for her. It was the one thing she could never do for herself. So once a week Don and she would come over and we'd do the same thing, until the night of her birth. Yes, her; Jacky had discovered the first time that I was carrying a girl. With Jacky there, who needed ultrasound?

The night of the birth Don got a call from Glenn, telling him it was time. Jacky appeared in my room. As Glenn and Don were running around like chickens with their heads cut off, Jacky and I became one. She felt every cramp, ache, and pain I felt. Sure, she could have stopped it, but she wanted to feel everything. I remember saying to myself, *Why in heaven's name would anyone want to feel every little pain of giving birth?* But not Jacky, she wanted the whole experience. She embraced it, knowing that she'd never have the chance again, if I could help it.

But I'll tell you, when it came down to that last minute, when our little girl was going to make her entrance, Jacky grabbed Don's hand and let out the loudest scream! I'm sure it could be heard all through the hospital. Don wasn't quite ready for that!

When the doctor put the baby on my belly I cried, but they were not my tears, they were Jacky's. For as long as she was a ghost, I never saw her cry or feel the way she did that night.

Don was one with her, and he knew they were tears of joy. He leaned over and kissed her on the forehead and told her he loved her.

When everyone asked me what I was going to name her, I said, "Jacquelyn." It was only fitting to name her after the woman who gave birth to her. Don't you think?

CHAPTER 37

So as time goes by, I sit on my porch watching Jacky and Don across the street playing with our kids. I'm also keeping an eye on the house built from love, so it will be handed down to the next generation. And knowing that if anything should ever happen to anyone in our inner circle, Jacky would always be there in our place, an insecure shy mischievous little girl who gave more of herself in death than in life.

And now you're wondering if this really happened. Is this still going on today, as you read this book? And why is the band so closed to outsiders after all these years? Did Jacky come back, like I said, because her love for Don was so powerful? Or do you believe that for a few minutes I died and came back because Glenn's love for me was so strong? Is the band really called The Boys of Summer? I guess we can debate that.

And now, when you see them in concert, and you're looking up at Don and he's looking out into space, do you think its Jacky he looking at? And when he sings that special song about love, is it her he's singing to?

Maybe you have to see for yourself. So if you're going to see the band in concert, look for clues. They're all there. Or maybe you'll never know, unless you're a part of our inner circle. And we'll never tell. So I think I'll let you decide for yourself.

And if you see a girl with long brown hair sitting in the front row, looking up at Glenn, and he looks down at her and smiles that smile he always had for her, just wave and I'll wave back.

I never see that eagle again. I guess you can say it was replaced by an angel.

TATE PUBLISHING & *Enterprises*

Tate Publishing is committed to excellence in the publishing industry. Our staff of highly trained professionals, including editors, graphic designers, and marketing personnel, work together to produce the very finest books available. The company reflects the philosophy established by the founders, based on Psalms 68:11,

"THE LORD GAVE THE WORD AND GREAT WAS THE COMPANY OF THOSE WHO PUBLISHED IT."

If you would like further information, please call
1.888.361.9473
or visit our website
www.tatepublishing.com

TATE PUBLISHING & *Enterprises*, LLC
127 E. Trade Center Terrace
Mustang, Oklahoma 73064 USA